STERLING STONE

L.B DUNBAR

Cover Design: Lori Jackson Designs

Cover Photographer: JW Photography & Covers

Cover Model: Timothy Giebel

Editor: Emerald Edits/Nicole McCurdy

Editor: Gemma Brocato

OTHER BOOKS BY L.B. DUNBAR

<u>Sterling Falls</u>

Sterling Heat

Sterling Brick

Sterling Streak

Sterling Clay

Sterling Fight

Sterling Touch

Sterling Stone

<u>Chicago Anchors</u>

Elevator Pitch

Catch the Kiss

Parentmoon

<u>Holiday Hotties (Christmas novellas)</u>

Scrooge-ish

Naughty-ish

Grouch-ish

<u>Road Trips & Romance</u>

Hauling Ashe

Merging Wright

Rhode Trip

<u>Lakeside Cottage</u>

Living at 40

Loving at 40

Learning at 40

Letting Go at 40

Silver Foxes of Blue Ridge

Silver Brewer

Silver Player

Silver Mayor

Silver Biker

Sexy Silver Fox Collection

After Care

Midlife Crisis

Restored Dreams

Second Chance

Wine&Dine

Collision novellas

Collide

Caught

The Sex Education of M.E.

The Heart Collection

Speak from the Heart

Read with your Heart

Look with your Heart

Fight from the Heart

View with your Heart

The Heart Remembers - a sequel

BOOKS IN OTHER AUTHOR WORLDS

<u>Smartypants Romance (an imprint of Penny Reid)</u>

Love in Due Time

Love in Deed

Love in a Pickle

<u>The World of True North (an imprint of Sarina Bowen)</u>

Cowboy

Studfinder

THE EARLY YEARS

<u>Legendary Rock Stars Series</u>

<u>Paradise Stories</u>

<u>The Island Duet</u>

<u>Modern Descendants – writing as elda lore</u>

For N, who said I probably shouldn't.
And S, who said I could.
Your faith in me and my ability to tell a story has meant everything
to me.

A NOTE

Some of the experiences in this book are not my own. Because of that, I've had sensitivity readers check those experiences and give me their stamp of approval.

1

———

April

[Stone]

Commitments.

After a lifetime of them, it should come as no surprise that I hate commitments. Especially the kind that lure me from settling into my easy chair, watching a ballgame, enjoying a beer, and soaking up rare moments of quiet.

But when a good friend retires from professional football, you want to celebrate that achievement with him, especially when you never had the same opportunity.

Neither the retirement nor the higher level of play.

As much as I hate the idea of commitments, I never hesitated when it came to making deeper ones. More important ones by the names of Clay, Judd, Knox, Ford, Sebastian, and Vale.

A rare smile curls my lips as I glance one more time at myself in the hotel mirror. My family is one of the few things I easily smile about. Their success stories. Their love lives in recent years. Their growing families.

Smoothing my hand down the silky tie over a crisply starched white shirt, I stare at my reflection.

"Not too bad, old man," I mutter, examining the silver that exceeds the black strands that once dominated my hair and the muted white playing a losing game of hide and seek in my thin-layered beard. Crinkles meet the corners of my blue eyes. Eyes that have seen too much over my forty-five years. The years that keep creeping toward fifty.

With a sigh, I swipe two fingers near my temple, although I don't have a single hair out of place.

I'm in Knoxville for the weekend. The timing worked out perfectly. I'll make an appearance at the dinner, stay for a drink, and then sneak away for my brother's fight.

He doesn't know I'll be there. He doesn't want me to know what he's doing late at night in the backrooms of certain bars, but I know everything about my siblings.

I should, as both the sheriff of Sterling Falls, our small West Virginia mountain town, and as their oldest brother.

My daily fight is feeling older when age is a privilege. I've lost too many people too soon—family members, good friends, and folks I couldn't save on the job—before they ever reached the same age I'm presently sporting.

On that note, I step into the quiet hotel hallway and tug my phone from the pocket inside my suit jacket. Scrolling for the Uber app my nephew helped me download, I double-check where I'm headed this evening. With my head lowered, I'm busy thumbing my phone screen when something hard and rather nondescript jabs my chest.

It isn't the force of the item so much as how startled I am that causes me to stumble backward, dropping my phone. At the same time, a woman propels backward in the opposite direction, and I reach for her before she'll completely fall.

With my hands on her upper arms, holding her steady, warmth drizzles beneath my large palms over her thin, long-sleeved shirt. Which makes no sense. Lowering my gaze, I note the offending object. The jarring poke came from an open book.

When I feel her stiffen beneath my hold, I release her.

"Are you okay?" I say at the same time she says, "I'm so sorry."

"I'm the one not looking where I was going," I assure her, as her apology isn't necessary. I bend to retrieve my phone.

"No, I had my nose stuck in a book."

I offer what I hope is a warm smile. No real harm. No foul.

"It must be some story," I say next, but then I catch on her face.

Because looking back at me is the most gorgeous woman I've ever seen.

Her skin looks like polished sunshine, shimmery bronze, and glowing just as brightly. Her hair is as dark as West Virginia coal, wild and loose around a goddess-like face. Then there are her eyes—a captivating grey-blue, almost silver, which feels prophetic considering my last name.

I'm Stone Sylver.

And she is striking.

She is also staring back at me, and we pass uncounted seconds just gazing at one another until I process our current position.

Tall, solid man blocking a slightly smaller woman in a hotel hallway.

Suddenly, I'm aware of my size and the awkwardness of simply staring at her. I clear my throat and slip my hands into my pockets as a subtle means to convey I don't intend her any harm. Her eyes follow the movement. I notice her shoulders relax a bit.

"Well . . . I'll let you . . ." I step to the left, intending to allow her to pass. Only she steps to her right, and we freeze in place again.

She chews at the corner of her lip, like she's fighting a smile. It's a losing battle, as her bright smile stands out vividly against the rich luster of her lips.

The corner of my mouth ticks upward in response.

As she holds the closed book against her chest now, trim dark brown polished nails tap against the hardcover, which faces outward. I arch a brow at the title containing *Daddy* and *Dom* in it.

"Uhm . . . have a good night." I try again to excuse myself, intending to step right this time.

Only she steps to her left.

And at the same time, we both move forward, nearly bumping into one another again.

Her book hits the floor with a resounding thud.

"Let me . . ." I start, bending at the waist to retrieve it.

"I got it . . ." she says, following my lead.

My fingers reach the book first, and I stand too quickly, thus knocking our heads together. This time, we both fall back, landing on our asses.

"Ow," she says, rubbing at her jaw.

"Jesus. Are you alright?" I immediately ask, reaching only briefly at the back of my head before scrambling forward to inspect her chin. Slender, long fingers stroke over the hard edge of her jaw, which she moves side to side.

"Let me look," I whisper, going into the protective mode conditioned by my employment.

Yet something deeper strikes within me. A visceral need to know I haven't hurt her.

With me on my hands and knees in my suit, and her on her

backside, knees bent upward, her long skirt shielding her legs, I'm practically in her face. The soft scent of honeysuckle and citrus tickles my nose. I take in the fullness of her lips. Then, I force myself to focus on her chin.

Her eyes widen, and I realize how close our faces are. Slowly, I lean back. "I've been told I have a thick head."

Her mouth curls again, in a slow, enticing way. Her eyes practically dance.

I point at the book which lies between us. "I'm going in," I teasingly warn.

She chuckles softly, the sound like the bright metallic jingle of a tambourine. I reach for the book that has fallen open, face down, and use my finger to bookmark the spot, then hold out my other hand for her. As I stand, she takes my extended palm, and that drizzle of warmth felt through her shirt only seconds ago becomes a crackle of heat spreading across my hand.

When we stand, I flip the book to the open page, eyes catching on a phrase.

"*And so the blue alien led her down the dark passage, heading toward a destiny she didn't know she'd eventually crave,*" I read aloud, before snapping the book closed and handing it back to her, suddenly realizing how close we stand. Less than the length of a book.

Her fingertips brush mine as she takes the book from me. Those pleasant pinpricks spread over my skin again.

"Your husband must get jealous of you reading that." I nod toward the book, speaking before I consider what I've said. The statement comes out of left field, sounding rusty, almost clunky, before I realize I'm curious if she has a husband.

Am I flirting with her? I'm definitely sensing some chemistry at work. Crackles and sparks. Heat and a rush of desire I haven't felt in a long, long time.

"Only my book boyfriend ever gets jealous . . . when I move on to a new book."

She tips the book forward, playfully knocking the edge against my chest.

"Easy there. That's some weapon you have in your hand." I smile wider to assure her I'm joking.

"Words are powerful things."

"They certainly can be." I've heard the best and worst of words. Both have hurt me in the end.

Shaking the negative thoughts, I note that she's slightly shorter than me, slim with wider hips. The perfect notch at her waist looks like an exact fit for my hands.

I shut down that thought as well.

Another moment of us staring at each other passes before I watch the column of her throat roll when she clears it.

"Well, thanks for the dance."

I chuckle in reference to our one-two misstep and scratch at the back of my neck. Pivoting a half pace to my right, allowing her the path forward down the hallway, I point in the opposite direction.

"I'll go this way, I guess," I state, uncertain why I've tacked on that disclaimer. Like I'm not ready to leave her when there's no reason to stay in this hallway.

"And I'll go that way." She flops the book forward, using it to point her direction.

I wave my hand, allowing her to go first so we don't have any more left-right dancing or head knocking.

As she passes me, I watch her move. The subtle sway of those hips. The brush of a long skirt in multiple layers that reaches her ankles. The fit of her long-sleeved shirt outlines her waist.

She moves with grace.

"Have a good night," I call after her, struggling to make my own feet move over the smooth carpet and away from this beautiful creature.

I'm aware I have somewhere to be, and she is headed in the opposite direction, presumably to her hotel room.

Is this what is meant when worlds collide but ricochet into the night?

Maybe it's more like that elusive moment. A brief glance. A possible chance.

And then the moment is gone.

She spins to face me one final time, walking backwards and holding up the book, waving it gently in the air. Her mouth slowly curls, and she digs her teeth into her lower lip again. "I will," she says in response to my wishing her a good night. "The story just reached an unexpected plot twist."

She winks and turns away from me one final time.

With heat in my cheeks, I shake my head. She was definitely flirty with me.

And if I didn't have a commitment, I might ask her if she'd like to grab a drink.

Instead, I resolutely spin in the opposite direction, edging closer to the elevator bank with every step. When I reach the short hallway, I pause, giving her one last glance.

Wondering if I'm about to walk away from an unexpected plot twist.

2

———

[Taxi]

Chewing on my lower lip, I fight the urge to giggle.

That might have been the strangest moment of my life.

It'd been my fault we collided. Nose stuck in a book, like I said. Escaping to other worlds. Living out a fictional couple's romance. Seeking adventure . . . of the sexy sort.

I can only assume he wasn't paying attention to where he was walking, either. He'd had his phone in his hand, but I somehow doubt he was reading about sensual encounters with aliens.

To my surprise, the second he clutched my arms to steady me, I didn't bristle like I normally would. He caught me so quickly, I don't think he was even aware he touched me. And thankfully, he did, or I would have landed on my ass. I'm typically not a fan of unexpected, unanticipated touches. However, a strange energy zinged down my arms and tingled all the way to my fingertips. Beneath the strength of his palms, a sense of calm blanketed my body after the initial shock. Like the first stroke of warm blue in the sky on a new day.

Could he have out-of-this-world powers, or was I just too lost in the fantasy of my book?

Daddy Dom Alien Invasion.

Don't judge. I'm in an extraterrestrial phase. Aliens appear better than humans most days.

And my little close encounter with a rugged man in a hotel hallway feels like something outside this realm.

His eyes were Montana-sky blue, soft and kind, and that mostly silver color cascading through his once-dark hair . . . *mm-mm-mm*. I chew my lower lip even harder, wondering if my next reading kink should involve a sexy silver fox.

At forty-three, most men in my age group are starting to gray in some manner, but this man took plain gray to stunning sterling.

As an artist, I'm hyperaware of the difference in colors.

I'm in Knoxville for a short-term assignment. Another wall mural to celebrate a diverse community. I'm excited about the upcoming project.

What I'm not excited about is the short-term housing in a hotel. For the most part, I live out of my VW van, but Gloria, as I've affectionately named the motorized love of my life, is on the fritz. So, while she's in the auto-mechanic hospital, I'm stuck in a random hotel.

As an accomplished urban artist, I've been all over the United States, using the world as my muse. My art is considered abstract, raw and edgy, and I embrace the communities I visit, immersing myself in them, exploring their residents, the neighborhood, the culture of their community. Of course, art doesn't always pay for a tank of gas, so I sometimes take side gigs in a new town as a waitress, a desk clerk, even a postal worker once. Anywhere I can meet people, observe others, get inspired by those different than me, I do it.

And the last place I want to enter is my hotel room, alone.

I consider myself a free spirit, which means I'm open to last-minute hookups and one-night stands. However, I'm on a random dude diet lately. As in, I've cut them out of my daily menu, finding them bad for my health. My appetite has been spoiled a little too often, and I told myself I'd do better. Be better.

I'm not watching my weight. I embrace my subtle curves. I'm looking out for my heart.

So as tempting as Mr. Tall, Sexy, and Silver was, I push against the pull to turn around and ask him if he'd like to join me for a drink.

Instead, I settle into my room, finish reading about alien invasions and domineering dudes, only to find I'm a little turned on and a lot antsy by the end. Artists keep odd hours, *they say*, so I head to a local barbecue bar in hopes of settling the itch inside me.

Knoxville is a beautiful city, especially down by the river, which reminds me of a place I once lived. The only place I considered a home, as much as my wandering heart can claim a base. I've always been restless, eager to move onward, but part of that jitter comes from never feeling secure in one place. A deep-seated fear lives inside me. One afraid of being plucked from a spot if I grew too comfortable and established roots.

As a child, my two sisters and I were dragged all over by our mother. An adventure, she called every new location. And every new man she was chasing.

I never wanted to be a chaser. At least, not of men.

Shaking off thoughts of my mama, I take a seat at the bar, noting my surroundings. The thick, wooden slab coated in layers of varnish with metal pipe accents gives a country-meets-industrial vibe to the place. My toes tap along with the country music blaring overhead, and I give a nod to the bartender.

Bartenders can be your best friend or the perfect partner for one night, but my man-diet whispers in my ear, so I order a liquid dinner and dessert instead.

"I'll have the pomegranate margarita, please. And a sweet potato cupcake sounds amazing." I haven't had one of these Tennessee favorites in years.

As I wait for my order, a man takes a seat to my immediate left, pushing his stool a little too close to mine when there is vacant space on the other side of him. He instantly glances my way and innocently asks, "Oh, this seat wasn't taken, was it?"

He's cocksure that the seat was available, and despite him being relatively good-looking, I'm already over his approach.

While I've been trying to protect my heart, my vagina has been on a long hiatus, and she wants a snack. The silver fox from earlier has been on my mind a little too much in the past two hours, merging an alien daddy into that tall sip of water whose large hands looked like they knew how to handle a woman.

His presence said commanding but somehow gentle. He released me instantly, almost like he knew he'd made me anxious at first. I didn't miss him slipping his hands in his pockets like a tender nod to say, *I'm not here to harm you.* But it might have been his smile that relaxed me the most. The crook of his mouth. The shift of his thick mustache. His smile was like a secret he rarely shared.

And he'd given it to me.

"I'm waiting on someone." The truth is buried deep within that statement.

I don't *need* a man, but I want one. That blue to my red that makes purple. A brick where I'm sand. A breeze that won't blow me away but collect the seeds of me. An everlasting love, like my Aunt Trudy had with Uncle Carlton.

"Sure he's still showing, sugar?" He clicks his tongue against his teeth, like he knows I'm lying.

"Sure as I'm sitting here," I mumble, giving the bartender a glance when he plops my fruity margarita in front of me.

Getting hit on in public is like the pages in a book. On the even number, it can be a flattering experience, and if I'm in the right frame of mind, innocent flirtations that lead to mindless fucking is not outside of my boundaries. On the odd pages, my body language might say *don't come near me*, as it presently reads, don't think it's okay to try flipping my pages, so to speak.

Tonight, the book is closed.

A waitress approaches from behind me and sets my dessert in front of me. The sweet potato cupcake is piled high with cream cheese frosting.

The man beside me tries again. "Some sugar for the brown sugar."

I stiffen, my jaw tightening. The term brown sugar is written into lyrics and waxed poetically as a compliment at times, but in this case, silence pours between us, allowing the air to chill, the words ash between us.

"I'm sweet enough already," I say lightly, but the cool undertone gives him a puzzled expression. I shift on my stool, deliberately angling my body away from him and roll my eyes.

While taking a sip of my drink, the stool on my right side is dragged against the hardwood floor. Out of the corner of my eye, I catch a glimpse of a man in a dark suit taking a seat. At least on this side of me, it's the only seat available.

Here we go again.

Then I do a double-take.

"There you are," I say a little too loudly, like I've been expecting a blind date. I shift on my stool, giving the man to my left my back. "Samson, right?"

The name pops out of thin air.

To my utter surprise, and strange relief, the Hallway Hottie from earlier gives me a questioning look before glancing over my head.

When his eyes meet mine again, he focuses on me and that strange warm sensation drips over me again. This time, it's a smooth honey-brown color, sticky and sweet, and thankfully playing along with my charade.

"Samson, it is."

I tilt my head, implying the man behind me. "Alien intruder."

"Ah." He lifts one brow, glancing around me again. "But I thought aliens were your thing."

I chuckle softly at the reminder of the book I finished reading before coming here and the fact he remembers the title. He read that passage earlier in a quiet but rugged voice that whispered through my head the remainder of my reading.

And I briefly wonder what he'd sound like whispering sweet things and sexy commands while over me.

"Need me to arrest someone?" He shifts on his stool, bracketing mine with the spread of his knees. His hand comes to the back of my chair, caging me in, and yet I don't feel threatened. More like protected. The tone of his voice suggested he might not be joking about arresting someone, and a slight shiver runs down my spine, but I ignore the chill.

Instead, I will my thoughts away from those thick thighs and ignore the temptation to wonder what a man his size might be packing beneath those slacks.

I'm not really a suit and tie kind of gal, and while this guy doesn't scream millionaire, he does give off a professional vibe.

Still, he's doing me a solid here by pretending to be the man I was waiting on.

Behind me, the stool scrapes angrily against the wooden floor. As the seat-confiscator steps away from the bar, I don't bother glancing in his direction.

Samson doesn't take his eyes off me, and eventually says, "All clear."

He leans away from me, removing his hand from the back of my seat, and a sense of disappointment blooms with his retreat. I try to shake off the unsettling sensation, but then my nose twitches, catching a whiff of something outdoorsy and fresh about him that lingers between us.

"Let me get your drink," I boldly offer. He did just play my hero.

"Don't worry about it." His smile is kind, but it doesn't reach his eyes as it did earlier. The lack of a grin is almost as mysterious as the crooked one he gave me in the hallway.

Stop analyzing his smile. Or lack thereof, Taxi. I mentally double pat my cheeks, like the slap will force some sense into me.

"I insist," I demand.

He tilts his head and tips a brow. "My mama would never forgive me."

I can appreciate a gentleman, and I accept his brush off of my offer, but I'm also slightly irritated, which makes no sense.

He orders a beer for himself.

"So, a mama's man," I say, hoping to keep him talking. He has a nice voice. Rugged but soothing, soft almost, like smoothing out a crumpled piece of paper.

"Once upon a time," he says before taking a drink of his beer and setting it on the counter. His attention returns to me, giving me those summer-sky eyes again.

"What about you? Mama's girl or daddy's?"

I chuckle, the sound instantly bitter. "Neither." You can't be a daddy's girl when you don't know the man, and as for my mama, well, she'd been absent since my formative years.

"You're from outer space, aren't you?" He leans forward like he doesn't want everyone else to know my secret.

I laugh. "Exactly. Traveling from lands far, far away, as aliens do."

The curve of his mouth curls higher, emphasizing the silver around those lips of his. Lips that look puffy and soft and ripe for kissing.

Nope. Stop it.

He chuckles as well, causing his eyes to flare. "Must be nice." The words are dull, like he hasn't been anywhere special.

"You from Tennessee?" I ask.

He shakes his head. "Just visiting."

I can appreciate a person keeping things tight to the chest, but his answer is so vague, I'm wondering if *he's* from outer space.

It doesn't matter either way. I don't need his street address. I don't even need his name.

"Well, Samson. Here's to landing in Knoxville." I lift my glass and tap the long neck of his beer bottle, then take a sip of my drink.

He raises his beer to salute me, pokes the corner of his mouth higher, and takes a short swig. "Greetings. What brought you to this illustrious mountain town?"

"Traveling artist." I'm not a fan of small talk or background-seeking chatter, yet I don't mind with him. "I've been commissioned to paint a mural."

His brows rise with interest. "Tell me more."

Truth? I've seen the glazed-over look of someone asking for details about my art only to not really care about my passion. But this guy looks truly curious, especially when he keeps his focus on my face.

"I've been hired by a local urban outreach organization to paint the side of a community center."

"Side?" he questions.

"The outside. Like a brick wall." I wave my hand up and down as if emphasizing the exterior of a building.

His eyes scan down my seated form. "Just you? Alone?"

"Meaning?" I arch a brow at him. Is he questioning my ability?

"I just mean, painting a single wall in my house seems like a daunting project. How do you envision something on such a large scale?"

I'm almost puzzled by the question when I know the answer. I hesitate even to give him my explanation, but the longer he stares at me, waiting on something without those eyes turning to a shield of disinterest, my mouth finally finds the words, and I explain the details, almost painting a picture for him of the initial mock designs, scaling proportions, and software I use to help map everything.

"I like to hand-draw it first, then use technology as a tool," I admit.

And the entire time I talk, he watches me, his eyes sharp, attentive, patient. He asks questions that make me realize he's really listening, not just waiting for a pause to speak.

He leans in, forearm on the counter, knees still bracketed around mine, like he's forming a cocoon around us and I'm the center of his attention. His head inclines. His gaze doesn't wander. It's intoxicating to the point I consider coming out of hibernation just for him. Handsome, enigmatic, controlled, and yet entirely present. The sensation is unnerving, but in a way that makes my pulse quicken.

"For this project, I'll actually be teaching my techniques to kids at the university. Art really saved me when I was younger, and I'm thrilled to pass on what I know to others."

His grin grows almost full wattage, like he hears my excitement and reciprocates it. I recall what he said about my book— a weapon of words. That smile of his at high blast might be just as lethal.

Eventually, I remember that conversations should be two-sided, and I ask what he does.

The corner of his mouth twitches, but it isn't as easy as I've seen. "Nothing as exciting as painting murals to emphasize the spirit of a community." He takes another sip of his beer, which he's been ignoring during my artistic deluge.

I smile at what he's excavated about my work, but still wish he'd share a bit more about himself.

"You gonna eat that cupcake or are you saving it?" he asks, changing the subject and nodding toward the dessert I almost forgot I ordered.

Digging a fork into the moist goodness, because I'd have frosting in my nose if I picked up the cupcake and bit into it, I hold the first bite out toward him.

"Ladies first," he says, waving his hand toward me.

As I wrap my lips around the sweet sensation, humming with pleasure, I notice the way his throat rolls as he watches me. Chewing slowly, I lick my lips, and his gaze follows the path of my tongue until I dig my teeth into my lower lip. The heat in his eyes proves I'm having an effect on him.

There's something about *Samson* that continues to give off warm tones of stable beige and denim blue in a comforting way.

His knee twitches, knocking into mine, and he clears his throat, sitting taller, making me realize how close we've been sitting. Glancing at the bar, he flips his phone, which I hadn't noticed on the counter, and he taps the screen, reading the time.

"Shit," he mutters under his breath.

"Big date?" I tease, hating how the words come out with a pinch of envy. Earlier, he hinted at me having a husband, and I noticed he wasn't wearing a wedding band. But that doesn't mean he doesn't have a woman still waiting on him.

"My brother has a fight tonight, and I'd hoped to attend, but I missed it."

"I'm so sorry." I swallow back a splash of regret along with the relief that it isn't another woman. "I've been so busy blab-bing about myself—"

"I like hearing your voice." His head swings upward, gaze landing on my lips, and I'm so startled by the admission that I stumble for a response.

"And it's not like he knew I was coming, anyway," he adds.

"Sounds like a story." I wiggle my brows and slice into the cupcake again.

"Definitely not as good as alien lovers, I imagine."

My book. I choke on embarrassment. I'm not ashamed of reading romance or ones as outrageous as alien lovers, but I still feel a little guilty about the fictional truth.

Alien dicks are big, and they know how to handle that girth.

With cupcake on my fork again, I hold out the next bite for him. As his mouth opens, and his lips wrap around the tines, he holds still a second, keeping his eyes on me before sliding his closed lips down the fork. Just as I'm about to pull it free from his mouth, his teeth briefly clamp on the metal tines. His mustache twitches before he releases the utensil and slowly pulls away, taking his sweet time to chew. The corner of his mouth holds a drop of frosting, and I reach out for it, swiping the mess with my thumb.

Without thinking, I set my finger against my own mouth and suck.

The flare in his eyes is a flame of brilliant blue and dark navy with a splash of sunshine.

"Anyway . . . " he says, like a punctuation on the night.

Panic strikes. I'm not ready for our time to end.

"I love this song," I blurt, although I have no idea what's playing overhead. Something sultry and country, and a bit too fast for my next comment. "We should dance."

He arches those thick brows.

"I mean sometime. In the future." *What the hell are you*

saying, Taxi? Implying you'll see this man again. Acting like futures are on your calendar. *Don't chase, dammit.*

"I just mean, you seem like a man who can dance. You had that whole one-two step happening earlier in the hallway." I good-naturedly mock him by digging my teeth into my lower lip, doing my best impression of a white man's overbite, then fist my hands in the air and pump out my chest three times, making a fool of myself.

He chuckles, thankfully, shaking his head. Then he surprises me by holding out his palm.

"Shall we, then?"

"Now?" My voice cracks unaccountably, when I propositioned him.

"It is the future," he teases, noting only the seconds that moved time forward. He slips off his stool and steps back, giving me space to slide off mine.

"Here?" I choke next, taking his hand. The bar is empty other than Kodiak, the bartender behind the counter, looking at his phone.

"You said this one is your favorite."

I still don't register what the song is, but I step closer to him, like I'm pulled by an invisible string, needing to be woven into the material of whoever he is.

Samson. We should exchange real names, and yet I'm loving the anonymity. He already knows so much about me.

With his hand notched at my hip and the other holding mine near his heart, which races to match the beat of mine, we sway to a song moving a little too fast, pulsing with a beat that doesn't coordinate with the rhythm he sets.

And yet, I don't want to move any faster than this moment.

3

____

[Stone]

She was utterly fascinating. And I was feeling a bit flattered that she pulled out that *I love this song* comment in order to prolong our night. Not that I was in a rush to stop talking to her or get back to my room alone. I could have sat at the bar all night, but I felt the weight of the bartender's eyes on us, possibly wanting to close up the empty bar.

Then she proposed we dance, and although I sensed she was joking, I decided *why not?*

It's been a long time since someone captured my attention and genuinely appeared to want mine in return.

We dance to some song where I wasn't even listening to the lyrics because I was so enthralled by how well my hand fit on the edge of her hip and how right her hand felt in mine against my chest.

She'd been on my mind since parting ways in the hotel. I'd

continued to wonder if I'd missed out on an opportunity to get to know her better while also wondering what attracted me so easily to her.

Sitting next to her at this bar, intending to pass the time before my brother's fight, had been complete happenstance. I'm not a man who puts much stock in Fate, or signs, or any of that mystical crap. But something put me in this bar tonight, in that exact seat, at the exact moment a guy wouldn't take a hint and leave her alone.

I don't know what it was. Instinct, training, or something older and deeper, but the second her voice rang too high, and she called me Samson, something in me locked into place. Protective. Automatic. Like stepping toward her was the only choice that made sense.

Then she started talking to me, telling me all about herself. She was easy to listen to. Her enthusiasm for art. Her excitement to share her talent with kids. The depth in her voice sounding like satin sheets and moonlight intrigue. I could have listened to her all night.

She could have brushed me off earlier, once that other guy took the hint. Instead, those bright eyes narrowed in, and I was drawn to her, feeling relief that the attraction between us, while unexplained, might be mutual. Like she'd been waiting to sit beside me as much as I'd been wanting to sit beside her without realizing it.

And I still didn't know her name.

"So, if I'm Samson, does that make you Delilah?"

Her laugh is so quick and sharp. "Something like that. But that poor woman turned to stone."

"That was Lot's wife," I correct. "And she turned to salt for looking back."

"Forgive me. My biblical studies are a bit rusty." Her smile is easy, those plump lips spreading wide.

"Doesn't matter to me," I admit.

Faith, skin color, creed—I don't judge people by any of it. I judge by what they do and why they do it. People can be good, bad, lost, and everything in between. People have situations thrust upon them. Some break the law to survive, not out of malice. A mother stealing formula to feed her hungry baby—the law calls it theft, but I can't see her as a criminal in the same way I see someone who preys on others for gain. The system isn't blind, but it's flawed. Racism, bias, and inequal opportunity. All of it shapes who ends up on the wrong side of the law. My job is to enforce the rules, yes, but my judgment doesn't stop there. I weigh intent, necessity, and circumstances. Some people are wayward because the world forced them to be. Others because they chose it. It's not always easy to tell the difference. But I try.

"Who was Delilah again?"

"She was a woman who worked in the sex industry," I state, careful to be respectful.

"Respect for the oldest profession in the world," my dance partner states, giving me another one of her big grins.

I like the shape of her mouth and the curve of her hip under my hand. Her honeysuckle and citrus scent tickles my nose again, and I want to breathe more of her in.

Instead, the song abruptly ends, but we keep moving another beat or two before she stops.

"I guess I should probably get going." She glances at the bartender, who is still looking at his phone like he's in no hurry to leave his casual position. Then again, it is getting late.

"Want to share a ride?" I realize asking her to join me in a car sounds risky, but an Uber driver would be an objective witness.

"Oh, I walked here. It's such a nice night, I'll just walk back."

I do not like the sound of that at all. The night is late, the sky dark, and she's a woman walking alone.

"May I walk you back to the hotel then?" I ask, not wanting

to cause her any concern about me while being concerned for her and her safety. "I don't like the idea of you walking alone by the river."

The space along the river has a nice cement path, but low-lit streetlamps and dark passages still pose dangerous opportunities for a lone walker.

She pauses a second, chewing her lip before she admits, "I'd like that." Still, she hesitates and glances at the bartender.

"Hey, Kodiak," she calls his name. "Think I should let him walk me home?"

The younger man stands tall and approaches the counter, sizing me up. Believe it or not, I think bartenders have a civic duty as well, and I'm pleased to see he isn't letting this woman go off with a stranger.

"Mind showing me your ID. We take safety seriously around here."

Pleased with his response, I step closer to the bar, pulling out my wallet and flipping it open so he can see my license. His gaze also catches on my badge. Using his cell phone, he takes a picture of both.

When he glances back up at me, he gives me a subtle nod. An understanding passes between us. I won't let anything happen to this woman. He'll haunt me to the grave if I do.

I pull out two twenties, offering them to him, before putting my wallet back in my pocket. "Keep the change."

He pats the top of the bar. "Definitely think you're safe with him," he addresses *Delilah*. "Y'all be safe and have a good night."

"You didn't have to do that," she whispers, standing next to me. "But I guess your mama would be proud."

Even though my mother is no longer with me, I strive to make her proud of me every day.

But that's not a conversation for now.

"Plot twist," I tease. "My treat." Then, I set my hand on the small of her back and lead her out of the bar.

Still wearing that long, form-fitting tee and loose skirt with sandals, she looks like an Egyptian temptress in modern form. She also shivers beneath the mountain chill.

"Here." I shrug out of my suit coat and slip it over her shoulders, keeping my hands there a second as she adjusts to the dwarfing size.

"Thank you." Her voice softens, and she glances at me before looking at the dark water rushing through this town.

The riverwalk is decorated with bright orange railings, celebrating the nearby university. The water looks like black silk as it weaves rapidly away from us. Streetlamps light our path, but I wouldn't want any woman walking alone along this trail. Just like I don't like to see the college girl with headphones running past us.

I hate that women live by different rules. I'm protective of my only sister, who continually teaches me how the boundaries are different between men and women. A woman can never be too alert, too self-aware, and it's been the mission of my life to protect whomever I can from evil that lurks everywhere.

Even in your own goddamn home.

Quickly dismissing thoughts of the past, I focus on the woman presently walking beside me at a leisurely pace. She doesn't appear in any more of a rush to end our stroll than I am.

"I grew up near a river," she says, keeping her eyes on the one beside us. "It was the only place that felt like home." Her voice lulls, the tone distant and a little sad.

"Anywhere I've heard of?"

"Probably not. It was a pretty small community." She leaves it at that, and I don't push for more than she's willing to give.

I'm just happy with her company. She's so beautiful, pulling my attention like the sun. Or in our current case, the crescent moon with a definite planet shining just off the corner. But it's more than her beauty that draws me in. I like her enthusiasm for art and her excitement to work with young adults. She also seems passionate about helping a community express their uniqueness.

She talked about vibes in art and celebrating a group of people, but I like the energy she emits. She's grace with a hint of eclectic. Humor and poise. *Her* vibe is contagious. Hell, I want to pick up a paintbrush, and I've never painted anything in my life other than an old house.

"Couldn't wait to get out of there?" I ask, knowing it's the stereotype of small towns. Either you can't wait to escape, or you never leave. There doesn't seem to be an in-between. From my own experience, my escape was cut short, and I'd been lassoed back in, permanently.

"Something like that," she admits ominously.

"I understand."

"Sounds like another story." She stops walking and glances at me.

Feeling the weight of those silvery eyes, I pause as well and brace my forearms on the railing to look toward the dark river.

"The short version is your typical tried to leave but got roped back in and stayed story." I crane my neck, glancing at her over my shoulder. "I have *not* traveled to places far, far away."

Leaning her hip against the railing, she stands close to me. Close enough that her breasts brush against my arm.

"Do you wish you had?"

"Yes," I confess, squinting back at the silky water. "There are lots of places I'd like to see in person. But my life has been full of responsibilities. Both professional and personal. I don't get much time to myself."

Tonight was a rare occasion.

And if I had gone off to see the world, I'd have missed out on things that happened at home.

Clay turning the family business around.

Keeping Judd grounded.

Ford becoming a professional athlete.

Sebastian getting his shit together.

Vale and Hudson.

Knox was the only one who went away for years, devoting his time to service in the Navy. As a former naval aviator, he's been everywhere.

My Delilah gives me a questioning look.

"Got a family?" she asks.

I snort. "A big one."

"One of your own?"

I pause, studying her face and catching on the soft glow of her eyes. "If you're asking if I'm married with children, the answer is no on both counts. Never had a wife." Although I came close once. "And no kids officially my own."

"Officially?" She tilts her head to the side, waiting for more information.

"Now that's a story too long to tell in one night." I chuckle. "What about you? Got a husband?" She mentioned a book boyfriend earlier, but I want a solid answer.

"Or a wife?" she counters seriously, then chuckles. "Zero on all counts. No husband or wife. No children, extraterrestrial or otherwise. I don't have that mom-gene women are assumed to carry."

I nod. I respect women who know who they are—or are not —when it comes to parenting.

"No one here saying you have to have kids," I point to my chest.

She smiles slowly. "Speaking of traveling, my family was a bit nomadic when I was young." She shifts, gripping the railing and turning toward the river. "Adventures, as my mama used to call them." Her voice lowers even more. "But then my mama went to jail when I was young, and I guess I continue a nomadic lifestyle because she's locked up and can't enjoy it anymore."

When she turns back toward me, something in my expression must show how sorry I am that her mother is behind bars.

"Don't feel sorry for me," she immediately commands, twisting to face me, straightening her body, and I stand taller to match her stance. "From ten to eighteen, I lived with my aunt, who was a wonderful, inspiring, unique woman. Then had art school. After that, I set off to conquer the world."

While she makes it sound exciting—art school and the world—sadness still rests beneath the surface. The loss of her mother must have been hard, and I can relate. Still, I don't pry.

She waved her arms out to emphasize the adventure of life and caught at the edges of my jacket to keep it on her shoulders.

Reaching for the lapel, I fasten the single button to keep the garment in place on her, needing a minute to distract myself from asking more about her mother. My profession makes me curious about the details, but I want to know about this strong woman, the survivor in her, more than her mother.

When I glance at her face, she's watching me. For some reason, I don't remove my hands from where the two sides of the jacket now link together.

Our eyes lock, and I lean forward, swallowing hard, feeling connected to her and desperate to kiss her. To bring that connection closer.

The setting is almost romantic. A dark river. The low streetlamps. A deserted pathway.

Only . . . the sudden stomp of hard soles running on concrete shatters the moment.

"Stop. He's got my bag."

With a quick glance behind me, I see a young woman running toward us, waving her arm toward the man who just raced by.

"Shit." I release my Delilah. "Stay here."

Running as fast as I can in hard-soled shoes, despite not having jurisdiction here, I chase the culprit. When he glances over his shoulder at my pursuit, he trips, stumbles, and tosses the bag at me, which I awkwardly catch. The distraction buys him time to get back up and take off.

With the backpack in my hands, I bend at the waist, drawing in deep breaths. I'm not typically on a chase, and the whiskeys I had earlier, along with a beer at the bar, have caught up to me. I heave in air before standing upright and turning back for the younger woman who stands near my walking partner.

When I return to where they wait, the young co-ed's face is flushed from her pursuit.

"Is there someone we can call for you?" Delilah asks, rubbing her hands up and down the younger woman's arms. "Maybe walk you somewhere?"

The girl shakes her head. "I was almost home when he tugged the backpack out of my hands." She sighs. "I wouldn't have chased him, but my laptop is in there, and I hadn't backed up my paper."

"Oh, sweetheart," Delilah coos.

"Where do you live? We'll walk with you," I add.

"I'm just over the bridge." She points toward a walkway leading over the river to a row of apartment buildings on the opposite side.

"Let's go," I say, motioning for her to lead the way.

First, she fumbles through her bag, then with a shaky voice she says, "I'm just going to call my mom while we walk, if that's okay?"

"Whatever you need," Delilah says.

We let the young college student walk a few feet ahead of us, giving her enough space to talk to the most important person in her life.

Moments like this make me miss my own mother something fierce. "My mom died when I was twelve," I blurt.

My walking partner swings her head in my direction. "I'm so sorry."

I bite the inside of my cheek before I add the rest of the story, including how my dad died when I was twenty-two.

When her hand comes to my bicep, I glance down at it. Her fingers are long and thin. Her hand slightly veined. Earlier, I'd noticed bright splashes of paint mixed with the rich brown polish and those splatters now make sense.

She surprises me even more by sliding her hand down my arm and slipping her hand against mine. She leans against my arm.

I link our fingers together, unable to recall the last time I held someone's hand. Her fingers felt right connected with mine. Two puzzle pieces coming together, easily clicking into place.

When we near the bridge, two other young girls stand by the corner. They race toward the co-ed in front of us, and all three girls embrace. Coos and questions, along with hands stroking over the stolen-backpack victim's hair and back, meet us when we draw closer.

The victim turns towards us as we approach. "Thank you. My friends will walk with me from here."

"Are you sure?" Delilah releases my hand and steps closer to the girl. For someone who says she isn't motherly, she tenderly pulls the girl toward her for a hug, whispering something that makes the younger woman nod.

"Thank you," she says to me one more time before Delilah and I continue walking.

She slips her hand around my bicep, but doesn't reach for my hand again. I miss the connection, but I like this position almost as much when she leans against me one more time.

"You lied, Samson. You really are from outer space."

"What do you mean?" I chuckle.

"Superman. He came from the planet Krypton."

I laugh a little harder. "I am definitely not Superman."

"Oh, I beg to differ . . . Superman."

And now she's given me another nickname.

I only wish I could live up to it for her.

4

———

[Taxi]

Eventually, *Superman* and I continue walking in silence. There's something so different about him. While I don't consider myself a good judge of character, especially of the male persuasion, part of the reason is that I'm guarded. I never want to be like my mama. Never want to be so attached that I can't function without a man. But something about this man says I can be who *I* want to be, and he'd be interested.

I can't believe I told him about Mama being in jail. That isn't information I readily share, if ever, and within a few hours of meeting this man, I'm spilling one of my deepest kept secrets.

I'm not proud of Mama, however I understand why she did what she did. Desperation leads to despair and poor decisions.

Although I don't typically pass out that nugget from my past, the words slipped easily from my lips in his presence.

While it was intoxicating to see him in superhero action, and there's no disputing he's a good-looking man, there's something beneath the surface that suggests he's inherently good. He won't judge. Like Clark Kent keeping Superman beneath the dress shirt and glasses, this man screams the same kind of cryptic secret with his kindness, his attentiveness, and his old-school manners.

Move over, Henry Cavill.

I would have kissed him right along the riverwalk if that young girl hadn't been shaking so hard from both pursuing her attacker and fear because she'd been robbed.

Moments before the distraction, Samson, or Superman, or whoever he really is, was about to kiss me, I was certain of it. The way those soft blues darkened. The way his gaze fixed on my lips. I don't know that I've ever wanted a kiss so badly in my life.

And I feel the same way right now as we stand outside my hotel room.

For a woman on a man-free diet, I'm hungry for more with him.

"Well, it's been an evening." His soft chuckle punctuates the night, and he scratches at the back of his neck, like he's nervous. On such a rugged man, his anxiety is endearing, almost cute. He's wearing a dress shirt and tie, like an uptight professional, but I've seen him in hot pursuit chasing a thief.

What's beneath the white button-up?

I lean against the hotel door at my back.

Neither of us moves.

I could invite him in, but something deep within me wants him to do the asking. Like, for once, I want someone to ask me to stay a while, which makes no sense as we're standing in a hotel hallway, the quintessential location for people traveling to and fro, not people who stay put.

He clears his throat. "I don't really know how to do this, but I'd love to kiss you."

"You don't know how to kiss?" I question, certain he's joking. His lips look like they were made for making out.

"Say good night," he admits.

I press off the door and lean toward him. "I guess a kiss might be the best way to say it." My voice drips, giving him every innuendo and indication that a kiss is exactly what I want.

Only, when his warm hand cups the side of my face, I stiffen. Not out of caution but in shock. Like the slow mixture of colors blending together. The heat of his hand is red to the blue inside me. The combination is a cool violet, full of lust and attraction, but also something deeper, something richer.

Then he kisses me.

The kiss is short and sweet but electric. A vibrant neon purple bolt of lightning rushes down my middle and cracks open my chest. His lips are soft, and the silver bristle around his mouth tickles, sending a second crackle straight to a part that hasn't felt a spark other than from my own hand in a long time.

When he pulls back, practically dragging his lips from mine, the gentle blue in his eyes has turned to fierce sapphire. He cups the back of my head, pulling me back for a second round.

They say lightning never strikes twice. Whoever *they* are has never kissed this man.

The instant our mouths meet again, the flicker of our first kiss is overshadowed by sudden fireworks. Charges of white light and explosions of bright purple. His lips are still soft and full but commanding, like he knows how to take charge while remaining tender. Everything in me wants to surrender to him.

When the tip of his tongue slides along the seam of my mouth, my lips part, like my heart expands, allowing him to greet my tongue. My lower half arches toward him, a magnetic force beyond my control. Like he's my new kryptonite. His other hand presses against my lower back, urging me closer to him, and sending more tingling sparks over my skin. Our tongues continue to sip and swirl, and we lock into whatever this strangely wonderful thing happening between us is.

Then a throat clears, and the soft patter of feet on carpet snaps us apart.

I step back, bumping into the closed door behind me, while my superman stretches his arms wide and braces his hands on the door frame, caging me in like he's shielding me from our newest intruder.

I chuckle, and he chews at his lower lip, fighting a smile and dipping his head as someone passes behind him.

"Well," I whisper, struggling to find more accurate words when I want to say, *Come in. Stay awhile.*

"Guess you better get inside," he says, keeping the position of his arms wide and protective. But those eyes of his spiraled another notch in the color wheel. The shade is an intense blue that rivals midnight on a snowy evening.

And I'm frozen in place. I want nothing more than to feel the weight of him over me. Feel the strength in those arms wrapped around me. I want his kisses on my lips and neck and down my body to places long ignored.

"Delilah," he struggles, the name strained.

Internally, I scream my actual name for him, wanting to hear it in the same way as this nickname.

"Go inside," he whispers, like he's hanging on by a thread, and all I need to do is invite him in. Give him permission to enter.

But I don't.

Instead, I suck in all this buzzing energy, swirling both around me and inside my belly, and spin for the lock pad, scan my hotel card, and slip inside the room with a final glance back.

He hasn't moved.

"Goodbye, Superman," I whisper before slowly closing the door, keeping my eyes on him until the last possible second. When I finally shut it, I fall against the barrier, like I'm spent from exertion. The sheer willpower to walk away. I tip back my head and breathe out a heavy breath.

What the hell am I doing?

That man has subpoenaed my vagina, but another organ overrules. My heart screams *be careful here.*

Still, I spin, peeking through the security peephole to find him standing in the same position for another second before he pushes away from the door frame and swipes both his hands down his face, like he's just as affected as I am.

Why didn't he ask to come inside?

Why didn't I invite him in?

But that's the crux of things.

I never invite someone to stay because I'm afraid they'll never ask me the same thing.

5

———————

May

[Stone]

"What's up, man?" My brother, Clay, only fifteen months younger than me, claps me on the back as he rounds my seat and takes his own at the table inside Milton Roadhouse. The bar has an old-time saloon vibe with dark, wood-paneled walls and wagon-wheel chandeliers. The three-sided bar has a large standing-room-only space surrounded by a smattering of tables, which are a mix of low barrels with circular surfaces and high tops.

My brothers and I try to get together at least once a month, just the guys. No offense to our one and only youngest sister, Vale, but men have guy things to share. And lately, my brothers are fixated on their love lives.

In the past two plus years, Sebastian stumbled into Enya. Ford met her sister, Cadence. Knox reunited with his high school sweetheart, Halle. Clay was rescued by Mavis. Only Judd and I remain standing, although we aren't exactly certain what's going on with our reclusive brother and the woman he's suddenly claiming as his fiancée.

Honestly, compared to that last man standing cliché, I'd like to take a seat. Preferably back at a bar in Tennessee next to one mystery woman I call Delilah in my head.

"Hey," I grunt as Clay takes a seat beside me. While I'm still dark in features, Clay has more gray with scruff on his face that matches the color of his short hair. His skin is weathered from years of outdoor work for our family business, Sylver Seed & Soil. The place was our mother's dream, and after her death, and our father subsequently running it into the ground, Clay rebuilt the business. Eventually, we roped Judd into being the chief accountant for the business in an effort to keep our quietest brother close. Judd's the one we most feared might slip between the cracks after the way our father treated him.

Knox also works at the Seed & Soil in the landscaping department, specifically in brick patio builds. He also volunteers for the fire department. Knox is built like me, more broad than tall, compared to Judd or Clay. We share the same dark features, but my brother is starting to gray near his temples.

He joins us next.

"Gentleman of the Round Table," he teases about the low top I'd snagged. Milton's isn't particularly busy for a mid-week evening, yet all the high tops were taken. He claps hands with Clay. The two of them have grown closer since his retirement from the Navy. Plus, Mavis and Halle have formed a special friendship.

"I need a beer," Sebastian huffs, falling into a chair, which slides from the force and bangs into Knox.

"You don't drink," I remind him, arching a brow, wondering what would prompt him to say he needs what he's given up for good.

"I know." He scrubs both hands down his face, tattoos on display, reminding me of how my brother has had a tough life until recently.

"It's just . . . the estrogen is so high in my house." He grunts, but then slowly smiles. His wife Enya is good for him, and along with their daughter Adara and their newest addition, Annabelle, he's surrounded by love he greatly deserves.

"Don't I know it," Knox speaks next, bumping his elbow against Sebastian, who sits too close to him. "Violet is still giving Halle a run for her money most days."

Knox's stepdaughter had trouble adjusting to life in Sterling Falls when she first moved here. She's turned herself around, also working at the Seed & Soil and babysitting for anyone in the family who needs one. She's a good kid, but on the cusp of going off to college.

"She's so like her mother." Knox slowly smiles as well, shaking his head. He dated Halle when she was seventeen, so his seventeen-year-old stepdaughter brings back memories.

"How's Dutton?" Sebastian asks Clay. His son likes to wear pink and paint his nails.

"He's good," Clay adds, his own smile joining the rest of them. "He's slowly growing into a Swiftie." Clay air-quotes the term used for a certain cultural icon in pop music and her enormous fandom.

"Speaking of Dutton . . . heard Winnie got in another fight at school," Sebastian informs the table.

Clay shakes his head. "Ford told me."

Our brother Ford's daughter, Winnie, is best friends with Dutton, acting as his silent bodyguard at school and often in trouble for it.

"Where is Ford?" I ask, glancing over my shoulder, like I expect him to appear. He doesn't go out as often as the rest of us. His three girls and pregnant wife keep him home, but after a successful career in professional baseball, he's happy to dedicate more time to his family.

"Cadence has him by the throat." Knox imitates being choked with his hands.

"You mean the balls." Sebastian mimics juggling a set in his hands.

"He's just in *love*," Clay drawls.

"Aren't you all?" I remind them as the sole man at the table not in love but still missing a woman who was never mine to miss.

"You know you could be," Clay counters. He arches a brow, when he knows Emerson Milton and I are nothing more than friends. The entire town thinks we are more, but we aren't.

"There's always Mabel Wilson," Knox teases.

I wrinkle my nose. Mabel Wilson is a sweet older woman who rotates between calling the fire department for false alarms, mainly because she wants to ogle the young men in uniform, and calling the sheriff department for some minor infractions like sheep in her front yard or a whispering noise in her attic, again only to invite one of my deputies into her house for cookies and tea.

My last interaction with Mabel, she mistakenly offered me dog biscuits as her homemade specialty. I send younger deputies whenever the department gets a call, warning them in advance not to accept any baked goods from her. My newest recruit learned to heed my warning the hard way.

Sebastian snorts at the reference to Mabel, while Knox leans into him, like they share the joke. Sebastian bumps Knox back with his shoulder, nudging him to get off him.

The scene is so reminiscent of when they were kids. The kids I raised.

I sigh.

Clay goes next with his suggestions. "What about Halle's

friend, Cookie Westmore? You already know she has a thing for handcuffs."

Sebastian and Knox roar into another round of laughter at my expense.

Cookie had a little mishap a couple of months ago. The single mother was attached to a bedpost when we got the call from one of her teenage children. Seems a little bedroom fun got out of hand and a one-night stand took the key with him.

"What about someone from Vale's book club?" Sebastian air-quotes around the club that's so much more than books to the women in this town, and might be where Cookie got those pink, feather-edged handcuffs in the first place.

"Pass." Not that there is anything wrong with any woman who is a member of the not-so-secret *Sterlets*, but I've grown up in this town, and I've seen too many things behind the scenes to be attracted to anyone local.

My mind is still set on someone who landed in Knoxville. And mysteriously disappeared into thin air the next morning.

I thought for certain I'd see her again. Maybe in the hotel lobby where they served breakfast. Even somewhere local. The city was a decent size, but as happenstance reunited us once, I bet on it bringing us together again a second time.

I'd been wrong. And I've been kicking myself that I didn't pursue something more that night.

Then again, I didn't want a one-night stand with her. Something about her said she's a woman you get to know on a deeper level, so you have all your nights with her. Which is silly because I'm not that kind of guy. The forever kind. I want to be, but I'm not.

I thought I was in love once, but it turned out not to be love after all.

Back then, I had siblings to raise and a house to keep, so I never made love a priority. At least not love between me and a partner. An equal who'd share things with me. A companion for summer nights and a confidante for the stormy ones.

"There's also Veronica Archer." But even Knox doesn't sound convincing when mentioning another single mother whose daughter plays on Hudson's travel baseball team. Ronnie is a widow, and while I'm sympathetic to her loss, she has a penchant for married men in the area. I'm too single for her liking.

"Don't worry, we'll find you someone," Clay says, reaching out and squeezing my shoulder. While I know he's teasing, and he's also well-meaning, I don't like the reminder that I'm alone. And that I haven't *found* someone for myself.

So, I blurt before I think, "I already found someone."

Brows lift. Eyes widen. Mouths gape.

"Emerson?" Knox draws out her name, shock lacing every syllable.

I've been rather open with my family recently that Emerson Milton, who is the town mayor, and I were never a thing. People have their perception of our relationship. We knew the truth. Or rather, I protected Em and her secret.

But since coming back from Tennessee, I've been more resistant to accept invitations from my friend. More reluctant to play a part in *her* story.

I shake my head, looking down at the rough wood on the tabletop.

"Who then?" Sebastian asks, leaning forward. His tone is serious, concerned even.

"Yes, do tell." Knox drops his voice while setting his elbows on the table and folding his hands beneath his chin, acting like an eager busybody wanting the latest gossip.

"No one you know," I state. Then add, "It was nothing." The difficult part in that statement was it didn't feel like nothing. Even if it was only a kiss, the moment was powerful, and the entire night felt a bit . . . magical. Which is not a term I'd ever use to describe something that happened to me.

Just as confounding, though, was her disappearing act.

"When?"

"Who?"

"Where?"

The questions fall in line like the ages of my brothers, from oldest to younger: Clay, Knox, Sebastian.

I double-tap the table and blow out a breath, sorry I've opened my mouth.

"Just met someone about a month ago. Thought the night was something special and hoped I'd see her again." I shrug. "But I didn't."

"Why not?" Sebastian questions, arching his brow.

"That sucks." Knox shakes his head.

"Shit." Clay focuses on me, his eyes soft with understanding.

"What are you going to do?" I state, like it's a non-issue.

The truth is I've spent most of my life reassuring my brothers, and Vale, that they deserve love. That their other half is waiting for them, seeking them out, because I believe there is someone for everyone. Just not for me, apparently.

My life is full while empty at the same time, but it's not something I'd ever admit to any of them.

I'm the oldest. I've always needed to be strong for them. It's written in my name. *Stone.*

"Sometimes things just happen," I use as a way of excuse for why it didn't happen for me and my mystery woman.

"Like a woman falls outside a bakery in a storm," Sebastian states, eyeing me while reminding me how he met Enya.

"Or returns to her hometown," Knox adds, a nod to his own story.

"Or she rescues you in the rain." Clay's story mirrors Sebastian's in that a rainstorm brought him Mavis, only he's the one whose truck broke down. She saved him.

"Yeah, well . . ." I really have nothing to add to their initial meetings with their soulmates.

A woman ran into me in a hotel hallway, rammed me with a book, then I knocked her jaw with my head. Not exactly a meet cute. Vale has explained that's how all romances begin.

We didn't have a romance. We didn't even have a fling.

We had one kiss.

An encounter that still haunts me.

Clay reaches over to squeeze my shoulder again, and I'm grateful when Emerson's youngest sister, Eleanor, arrives at our table to take our order and pull the spotlight off me.

I'm better at letting them talk while I listen.

That's what I always do.

6

[Taxi]

"That looks beautiful, Kendra." I compliment the budding artist's delicate work as she adds additional flowers to the mural on the community center's exterior. Passion flowers are Tennessee's official wildflower, and the intricate design adds a burst of exotic to the complex image that combines the familiar faces and symbolic images that represent this community. The flowers are often muted lavender with white accents, but sometimes white with blue striping.

And that blue reminds me of the color of a certain someone's eyes that I should have forgotten by now.

The star-like flower feels appropriately named as I tell myself that night was only one of false passion. Not the deeper sensation my rose-colored glasses believed I was experiencing.

Yet. Deep inside, something still tells me I'm wrong.

As much as I thought Samson-slash-Superman-slash-whoever-he-was did me wrong, I somehow feel like I'm the one not right. Not confident about what I saw when I saw him the next morning, eating breakfast in the hotel lobby.

"Like this?" Maxim asks, wanting me to assess his technique. The one I didn't try to correct, but made a suggestion about. If he held the brush differently, the hand cramps he has complained about might dissipate. Then again, I didn't want to fix what wasn't broken yet. An artist has their own unique interpretation of a work and how to create it.

"That's amazing, Max." I offer the shy young man a patient smile. He reminds me in some ways of my nephew. A smart but timid boy blossoming into a precocious and mindful one.

My thoughts leap back to another person I considered thoughtful and kind. Gentlemanly as he walked me to my hotel door and kissed me like he'd been waiting for me his whole life.

Then again, that was only me projecting once again on a man.

The idea scares me.

I'm restless by nature, although some might argue it was nurture. Mama and her adventures, which weren't anything other than running after the unattainable.

That restlessness inside me feels somehow inherent, and it's caused me to fear chasing any man. I've seen the disappointment it can lead to, just like I'm currently disappointed in Mr. Tall, Silver, and Sexy, a man I can't stop thinking about every time I walk down the hotel hallway and stop in front of my door.

Because that's where he kissed me senseless.

I sigh, and watch my current charges work their magic, filling in the mural I sketched out in grand form for them to color.

Jungle greens. Rich browns. Deep blue. Sunshine yellow.

The image is alive.

While I'm silently dying inside. *Okay, dramatic much, Taxi?*

However, my displeasure feels like grief. A loss of something I didn't have in the first place, but felt the trust slowly opening the door of my heart.

I mean, I told him about Mama.

And as much as I'm always on the move, I want to stop. I want to be grounded somewhere, where someone is waiting for me. Wanting me to stay put.

One reason I immerse myself in various communities is because I'm secretly searching, hoping, seeking that sense of permanent connection that can keep me planted.

Yet nothing scares me more than setting down roots, only to be left behind.

The thought brings me back to my aunt. Living with her was a moment of stability, and yet I never felt like I belonged there. Not because of anything she did, or my uncle did, but just a feeling I'd conjured. Like I shouldn't get too comfortable because I didn't deserve to be there, living with them. Not after what happened.

That sensation drove me away from the only home I'd ever known, prompting decades of wanderlust.

In my forties, I have a new perspective. I've been running my entire life out of fear, and if I leave first, I can't get hurt. So, I seek belonging and stability, but uproot myself before anyone can ask me to stay.

Because I'm afraid no one will ever ask.

Silly, really, to still harbor such feelings. I make my own destiny, and if my destiny is wherever I go next, I should plant those roots. I should invest in people and forge relationships. But something always whispers that I still haven't found what I'm looking for.

Because I want someone to be looking for me.

I'm holding that seat, still waiting on the *right* man to take it.

And I thought he had. At least for a few hours, I started to believe.

"Miss . . . Taxi," Kai corrects himself, holding out a bucket filled with the bright green paint intended for the tree leaves he's about to decorate.

The community organizer wants the kids to address me as Miss Alexander, but I told them I prefer Taxi. I appreciate teaching them respect for elders, but I'm not that old. Not yet. I might be the master here, but I see the artistic ability in each and every student ready to surpass me.

Their talent is refreshing. Art was such a godsend for me. Art is where I found grounding and a release for energy and emotions I couldn't describe or confine.

And Aunt Trudy always supported my dreams.

At one point, I even believed the elusive thing I was chasing was a dream. Then I realized I'm living that dream. I travel. I paint. I meet interesting people. What a grand life.

But I want that one person. The right person. For me.

I nod my approval at Kai's selection, before calling out to another student. "Looks good, Ariel." The young woman looks like the mermaid princess who is her namesake. She gives me thumbs up as best she can with a paint brush in hand.

They are such a great bunch of young adults. Their futures lie ahead of them. Their hearts open to possibilities. Their minds sharp. Their creativity endless.

I remember that energy.

Out to save the world, I'd told myself then. Have real adventures, not the false ones Mama called our aimlessness.

But now, I just want to save me.

7

July

[Stone]

My sister has been dating my former best friend behind my back, and it comes as quite a shock to learn they are in love.

Cortland Haven is twelve years older than Vale, and I am overly protective of her, having raised her from birth.

Not to mention, Cortland committed the betrayal of all betrayals when we were younger, and I was at my most vulnerable. I don't trust him, but I trust my sister. She's had her own difficulties in life, but she has a good head on her shoulders, being a single mother to the most amazing eleven-year-old, my nephew Hudson.

Another child I've felt responsible for since birth, as Vale and I have shared a house since Hudson was born.

Family is important to me. I've made them the center of my

world. The one commitment I embraced, instead of steering away from. They are my sun, and I'm simply a planet circling around them, trying to keep them safe and warm and protected from things that might burn.

And because family is sacred, a long time ago, I instituted a mandatory Sunday evening meal that fluctuates between afternoon barbecues in warm months to football days in the fall and casual dinners in the winter.

Our newest tradition began when our younger brother, Ford, decided to move home. He cleared an overgrown meadow on our property to make a baseball diamond. Now, we have our own little Field of Dreams right here in Sterling Falls, West Virginia. Because his birthday is close to the Fourth of July, we celebrated his special day with our first family baseball game a year ago. This is our second season. Over the course of twenty-four months, our family has grown, like the wild weeds once occupying this once-ignored field.

"You okay with this?" Clay asks, questioning me about the newest relationship in our family.

He means Cortland and Vale.

"Guess I'm going to have to be," I say, squinting toward the lovebirds in the driveway just outside the fence line where they are awaiting extra visitors to this year's game. Observing them, I note their contrast. Cortland is tall and dark, though his hair is graying just like mine. Vale has long, honey-colored hair, like our mother's, with the signature blue eyes of all the Sylvers.

While I like to keep things just the seven of us and our newly expanded family members, reinforcing my protective nature, Vale convinced me to allow some additions to this year's festivities. People who we need to remember helped us, once upon a time.

Like Mary Haven, Cortland's mom.

"Don't know that I even understand what is happening lately," I whisper, meaning the attraction between Cort and Vale.

He fucking helped me change her diapers.

Clay chuckles beside me and claps my shoulder. "Love, man."

At that exact moment, my sister kisses my former best friend.

Forcing myself to look beyond Vale and Cort, I stare at the house behind them. The two-story Cape Cod with dormer windows and a wraparound porch is in its best form. It took years to restore the white clapboards and replace the worn roof. Years before I had the means or money to do internal fixes, like a better furnace and an updated kitchen. But beyond the line of vehicles that make the driveway look like a used car lot, the house stands tall and glistening, almost prideful.

Like it might be smiling at me. Pleased with me for opening my yard to people who haven't been here in more than two decades.

"Guess I'd better get this over with," I grumble to Clay, about greeting our additional guests as another car pulls up.

Outside of Cortland and his mother, I hadn't expected Cort's spitfire younger sister, Trinity, or his laidback brother, Clinton, along with his little girl, but at this point, the more the *wearier*.

As I approach the edge of the driveway, Cort instantly lifts his head, greeting me over Vale, who leans into him, with a short, sharp, "Stone."

I tip up my chin, still finding it difficult to say his name after all this time. My heart is no stranger to wounds, but some cuts are deeper than others. Cort's betrayal has dulled, but still aches on occasion. I've asked Vale to give me time to wrap my head around their relationship. I don't want to ostracize my sister for her love match, even if I don't particularly like it. She's a grown woman. Her heart. Her choice.

"Stone Sylver, it's been too long." Mary Haven's voice cuts off the staring contest between Cort and me and yanks me back, like a yo-yo, to being a kid. To a time when I hung out at the Havens' home more than my own. Her voice gets me every time I see her around town, asking how I'm doing, asking if I need anything, like I'm still a twelve-year-old boy, living with a father who shut down after our mother's death and left me to raise a baby along with a few toddlers.

Mary must be somewhere in her late sixties by now, but she looks as young as ever with a short, white bob in loose curls. She lost her husband about ten years ago.

I welcome her embrace, overwhelmed by a hug I remember almost more than my mother's. Mary was like a second mom because Cort and I had been inseparable as children. From cradle to college, he was a brother from another mother, and as important to me as Clay and the rest of my siblings.

Eventually, I pulled back from the rest of the Havens because of Cort. For my own sanity, I had to let them all go.

And now wasn't the time to work through the emotions brought about by our slowly developing reunion.

"Thank you for having us," Mary addresses me when she ends our embrace, but keeps her hands on my shoulders, eyeing me like the mother she is. Like she knows I'm struggling with this new development.

Cortland and Vale. My former best friend and my sister.

"Of course," I offer her the strongest smile I can muster, and then greet Trinity and Clinton, while watching Clinton's little girl, Ruby James, run toward my niece, June. The two girls hug like long-lost friends when they are only five.

"Now, where is Trudy?" Mary questions, looking around my shoulders. "I heard she and I are team moms. One for each."

This is the first I've heard we will have even *more* guests, and I mentally calculate if we have enough burgers and brats for everyone. Then again, I left Vale in charge of food shopping for today's meal, so I smile at the mention of Trudy Wallace.

Trudy had been our mother's best friend since high school.

She's a pillar in this community. Once a foster parent to her nieces and nephews, and anyone else who needed a place to stay, she would have adopted all of us Sylvers if it hadn't been for our father's intervention. And even once he passed away, she suggested taking in the younger set so I could follow my dream.

Instead, I chose the road already traveled and stayed. Trudy had enough responsibilities.

Cort chuckles at the mention of Trudy. "We're a little old for team moms."

"Says the man hiding behind his," I mutter, knowing Vale's invitation to include Mary Haven was intended to soften Cort's attendance.

My comment wasn't meant to be heard by everyone, but somehow, it was. An eerie silence falls behind me when only moments ago the baseball field was full of chatter and the sound of a ball hitting a bat for batting practice.

"Don't be a dickhead, dickhead," Cort says. His tone is light, teasing even, cautious. Like he's offering me an olive branch through a joke. Through a comment we might have said to one another when we were still inseparable teens.

"I'm not a dickhead, dickhead." My face is tight for a second. Jaw clenched. Back teeth snap together, but I can't seem to fight a smile.

We might be too old to tussle in the yard like we once did, but I *feel* a little like a middle schooler as we toss insults at one another.

"Okay now," Mary says, swinging her gaze from her son to me and back. "That's enough talk about dickheads."

Spoken like a true mother.

"Mom," Trinity barks before laughing. Cort's younger sister falls somewhere between Knox and Ford's age. The short blonde is a force as the only sister in the Haven clan.

"I brought my famous lemonade with me." Mary winks at

me. "One for the kiddos and one for adults who aren't dickheads."

I choke on a laugh while my mouth waters. There is just something special about Mary's lemonade. She makes it from scratch with the right combination of real lemons, sugar, and ice, and a pinch of something I can never discern.

"I call Mary," I holler, slipping my arm around her shoulders, claiming her as *my* team's mom.

Our family teams are led by Clay and me, which feels about right as he often played good cop to my bad. Ironic that I'm now the town sheriff, but once upon a time, we needed a family disciplinarian, and that role fell on me, while Clay was the softer, more philosophical side of our pair. We took on the roles we *thought* a mother and a father might offer our younger siblings.

I would never have survived raising the younger set without Clay.

As I'm escorting Mary to the actual ball field, another car pulls into the driveway. Assuming it's Trudy Wallace, I pause and turn back toward the drive, while Mary continues onward.

The back door of a sedan flings open, and a young boy rushes out like he's been sprung free from a cage.

Simon Gilbert is a dark-haired nine-year-old Trudy has claimed to be her grandson, and he's particularly attached to our brother Judd in a sort of big brother relationship. With a mitt and a ball in his hand, he's running toward the field when Trudy exits the passenger side of the front seat and says, "I'm not raising no Tasmanian devil here."

Her kind but strong voice has the young boy doing a one-eighty, racing back to the vehicle to close the car door.

Trudy is roughly the age my mother would have been, so in her late sixties, like Mary. She's a robust woman with ebony skin, and her current hairstyle is a short cut with sharp bangs. Because she exited the passenger side of the vehicle, I squint in the direction of the driver's side, curious about who else is joining us today.

Trudy greets Cort and Vale first since they stand closest to the drive.

My gaze, however, is aimed at Trudy's car, like I can't seem to look away until I know who drove her and Simon here. The pull to that vehicle is unsettling, pleasantly eerie. Like the air almost crackles, yet it's a perfectly sun-filled day.

Must be the heat, I decide, until a feminine form finally slips from the driver's side, standing tall and curvy in all the right ways with a ponytail of wild, dark curls on the top of her head.

I'm frozen in place, watching as she shuts the door, and then approaches where Trudy stands near Vale and Cortland.

Large, dark sunglasses cover her eyes, while she wears bib overalls with a skin-tone tank top underneath. She looks like a fucking supermodel. The air around her says don't speak to me. And yet, without seeing her eyes, I already know what they look like.

Mercury and magic, and haunting, because I haven't been able to get them out of my head for three long months.

Three months where I've been kicking myself for not asking her if I could come into her hotel room. If I could have her real name and her phone number.

Three months where I still feel her lips against mine.

Three months of imagining all the ways she'd press against me, beneath me, above me. With my hands on her hips, like my palms were made to fit there.

"Vale, I don't know if you remember my niece, Tallulah."

My head swivels from the tongue-tying beauty to Trudy Wallace and back.

What?

Tallulah? How close the name is to the nickname I'd given her . . . Delilah. When she'd called me Samson at first and ended the night calling me Superman.

Hell, her voice has been haunting me as well, saying things she didn't say, like she wanted me to invite me into her room, wanted me inside her body.

Eventually, I feel my toes and move my feet, crunching over the gravel to approach this new collection of guests.

Vale is hugging Trudy while I stand just off Cort's left side.

While I've finally been able to move closer to them, the one thing that refuses to shift is my gaze. From her. Tallulah.

"Stone," my sister says, at the same time as Tallulah looks in my direction and quietly gasps. Her lush lips separate only for a brief moment before she slowly removes her sunglasses.

The resemblance to Trudy is non-existent, aside from their similar jet-black hair. Tallulah is almost willowy on top with wider hips. Her eyes are shaped differently, sharp and silver compared to the warm, rich brown of Trudy's. And her lips are deeply pursed.

Remaining stuck in place, like a deep-rooted weed, my tongue is knotted, my eyes transfixed, until she catches on them and immediately looks away.

Stricken.

Like a baseball bat to the gut, I feel the hit.

What the hell was that expression all about?

Finally, I find my manners and move my feet again, stepping toward this surprising, stunning, puzzling newcomer.

"Um. Hey. Welcome to my home." I sound like a fucking robot as I extend a hand, equally robotic in action, when I've had my lips on hers. When I've already felt the warmth of her palms and the curve of her hips.

When she finally sets her hand in mine, we don't shake as much as hold our hands together. Wrapping my fingers tighter around hers, a sense of rightness circles me.

She's here. This is her. Destiny did not fail me.

Only, her hand lies limp in mine, like I'm holding a dead fish.

What the hell?

I apply more pressure, almost refusing to let go until she looks at me, meets my eyes again.

Except she doesn't. She blatantly refuses to look at me, instead glancing around me like I'm not standing here, holding her hand, squeezing, straining for her attention.

What am I missing?

"The name is Taxi," she corrects her aunt in a bored tone, like she's been forced to greet me, and doesn't like the introduction. Like we've never met. Like she's never seen me before and isn't seeing me now.

Somewhere behind Taxi, Trudy scoffs, then chides, "Tallulah Alexander."

Tallulah's gaze flings back to me. "Nice to meet you." The afterthought to her aunt's scolding suggests she'd rather spit in my eye.

Taken aback, I blink as I stutter, "Yeah, nice to meet you." The sound of my own voice is unrecognizable. Monotone. Flat.

Trudy chuckles. "You two have met, you just don't remember."

A breath catches in my throat, and I choke. *Of course I remember.* One does not forget kissing Tallulah Alexander. *Taxi.*

How does Trudy Wallace know we've met? Did Tallulah—Taxi—tell her about me? About us? And if Trudy knows, why is Taxi acting like it never happened?

"She was the one always running around the yard, causing chaos as a child, painting my shed a nifty shade of purple with green accents." Trudy chuckles. "Never knew where she got the paint. Or the energy."

"Aunt Trudy," Taxi groans, her hand tightening in mine for a split second, holding on like she's grounding herself.

I chuckle at the thought of her younger, wild spirit. Sun-kissed skin. Dark, flowing hair. Fierce energy. Totally unstoppable. That spunk she might have had as a child? I see it in her now and it makes her utterly magnetic.

So magnetic that I'm still holding her hand.

"Beautiful," I whisper aloud, picturing it; her in her element, painting buildings, expressing her love of art.

Taxi drops my hand and slips her sunglasses back on her face to shield her eyes, but I don't miss a tremor in them before she tucks them into the deep pockets of her bib overalls.

She glances around me once more, like I'm a door instead of a window.

"Heard there's a baseball game. Are we going to play ball or what?" Her voice lifts, rising like when I met her in that Knoxville bar, and she practically shouted a name. *Samson*. The raised cadence is a distraction I instantly remember and recall how it led to a momentary game, only I'm not part of this new match.

Irritation takes over. An itch that demands to be scratched. Just what the fuck is she playing at here? Why is she acting so cold? What is she doing in Sterling Falls? And why, if I apparently know her, did I not recognize her in Knoxville?

"Oh, we're going to play alright."

Because dammit, I want to know where she's been all this time. And more importantly, why I feel this visceral need to know more about her when she so clearly wants nothing to do with me.

I step aside and wave my arm, inviting her to step forward. The second she does, I step up behind her, as close as I can get.

"So, it's Taxi?"

She doesn't respond. Head high, hands in her pockets, she acts like I'm not a shadow at her back, trailing behind her, chasing her.

"Why are you here?" That itch for knowledge is darn near painful. "Or better yet, why are you acting like this?"

Without acknowledging me, Taxi walks right up to Clay, like she's assigning herself a spot on *his* team.

Glancing at my brother, his eyes widen at her brazen approach. I'm certain he can read my face. A question that's become a theme is blinking in his gaze like a neon light.

What the hell is going on?

Have I entered an episode of *Twilight Zone*? Maybe I've been beamed up into an alternate universe?

First Cortland Haven and half his family are in my yard.

Then Trudy and her grandson.

And now this. Tallulah Alexander and her cold shoulder.

Definitely feels like a second Ice Age on this planet.

8

[Taxi]

Stone Sylver.

He's *the* Stone Sylver.

Talk about a plot twist.

And how the hell did I not know this about him?

The initial shock of seeing him again immediately wore off when I remembered why I should *not* be excited to see him. That ongoing war within me, battling over the best kiss I'd ever had and the unexpected betrayal from the next morning. The continuing skirmish between feeling a deep-seated gut instinct that he was different, and then finding out he wasn't, and yet *still* being conflicted by the obvious.

I saw him with another woman the following morning.

You don't get a more meaningful message from the Universe, even if a teeny tiny niggling sensation tells me I might have had it all wrong. I ignore that miniscule smudge of unease because the broader picture is that Stone wasn't who I thought he was.

And now I'm really discovering he isn't who I believed him to be—just a random man I met in Knoxville and haven't stopped thinking about for months.

Because he's a fucking Sylver!

Let's take his name out of the equation for a second and focus on the uptick in my pulse at his nearness behind me. His breath against my neck and the edge to his voice, as if *I'm* the one who'd done wrong in this situation.

What am I doing here? he asked.

I haven't the faintest idea. One minute Aunt Trudy invited me to visit Sterling Falls for a few days over the holiday, and the next thing I knew, I was attending a baseball game slash barbecue at the home of a well-known family . . . and one of my best friends from high school.

I briefly glare in the direction of Judd, but first I have another brother to approach.

Trudy already explained the basics. Two teams led by the oldest two brothers.

Stone. His name whispers through my head again, but I shake the thought along with a shiver as I sense his presence still behind me.

I wasn't particularly athletic. Didn't even know the rules of baseball, but I knew one thing: I could not be on Stone's team.

Walking directly to Clay, who looks just like he did as a kid only a little more weathered and a lot more silvered, I stick out my hand.

"Taxi." I boldly reintroduce myself. "I want to be on your team."

I haven't seen Clay in years, although I know he runs the Sylver Seed & Soil, a new destination in our small town, putting Sterling Falls on the map.

His blue eyes are similar to his older brother's. Soft and

kind, but more playful, less guarded, and I hate that I catalogue all this information with a mere glance. Hate that I remember so easily how *Stone* looked at me. With hunger and restraint. With desire and reserve.

Clay glances around me.

Stone's continues to linger behind me even though I wanted to leave him in the dust, crossing this baseball diamond as quickly as I could without making more of a scene.

When we shook hands, mine trembled within his hold. Attempting to act unaffected by his touch, my body betrayed me, especially when Aunt Trudy shared that little nugget about painting her old shed. I clutched at Stone like I needed him to ground me when I don't want to be grounded. I revel in being permanently untethered, or so I tell myself every few days.

And Stone is still behind me, staring at me, whispering more questions he isn't speaking aloud.

I have my own set of questions that don't really need answers.

I thought you were different.

Well, he wasn't, I remind myself, ignoring the pitch in my belly.

Gazing back at me, Clay chuckles and shakes his head. "Sure, darlin'. What position do you want?"

Since I haven't played baseball in . . . ever . . . it's probably best to put me at . . . "Shortstop is good." My quick recall of the position from a mandatory session during high school physical education classes surprises me. I'll be between two bases and able to let either of those basemen cover any ball hit my direction.

"You got it." Clay winks at me and glances around me one more time. Then he laughs harder. "Oh boy," he mutters to himself, passing me and heading toward his older brother.

I will not look. I will not look. I will not look.

Instead, I focus next on Judd Sylver. Once upon a time,

Judd had been my best friend, running around this yard, like Aunt Trudy shared. He was quiet to my loud. Soft to my hard, but I adored him because he was one of the first friends I'd made when I arrived in Sterling Falls at ten years old.

The greasy-haired, hand-me-down-wearing kid who loved math and poetry eventually turned into a brooding heartthrob, sporting dark-rimmed glasses and tight-fitting, dark tees in high school. But math geeks and art nerds didn't always cross paths, and eventually Judd and I went our separate ways.

We've only recently reconnected. Because of Simon.

I don't know Simon well as he'd only come into Trudy's life a little more than a year ago but with this visit, I'm making it my mission to learn more about the young boy left behind, like me and my sisters once were. I intend to assure him about who *I* want to be in his life—Aunt Taxi.

I might leave, but I'll be back.

"Hey you," I greet Judd, going in for a hug that would have once made him uncomfortable. Now, he easily embraces me, confident in our connection as old friends.

"Hi, Taxi." With his arm only momentarily around me, he leads me toward a spunky-looking girl with short hair in loose brown and blonde waves.

"Genie, this is Taxi."

Judd releases me and steps over to Genie, pulling her into his side, and smiling in a way I've never seen Judd smile. Aunt Trudy told me about Judd's recent girlfriend, a reunion between him and a different friend he had in high school.

My quiet, aloof, best-friend-from-childhood looks really fucking happy.

Genie steps out from underneath Judd's arm and right up to me, hugging me like *I'm* a long-lost friend. "It's so nice to finally meet you."

"You, too." My response sounds hesitant at first because her embrace startles me.

Again, I'm not a person who likes unexpected touches, so I'm taken aback, especially considering Genie and I never connected when we were younger. Virginia Webster, AKA Genie, is younger than Judd and me and from a crowd I never crossed paths with in high school—the rich kids. The new money of Sterling Falls did not mingle with those of us who had less than.

However, Genie's warm welcome feels genuine, and too easily, I melt into her hug, finding myself reciprocating it. Her attention endears her to me on Judd's behalf.

When we pull apart, Genie additionally surprises me by capturing my hands. "I've heard so much about you." She smiles pleasantly. "We need to be fast friends."

A statement like that could be off-putting, but Genie is just too bubbly to deny her sincerity. She focuses on me, like she won't let me go as a potential friend. It's a heady sensation.

People don't tend to hold onto me.

And my thoughts fling to a man somewhere on this baseball diamond.

He played me, and I've never been more grateful *not* to invite a man into my hotel room. He was exactly what my heart tried to guard me against. Acting a fool, like my mama. Getting my hopes up that another random man would be different.

This time, Mama said too many times.

And Stone turned out to be just like a lot of other guys I've encountered over the years.

A cheater. A liar. A thief of hearts.

Thankfully, I hadn't quite given my heart, or my body, as the two have issues separating themselves and *this time*, I was grateful.

Still . . . the way Stone had looked at me. So intently. So interested in my art and my work with the students. He listened to me mention Mama and jail without passing judgment or asking for details. Then, the way he went into superhero mode, helping that young co-ed. He appeared so solid, in control, protective even, and I leaned into that sensation. Something inside me said *you're safe with him, Taxi.*

But I couldn't trust my head or my heart. And my body? Forget about it.

That goodnight kiss has haunted me for three months. The command of his lips. The tenderness in them. The whisper of a promise in them.

My man-free diet hit a plateau after that night. I didn't hunger for anyone else because a phantom kiss lingered on my lips. A ghost of a snack that was decadent and rich. Like a sweet potato cupcake and cream cheese frosting. A little spice. A little sweet. In combination, perfection.

That night I took care of myself as I've done too often in the past year, and I came like I've never come before. The release was so powerful, I still remember it as well, when I used to hold the belief that an orgasm was an orgasm.

Duly noted from that night henceforth, not all orgasms are created equal.

And it was only the mental image of what Stone could do for me that brought about the release.

Imagine what the real man could do for you?

I refuse. Because I wasn't seeking something physical from a man like him.

And that was the crux. I thought he was different.

When I finally glance in his direction, giving in to the temptation, like it's okay to look at the delicious cookie display as long as you don't take one, my brows crease when I witness Stone looking back at me with equal irritation.

How dare he be annoyed with me!

"You two playing or what?"

Sebastian Sylver, the youngest brother in their family, pulls my attention away from the oldest, but I can't ignore how my pulse still races.

Sebastian had been a real wild card, from what Aunt Trudy told me, and he eventually got into trouble with the law. He even did some jail time.

I shiver at the thought, knowing where my mother spends her days.

The reminder yanks my gaze back to Stone, who is watching his youngest sister, Valentine—Vale—kissing a man just beyond the baseball diamond confines.

Apparently, Sebastian was not addressing Stone and me, but the couple who appear madly in love with one another.

I sigh over the obvious attraction and deep display of affection, causing my gaze to return to Stone.

Dammit. I don't want to look, but his focus remains on the approaching couple. His broad shoulders tense. His jaw tight. Even his mustache looks stern as he squints in their direction.

His body language suggests that beneath the surface, something is bothering him, and I remind myself I don't care.

He isn't my business.

I shouldn't feel even a twinge of sympathy for him.

Still, he's instantly black when he's typically soothing blue, and I question only briefly what could cause such a sturdy man to look momentarily battered.

Again. Not my concern.

Until his gaze suddenly locks on me.

There are so many shades to Stone.

The hesitant hue of stalling in a hallway, lingering to look too long at me. The playful palette, momentarily pretending to be my blind date, and then shifting into a comfortable color of communication. Talking and listening. Teasing and sharing. When we danced, he was the soothing sound associated with blue water. Eventually, he was a cobalt flame of desire, the flick of a flare when he kissed me.

And all those sapphire shades were tainted, dull and dim,

when I learned he had good reason not to invite himself into my room.

He should have never kissed me in the first place. And I'm the stupid one who let him.

Forcing my gaze to unlock from his, I turn my attention back toward Clay, waiting on my new coach to give instructions.

Being involved in a game is like being placed in another community. Players find a sense of belonging and common initiative. *Go. Fight. Win.*

Being among this lot is an entirely different experience from the average competitiveness of an athletic game.

The teams are as evenly divided as they can be. Partners get separated, leading to flirty innuendos about going down and future promises. Children get included, right down to a pair of five-year-olds. The six Sylver brothers divide down the middle.

Stone, Ford, Sebastian. Clay, Judd, Knox.

As the game begins, I'm surprised by the overall athleticism of the boys, now men, and their playful banter. Jabs and jokes about age and ability are tossed around the diamond.

The night I met Stone, he said he intended to make his brother's fight, and I realize now he meant Judd, who'd been boxing in bars for a number of years.

My gaze slings between the two, wondering how I hadn't made the connection. Then again, Judd is a little taller than his older two brothers. He's lean like Clay but muscular and strong like Stone. His eyes are more cobalt blue than the softer tone of the older two, and honestly, I wasn't thinking about my old friend when I gazed upon the kind glow of his oldest brother.

Fool me once, shame on me. I will not be fooled again, and I pull my gaze from Stone and his position as pitcher on the mound.

As a weak link on my team—even the kids are better than me—I'm at the bottom of the batting order, so when it's finally my turn up at bat, I try to concentrate more on the ball than the silver fox pitcher.

Easier said than done as he's looking at me from beneath the brim of a low-slung ball cap, sizing me up and down, making me feel like he's mentally undressing me. Pop would go the fastenings on my overalls. Down comes the denim. Off comes the tank top.

Yeah, not happening.

"You gonna pitch that ball or just stare at me?" I taunt, unable to stop myself.

For some strange reason, it isn't only that I want to attempt to hit that ball, envision it being smacked out of this makeshift ballfield, but I want to prove I'm a player too.

I belong on someone's team.

Stone slowly lowers the ball to his waist, eyeing me like he's surprised I spoke.

"Cat got your tongue, old man." The teasing jab comes from one of his siblings.

"More like the girl has his attention."

Flustered by the comment, I turn toward Sebastian who is crouched behind me as the catcher for his team.

Does he know Stone and I met? Has Stone mentioned me? How could he after what *he* did?

While I'm distracted, Stone lets the ball sail. It narrowly misses me. Thanks to the quick reflexes of Sebastian, he catches the ball.

"What the hell?" I mutter, turning back toward the pitching mound and taking up a batting stance again.

I will not strike out. I will not strike out.

The mantra seems to shift in my head.

You will not regret me. Say you will remember me.

Sheer determination has me swinging, connecting the bat with the next pitch, and sending the ball between second and third base. As Stone's team has one of his young nieces covering the shortstop position, he runs toward the spot to help her retrieve the ball.

Because I'm so excited I made a hit, I race toward first and round for second like I'm a newly drafted professional when my exercise regimen consists of occasional yoga and a rare walk. Focused on second base, I don't pay attention to Stone making his way to the same spot. I should slide, but that isn't going to happen in my cute overalls, not to mention I don't know how. Plus, flinging myself into the dirt and gliding over it seems like it would hurt. Badly.

Stone tags the base with his large foot, which is a certain out, the last one of the inning for my team. Only my momentum keeps me going and I barrel straight toward Stone who catches me around the waist, spins me around, and hikes me over his shoulder.

"Out," he cries, loud and proud, further confirming what I already knew.

However, he doesn't set me down. Slung over his shoulder like a sack of seed, he carries me slowly toward home plate.

"What is your problem?" I snap, gripping the back of his warm shirt.

"What is yours?" His tone is equally sharp.

"Definitely not you," I grunt as his shoulder wedges into my belly. All the blood is rushing to my head, and I try to lift it. He's wearing a dark green Sylver Seed & Soil tee that's sweaty down his back, and yet he still smells good. Like mountain spring and fresh air and all man.

Fuck!

"What's that even mean?" he hums, taking his time to return me to my team.

"Don't worry about it." He'd said the same thing the night we met. He wanted to be a gentleman. He wanted to please his deceased mama.

How pleased would she be to know he was a liar? A cheat? *He* should be wearing a giant scarlet A on his chest.

Thankfully, we've reached my bench, which is made of blankets spread on the ground and collapsible camp chairs. He sets me on my feet, but I stumble from the sudden rush of blood to my head. Wobbling, I reach out to steady myself and grip Stone's strong arms where the cuff of his sleeves meets his biceps and the heat of his skin warms my palms like they did the night he walked me to our hotel.

When he held my hand, cupped my face, and kissed me like I've never been kissed before.

Pulling my hands back, like touching him scorches me, I try not to glance at the ink he has down his forearm.

We could have had so much fun with him, my body teases.

No, we could not have, my heart screams.

I pat his chest placatingly, immediately noting how firm he is beneath that second-skin tee he's wearing.

"Well." I chuff. "Thanks for the ride."

Unaware he'd been holding my hips, I miss his hands when he releases me.

"Anytime, *Delilah*."

"Tallulah," someone corrects him.

"Don't," I snap. The nickname hits a mark. Like a private joke shared by a couple. One that feels strangely intimate.

The kind of inside joke that had me searching for my Samson the following morning, hoping he might be lingering in the hotel lobby for the free breakfast, or at least, a coffee.

And he sure was. *With her*.

9

[Stone]

I do not know what her problem is, but the longer her issue appears to be only with me, the more irritated I grow.

And if I thought my family would be focused on her, like I've been unable to pull my gaze away from every move she makes on this field, I was wrong. Because all eyes are on me once I set her on her feet, and she placates me with a patronizing pat on my chest before walking over to a blanket she shares with Genie.

"What?" I snap at Clay, like I hadn't just made a spectacle, carrying Taxi over my shoulder like I was flirting with her. Like I was familiar with her. Like I knew how her lips melted against mine.

In response, he only chuckles.

For some unknown reason, I glance over at Cort next. Why I do that, I have no idea. As if some long-suppressed habit forced me to look at my former best friend for reassurance or backup in this situation. And he's watching me with a cocked brow and a smug grin, like he knows as well as Clay that I have a secret.

One that's about five-eight and weighs less than a couple bales of hay, with eyes that match my last name and dark lashes to boot.

Fuck. Why is she so fucking stunning? And just what's with the attitude?

"I'm gonna start the grill," I announce, needing space from . . . everyone. I don't consider myself a quitter, but I'm forfeiting.

"What about the game? We need a pitcher," Sebastian whines, like he's still ten and in competition with Ford.

"Hudson can do it. It will be good practice for him," I toss over my shoulder about my eleven-year-old nephew who plays baseball for the Haven Hitters, the 12-and-under travel baseball team Cort coaches.

I'm aware of the irony.

Cort. Cort. Cort. It's all I've heard for weeks.

And now this.

Tallulah.

"He's already pitching for Clay's team," someone hollers back, but I keep walking, tucking my mitt underneath my arm.

"Stone." Vale's soft, concerned voice follows me. Her feet thump behind me.

"Not now." This isn't about her. With my back to her and my arm raised, I flick my hand in a signal to stay back. "I'm just gonna start the grill," I lie again. Last year, we waited until the game ended and beers were shared before anyone left the makeshift field.

As I continue to stomp toward the house, the soft crunch of gravel behind me eventually has my head turning.

Hope rose, but instantly falls when I realize it is not Taxi.

"Why don't you let me help?" Mary Haven's motherly voice

stalls me in my tracks. With a tight nod, I agree, allowing her to catch up to me.

Walking side by side, she squints at the house. "Place looks good, Stone." Pride fills her voice, like she knows the effort it has taken to restore this place. A house is just a house, but I've worked hard to make it a home. Give this place curb appeal on the outside and love on the inside.

"Thanks," I mumble.

I wait for her to say what so many others say. *Your mama would be proud.*

I hope so.

Most people don't like to mention my father.

I'd want to make him proud as well, although he doesn't deserve the sentiment. He'd turned into such a disappointment. Into someone I no longer recognized. Eventually, I could hardly remember the man he'd been, the dad he was, compared to the father he turned out to be.

Most days, however, I don't like to be told I'd make either parent proud because it makes me sound like a saint when I am definitely not worthy of the praise. And I'd give anything to have them both back.

Seeming to read my mood, Mary quietly follows me into the house.

"I'm just gonna take a quick shower." Typically, I wouldn't care if I stink. No one else is going to freshen up after playing in the sun and heat. I have no one to impress, but my mind leaps to Tallulah. Taxi.

My Delilah.

"Take your time," Mary suggests as she heads for the kitchen like she's been here only yesterday and not twenty years ago. I take the stairs leading to the second floor, skipping every other step.

On the first floor, I have a bedroom and a space I converted into an office, and my personal bathroom is the one across the hall down there, allowing Vale and Hudson to have the second floor to themselves. Wanting distance, I intend to use the upstairs bathroom for a shower instead.

With thoughts of Taxi in my head, my dick stands at attention, and my personal punishment is to refuse to touch him. I will not get myself off to thoughts of a woman who is refusing to look at me. Refusing to acknowledge me. Like that mind-melting kiss never happened.

For half a second, I hang my head, pressing my hand against the tiled wall and glaring at my erection.

Images of Taxi on her knees in front of me fill my thoughts. Then come images of my hands on her hips and me gliding into her.

I tip my head back, blinking up at the steam-filled ceiling, groaning, "Why?"

Why is she here? Why is she acting so cold?

Realizing I don't have time to process my questions or calculate answers, I shut off the shower, slide aside the curtain and reach for a towel.

And the bathroom door flings open.

A shocked expression strikes the face of one beautiful woman.

Lips in a pretty little O. Eyes wide and sterling bright. Hand on the doorknob.

Taxi doesn't move.

Instead, I do, taking my time to swipe the towel underneath my chin and down my chest, letting it drape in front of where I'm long and hard, practically pointed at her. Every slow movement is deliberate. She shouldn't be in here, and that's exactly why I don't cover myself.

My house. My bathroom.

My body wants her, yes, but my head is fully aware, fully in control.

She's in my home, watching me like she owns the show, and

I let her. I'm throwing down the gauntlet, daring her to react, letting the tension build with every inch of my measured moves.

Down my chest.

Over my abs.

The challenge hangs heavy in the air.

And neither of us speaks.

When I get to my dick, using the towel to keep me covered, but still rubbing it around the appendage, she finally turns her head.

"Lost, little girl?" I tease.

With her hand still on the doorknob, her cheek aimed in my direction, I watch the subtle roll of her throat as she swallows. "I needed the bathroom. Vale sent me up here."

Clearly, this space is occupied, but I don't want her to leave yet.

"We need to talk," I state instead.

Noise in the hallway causes her to glance back in my direction. Hastily, she steps forward, shutting the door behind her, locking us both in the narrow, steam-filled bathroom.

I step out of the tub, keeping the towel in front of me, letting my ass hang out as we stare at one another.

"What am I missing here, Taxi?" I lower my voice, trying to keep it steady, like I'm interviewing a potential suspect or a skittish victim.

She crosses her arms, glances at my waist, and then turns her head toward the mirror over the sink. From her angle, she can see my ass in the reflection.

I allow her to check me out a second longer, before discreetly working as best I can to wrap the towel around my waist and securing it just above my hips. I swipe a hand through my hair, making it stand up at all angles.

And all the while Taxi watches me through the mirror. Her chest slowly lifts and lowers, like she's trying to control her breathing. Her nostrils even flare once. She swallows again and licks her lips.

Dammit, I want to press her against the sink and kiss her senseless. Jar her memory because I'm certain she felt something when we kissed that night. When she kissed me back.

Stepping closer to her, I risk cupping her jaw and making her eyes meet mine. "Taxi, talk to me."

"You played me," she says, loud and sharp and tugging her face back so I'll drop my hand.

"What? No," I state almost as loud, fisting my hands at my sides.

"I saw you."

"Saw me?" I have no idea what she's talking about.

"The next morning. I came down for coffee, and there you were, all smiles and bright eyes with a beautiful blonde and—"

"A blonde?" I interject, racking my brain, completely mystified by this accusation before things eventually click into place. "Oh no. No, no, no, Taxi."

I grip her upper arms and lower my head to level my eyes with hers. "*That* was not what you think."

"I think . . . you had her all along and simply played me." Her eyes widen like she's suddenly thought of something else. "Or you picked her up after you left me."

"No," I bark, distinct and adamant. Clearing my throat, I try to lower my voice. "No, that is not what happened after the best kiss of my life."

Her long lashes flutter as her breath hitches.

"I . . ." How do I explain the situation? How do I explain who Emerson is? "That woman was Emerson Milton. She's a friend."

Taxi scoffs, yanking herself out of my grasp like the words sting. She takes a giant step away from me, which forces her shoulder blades to hit the closed door.

"People assume . . ." I swallow thickly, scrubbing my hand

down my face. "I don't care what people assume. We've been friends for years. And she—" I pause again. "Her story isn't mine to tell. But I swear on each of my siblings and my dead parents, I did not cheat on you with her."

"You can't cheat on someone you aren't with," she says, her flat voice matching the sudden lack of shine in her silvery eyes. She's closing in on herself, like putting up shutters, blocking out a storm.

"Taxi." I step toward her, but she stiffens her spine and lifts her head, plastering herself even tighter against the door.

With my hands up in the air, I whisper, "Delilah."

"Don't." Her voice is sharp-edged, jarring and direct, as it was outside when she used the same command. A solid wall goes up between us.

My confusion hits a new level. We felt so connected that night. The thread between us easy and refreshing, so I don't understand this moment, where she isn't willing to hear me out.

"Explain this to me." I lower my hands and point between us. "Explain what I'm missing. Explain what happened. Give me something."

I'm not above begging, wanting to understand this shut down, that's even colder than the chilly behavior outside.

"You don't deserve it," she whispers, like I've scorned her somehow.

The edge to her voice has me flinching.

I could blame Emerson for the charade we've built. Town mayor. County sheriff. Visually, we make sense, but Em and I have never been together. That's the image *she* wants to portray to cover her secrets. As her friend, I want to protect her. It started as a united front. A fundraiser. A public event. But as the rumors grew, so did the lie.

For my own part, I might have used Emerson as well. Hanging out with her allowed me to avoid the complications of a real commitment. Protect myself from ever getting in that position again. I haven't had the time or interest in dating anyone seriously, so Em was convenient for me.

Our little arrangement even worked for getaways. A false weekend here or there that allowed Em to go where she goes and me some rare time off, which is how we both ended up in Knoxville.

Not together, but seemingly together.

And I see now I've really messed up because what was always intended to skew perception has turned into a giant misunderstanding.

"Emerson and I were not together that weekend. Or any weekend ever. She wanted a weekend with—" I cut myself off before I share more than necessary. This isn't about Em. It's about me. "The timing was just convenient. She wanted to go to Knoxville, and I had a retirement party for an old college buddy. Plus, I wanted to check in on Judd. See his fight." I pause. "Then I met you."

A second encounter that I considered a twist of fate, when I didn't believe in fate.

And yet, here Taxi is again, staring at me with narrowed eyes like she doesn't believe a word I'm saying. On the flip side of that disbelief is the fact she isn't moving yet. Isn't opening the door behind her and shutting me out completely. Which leaves me questioning once again what she's doing here. If we had our chance, and lost it in Knoxville, what is Taxi doing standing in my bathroom, arms crossed, glaring at me like a bull prepared to charge a red flag?

I am not a red flag. I'm as green as they come, but that doesn't mean I'm one-thousand percent innocent. I wear guilt in many areas, but not in relationships with women.

"I've never touched Em. Not like you might think. We aren't involved, not even interested in one another, other than as companions in our respective civic duties. She's the town mayor."

Once upon a time, I might have been a bit enamored with Emerson. She's pretty and intelligent, kind and devoted to this town, but Em loves someone else, and that's her secret to keep.

And this moment right here is teaching me a hard lesson.

I can't be the guardian of that secret any longer, because it is keeping me from what I want.

Taxi.

"I've never kissed her. Never kissed *anyone* the way I kissed you."

Taxi's eyes soften only a fraction at the truth.

"And like you kissed me back," I add, because I felt it. I couldn't be completely wrong. There was a connection, at least briefly.

Her chest heaves again, and her nostrils flare once more. She doesn't break from lasering those sterling eyes on mine.

Slowly, hesitantly, I lift my hand again to cup the edge of her jaw and stroke my thumb over her smooth skin, marveling at the softness underneath the rough of my hand.

I watch how she licks her lips. Her voice is quiet when she finally speaks, "Why didn't you tell me? That night."

"Because I wasn't thinking about Em when I met you."

Emerson and I didn't stay in the same room. We didn't even stay in the same hotel. She went where she goes and met me in the morning for breakfast.

"What you saw in the morning . . . that was me telling Em about the incredible woman I'd met the night before."

I lean closer, feeling the cool metal of her bib overall clasps brush against my bare chest. Her gaze drops to the thick dusting of hair just below my collarbone. Slowly, ever so slowly, she lifts her hand, placing it over my heart, where it races beneath my skin.

The second she touches me, my flesh pebbles and my dick

jolts, poking at the loose, hip-hung towel and nudging toward Taxi. If she notices, she doesn't react. Instead, she keeps her hand on my chest another second, both of us watching where she's touching me. Where sparks fly and my skin sizzles like she's branding me. Then, she moves her hand, gliding it up and over my shoulder.

My eyes close, like I can't handle the sensation, when I'm drinking in every atom of her palm against my flesh. It's been so long since someone has caressed me, held me, fucked me.

The urge to rush this woman is almost overpowering, and yet, I don't want this moment to end. Her slow map of my skin. The heated touch of her hand on my chest.

"Why didn't you ask to come into my room that night?" she whispers, coasting her hand down my arm. The heat of her palm leaves a lingering trail of sparks, crackling and tickling my flesh.

"Why didn't you invite me in?" I counter, low and deep, as I open my eyes and focus on her mouth again.

She shrugs, subtle and hesitant.

"I don't do things like that, Taxi. I don't meet women at random or invite myself into hotel rooms for one-night stands."

It isn't like I haven't had them. I just haven't had one in years. Watching my siblings fall in love, one by one, over the past twenty-four months has made me yearn for something I didn't think I'd ever have. Didn't dare to hope for. Something I'd given up on as a possibility.

As much as I've tried to reassure every one of my siblings that love exists, that they are worthy of it, that they deserve it, I haven't bought into the philosophy for myself.

But now, I want it.

And I want it with this woman who felt unique and special that night. What are the chances of not only a strange encounter in a hotel hallway but a second meeting in a bar? And the way she batted those lashes at me, laughed with me, told me passionately about something so significant to her as her art. Told me with heartbreak in her voice about her mother. Taxi was beautiful on the inside as well as the outside, and something deep inside me cried out for more with her.

I couldn't explain it, but I wanted it.

And here she is a third time, taunting me with her presence and her saucy attitude, and making me question everything again.

"Why should I believe you?" she asks, the question honest and raw.

I want to beg her to trust me, but it's never that simple. "Let me show you who I am."

Taxi focuses on her hand, blazing a pattern against my chest, over my shoulder, down my arm. I'll get a tattoo to permanently mark where she's blazing that trail over my skin.

But then her hand abruptly stops right over my heart, and she applies light pressure, extending her arm, gently forcing me back.

"I can't." No more whispers. No more caution. Her voice is strong and firm.

Why? It's on the tip of my tongue when a sharp knock rattles the door behind Taxi, and we both jump.

"Uncle Stone, you about done in there. I'm starving."

Hudson. My innocent eleven-year-old nephew. I'm going to strangle whichever brother sent him up here. Or maybe it was Vale.

While I pride myself on being the grill master for every special occasion, I want to shout, *I'm busy.*

I'm trying to woo a woman who doesn't want me.

The truth stabs me in the sternum.

"Be out in a minute," I say over Taxi's head, toward the thick barrier behind her.

Pausing a second, I wait for Hudson to disappear down the hallway before I glance back at Taxi.

I don't know what to say. Her mind seems to be made up.

Whatever I thought we had, thought we shared, hadn't happened. At least, not for her.

Taking a giant step back, I tighten the towel around my waist, struggling to keep it on my hips because my dick hasn't gotten the memo yet.

Taxi glances down at where my hand fists the twisted terrycloth. She digs her teeth into her lower lip, but as much as I want to read that reaction as a sign that I'm affecting her, she's already said I'm not.

I hang my head, avoiding my own eyes in the reflection of the mirror. I know what I'll see. A man aging alone. A man who already lost a girl once, a long time ago, which caused him to never put his heart out there again. Never trust that love would happen.

Taxi felt different, although I can't put my finger on why.

I'll never have an answer. There isn't one.

Quietly, she spins for the door and opens it, cautiously checking the hallway before slipping out of the bathroom.

When she closes the door, I take another minute for myself.

Inhaling a deep breath, I reconstruct the shield I often wear to keep emotion away from logic.

The emotion being the desire to pursue this girl.

The reality is saying *step back, old man.*

She's not the One. Again.

10

[Taxi]

et me show you who I am.

The moment I close the door behind me, second-guessing myself kicks in.

Here is a man practically begging to prove to me he is a good person.

Not in a way that a bad person tries to say he has good character, but the way a truly good person knows his character is safe and sound.

Still, I didn't trust myself or this situation. Stone was still vague about Emerson. What was her secret? Why couldn't he share it with me? Why didn't he trust me enough?

Then again, we hardly knew one another, and I didn't believe we ever would.

"I'm not staying anyway," I whisper, as if that statement further justifies my conviction.

Stone is planted while I constantly uproot. Commissions call. Adventures lead.

Once upon a time, Sterling Falls was my home, but was it really? I'd felt safe with Aunt Trudy and Uncle Carlton, but never truly secure. In the recesses of my mind was the fear that someone would come forward and claim my sisters and me. They'd take us away from Trudy and Carlton like we'd been taken away from our mother.

Of course, our mother made that choice for us.

And as for my father, I'd never known the man. He'd made the decision to never know me.

Then again, I recognize the urge to flee. Not so much a desire to run as a fear of staying in place.

I was only here for a visit.

At the sound of chatter from the lower level, I release the doorknob and walk down the hall, taking the stairs slowly as I still need to use the bathroom.

Stone Sylver has a nice house. One filled with soothing colors and personal touches. Steel blues and sandy browns fill his living room, where a large fieldstone fireplace that looks original is the major focal point. Old farmhouses like this one have character, and I'm pleased to see the Sylvers have not removed it, while adding modern updates.

A large dining room leads to a remodeled kitchen with an island that separates the workspace from a table that seats eight.

Seven siblings plus one.

From what I've learned today, each sibling has a partner. Clay and Mavis. Judd and Genie. Knox and Halle. Ford and Cadence. Sebastian and Enya. Vale and Cortland. Not going to lie, I was starstruck to meet Cadence, one of country music's sweethearts, even if I'm not a country music fan. I also have an instant girl crush on Genie and understand why Judd has heart-emoji eyes every time he looks at her.

Only Stone is alone.

Whether I believe his story about Emerson Milton or not is yet to be determined. What I do remember is the way his eyes were lit and his smile easy with her. And how her hair was long and straight and beautifully blonde.

Curly-haired girls almost always want that smooth, sleek look, while women with stick straight hair want curls. Sometimes, women are never happy with themselves.

I didn't see her face, but I'd bet Gloria, my van, on Emerson being a beauty.

This mountain is named for the Miltons. Milton Peak. Milton County. And apparently, Emerson Milton is the town mayor. Five girls in their family, if I remember correctly. Suddenly, I recall little blondes with perfect bows in their hair. I wasn't in their circle when I lived here. I got the impression they didn't want anything to do with poor foster kids like me, living with my aunt while my mother rotted in jail. I learned early to keep my distance, to watch, to survive, but never to belong.

Just another reason not to trust people so easily. I've built walls so high I don't even notice them anymore. I'm not certain even I can climb over them.

And yet . . . there's something about Stone Sylver. Something that makes me question the rules I've lived by. He's different. Unpredictable in a way that makes my chest tighten.

Let me show you who I am.

And he's scaling those walls, rattling my foundation.

When I eventually make my way back to the kitchen, I step closer to Aunt Trudy, who is standing on the opposite side of the kitchen island, across from where Mary Haven is cutting lemons. I'd been long overdue to pay my aunt a visit, so when she asked me to come here, the timing worked because I had a few days between jobs.

"The bathroom upstairs was occupied. Is there another one?" I ask, like Trudy is familiar with the house.

"There should be one around the corner," Mary points with the knife she'd been using toward the refrigerator and a hallway beside it.

At the same time, Stone rushes into the kitchen wearing only a towel.

He stumbles and stalls. "Oops," he says, then quickly nods. "Ladies." He rushes through the kitchen toward that hallway beside the fridge and disappears.

My gaze follows his retreat, wondering once again if I've made a mistake.

Mary and Trudy giggle like schoolgirls.

"Well." Mary clears her throat, although her eyes are still laughing. "He's grown up very nicely."

Stone Sylver is one *fine* man. Those broad shoulders. That thick patch of hair on his chest. The apparent strength in his arms. I didn't miss the shape of his ass when I caught a peek in the reflection of the mirror. I also didn't miss the outline of another appendage. One long and thick and poking in my direction through terrycloth.

"Mm-mm-mm," Aunt Trudy hums, shaking her head. "And such a *good* man. Who would have thought?"

"What do you mean?" I ask before I can stop myself.

"Man's had a hard life," Aunt Trudy says, turning back toward the counter where Mary is back to slicing lemons. A large bottle of vodka rests just off the cutting board next to a pitcher filled with ice.

Oh my. So, it's going to be that kind of lemonade.

"He sure has," Mary agrees with Aunt Trudy, keeping her voice quiet while she pauses from slicing lemons. She glances at Trudy. "I'm just grateful he has patience. I don't know if he'll ever truly forgive Cortland, but I see him trying. Or at least giving him grace for his sister's sake."

"What are you two talking about?" I demand, whipping my gaze from one woman to the other. Town gossip is *not* my thing, but curiosity has risen like the hairs on an agitated cat.

"Stone was engaged once," Trudy explains.

"And Cortland stole the girl," Mary adds, her shoulders falling in disappointment. "Worst mistake he ever made. Both the girl and losing his best friend over her."

"But you got Josh," Trudy gently states, like a pleasant reminder.

"But I got Josh." Mary smiles.

"Who is Josh?" I ask.

"My grandson. He's almost twenty-four." Mary's smile grows even larger as she mentions the young man.

"And he looks just like his daddy," Aunt Trudy confirms with another hum, giving a stamp of approval to the young Haven family member.

With my mind still reeling over Stone once being engaged, losing both the woman and his best friend to betrayal, he makes another appearance in a pair of loose, camel-colored hiking shorts and a light heather-gray T-shirt.

There'd been jabs and quips about Stone being reserved and stalwart during the baseball game, but I hadn't really seen that side of him.

I only know a man with a sly smile who bumped into me in a hotel hallway.

I also know the man who leaned into faking he was my blind date and then did not feign interest in learning about my art commission.

He even stepped up for a single dance, walked me home so to speak, and kissed me goodnight like I was his next breath.

He'd been a bit of an illusion that night but knowing that he's endured loss and come out steadier for it makes him seem even more grounded, more real. I think back to the tight expression on his face when he watched Vale and Cort kissing by the driveway. His emotion held back. The patience Mary Haven mentions firmly intact.

He wasn't Superman so much as human.

A man who's been hurt but survived. And suddenly, I see him a bit differently again.

We've all been hurt at some point. We all have heartbreak stories to tell and secrets to keep, and it wasn't fair of me to judge him for his.

Emerson Milton. She's a friend.

Still, I wasn't staying. I didn't know why I keep finding myself on a path facing Stone Sylver, but I'll be making a U-turn soon.

But dammit, why does he have to look so good? The T-shirt looks worn and soft, and I bet it smells like him. Mountain air and freshly showered. A swirl of dizzy green and comforting blue.

I close my eyes like it will make Stone disappear, but behind my lids all I see is his face. The confusion when I accused him of playing me. The hurt. The adamant tone of his voice rings in my ears. When he told me he hadn't been with someone else and explained Emerson Milton. Explained that he'd been telling her about an incredible woman he'd met the night before.

He'd been telling her about me.

But why hadn't he told me about her?

Opening my eyes, I find Stone's gaze on me, blatant and direct, and building the tension I'd felt upstairs, while trapped in a small bathroom where the freshly showered scent of him overwhelmed my senses. His heart was racing under my palm. His skin warm and tight.

Like his jaw right now as he stares at me.

Ah, there's the stalwart, reserved man I've heard about.

Out of the corner of my eye, I catch Mary Haven glancing between Stone and me and feel Aunt Trudy's narrowed gaze on the opposite side of my face.

"Seems the bathroom upstairs is finally vacant," Aunt Trudy mutters in that knowing tone she has. Like she hadn't missed how I was upstairs. And so was Stone. And she knows he and I shared a moment.

Never kissed anyone like I kissed you. And like you kissed me back.

Had he felt it? Did he feel like I was someone as unique to him as he'd been to me? And why would any of this matter?

I wasn't staying, I scold myself internally, gritting my teeth, and clenching my fist, like I'm arguing with myself. Starting a new battle within me.

I couldn't stay in Sterling Falls, could I?

I glance at Aunt Trudy, missing her with an ache I hadn't known existed until I saw her again. It's been almost a year since Simon came to her and I came to check on both of them. Guilt hits me hard. I should do better, be better, about visiting, about spending time with both of them.

For some unknown reason, I gaze back at Stone.

Do not make him a reason to come back as well. No chasing, Tallulah Alexander. We don't do that.

With Stone still staring back at me, there's no doubt the two women in the room witness the way we look at one another. Both of us reserved, while a hint of hunger lies behind his eyes. Or maybe that's lost hope.

He wants me to trust him, and I want to, maybe, but I don't know how.

And the longer he keeps me ensnared with his gaze, the more I want to rush across this kitchen and beg him to show me who he is, like he asked upstairs.

Because a man wanting to prove himself to me means he thinks I'm worth proving something to, as if saying, you're safe with me. I've got your back. And your heart.

The thought rattles me. It's too much too fast, and I'm ready for Mary Haven's special lemonade to clear my head. Or better yet, erase any crazy ideas, like learning more about Stone Sylver.

Thankfully, Stone breaks first, though I don't miss how his shoulders fall in defeat.

As for me, my belly sinks, and I roll my lips inward, chewing at them as he gives me the side of his face. Instantly, I note the strong line of his nose, the puff of his lips, and the hard edge of his jaw. Plus, that thick mustache.

He's grown up very nicely, as Mary said.

Quickly, he looks back in my direction but addresses Mary and Trudy. His voice is that tender, rugged tone that tickles my skin.

"Ladies, thank you again for being here today. You've both been important to our family, and I apologize that it's been so long since we've had you here for supper."

Heavy silence fills the room, and my stomach drops another notch. Something deeper exists in the quiet seconds that pass. And I recall all the times Judd Sylver hung out at Trudy's place, sheepishly accepting the meals she offered him. The Sylvers had been no better off than us. Then again, Sedona, Jolene, and I had the love of Trudy and Carlton. Judd had a mean daddy, which meant—

My attention snaps back toward Stone.

That evil man had also been the father of the man offering his full gratitude and sincere apologies to Mary and Trudy.

A new desire to rush him takes over. One which wants to offer him sympathy and understanding. To hug him and hold him and tell him how sorry I am that someone so vile as *his* daddy was his dad.

We all live diverse experiences. And our perspective was judge and jury on the experience of others. Have I misjudged Stone again?

Shit.

"Stone Sylver, don't you dare make me cry," Trudy warns, crossing the kitchen toward him.

Mary simply sets down her knife and reaches for a paper towel to dab at her eyes.

Fuck. The air feels clogged with something bigger than Stone and me and our interlude upstairs, and suddenly, I don't know what to do with myself.

When it came to Stone Sylver, every new layer revealed twists me all up inside.

He's certainly a kaleidoscope of color.

11

———

[Stone]

For the remainder of the afternoon, I play the perfect host toward Taxi, keeping myself cordial but distant.

"Did you get something to eat?"

"Would you like another drink?"

And at one point, absentmindedly, bringing her a dessert.

Sebastian owns the local bakery, Curmudgeon Bakery, and he's best known for his baby bundt cakes. His wife, Enya, is partial to the lemon ones. Today, he brought an assortment of cupcakes, using the family as his test samplers.

Handing one to Taxi, I say, "Sweet potato cupcake. Met an extraterrestrial in Tennessee once. She said it was her favorite."

I ignore the sudden lift of Clay's head, like he's put two and two together from that night at Milton Roadhouse when I spilled that I'd met someone. A night that meant nothing . . . at least to her.

Taxi's eyes fix on mine a second before she takes the

wrapped treat from me, brushing her fingers against mine. I revel in the sparks crackling over my skin but break eye contact first, like I did in the kitchen, knowing it's best not to stare too long.

My mind already holds a permanent snapshot of Taxi. One where she smiles widely, loves books with romantic aliens, has a passion for vivid art, and appreciates spicy cupcakes.

I give her my back because I'm not strong enough to stop looking at her. I want answers when I have no right to ask more questions. I don't understand, and this is why I'm not involved with anyone. I know my limits. My heart is too vulnerable to open up.

"What was that?" Clay whispers, stepping up beside me as I scrape the grill that's already been scraped for grease and crud from cooking burgers and hot dogs.

"I don't know what you're talking about," I say, keeping my gaze aimed at the slats of the grate, scrubbing harder and harder with the steel wire brush.

"What's going on with you and Taxi?" he asks outright.

"Nothing," I whisper.

"Heard that before." He pauses, but I don't look up. "She's the one, isn't she?"

I still don't glance at him, scouring that grill like I can scrape through the cast-iron slats.

"What one?"

"Don't play coy with me." Clay chuckles.

My brother knows me well, and he's also good at pulling out truths from others, but I'm not up for a confession right now.

Instead, I want to stew.

"You can't be closed off forever," he states quietly.

My head snaps upward. "Okay, pot." *Pot meet kettle.* Clay has a big heart, and he's taken in stray animals and lost souls most of his life, but I'm not one of them. I don't need saving by the savior in the family.

"I'm good," I mutter, returning to my scrubbing.

"But are you?" Clay counters.

I shrug, tying the motion into my current action. "I always am."

Clay chuckles and claps my shoulder hard, pinching me at a pressure point to get my attention. "One of these days, you're going to fall. And fall hard."

"Not me," I argue. "I'm sturdy on my feet."

Still standing, I want to remind him of how couples compare individuals not in relationships.

I don't admit again how much I'd like to take a seat. Pull up the chair for that someone. I'm still saving a spot. I'm just not sure anyone wants to take it.

"Think it's clean," Clay says, another smile in his voice as he tilts his head toward the grill.

"What?" I stammer, meeting the twinkle in his eyes before glancing down at the grate, where I've rubbed so hard the black almost looks worn.

I toss the wire brush onto the cool grate and close the lid of the grill.

"I'm going to find the kids," I mumble. "Maybe Zelle wants to teach me another dance from the TikTok."

Clay laughs loud and hard. "There's no *the*."

"Whatever," I snap, needing a distraction and using my niece as an excuse. She's always trying to convince me to learn some trendy dance. Now might be a good time to take up the offer.

The last dance I had was in an empty bar, holding a woman who felt right in my arms and listening to a song about someone who looked like I'd miss one day.

And that's exactly what happened.

Or maybe it's just the *idea* of Taxi I miss. She could have occupied that vacant seat. My dance card permanently filled. My nights and days complete.

The remainder of the afternoon passes with the kids running around the yard. The adults linger either at the two picnic tables placed end-to-end to hold our expanding family or in a circle of seats Vale has set up, which includes a yard swing, two Adirondack chairs, and spread blankets. The drinks flow for those who drink, and I keep an eye on everyone's consumption, knowing we have plenty of room for those who overindulge and need to spend the night. Desserts make another round.

And all the while, I try to ignore the tambourine laughter of Taxi as she befriends Genie, intrigues Vale, and gushes over the newest baby in the family.

She is cautious with Simon, anxious even, but still evidently cares about the child. She often checks on his well-being, although he's been quickly absorbed into play with Hudson and Zelle, being roughly their age. She glances at Trudy with fondness but also concern. However, Trudy's in her element, guffawing with Mary Haven and giggling over shared history.

And every once in a while, Taxi watches me.

I give her a tight smile and soft chin tip, glad she's enjoying herself in my yard, making herself at home among my family. It gives me joy that my siblings are a welcoming bunch, each of us knowing in our own right what it's like to feel like an outsider, even in our hometown.

When the sky grows dark, Knox and I head out to set off fireworks. With him as a firefighter and me as sheriff, we have an assortment that may or may not be legal. We supervise those who want to help us set off the colorful displays. Chief among the kids is Hudson, whom I watch as if he's my own son. It's hard to shut off the protective-father stance. Being that I've been doing it since I was twelve, I can't seem to help myself.

On that note, I gaze across the meadow in the direction of Cort and Vale. If their relationship continues, and Cort boldly told Hudson it would, Cort could potentially be Hudson's stepfather someday.

The idea ignites a whopper of an explosion in my belly.

Cort already has a son. And although I'm long past the idea that Josh could have been my boy, because he wasn't, it still stings that Cort has a child when I'll never have one of my own.

Not that I need kids. I've raised my siblings. Hell, I've raised Hudson alongside my sister.

Still, he isn't my boy. I don't have a child who's all mine.

Funny how family comes in all forms.

Trudy Wallace is a good reminder.

She and her husband Carlton never had kids either. Trudy once explained she couldn't. It was a different time, a different era, and she and Carlton didn't have all the medical assistance couples have today.

Trudy never held a grudge against biology. Instead, she took in a nephew, then three nieces, one of whom was Taxi, who went by Tallulah then, and I still can't believe I'd forgotten. Or that I didn't recognize her as an adult. Then again, I spent more time with the Havens as a child.

Trudy also took in a stray teen or two, which is how she ended up with Simon, the boy she calls her grandson. She'd been listed as next of kin for someone who'd gotten himself into trouble. Simon is a cute kid. Whip smart while deep-souled, like Judd, and I'm pleased the younger generation of Sylvers is equally welcoming of Simon today.

Thinking of the Wallace clan, I easily find Taxi laughing again at something Genie says. The two of them have been acting like long-lost friends all afternoon. Currently, Genie sits cradled between Judd's bent knees. His body language says she's all his, and I've never seen my reserved brother happier.

Although I'm struggling with Cort and Vale's relationship, the positive effects of love on each of my brothers is evident. Good women make all the difference to troubled men, like

Sebastian and Judd. And a feisty woman can change a sour heart, like Cadence did with Ford. Halle and Mavis are more reserved, experience bringing gentle wisdom that complements the stability of Knox and Clay, respectively.

Which leaves only me as a party of one.

In moments like this, a part of me finds sympathy for my father. He couldn't handle being alone. When he lost our mother, the love of his life and the pillar of our family, he lost himself in booze. I'm not a heavy drinker for fear I'd turn out like him, when deep down I know I'd never be like that.

I lost the woman I thought was the love of my life. Not by death, though. Not like Dad.

Bailey Cummins turned out *not* to be the woman I thought she was.

My gaze leaps to Cort again.

Some say I dodged a bullet with Bailey. Cort caught the shot instead. Doesn't seem either of us fared particularly well when it came to her.

With a heavy sigh, I remind myself I've always wanted the best for my old friend. Even if he stole my girl, I didn't wish him ill, and I certainly never wanted what eventually happened to him and his son, Josh.

I'm not vindictive. I don't seek revenge.

I only want what's best for everyone.

With that, I give a final glance at Taxi, accepting that apparently, I'm not what's best for her.

12

———

[Taxi]

It's hard for me to define myself. With my humble beginnings and nomadic upbringing, I can't say I'm a country girl or city woman, but I embrace the part of me that works with urban communities.

However, Stone Sylver put a light-colored cowboy hat on his head at some point during the day to shield his face and neck from the sun, and I realize I might have an inner cowgirl streak down deep. He's still wearing the hat at night, and I might be a teeny-tiny bit tipsy from Mary Haven's extra special lemonade.

My head is a mess, but my body is screaming: *Save a horse, ride the sheriff.*

"What?" Genie giggles beside me. Her head turns from me to Stone and back, causing her short curls to bounce around her head. "You got the hots for Stone?"

Shit. Did I say my thoughts aloud?

Genie knocks her shoulder into mine as we share a blanket again, watching Stone and Knox set off fireworks a safe distance from the party.

I simply hum in response to her question, keeping my gaze fixated on the man who is hard to make out in the dark except for that cowboy hat. But I know him. In the sense, my palm is still tingling from where I touched him earlier, feeling the firmness of his chest, heart racing beneath shower-fresh skin.

"He's the best," Genie adds, as if that word encapsulates everything when it sums up nothing.

I don't know what the best even means, but the more I stare at Stone, the more I want to find out.

"Meaning?" I ask before I can stop myself.

"Well, first, there's the fact he raised his siblings while his dad was deep in the bottle." Genie makes a sign with her hands, tipping her thumb toward her lips while her pinky rides up in the air.

"Then, you've got him giving up his future to raise the younger set after his dad died."

"What?" I whisper, staring into the darkness around Stone, watching a flame flicker from a long-necked lighter as he sets the firework container alight.

"Yeah. After Judd went to college. Guess that makes it around the same time you were in art school," Genie adds, because we've already traded our paths. Both art school attendees. Both artists in our own right.

"Stone came home to raise Knox, Ford, Sebastian, and Vale." She tilts her head, questioning me.

I pause a second, continuing to watch Stone, holding my breath when a firework pops into the air with a woosh. But the real reason my breathing falters is that I hadn't known this fact in Stone's history. As Genie said, it happened after I'd left Sterling Falls.

Another similarity between us.

When our mother was taken away, I felt responsible for Sedona and Jolene. Not that a ten-year-old had the where-withal to be accountable to a one- and three-year-old, but I'll never forget huddling in the back of a police car, holding my sisters to my side, frightened about what was happening, while at the same time wondering how I was going to take care of them.

Thankfully, I didn't have to worry long. Trudy Wallace was our next of kin. At least for them. Their daddy and mine were two different men.

"I . . . I didn't know," I say weakly, keeping my gaze fixed on the man, lit up by the explosion overhead. The burst of incandescent yellow. A crackle of rusty orange behind it.

"Anyway. Stone is just a really great guy." She chuckles. "Well, he's more like a good man. There's a difference."

Strangely, I know what she means. Some guys are just guys. Fun to be around, great for a good time, easy to hang with. But a man . . . he's different. He's sturdy and confident, compassionate and playful. He isn't just a good time but a rock when things go bad.

The day has been full of surprising bursts of information, like a firework dangling overhead before disappearing into the dark.

Stone had been engaged. Stone lost his best friend. There'd been mention of both his parents being dead. He'd raised his siblings.

And another plot twist, he's the town sheriff.

I guess I knew this information as well, but had somehow placed it aside in my mind, blocking anything that involves law enforcement. My relationship with the law leans toward a distrust of the system. A lack of enforcement resulted in a loss of faith in them.

But those thoughts are heavy for a brain already weighed

down by the other things I've learned about Stone Sylver as I've observed him throughout the day.

He loves his family, first and foremost. You can see it in the subtle smiles he gives to them, or without them noticing. When he dips his eyes, but curls his lips, at something they said, either to tease him or each other.

He has grace for those who have done him wrong, as I've surmised from the snippets I've gathered about Cortland Haven and Stone's past friendship. The loss of that relationship. And the patience he's offering his sister, who is so obviously in love with his former best friend.

Stone is also kind. He doted on Trudy and Mary throughout the day, even giving in to their slightly tipsy behavior, letting them tease him about how handsome he's become and what a fine partner he'd make for any woman.

There was even a jab or two about Emerson Milton and her loss. How she was a fool when it came to him.

And all these tidbits had me questioning myself even more.

I'm not staying.

But—for hypothetical sake—what would it feel like to be involved with a man like him? A man who cherishes family, lets two old ladies flirt with him, and offers gentle tolerance to a complex situation. A man with a beautiful home and a steady job, albeit that employment conflicts with something deep-seated inside me.

That last one might be the hardest to overcome, and I weakly use it as another excuse not to get involved with Stone Sylver.

I'm not staying.

My what-if scenarios are as devoid as a spent firework.

Shortly after the finale of the celebration in the sky, everyone starts packing up. Blankets are folded. Chairs collapsed. Trash picked up. Exhausted little ones have fallen asleep.

Eventually, with Trudy's arm looped in mine, I assist her to the car, which she'll need to drive because I've had an extra Mary-Haven-lemonade my mixed-up emotions didn't need.

Simon climbs into the back seat.

As I hold open the driver's door for Aunt Trudy, an electric ripple crackles down my spine. The sensation rivals the firework show and has me standing straighter, hyperaware of his approach before Stone reaches the side of the car.

"I want to thank you all for coming." His voice is low, quiet and rugged, and I close my eyes for a moment, allowing the sound to wash over me, imprinting itself.

How would he speak if he were over me? Under me?

I shake the thought and spin toward him. Trudy gives Stone another easy hug before slipping into the driver's seat, leaving us alone.

Stone and I face off. His eyes are on me in a way that's steady, assessing, almost measuring, but there's heat in those soft blues, barely contained, and easily discernible, even in the pale moonlight. His jaw tightens, shoulders broad and still, a quiet tension in his stance that makes my stomach twist.

My pulse spikes and I realize I'm pressing my weight slightly forward, wanting on . . . what? To see him better? To challenge him? My fingers twitch against my leg, and I can't prevent the faint heat creeping up my neck.

Eventually, he holds out his hand. The movement is stiff, business-like, controlled.

"Taxi." He pauses on my name, and anticipation builds, stealing my breath as if I'm hopeful of what he'll say without knowing what I want that hope to mean.

"It's been a pleasure," he finally adds, but his eyes tell a different story.

"Same," I say, forcing my hand to meet his. His skin is warm and firm, and the contact sets additional sparks through me. My knees feel oddly weak, but I plant my feet. Conflict rises like a tide. I don't regret his touch. I want more. My mind protests, but my body betrays me, leaning slightly closer even as I try to remain aloof.

"You ever need anything . . . " He exhales softly. "I'm always here for you."

We pause another beat, one matching the skip in my chest.

He's here for me?

Then Stone nods once, releases my hand, and steps back, calm, composed, cracking the tension between us.

"Y'all drive safe."

Instantly, I want to reach for his hand again.

Instead, in my head I whisper, *Goodbye, Samson*.

13

———

[Taxi]

If I thought Aunt Trudy was going to let my strange interactions throughout the day with Stone slide, I was wrong.

Her keen motherly sense didn't miss our continued glances and locked stares. Or the way he doted on me, checking that I had enough to eat or another drink or even that damn cupcake.

Sweet potato cupcake, an extraterrestrial favorite.

His brother Sebastian explained how Stone suddenly had a craving for the dessert after a trip to Knoxville in the spring, and the curmudgeon baker has been trying to perfect the cupcake as an alternative to pumpkin ones during the summer months.

"Want to tell me what's going on with you and Stone Sylver?"

A while back, Trudy sold the larger home where she raised

a handful of kids, opting for what she calls a cozy cottage with two bedrooms and a single bath. The house is actually a single-story ranch with a small kitchen she had refinished with white cabinets and blue accents.

"Now that I don't have children buzzing around, making messes, I can have a white kitchen."

There's a strangeness in being here. As in, this is Trudy's home, yet not home. Not the house I stayed in when Trudy took in me, Sedona, and Jolene. That house felt grand with a spacious yard and outbuildings. The rooms were crowded, but the house overflowed with love.

Trudy's original farmhouse was large, almost rickety, and not to be confused with the Wallace Farmhouse, which was a dilapidated house off the highway outside of town and eventually purchased and restored a few years ago. In Trudy and Carlton's former home, the floorboards creaked, the back door needed an extra shove to close, and one bathroom or the other was always taken, yet the house was full of love. Love for my two sisters and our younger cousin of sorts, and any other teen that filtered in and out of their place.

One of those teens was Simon's father.

This new place is sweet but unfamiliar, causing that unsettled sensation again. The reminder I don't belong here.

With Simon present, the second bedroom is his, so it will be sofa city for me. "Nothing to tell," I lie, flinging a bedsheet over the cushions.

Aunt Trudy hums somewhere behind me, knowing when I don't tell the truth.

While Trudy might not have been my mother, biologically or otherwise, her motherly instincts often surprise me. Like how she knew when I was missing Mama as a child and didn't fault me when she had much to find fault with my mother. Trudy allowed me to grieve the loss, as if Mama had died, because that's what it felt like.

The truth is, Mama abandoned me and my sisters, refusing to allow us visitation.

She didn't want us to see her in her new adventure.

Reality eventually seeded inside me. I'd been left behind.

Trudy and Carlton made every attempt to make me feel welcome in their home, and I did. But I also didn't. I kept myself guarded, afraid that one day they'd realize I came from someone who'd done a bad thing. Then, they'd turn me out.

I left before that could happen.

Headed off for art school and my own adventures. Real ones.

I'm quiet for a second while I tuck the sheet around the cushions and slip a pillow into a case. And all the while, Trudy waits behind me, giving me space that she'll eventually invade with good intentions.

"I don't want to talk about him." I keep my head low and my voice even lower as I pause, hugging the pillow to my chest like a shield.

What do I even say about Stone Sylver? He kissed me. I'm confuddled by him.

When I turn in her direction, I don't look up at my gracious aunt but plop onto the cushion, feeling the sudden dip in the worn stuffing.

Still holding the pillow tight to my chest, I whisper, "Did you know he was the sheriff?"

Of course she knew. She probably told me at one time, but I hadn't connected the dots. Hadn't known that Stone Sylver, small town sheriff, was Samson Superman, sweet talker, silent dancer, skilled kisser.

Aunt Trudy steps closer to me. Her spicy patchouli scent invades my nose, and I close my eyes. Funny how a scent can bring back a memory.

Aunt Trudy holding me as I silently cried as a child, some nights not even aware I'd had a nightmare.

Aunt Trudy fixing my hair in braids, a multitude of bow-shaped barrettes to keep them in place.

Aunt Trudy tapping the sharp-scented oil against my wrists before I graduated from high school, smiling in the mirror from behind me, telling me Mama would be proud, when I'd long forgotten my mother and was in a rebellious stage of unforgiveness.

"Baby," Aunt Trudy says softly. No sass, just weight in the word. "I know what police can be like. Lord knows I've seen enough to last me a lifetime." She moves closer and takes a seat beside me on the couch, forcing me to edge over to accommodate her.

"And I know why your hackles go up. You grew up learning cops meant trouble, and half the time they did."

She reaches for my hand and tugs it into her lap while I continue to clutch the pillow against my belly.

"But don't go taking all that pain and slapping it on one man just because he wears a badge."

Trudy pauses, a classic move from her, letting the truth settle.

"That boy didn't put your mama in jail. He didn't leave you and your sisters lost. Don't let hurt that you didn't ask for decide who he is before you've even had a chance to know him."

My own pause follows her words, reflecting that she's right. She's always right, and I've always strived to be as open and mindful as her. She sees it from both sides, and her wisdom calls out assumptions that stop being proactive and start being prejudices.

But I'm never quite as good as Trudy.

"My mother killed your brother," I whisper, keeping my head bowed. Aunt Trudy doesn't need the reminder of what Mama did . . . and yet . . . "How do you so easily forgive?"

Aunt Trudy pats the top of my hand in her lap, humming again.

"Forgiveness." She pauses. "Such a burden to bear when it should set you free."

I glance over my shoulder at her, but Aunt Trudy is staring at the wall on the opposite side of the room.

"My brother also beat your mother," she says quietly, as if I need the reminder of the devil he'd been. Sadness lingers in her voice, exemplifying the difference in siblings.

One sweet and kind, forgiving and accepting. The other angry at the world, assuming he was owed everything, including obedience from Mama.

When he went for one of my sisters, so innocent and fragile, but crying, annoying him, Mama took the law that had failed her into her own hands.

"The law wasn't on her side." It's more of a statement. More declaration than a necessary reminder neither of us needs.

"Didn't give her the right to decide what was just."

Trudy squeezes the hand she holds, triggering another memory. She was the first to show me true affection. Not that Mama didn't occasionally offer a hug, but as I grew older, her attention grew more distant, sparing embraces only for my younger sisters.

"Good people can make bad decisions all the time," Aunt Trudy states. "Just like bad people make wrong ones thinking they're doing right."

Aunt Trudy and I both remain quiet, and the current climate of the world flashes through my thoughts. I strive to be open-minded but I'm also mindful that the rules are not equal everywhere.

"Life can be difficult some days. Hard at times. Sometimes things don't make any sense, but hate breeds hate, and you cannot let that happen. In between the crooked cracks is light, and that's where I choose to focus."

Aunt Trudy lets out a deep exhale.

"You and your sisters came to me during some of the darkest days for Carlton and me. And through some truly unsettling circumstances." Her voice shifts as does her attention, eyes landing on my face and offering me a warm smile. "And yet how blessed was I to have had the sheer pleasure of raising you. All three of you rascals. You were light in those dark times."

The three of us, but I hadn't really counted. I wasn't one of them.

Sedona and Jolene.

Our mother killed their father. They'd lost two parents at once.

For some reason, I think of Stone. He'd lost both his parents when he was young as well. He'd stepped in to raise the younger set.

What a noble man. He's not a superhero; he's a goddamn saint.

I fixate on Trudy, finding a resemblance, not in physical appearance but in temperament, to Stone.

Quiet strength.

"And look how you turned out," Aunt Trudy states, her voice a little louder, a little lighter, intruding on my thoughts of him. "Exactly as you are. Beautiful. Smart. Talented. Successful."

She claps over my hand once. "Because you are loved."

Rarely shed tears prickle my eyes. Trudy isn't taking credit for who I am, but how I was raised. Her compassion and education kept my heart and mind open to differences in people, to acceptance of others. And her love saved me from making bad decisions.

I could have turned out like Mama, chasing after men because I didn't see the value in myself. I could have been lost like Mama, who thought she needed a man to anchor her, instead of being her own iron-steel. She was an untethered boat, and she took Sedona, Jolene, and me on the ride. But I want to be on the shore.

I crave security despite my wandering soul. And I've had some sense of stability, because of me, and my talent, and Trudy and Carlton's support.

"I don't mean to be spilling beans, but what I'm about to tell you isn't a secret. You remember how Judd used to come to the house, hanging out like he was one of you." She smiles warmly, loving Judd like she loved all the rest of us. "Lost souls have a way of finding me."

She bumps into my shoulder, teasingly.

"I'm no angel." She laughs at herself. "But I recognize ones when I see them, and Stone is one of them. He could have turned out like his father. Mean, ornery, hateful. I don't excuse Flint's behavior, but that man was hurting. Love of his life gone. Babies to feed. He didn't know how to love without Violet."

Aunt Trudy sighs, recalling a woman I'd heard about often as a child. Her best friend, sadly taken from this earth too young and so tragically, although I can't remember what happened to her.

And it strikes me again that Trudy's friend is Judd's mama, Stone's mother.

He's felt the pain of a mother's absence.

Mama's man?

Once upon a time.

Oh, Stone.

"But Stone's nature is to protect, and he's been a rock for his siblings, giving them a soft place to land when they each falter. He isn't infallible. None of us are, but he's damn near perfect."

Her voice is fully restored to light and praising, almost wistful.

"And if a man kissed me well enough to curl my toes, I might want to cling a little."

I chuckle, the sound watery. "He didn't curl my toes."

"Shame. He seems like he might know his way around a woman."

"Aunt Trudy!" I laugh, the sound a bit choked with the unshed tears in my throat.

She pats my hand again, back to her teasing self.

I swallow the thickness in my throat and question, "How'd you know he kissed me?"

"Let's see." She taps her chin. "Was it the steamy stares? Or the way he tracked you around the yard?" She turns her head to face me. "Or the fact he couldn't take his eyes off you in general?"

"Trudy," I whisper, shaking my head like she's making these things up.

"Might have been you reciprocated that stare. More like an angry glare." She pauses. "Are you mad you kissed him? Didn't like it?" She wrinkles her nose.

I shake my head again. "No. I liked it." I liked it a little too much.

Suddenly, I straighten my shoulders and sit taller. "But it doesn't matter. I have commissions to fulfill. More adventures to be had." I hate how much I sound like Mama, and almost weak, as if I no longer believe in the thrill.

I love my art, and I've developed a newfound love of teaching, but I'm growing weary of hopping from one place to the next. Always chasing something that seems out of reach.

"Sometimes, adventure can be found right in your own backyard."

"Bloom where I'm planted? How very *Wizard of Oz* of you," I joke. "Plus, I don't have a backyard."

"Yes, but whose fault is that?" Aunt Trudy holds her dark, rich eyes on me, imparting wisdom I don't have the bandwidth to read.

I'm tired. I've been drinking. It's been a long day of information overload and puzzling reunions. And some heavy sexual tension.

But most of all, I'm questioning me.

What do I want?

And why *don't* I have a backyard?

14

———————

September

[Stone]

"Uncle Stone, you got a postcard."

"A postcard?" Stepping over to where Hudson stands by the kitchen island, I take the piece of mail from his hand and scan the picture on the front, then flip to the back.

MY LATEST COMMISSION IS COMPLETE. Thought you might like to see what little ol' me can do with the side of a building.

Also heard you and your brother re-roofed Aunt Trudy's house.

Thank you.

—Delilah

. . .

Flipping the postcard over again, I observe the image on the front a bit longer. The side of a two-story brick building has been used as a large canvas and transformed into a giant mural. One covered with sharp angles and dramatic edges, representing a community in Philadelphia. The mural holds symbols of America along with blue-collar icons and pieces of history not as openly shared. It's striking and beautiful and all Taxi. I hear her laughter in the faces of the people she painted and better understand her style. Bold colors. Graphic but rich. I note the name of the organization that sponsored the project at the bottom of the card and plan to look into it.

"Who's Delilah?" Hudson asks, breaking into my thoughts. Nosy little man has apparently already read the postcard.

"Private joke," I mutter, continuing to stare at the mural.

But was this a joke to her? Why send me something when she could hardly look at me back in July?

Her gratitude for fixing her aunt's roof wasn't necessary. My family would do anything for Trudy Wallace.

"Pretty."

I lift my head, finding Vale standing at my elbow, staring down at the picture.

"Yeah," I whisper, my throat suddenly thick.

Then I slip the postcard into my back pocket like I'm not affected by it and search blindly through the remainder of the mail like I give two shits about the electric bill.

After what I surmise is a reasonable time to pretend to check out the mail, I turn for my office off the kitchen. Once inside, I prop the postcard against the base of a lamp, torturing myself while silently pleased that Taxi is still pursuing her dreams.

Living adventures. The kind of her own making.

15

October

[Stone]

Took a little detour. *The leaves are changing. I love this time of year. Autumn always feels like entering a new season of life. Sounds a bit over philosophical, doesn't it? Then again, I'm in my forties. Times are a changin'.*

I landed another teaching opportunity with a group of kids near Detroit. Their excitement for art fuels me.

How about you? Performed any Superman heroics lately? Hope all is well and safe in Sterling Falls.

Trudy told me you raked up her leaves.

Thank you.

—Delilah

. . .

THE POSTCARD IS MORE ICONIC, like she grabbed it at a visitor center or a truck stop. The image of autumn leaves in flaming orange, brilliant yellow, and rustic brown fills the space.

A detour, she said. She's evidently on a road trip in Michigan.

As I stare at the image, I'm curious why she has sent me a second postcard. The questions are endless. Is she only thinking of me because I've done something for her aunt? Or is she thinking of me? Does she, dare I wonder, miss me somehow?

I snort as I lean back in my office chair, the furniture on rollers squeaking as it strains under my weight. I should replace this old thing. I should change a lot of things, but one thing I wouldn't change is the memory of her.

I don't have a way to respond to her short letters. Perhaps that's the point.

Maybe sending me these postcards keeps up the anonymity.

Samson and Delilah shared a night, not Stone and Taxi.

16

December

[Stone]

Happy Holidays.

I hope you don't mind me sending you these little snippets of where I've been, what I'm doing. You once said you hadn't been anywhere, and you want to see all the places for yourself. Maybe one day soon you can.

The holidays never feel the same without snow. I miss the mountains of West Virginia.

Strange, right?

—Taxi

WHILE THE PAPER is a sturdy cardstock, the image looks hand drawn and includes a cactus with snow dripping from the sharp needles of the waxy plant. Quite a juxtaposition, but then again, she's in Arizona with Trudy and Simon. And I know this only because I offered to watch Trudy's home while she's gone.

I stare at the image for another second. This one has no color. Just pencil art, shaded here and there, like it's a template for a mural.

Then again, could she have drawn this specific artwork just for me?

A large rock, almost near boulder size, sits beside the desert plant.

A cactus with snow melting on it, next to a giant stone.

I could read more into the drawing, but I don't. I don't understand why these letters keep coming to me, every six weeks almost to the date. Like she's journaling her adventures for me.

She questions how strange it might be to miss the mountains at this time of year.

The only strange thing about this latest postcard is that she finally signed it with her name.

Taxi.

And no, I don't think it's strange to miss West Virginia.

It misses her, too.

17

February

[Stone]

An envelope arrives with a smaller envelope inside, and a rectangular card within the second enclosure looks like an old-school Valentine's Day card. The cartoon caricature of Superman holds a heart-shaped piece of glowing green kryptonite.

TAKES MORE *than a cape to be a superhero. It takes heart.*

A LOOPY HEART-SHAPE accompanies her name.

I don't know what to make of the mail that comes every few weeks, I only know I don't want them to stop. Because some sick part of me believes she's sending these notes in hopes I'll think of her.

And I want to believe sending them means she's also thinking of me.

MARCH FOLLOWS suit with another postcard from Chicago, where Taxi attends a baseball game. She admits she doesn't understand the rules of the sport. She was a literal one-hit wonder last summer, connecting with the ball and running like she'd scored a home run when she was an easy out.

We were a one-hit wonder as well.

But this card is a little fuller with details, one that explains how she has another commission working with kids and how much she enjoys teaching. She even hints she might like to retire one day. Maybe find a permanent teaching position.

Not that Sterling Falls has a university, but there is a small college outside of Huntington, only forty minutes from here. Then again, the mountainous terrain doesn't exactly say urban outreach.

And I refuse to hope this means Taxi will settle here.

Still, I'm happy for her. She's finding a new way to share her passion.

I only wish I could see her art in person.

IN LATE APRIL, it's like the great unknown heard my request and I receive another postcard that's a collage of images. More like a giant mural of murals that form Taxi's face with skewed angles and odd shapes.

· · ·

DON'T THINK *I've ever mentioned I have an Instagram. If you ever want to know where I'm at or see my latest work, check it out.*

Hugs, Taxi

HUGS. I focus on the word, reading more into it than I probably should as a man nearing fifty, not some love-sick fool of fifteen.

The sheriff's department has an Instagram account for public service awareness, and we have a few burner accounts for surveillance, although the last time I needed to use Instagram was to investigate kids cyberbullying one another.

Being that I don't have a personal account, or any social media for that matter, I holler for someone I know who does.

"Hudson," I shout as I stand in the kitchen leaning against the island counter.

The pattern of mailed postcards has picked up pace, arriving at least once a month, typically right in the middle. I've learned not to anticipate one any sooner, and I anxiously await the one that might come later.

Heavy feet thunder down the upstairs hallway and then thud down the staircase.

"Yeah?" he asks, sounding breathless despite being an athletic kid. He's learned that I do not tolerate resorting to a text or phone call to get his attention within our own house.

When I call out for him, he needs to answer.

"Yeah?" I scoff, mocking his teenage tone, then offer him a slow smile.

I love this kid so much, and I feel him slipping away from me. Not only because of Cort's recent involvement in his life but also his age. He's on the cusp of being a teen, starting middle school next fall.

Another Sylver boy growing into a complex man.

"What did you need, Uncle Stone?"

"Right." I shake my head and stand taller. "Can I use your Instagram?"

"Why?" He tilts his head.

I tilt mine. "Got something to hide on yours?" *He better not.*

"No. I just . . . are you looking for something?"

I pause a second, weighing whether I think my now-twelve-year-old nephew is guilty of hiding something from me. Deciding he probably isn't, I explain myself.

"I actually want to look up an account."

Hudson lifts his phone, taps the screen, and waits.

I stare at him. He stares at me.

"Tell me who to look up," he says, holding in his exasperation.

"Oh. Um . . . T2urbanartist."

I wait as he types with his speedy thumbs, then turns the screen toward me. "Since when are you into art?"

"Since mind your own business," I tease, reaching out for his phone. He doesn't relinquish it at first, and I give him another look. A warning glare that if I believe he's doing something he shouldn't be doing on that device, I'll be getting his mom involved.

Hudson and I have a pact. We're pals. But I'm also the only father-figure he has. I'm good cop to his mother's bad, but I'll be turning him in if I need to. In twelve years, we've never had a problem.

Reluctantly, he hands me the phone, and I stare at the images on the grid. Slowly, I scroll through the account, landing on an image that stops me.

Among the photos of her artwork and some initial sketches is a singular graphic.

A dark-haired man in a cowboy hat. Head tipped forward. Sly smile on his lips. Large mustache.

The caption reads: **Cowboy kryptonite. Leaps mountaintops. Melts hearts.**

I stare at the image, re-reading the words over and over like they aren't already imprinted in my brain.

At the top of the screen, a notification pops up, interrupting my thoughts.

Amelia, reads the name. Three heart emojis follow.

I glance up at Hudson, knowing his secret and giving him a gentle grin. His first experience with love.

Here's hoping he can protect his heart.

By May, I'm almost angry that the postcards continue. Like a little tease that she's out there, experiencing the world and wants to be anywhere other than Sterling Falls.

Trudy's dropped hints about Taxi's whereabouts, but I never give in to her teasing nature.

If Taxi wanted me to call her or respond to her notes, she'd share her number or reach out in another manner.

Instead, she's still as fleeting as a dandelion seed in the wind.

And I'm the fool who now has an Instagram account.

While I'm happy for her, I resolve that her postcards are nothing more than friendly mail.

18

—————

August
One year, one month, and thirteen days
since last seeing Taxi.

[Stone]

For years, I've grumbled internally about wanting days of silence. Peace and quiet and space to myself.

And yet, as I stand inside the house I'd slowly, but surely, restored, the silence is almost deafening. The stone fireplace mocks me. The pictures of my family on the mantel say, *you got what you wished for.*

Vale and Hudson have moved out.

Today is his first day of middle school. Typically, I'd drive him on the first day of a new school year, make a show of my sheriff's truck, a subtle warning not to mess with my nephew. Now, he's living in Rogue River, the next town over.

Vale and Cort are probably taking him to the new-to-Hudson school.

He's twelve years old, and that means another dozen years of raising a child that wasn't biologically mine yet tied to me through biology.

With my hands on my hips, wearing my crisp, dull-brown uniform, I stare around the living room like I've never seen this space before. The sandstone-colored walls. The sky-blue chairs. The deep brown leather couch. Vale made a mark on every inch of this home while respecting that *we* shared this place.

Now, I live here alone.

Is this what my father feared? Had his loneliness for my mother driven him to push away the seven children surrounding him, willing to love him, wanting his love in return?

My siblings didn't move out because I was a curmudgeonly older brother. They left because that was the nature of growing up. Because moving out, falling in love, and starting their own families was how the cycle should work.

It'd only taken Vale most of her life for it to happen. And she took Hudson with her. Of course, she did. It's as it should be.

But standing here, the silence is nearly too much. No thundering footsteps from Hudson, rushing across the upstairs hallway and clomping down the staircase. No Vale hollering for him to hurry up. No grumbled good morning.

"Have a good day," I mutter to the empty room before swiping a hand down my face.

What the fuck?

I should be over this shit. Cort and I have an unspoken agreement. We tolerate one another. We don't mention the past. We don't talk much here in the present. But he did come to me to ask for a future with my sister.

They don't need my permission. Vale is a grown-ass woman, and I am not her father. Still, I appreciated the gesture.

Jesus, Cort will be on his second marriage, and I've never had a first.

I'm long over the reasons why I don't have Bailey, but the general concept of not having a partner in life is still a bitter pill to swallow some days. Like today, when I'm standing here alone, knowing I'll come home to the same silence at the end of the day. The same empty nest.

A sharp crackle on the radio attached to the vest over my uniform causes me to jump.

"Sheriff?" Fern is our new dispatcher, and she's still learning the ropes.

"Fern," I state, squeezing the sides of the radio.

"Sorry to contact you like this, sir, but you weren't answering your phone."

Reaching for the device in my back pocket, a few notifications pop up, all missed calls and text messages from the department.

> Sir, I need you to call in.

> This is urgent but not an emergency.

> Sheriff Stone?

"What's going on?" As I read the messages, my brows cinch. *Urgent but not an emergency?*

My thoughts leap to Hudson.

"It's Trudy Wallace, sir. We got a call this morning from her grandson. She's been taken to Milton County General."

Our small-town community is roughly forty minutes from Huntington, and the hospital is just outside the larger town's limits. We have a clinic in Sterling Falls for minor emergencies but *rushed to the hospital* sounds like something major.

"What happened?" I ask.

"Massive heart attack, sir. I thought you'd like to know."

"Where's Simon?" The boy is ten now. Trudy is his entire world, next to Judd and Genie.

"He demanded to be allowed to go with Trudy."

"Copy that. Over and out," I click the radio as I rush toward the front door.

The department has strict orders to contact me regarding anything related to my family and Trudy Wallace. The list of strict-order-contacts could go on and on, but I narrowed it down to my siblings, their partners, their children, and this one woman because of all she tried to do for us. All she'd been to our mother.

Thick as thieves, my mom used to tell me.

Violet Beauchamp moved to Sterling Falls during her high school years. She'd say starting a new school felt like the most difficult thing in her life. Then she had children.

For half a second, I can almost feel my mother tapping the tip of my nose and witness the smile on her lips as she teases.

Trudy was the first person Mom met when she came to Sterling Falls. My father was the second.

It was not *love at first sight*, Mom would say.

It was definitely love at first sight, he'd argue.

Settling into my department-issued truck, I speed out of the gravel driveway, kicking up rocks, and head for the highway leading to Huntington.

"Call Judd," I grunt to the voice-activated equipment in the truck that links with my phone.

"Stone." Judd sounds breathless.

"I got a call from—"

"Simon called me. I'm already on my way."

Logically, both of us don't need to be headed to the hospital, but Judd's relationship with Simon kicks him into big brother mode.

Trudy hadn't wanted Simon to have a cell phone, saying ten was too young for the device. Judd demanded that the boy have it for emergencies.

This moment reinforces Judd's argument. He'd been worried about the nearly-seventy-year-old woman living alone with a young boy.

"I can call you when I know more," Judd states.

"I'm headed there anyway," I bite out. Not that I'm angry with Judd. I'm anxious about Trudy. And Simon.

And Taxi.

Does she know? How could she? She's been gone for over a year.

I don't often ask about the wandering artist when I see Trudy, but the proud aunt eagerly shares all the doings of her niece.

Tallulah is in Montana. Strange that a woman with an urban vibe to her art was called up for a commission in a mountain town, but she loved it out there.

Tallulah is in Florida. Says she hates the humidity. And the bugs. Lord, do they have bugs down there.

Tallulah didn't make it home for the holidays. Flight was cancelled due to a storm.

Tallulah was sorry she couldn't make another Sylver Fourth of July baseball game.

And on and on, giving me updates I didn't request or require. My heart was full of pride for Taxi and her map-hopping career. She was obviously sought after and successful.

And I had my postcard collection.

I still questioned what happened between us, but then again, she'd made it clear she wasn't interested in anything other than our one night. Samson and Delilah. Superman and a mystery woman.

No regrets. Just a lingering disappointment.

I don't live a life of what-could-have-beens. I couldn't

afford to live that way. All that I'd lost didn't measure up to all that I'd gained, even if it wasn't apples to apples in comparison. I was grateful for what I had and tried not to dwell on what I didn't.

With a deep sigh, I flip the light on my truck, abusing my authority, but allowing myself grace while warning other vehicles about my extreme speed, as I dash down the highway with growing concern.

"Massive heart attack," the young female doctor confirms to Judd and me as we stand inside a stark waiting room.

Her gaze shifts to Simon, who'd fallen asleep in two chairs Judd had pushed together.

"She's lucky the boy was trying to administer CPR."

Judd is a few inches taller than me, and his shoulders lower when he hangs his head. A soft smile curls his mouth. He'd been insistent on Simon knowing basic lifesaving skills. *I'd* made it mandatory for all my siblings to learn CPR after losing our mother the way we did. Not that CPR would have saved her, but . . .

"She would have died without his quick attention."

The doctor's honesty is appreciated. I won't even pretend to know how a ten-year-old placing pressure on Trudy's chest saved her. I'm just grateful she's still here. For him. For her.

"She'll need to stay in the hospital for the next few days," the doctor continues.

Judd glances back at Simon. "I'll take him home with me."

Easy enough solution, as they are close and Simon has had sleepovers at Judd's home.

"Are there any other family members to be contacted? Perhaps an adult child?" she questions, glancing at the tablet in her hand.

"Is there something else?" I question. Something that demands an adult's attention.

The doctor shakes her head. "Nothing immediate, but Miss Wallace is going to need some assistance once she returns home. We don't have an emergency contact for her in our system."

"I'll call Taxi," Judd blurts, and I swing my head in his direction.

He'll call her?

It should make sense. They'd been friends as children, although Judd was more of a loner once he entered high school. I missed a few of his years when I went to college. Then, he went to college once I returned home. I hadn't considered that he was still in contact with Taxi or even had her number for emergencies like this one.

My brother had her number all along and I could have gotten it from him.

Not the time. Not my concern. The two thoughts collide and knock each other out of my head.

"What's next?" I ask.

"Rest. Recovery. Eventually, physical therapy. She's heavily sedated for the moment, but if you'd like to see her, you can." Her eyes shift toward Simon again. "We've moved her temporarily to ICU. Typically, we don't allow children under sixteen in the unit." Her hesitation suggests she might consider breaking hospital protocol.

"I don't want him to see her with tubes and equipment anyway," Judd immediately states, like he's suddenly in charge of Simon's well-being. "He's already seen enough."

The little hero made some thoughtful, quick decisions when he could have been scared out of his mind. Maybe he had been, but fear turned to action. He saved Trudy's life.

When the doctor excuses herself, Judd and I each take a turn visiting Trudy, who isn't aware of our presence. A heart monitor measures the slow but steady rhythm of her recovering heart. A mask covers her mouth, administering oxygen, while various other tubes and wires cover her body. Her youthful face looks like she's aged ten years.

I feel utterly helpless. Seeing this powerhouse of a woman lying here reminds me how mortal we all are, and the one area I cannot protect anyone from is death. I've witnessed the inevitability of life too much in my forty plus years. I'm not ready to lose Trudy Wallace.

Eventually, I convince Judd to take Simon home with him.

"I'll stay." I don't have anyone waiting on me, like Genie and the new baby are waiting for Judd. Plus, Simon doesn't need to hang out in a hospital.

After Judd contacted Taxi, he told me she was hopping on the first flight out of Alabama.

Taxi will be in Sterling Falls soon. I wished her return was under better circumstances.

For hours, I try to distract myself from the thought, as I sit at Trudy's side, using my phone to occasionally conduct business, but mostly letting my deputies take over for the day.

The ICU doesn't allow more than two visitors at a time and regulates how often those visitors can enter a room. The nurses let me stay full-time, but eventually, there are three of us in Trudy's room.

Emory Milton, the matriarch of the Milton family, and not any kind of kinfolk to Trudy, somehow talked her way in here. With her daughter, Emerson, at her side, I have no doubt Em tried to use her pull as the mayor of a nearby community to get her mother through the ICU security doors.

The senior Milton pays no attention to me as she rushes to Trudy's side, hovering over her friend's body before wrapping her hand around Trudy's.

"Oh, Trudy," Emory whimpers, blinking several times.

While Emory Milton was never friends with my mother,

and rather down on all of us Sylvers, I've learned the reasons behind her hatred from her daughter.

Once upon a time, Emory Milton, the most popular girl in area, had been dating Flint Sylver when Violet Beauchamp moved to town. And while Mom said it wasn't love at first sight because Dad ignored her, Dad argued he only ignored Mom because he was so attracted to her. The facts remain. He was already dating someone else.

He dumped Emory to be with Mom.

And all these years later, Emory has never forgiven Violet for arriving in Sterling Falls and taking her boyfriend.

"How are you doing?" Emerson asks me, sticking to the back of the room where I stand, allowing Emory a moment with Trudy.

"I'm good." The chair hasn't been particularly comfortable, and I could use something to eat and better coffee, but those feel like trivial things compared to Trudy's position.

"Mama made me come with her," Emerson continues, clarifying why she's present when she doesn't really owe me an explanation.

After all that happened with Taxi and the misunderstanding of what she'd seen between Emerson and me, I told Em I couldn't pretend anymore. I couldn't make public appearances and feed the rumors about a relationship we *didn't* have. Em either had to come clean, or we needed to break what was never glued together.

She opted for a breakup.

Which led to another notch in Emory Milton's dislike of someone with the last name Sylver. According to Emory, another Sylver broke the heart of another Milton, although that wasn't even half the truth. The other half was Emerson's to tell.

And Emerson and I are still friends. Just work-related ones.

As Em and I stand at the back of the room, the sliding door

open with flair, and a force of wild dark hair; beautiful, bronzed skin, and vivid color arrives wearing bright pink overalls covered in paint splatters.

She rushes to the bedside opposite Emory and stares down at her aunt.

When her cheeks drain of color, she turns her head and her silvery eyes collide with mine.

Taxi is back.

19

[Taxi]

When Judd's number popped up on my phone, I almost ignored the call. It was early in the morning. I'd just finished a project, and I was looking forward to a long day of napping in Gloria. My van had seen more miles in the last year than I'd put on her in the past five.

Chasing, my mama would say. The next adventure when it was really about pursuing her latest man.

Running, Sedona would argue, like she was anymore planted than I was.

Working. I'd overused the excuse as a reason not to return to Sterling Falls and face my aunt.

Or him.

A man I'd been sending postcards to for almost a year but had no way to know if he received them. It was better this way, I'd told myself. Sending a note without a return address meant he couldn't reject me by not responding. I hadn't given him the choice.

Then again, I'd hinted at having an Instagram and I thought he'd DM me there.

He never did.

Let me show you who I am.

I hadn't done it, and the words shouldn't have been chasing me everywhere I went this past year.

Maybe I *had* been running, like Sedona said.

None of this should matter now. Not with Trudy lying in this bed, so frail looking, so drained of energy.

And yet, I'm seeing red at the proximity of that pretty little blonde standing so close to Stone.

Rich crimson that bleeds with an irrational amount of jealousy and anger when I have no right. I'd been the one to leave. I've been the one conducting one-sided communication. I walked away from him.

But had I? Had I really let him go?

Those thoughts were neither here nor there right now.

I force my gaze from the perfect-looking couple. Her, in a sharp, fitted, navy blue suit, and him in his dull brown uniform. The town mayor and the sheriff.

With my gaze firmly on my aunt, my vision blurs. Tears I rarely shed come from a collision of emotions. The initial shock. The rush to get here. The exhaustion. And now this, Stone and Emerson again.

I blink back the clouds in my eyes despite it all being too much.

My focus and priority need to be in one direction. The woman in front of me. A strong, robust female who suddenly looks so helpless, attached to tubes and monitors.

A massive heart attack.

How did this happen? Her heart is too big, too strong, too

full of love. There is no way it attacked itself. Trudy Wallace would not have allowed it.

Uncle Carlton had a heart attack as well, and Trudy made a sad joke after his funeral.

"We're just heart people. Some people suffer strokes. Some deal with cancer. We're destined for heart trouble."

Had she been troubled? Was she not taking care of herself? Had she been eating poorly? Not exercising? What caused this?

I was desperate for something to blame other than genetics.

Heart people loved. They took in three girls who were not their own. They cared for the little girl whose mother caused them heartache. They made her feel like she had a home for a little while and a family for a little bit before the three sisters scattered like migrating butterflies.

Sedona was in England; Jolene was God knew where. As for me, I've been driving all over North America, painting murals on buildings, reinforcing communities, when I didn't have one of my own.

But didn't you, Tallulah? Don't you have this woman lying here? And Simon, too?

Why don't you have a backyard?

Slowly, I lift my gaze to the woman standing on the other side of Trudy's bed.

Emory Milton. I don't understand the relationship this posh, uppity, pillar of the community has with my adoring, kind-hearted, generous aunt, but the two opposites are friends. Maybe because Trudy never lets Emory get away with her inherent rudeness. Or maybe because Emory needs the tough love Trudy offers.

Either way, I don't begrudge Trudy having a friend. I just want everyone out of this room so I can process what has happened.

Aunt Trudy had a massive heart attack. I could have lost

her. And what did this situation mean for her future? Selfishly, what did it mean for me?

Another person hits my thoughts. "Where's Simon?" I demand, turning my attention back to Stone, like he's the authority in this room. He is the only person standing tall and stiff, fully in command of his emotions.

"He's with Judd."

Right. Of course. Now, I remember. Judd mentioned he'd take Simon home with him.

Relief washes over me at the sound of Stone's rugged, quiet voice, which makes no sense. The relief is knowing Simon is cared for. Stone's voice should mean nothing to me, especially as he's still standing so close to Emerson Milton.

The synapses in my brain feel like they're firing in all directions.

Trudy. Simon. Stone. Emerson.

Turning back toward Trudy, I simply stare at her, uncertain what to say, what to do, how to react, and knowing I won't voice anything in front of this little crowd. I want to be alone with my aunt.

Within seconds, a nurse enters the room.

"Um . . . Hi, everyone." The petite brunette clears her throat. "Y'all can't all be in here at once."

"I'm family," I blurt, warning her with a glare that she'll have to fight to remove me from this hospital room.

Stone lets out a little choke, more like a cough covering a laugh, and I swivel my head in his direction next.

Get out.

Please stay.

Someone hold me and tell me Aunt Trudy will be okay. Let that someone be him, the strong-looking man wearing a uniform I detest but emphasizing the strength of his arms. Arms I'd been anticipating wrapping around me when I have no right to think such thoughts.

Stone holds up both his hands. "Why don't we all give Taxi some privacy here?"

"I'm her best friend," Emory whines, whipping her attention from Trudy to Stone to me, in a triangular route of anguish and irritation. "She'd want me to be here."

"Mama, please," Emerson counters.

When Stone places his hand on Emerson's lower back, my stomach clenches, like a gut punch, when I have no right.

I walked away from him, and yet that earlier jealousy snakes through me despite an immediate scolding.

He is not mine.

I drag my gaze back to my aunt, forcing my thoughts elsewhere

Still holding her hand, I stroke her hair, which shifts. Puzzled, I notice her wig isn't as secure as it should be, like someone placed it on her head in haste instead of properly fastening it.

What happened here?

I glance at Stone once more, like he would hold the answer, when I doubt he has any idea about women and wigs.

His hand is no longer on Emerson's back. The blonde has already left the room, and Stone waves out his arm, suggesting Emory do the same. Ignoring Emory, I look at Trudy once more, thoughts racing so fast, nothing lasts more than a second.

When a firm hand comes to my lower back, I flinch in surprise and meet the warmth of sky-blue eyes. His gaze is steady while concerned, reminding me of the last time I saw him. When we just stood and stared before parting ways again.

He takes a slight step away, yet the heat of his hand still lingers on my back.

"Do you need anything? Food? A coffee? Something for Trudy?"

I swallow the thickness in my throat, barely holding everything inside. His sudden kindness feels like too much.

My brain can't compute anything other than what he's already suggested. "Privacy."

He nods once and rolls his lips inward before restoring them to their full lushness beneath a mustache.

"Okay. But if you think of something, I'm here for you."

I weakly nod my gratitude and watch him exit before recalling he'd said the same words to me almost a year ago.

He is here for me.

And for some reason, the thought crashes with everything else that has happened today. The fear of losing Trudy. The rush to get to her, hoping there was still time.

The tears I'd been holding at bay for hours finally break free.

20

[Taxi]

I don't know how long the tears fall, but eventually I fall asleep with my forehead against Aunt Trudy's arm. A gentle nudge to my shoulder has me lifting my head with a sudden jolt, causing my neck to crack. Tipping my head forward again, I squeeze on the kink in the back of my neck before noticing someone standing close to my side.

"I didn't mean to startle you." The deep, but quiet tenor has me looking up and up and up at the tall figure beside me.

Stone. *He's still here?*

Our eyes meet only briefly. His are kind and concerned as he puckers his mouth, causing that thick mustache to twitch above his lip.

The sound of machines humming and steadily beeping must have lulled me to sleep. The dim room suggests it's late.

"What time is it?"

"Actually." He pauses. "It's time to go." He glances toward a nurse entering the room.

"I'm sorry, but visiting hours are over," she cheerfully announces.

Visiting hours? I'm not visiting. I'm family.

I swivel my head in the direction of Aunt Trudy. Earlier, I removed her wig and wrapped her head in a silk scarf I had in my bag. The vibrant burst of color next to her dark skin only slightly brightens the stark image of wires and tubes and a hospital bed.

And I don't want to leave her side.

"Do I really need to go?"

"Hospital rules," the nurse says, smiling sympathetically. "We open again at eight a.m."

Eight a.m.? What will I possibly do all night?

"I can give you a ride somewhere," Stone says, as if reading my thoughts. "To Trudy's. Or maybe Judd's." He hesitates a second. "You could even stay at my place."

As much as I don't want to be alone, I cannot impose on Stone, nor do I want to disturb Judd. He and Genie have a newborn baby, plus Simon is there right now. I need to see Simon, but I'll hold off until tomorrow when I have a better grip on my emotions and this situation.

Without answering where Stone should take me, I give one final glance at Aunt Trudy.

Don't you dare die on me. It's a harsh prayer but a desperate plea. As much as I might not feel like I have a physical home to return to, I've always had her. She's my home base.

With my sisters scattered, I'd be even more untethered without Aunt Trudy.

And what about Simon?

Slowly, I rise from the plastic chair and lean over Aunt Trudy, placing a kiss on her forehead.

Guilt slams into me. I should have visited her more often. I should have told her more things. How I felt about her. How important she is to me. How I selfishly still need her, need to know she's still here for me.

Stone steps to the side when I push back my chair, allowing me to step in front of him. He picks up the duffel bag I hastily packed and dropped as soon as I entered the hospital room. He places his hand on my lower back, much like he did earlier, allowing the heat to seep into my skin, which I hadn't realized was so cold.

With the gentle pressure at the base of my spine, he guides me out of the ICU and down the quiet hospital hallway to an exit. When we reach his sheriff's truck, he opens the passenger side door for me and holds out his hand to help me up. Ignoring his offer, I reach for the bar on the edge of the door frame and hoist myself into the passenger seat.

When he shuts the door, my pulse begins to throb as I spy all the equipment between the seats and a computer screen attached to the dashboard. I swore I'd never be in a cop car again. Like the one where they put my sisters and me, huddled together in the backseat, clinging to one another, uncertain what was happening to us or where they were taking our mama, who was placed in another car, separated from us.

I shiver at the memory and flinch when Stone slams his door after taking the driver's seat.

"Sorry," he mutters, noting the jolt in my body. He adjusts in his seat, presses the ignition button, and turns on the heat, although it's still the middle of August.

"It's too warm for heat," I comment.

"I know, but you're trembling."

Glancing down at my fisted hands, I straighten my fingers to find them shaking. I slip them underneath my thighs as if that will stop the tremor.

"Where to?" he asks, all reserved and business-like. Like I'm any other person he'd give a ride.

I shouldn't be thinking about how he kissed me once upon a Tennessee evening. Nor how much I could really use a hug, and I remember his hands being strong and his arms solid.

Swallowing, I stare out the windshield. "I guess take me to Trudy's, please."

I catch Stone's nod in my peripheral vision, and he reverses out of the parking spot. We spend the next half-hour in silence, letting the hum of his tires on asphalt be the soundtrack in this truck.

When we arrive at Aunt Trudy's, he cuts the engine, and before I even reach for the handle, he's around the front of the truck and popping open my door. He grabs my duffel from the back.

I could argue that he doesn't need to walk me in. The distance is only a few feet, but I don't have the energy. I fumble through my oversized tote for the beaded keyring that has actual car keys needed for Gloria and a single house key.

Pulling the screen door forward, Stone props it open with his body, while I fumble with the house key. My fingers are still shaking.

Eventually, he covers my hand with his and guides the key into the lock. With his hand over mine, he twists, forcing the key to turn and pop open the front door.

"Appreciate the—What the heck?" As I'm thanking him for the ride, he follows me into the house. "Just what the hell are you doing?"

Without an ounce of chagrin, he states, "I'm not leaving you alone tonight."

Crossing my arms, I glare at him in the dark entryway. "What if I want to be alone?"

"Then I'll sit in another room, but I'm not leaving."

"You can't *sit* in another room."

What's he planning to do, spend the night in a chair?

Ignoring my statement, he turns to close the front door and

flip on the hallway lights, appearing rather familiar with Trudy's home.

The layout is simple. The entryway is a short hall with the small, square kitchen to the left. The hallway ends in the living room, which is long and narrow. Another hall leads off the living room to two bedrooms and one bathroom.

Pretending as if Stone isn't present, I make my way to the linen closet and return to the living room, where Stone has taken a seat on the couch.

"You're on my bed," I snap.

He glances left, then, right before looking up at me. "You sleep here?"

"Sofa city. Trudy only has two bedrooms. Simon's and hers." She'd bought the smaller place because it would have less space to keep clean. Plus, she expected visitors in that extra bedroom, not a permanent resident. She would never begrudge Simon's presence. She loves him, but I've sensed her struggles when we've spoken on the phone. She's already raised children. In her retirement from foster care, she took on a second career as a real estate agent. She loves finding new homes for people.

Stone stares at me for a long minute. Those blue eyes remind me of my recent visit to Montana, and he gives me a puzzled look before he hefts himself off the couch and enters the kitchen. While I fling the sheet over the cushions and cover a bed pillow with a silky case, I hear Stone rustling around in the kitchen.

"Don't even think about stealing Trudy's food," I holler, like he's conducting a jewelry heist in the other room.

When the couch is made up, I sit heavily and tip back my head, staring at the ceiling. Sensing Stone's approach, I glance at him.

With a plate in hand, he says, "I made you a sandwich. Turkey on wheat. It's all she had."

I stare at the dish. Aunt Trudy's trusty 1970s Corelle. A white dish with a gold floral pattern around the rim. Then I take in the sandwich. Brown bread. White meat, neatly folded between the slices. Beside the sandwich are apple slices. He holds a can of cola in his other hand.

And I burst into tears.

What is with all this emotion?

Covering my face, I pitch forward, bracing my elbows on my knees. Stone is suddenly sitting beside me, hand cupping the back of my neck, and I tip into him. He wraps his arm around my back and the other around my front, pulling me tighter into his side.

I'm typically not a crier, so I don't know what's come over me.

I allow myself a moment in the strength of his arms and the press of his forehead into the back of my head before I hastily swipe at my cheeks and straighten. Instantly, I miss the warmth of him holding me, but that's not why he's here.

"You haven't eaten all day. Take a bite." He picks up the plate he'd set on the floor and holds the sandwich toward me.

"Thank you," I whisper as my throat feels too raw and my tongue too thick. The first bite is like an explosion in my mouth. He's right. I haven't eaten all day, which makes me snippy when he doesn't deserve my hangry tone. Of course, he wasn't stealing Trudy's food.

While I hold the sandwich, he sets the plate on his thigh and reaches for the soda can with his other hand. Popping the tab, a sharp hiss fills the room. I'm not a big soda drinker, but I take the can he offers me.

"You need a little sugar to settle the nerves."

Seems counterintuitive to calm the jitters, but I don't argue. Instead, I take a sip and set the can on the floor near my feet.

"Another bite," Stone softly commands, and I take a second one while he watches me.

"Why haven't you asked how I'm doing?" I question for some reason.

"Because I'm assuming from the shakes, you're still in a state of shock, resulting from lack of food and decent sleep, and the struggle to process what Trudy's heart attack means. What it could have meant." He pauses for effect.

We both have the same thought. Trudy could have died today.

"But you tell me if I'm wrong. How are you holding up?"

Befuddled by his accurate assessment and observation of me, I don't respond. Then I remember his position. His career. He probably deals with this kind of thing all the time. The shock. The loss.

Only I didn't lose today. Trudy is still here.

"What happened?" I whisper, like I haven't already heard the particulars from Judd and then the doctors. Several thoughts slam together at once before he can answer my rather rhetorical question.

"I should have been here. She should not be raising Simon on her own. She's growing older. She needs to take better care of herself. I should be taking care of her."

"Whoa, whoa, whoa. Slow down." His hand swipes up my back again, and he gently squeezes the nape of my neck.

I bristle, but not for the reasons he must think, and he instantly removes his hand. His touch was firm yet tender. The heat of his palm caused me to shiver again. And I wish he'd put it back on me.

Instead, I take another sip of soda.

"I don't think any one thing, nor a single person, is to blame for Trudy's genetics. Heart attacks happen."

Stone speaks like Aunt Trudy simply tripped when the doctor explained how Trudy has been having heart issues for years. She's never mentioned it to me. Had Sedona known? What about Jolene? Neither of them ever said anything about

Trudy's health the last time I talked to them. Then again, between the three of us, I'm the closest to Trudy.

"Why didn't she tell me?" I whisper, more to myself than Stone.

"Because that's not who Trudy is. She doesn't want people to worry about her. She doesn't want anyone to make a fuss." His voice is gentle, a smile in the corners of what he's saying. He knows my aunt well. She's someone who cares about others, but apparently isn't taking care of herself.

I snort and take another bite of the sandwich. I'm not certain turkey on whole wheat has ever tasted so good. When I eat an apple slice, I'm suddenly full and sleepy. I should shower, but my limbs feel too weak to bother.

I pick up the other half of my sandwich and push it toward him. "Here . . . you should eat too."

He glances at it, then at me, those blue beams of his eyes catching mine. For a second, he studies me, like he's noticing something new.

I shiver again at the intensity. At how deeply it seems this man observes me, sees something in me. The sensation from the night we first met tickles over my skin. Like he is different. Special, even.

"Thanks," he says, voice low, a hint of a smile tugging at the corner of his mouth. He lifts the sandwich carefully, as if the gesture matters more than the food itself.

While he eats the remainder of the sandwich, I settle back against the couch, letting the quiet linger, small and comforting.

Thinking this is how having a home might feel.

21

[Stone]

I appreciate that Taxi wants privacy, but I'm not about to leave her alone. She was woken by bad news, raced to an airport, and rushed to a hospital, then napped hunched over beside her ailing aunt's bedside. I didn't trust her mental capacity or physical ability to be alone.

And I was also being fucking selfish.

I was one-thousand percent certain Taxi could take care of herself, and yet I wanted to be here for her, whether she wanted me to or not.

This was my way of trying to process what happened to Trudy. I needed to do *something,* and that something was to be present for her beautiful, yet annoying, niece.

Being tough skinned, I could take her little jabs and sharp tongue if she needed someone to lash out on. Needed some way to make sense of a frightening heart attack striking her beloved aunt.

After my mother passed, and my father changed, I'd built resilience. With every insult he hurled, I reminded myself he was hurting. He'd lost the love of his life. He was left with seven children to raise when she'd been the nurturer. But when his insults turned to something deeper, more sinister, my compassion wavered. My sympathy waned.

However, Taxi is not my father.

She is hurting in a different way. Fear. Confusion. Relief because her beloved aunt will live.

As I busy myself cleaning up the kitchen and washing the plate I used, I hear Taxi move through the small house. Her path to the bathroom. Her return to the living room. The light goes out in the other room.

I meant what I said. I'm not leaving. She can ignore my presence all night, but I'll be parking myself in a hard-backed, wooden chair in this square kitchen. In the morning, Taxi will need a ride back to the hospital, and I use that as an additional excuse to stay.

I'll be here for her.

In truth, I'm relieved Taxi is here, as we don't know what is next for Trudy. Or for Simon, for that matter. Because a ten-year-old boy cannot be the caregiver for a recovering heart attack patient, not that Judd or I would let that happen. Especially Judd. Recalling my own childhood, and the way things flipped from my being a pre-teen to practically a parent, I don't want that kind of responsibility falling on another child, even if Simon is excessively competent.

When I pull the kitchen chair away from the table, it scrapes on the linoleum flooring, and I wince as the noise sounds like thunder rattling the shingles on the roof.

Taxi needs her rest, and I take a seat, setting my phone in my hand to send out an update in the family group chat about Trudy's condition and Taxi's present location.

As if just thinking of her conjures her, she's suddenly

standing in the entrance to the kitchen. Her wild dark hair is tied up on her head and she's wearing a deep magenta velvet robe that looks three-sizes too large for her.

"It's Aunt Trudy's," she says, glancing down at herself before leaning against the opening to the kitchen. One leg crosses over the other, separating the fold of the robe and exposing the shapely length of her leg. Her head tips to the side as she tugs at the two ends of the robe's belt.

"I can't sleep."

Once upon a time, I'd argue with Hudson or one of my younger siblings that they hadn't given sleep enough of a chance. They'd want a drink of water or need to use the bathroom for a third time.

Only ten minutes might have passed since Taxi told me she wanted to lie down.

"I need a distraction." Her silver eyes are exhausted and sad, but also sheepish, and she quickly dips them, glancing down at her toes. "Want to take my mind off things, Superman?"

Leaning back in the hard chair, I stare at her for a long moment. Taking in how she's avoiding a glance in my direction, while her voice drops lower. Low, but tired, despite what I *think* she's proposing.

Her shoulders hunch forward. Her hand clutches at the two folds of the robe before both hands slip into the giant pockets.

She doesn't really want what she's suggesting.

As much as the nickname she'd given me once upon a time sends my belly swirling, tonight isn't the night for anything other than rest.

And the longer I stare at her, I realize her ask might be a silent cry for comfort and support, not one of desire.

Her vulnerability tears at my sternum.

Slowly, I stand from the kitchen chair and close the

distance between us, scooping a few loose strands of her hair around her ear and cupping the back of her neck.

Taxi shifts, releasing her hands from her pockets and crossing her arms over her chest, like a small barrier between us. A wall between what she's asking for and what she really needs.

Tipping my head forward, I bring hers to mine, resting our foreheads together.

"Tallulah Alexander, I'd give you anything you need, but I won't do this." My tone is quiet but firm. I'm not rejecting her, I'm accepting her pain. I'm sensing she'll regret any decisions made under stress and exhaustion.

"Because of Emerson," she quietly asks.

I shake my head gently against hers before pulling back and tipping up her chin, so she'll look at me. Those silvery eyes that I recall as so playfully gleaming are dull, almost gray, cloudy on the verge of a quiet storm.

"Taxi, I already told you that Em is nothing more than a friend, but I'll reiterate it again. Nothing ever has, and nothing ever will, be more than a work friendship between us." I stare into those eyes that make my knees a bit weak. "I haven't been with anyone since long before last summer."

The last bit of information isn't necessary for our current position. The one where she is vulnerable and I'm trying to be an upstanding man, but I want her to know that just like I told her a year ago, I don't sleep around. Not randomly, not casually, and that includes Emerson.

Her eyes briefly widen before she must decide on something. She nods once as if accepting that Em is important to me, but not more than any other friend.

It takes every ounce of strength I have not to tug Taxi into my arms, hold her against me, press her where my heart hammers, and wrap my arms around her to protect her. Protect her from herself and her pinging emotions.

I can only imagine the thoughts in her head. Her fears for her aunt. Her concerns for the future. Her guilt, as she expressed earlier.

But tonight, I don't want her thinking about any of that.

"I'm here for you," I say, hoping to impart my meaning. Let me be her rock, not her distraction.

She nods like she hears me, but I'm not certain she's really listening.

Bending at the knees, I scoop her up, and she screeches in surprise before quickly wrapping her arms around my neck. She lets out a sharp laugh, reminding me of that tambourine tingle from the night we met. The sound travels down my chest to a place that won't be gratified.

I carry Taxi back to the living room, which is now doused in darkness, and set her on the couch she made up like a bed.

She huffs as I release her, then reaches for the side of my pants, gripping the strip that runs down my outer thigh.

"I was jealous," Taxi quietly owns. "Earlier. Seeing you with Emerson. I didn't like it, which wasn't fair to you."

I fight a smile, warning myself not to read more into her admission of jealousy.

"I'm right here," I remind her, stroking a finger around her face.

"Don't leave," she whispers, looking up at me with eyes I can't quite make out but know even in the dark because those eyes appear behind my lids when I close my own. They've haunted me and teased me and played out in fantasies I don't dare admit.

And something deep inside me opens even wider, drinking in the drops this woman gives me.

"Just give me a minute," I respond.

Trudy has a recliner in her living room along with the couch, but I'm not interested in rearranging her furniture. Instead, I opt for bringing a kitchen chair to the side of the couch, staring at Taxi as she lies on her back, face aimed at the ceiling.

I can't imagine she can fall asleep any easier with me watching her, but after she's asked me to stay, I won't leave her side.

Eventually, she drapes her arm over the top of her head, causing the long sleeve of her aunt's robe to expose her forearm.

She sighs heavily before saying, "I've been so unfair to you." Her voice remains quiet, puzzled and apologetic.

My brows lift as I lean forward in the chair, resting my elbows on my thighs. "How?"

"Last summer."

"Taxi," I groan. "We don't need to go back there." We don't need to rehash the kiss that meant nothing to her and everything to me, or the day she spent at my home, where she rejected me.

"I was wrong."

Her statement puts a hold on any argument I was about to offer.

Her head shifts so suddenly on the pillow that I sit back in the hard chair. She rolls to her side, tucking her hands underneath her cheek. With the light streaming from the kitchen into the hallway, a sliver of illumination enters the room, and I catch her eyes focusing on me again.

She swallows thickly. "What do you know about me?"

"Other than you're the most beautiful woman I've ever met?" The intention was to keep my answer light, almost teasing, but it comes out sharp and direct, and I bite back the additional comments fighting to be added to that assessment. Ones that recall a kiss in a hotel hallway. The feel of her hips in my hands and the taste of her tongue. The way her breath hitched, and her body arched toward mine.

Her smile is weak. "I mean, about my history. My backstory."

"Your history doesn't change who you are," I admit. Oftentimes, we are who we are because of our backstory. How we resist it, persevere through it, survive it. "But if you'd like to tell me, I'm willing to listen."

Because sometimes, even when the backstory doesn't matter in the present, it needs to be told. Or it *feels* like it should be shared.

Maybe talking about herself and her aunt will ease her mind. Bring up good memories and settle her into her sleep.

Or, maybe, Taxi is finally opening up to me.

22

[Taxi]

I didn't know where to start. Didn't know what he already knew or didn't know about me. As neither of us recognized the other as adults, I didn't know what he'd remember from *my* childhood. My brief time here in Sterling Falls.

Judd was often at Trudy's home, which made our friendship easily bloom, but I didn't have much interaction with the eldest Sylver or his brother Clay, who was second in line. Both boys were teenagers, and just ahead of Judd and me in age when I moved here.

I also didn't have much interest in boys back then. My world was my sisters and our younger cousin of sorts, Rowan. Our time together included running around the yard, making up games, and using our imaginations, which sometimes resulted in innocent trouble, like painting the side of Aunt Trudy's shed purple and green.

Trudy and Carlton's home was full of fresh food, clean spaces, and land to roam free.

Grand adventures were had in their backyard.

Heaven in West Virginia? I believed I'd arrived.

But the darker side of landing a dream placement as a foster kid was the reason I was in Trudy and Carlton Wallace's home in the first place.

"My mama . . ." I begin, licking my lips. "She didn't make good choices when it came to men."

Stone lowers his gaze and nods, like he already understands my meaning.

"I never knew my daddy. He was long gone by the time Mama met Trudy Wallace's older brother. Sedona and Jolene are *his* daughters."

Stone's head lifts, and his thick brows pinch, hinting he already knows where this story might be headed.

"He was a mean man." I exhale. "He loved my mama something fierce and then acted the opposite with the flip of a coin." Love was not the right word to describe what my mother and Trent Wallace had. I wasn't deaf to the noises coming from my mama's room or blind to the way he'd sometimes kiss her in front of us. Like he wanted to swallow her, bring her into his chest, and keep her near his heart.

"They were not good for one another. Toxic." Stone's face has my attention, but my mind is years behind me. The insults. The fights. The results.

"She went to the police."

Stone's head starts to bobble like he knows how this story played out.

"When they didn't help her, she took the law into her own hands."

Stone closes his eyes, scrubs a hand down his face, the rasp of his scruff loud in the otherwise quiet room. He leans against the high back of his chair.

Shame washes through me. The stain of my mother's decision was like paint I can't ever seem to remove. And I don't know why I'm telling him this story when I never share it with anyone. Traveling here and there doesn't lead to long-term relationships or anyone getting close enough to need to know, want to know, these details from my past.

Water under the bridge, Trudy might say. But when the tide rose, a flash flood of memories could drown me.

"She was found guilty and sentenced to life in prison." I swallow thickly. "And we never saw her again. By her choice."

I tried to reach out to Mama when I got older. Sent her a handful of letters to tell her about art school, and Sedona and Jolene. How we all fared well with Trudy and Carlton.

The letters were returned in a bundle, marked Return to Sender. I never reached out again.

Maybe that's another reason I sent Stone all those postcards without a return address. I couldn't take that kind of rejection again. If he tossed them in the trash, I wouldn't be the wiser. But if he sent them back to me, I couldn't handle that kind of dismissal.

Stone leans forward again, slowly, deliberately, like he knows he's approaching someone fragile. Someone on the edge of cracking, despite the strong exterior I display.

He reaches for my hands and tugs one toward him. Cupping both his hands around mine, he strokes the thick pad of his thumb over my knuckles, focusing his gaze on where he touches me.

"I'm so sorry that happened to her." He pauses. "That she sought help and didn't receive it. And I'm sorry she felt desperate enough to make a decision that altered her life, and Trudy's brother's life, and yours and your sisters' forever."

He pauses again and pulls my hand up to his lips, pressing them to those knuckles, lingering there.

"The sins of the father . . . the sins of any parent . . . should never be held against the child."

With a suddenly sharp look, Stone's eyes say everything. He isn't going to hold my past against me.

"You're the sheriff," I swallow thickly, shame rattling inside me, remembering what Trudy said. My mama's situation was not Stone's fault. "I hope you can understand—"

"You don't trust the law."

I shake my head, acknowledging his assessment.

With his head bobbing only slightly, he lowers my hand, still held snuggly in both of his. He stares at the back, continuing to paint even strokes over my skin. My fingers are long and thin compared to the thickness of his and the pad of his palm. His hold on me feels reassuring, soothing, calming.

"Taxi." He lifts his head. "I'm not asking you to trust something you can't. But I am asking you to trust in me. As a man. A man who wants to get to know who you are in the present, not what happened to you in the past."

"One defines the other."

The corner of his mouth flicks upward, forcing that mustache to twitch. His voice is sad.

"Yes, it does, but I never want to be held accountable for things out of my control. Things I navigated the best I could and became determined never to be."

He pauses a beat. "My father . . . he was mean, as I suspect Trent Wallace might have been. And he took his heartache out on his children."

My eyes widen, remembering bits and pieces of Judd's experience. His tears. His hatred of their dad.

"Did he . . ." I swallow thickly. "Did he hurt you?"

"Not in ways you might think. But words can do their damage despite the old saying. He was worse toward a few of my brothers." He swallows thickly.

Sticks and stones can break my bones, but words will never hurt me. Easier said than believed by some.

"But I'm explaining this so you know where I'm coming from. I believe in the law and the rightness it should follow. The rules. The regulations. Because I didn't have anyone protecting me . . . me or my siblings . . . I went into law enforcement to *be* that protection I didn't receive for others."

I watch his throat roll, sensing there's a story here. One with more depth, despite the past I knew about Judd, and this new admission from Stone.

"I just want to assure you I'm on the right side of things. I'm not perfect, but I try my best to be fair. To see all sides of a story."

He stills his thumb over my knuckles and focuses on my face.

"I'm sorry the law didn't do its job, do what was right by her, but the whole reason I'm a sheriff is to make certain the law does what it should. Protect those who need it."

Like Mama.

Like his siblings.

My body practically squirms, the desire to sit up and crawl into his lap and reassure him in some manner. Confess my guilt for unfairly judging him and express my sympathy for all that happened to him as a child.

We're almost two peas in a pod. Almost.

Instead, he startles me by patting the back of my hand once, gently. "Now, this isn't exactly bedtime story material. And I really do think you need some sleep."

He runs his finger around my face again and settles just underneath my chin. "Get some rest. I'm right here."

I lick my lips, nodding to agree with him, but still overflowing with new thoughts.

His past. Mine.

He's already rejected my proposition for distraction. Saw

right through my proposal and gently shut me down. Rightfully said no. I'm not in the headspace for sex.

I want something more.

"Stone?" I swallow a thick lump in my throat. A stream of panic lances through me. Fear that he'll say no, but still so desperate for a yes.

"Would you . . . could you . . . maybe just . . . lay here with me?" It's a big ask, especially after what I told him, how I've treated him.

"Sure." He answers without thought, quietly sighing as if in relief.

Slowly, he stands. Stone Sylver could look imposing if he wanted to, the uniform adding to that power stance. Instead, he looks like a safe space to root, a soft place to land.

At least for tonight

"That uniform looks uncomfortable," I admit, uncertain how he'd sleep in that thick belt with that badge on his chest.

He chuckles softly, placing his hands on his hips and shaking his head. "Still trying to get me out of my clothes, Tallulah?"

"Want to know if there's a giant S for Superman underneath that stiff shirt."

His laugh comes a little louder as he slowly unbuttons his uniform, but his tone sobers when he says, "I'm just a man, Taxi. No superpowers. Nothing special."

I beg to differ, but tonight I don't have any arguments left in me.

Silently, I watch as he strips off his shirt, peeling back the two halves and rolling it over his shoulders before draping it neatly over the back of the kitchen chair. His belt makes a distinct clatter when he removes it, setting it over the chair, as well, before toeing off his shoes.

He's wearing a plain white tee beneath the uniform. No S on his chest, other than an invisible one.

One for steadfast, sturdy, solid. Stone.

"You can take off your pants if you're uncomfortable." I lick my lips. "If it makes *you* more comfortable."

He chuckles again. The sound light, but a little choked. "Still trying to get in my pants, darlin'?"

I laugh, feeling a little lighter myself, before chewing at my lower lip to bite back a response.

When his pants come off, he lays them neatly on the chair seat. In white boxer briefs, he looks like an underwear model, advertising something pure and dignified with all that starkness, but I briefly see the outline of something not so little that gives me impure thoughts.

Looking away, I close my eyes as Stone reaches behind me and tugs the back cushions free from the couch to offer him more space. I don't know how we'll both fit on this old sofa and second-guess my suggestion until Stone climbs over me, slipping in between the back of the furniture and my body.

And then, he spoons me. And I do not mean a casual big-spoon, little-spoon nesting together.

Stone Sylver knows how to *cuddle*.

He slides one arm underneath the pillow and settles his nose against the nape of my neck. Then he drags his hand down my arm and over my hip, where he flattens his palm against my lower belly, pinning me to him.

Back to chest.

Ass in lap.

Knees behind my knees.

He's lined up with me in every way he can be, including his feet underneath mine, propping the pads of mine on top of his.

He bends the arm beneath the pillow, slips his hand into the robe that's too big for me, and cups my opposite shoulder. His palm is warm against my heated skin, and he tickles that thick mustache into my nape before mumbling, "Good night, Tallulah."

In some manner, I should feel trapped by our position, caged in, pinned down, however one wants to define the confinement.

Instead, Stone coiled around me makes me feel cradled, coddled . . . safe even. And while my body first wanted sex as a distraction, to experience his flesh and disappear from my head, the zing zipping down my middle is nothing compared to raging desire.

It's the slow melt of an ice cap. The trickle of a refreshing stream. The cool mix of deep blue with bland white, resulting in a pretty periwinkle. A color that always feels soft and feminine, and taken care of.

Like Stone does for me.

And I slip into a restful sleep.

23

[Taxi]

In the morning, Stone and I both wake, apparently rested, despite a lumpy couch beneath our sides. My alarm goes off because I want plenty of time to get back to the hospital.

Stone and I are quiet together, giving each other hesitant smiles. I give him privacy to redress while I use the bathroom, giving myself a pep talk about making it through another uncertain day.

While I refuse breakfast, Stone stops in Sterling Falls at his brother's bakery, Curmudgeon Bakery, where he picks up muffins and coffee.

"In case you get hungry later," he tells me, taking care of me in another small way. I've been solely responsible for myself for so long, his care and concern thrill me in a way that seems almost foreign.

We exchange phone numbers, and I tell him I'll call him with any updates. He offers to return after his shift.

I'm grateful he'll be back, although I don't want to be a burden. I'm set to argue that I can call him when I need a ride back to Trudy's, but he holds up a hand, stopping me before I can speak.

"Just let me be here for you."

The words stop me short.

Late in the afternoon, Judd and Genie bring Simon to the hospital to see Trudy. She woke up only once, earlier. The doctors have warned she'll need plenty of rest at first. Then lots of home care, including rides to appointments and eventually physical therapy. It's a lot to consider, and unfortunately, Simon hears the tail end of a conversation about next of kin and responsibility.

Judd suggests we all go to the cafeteria for a treat, although I'm not necessarily hungry, but I would like a minute with Simon.

Genie is also an artist, designing quirky calendars with fun, non-traditional dates in them, and she has a sketchbook with her and a set of colored pencils she offers Simon.

I sit beside him, silently sketching out an image while he attempts his own drawing on the opposite page. Judd and Genie sit across from us with Nolan strapped to Genie's chest.

Judd and I are discussing Trudy's future again, when I finally say in exasperation, "I'll take care of it."

I'm tired of hammering this point home with Judd. He's an amazing human being who has been dutiful and kind to Trudy, but she's my aunt. Judd also has a special relationship with Simon. The two are extremely close, so I know I need to tread lightly here. I just want Simon to know he's loved by many, not just a few.

Suddenly, Stone appears at the edge of the table, looking

refreshed in a pair of worn jeans and a beige, denim shirt that reminds me a little bit of his uniform.

"You'll take care of what?" he asks, glancing from me to Judd and back.

"I'll take care of *her*," I emphasize. "Trudy."

Stone looks at Judd, then me again, like he's confused.

"There was just a little mix-up in Trudy's personal information with the hospital. She didn't have anyone listed as next of kin," Judd explains.

I nudge Simon's shoulder with mine. "And I'm trying to reassure my little man that I'm here to take care of Trudy. And him."

I smile affectionately at Simon, who doesn't look up at me. He's been exceptionally quiet, which is understandable considering all he's been through. Thank goodness he's already in therapy.

When Simon doesn't look at me, I glance back at Stone.

"There's also a concern for Trudy's ongoing care," Judd explains. "Who will assist her with her personal needs, follow-up appointments, and physical therapy sessions?"

I turn toward Judd again, narrowing my eyes at him. "And I already said I'm here for them."

Glancing back at Simon, he appears to be focused on his drawing, but his hand has stilled. I'm not comfortable having this discussion in front of him, and I cup his chin, gently turning his head so he'll look at me.

His hair is dark, hanging longer in the front, and brushing the tops of his dark-framed glasses. He looks like a miniature Judd with his bright blue eyes and these glasses. He worships my old friend, but I'm trying to assure Simon that I'm family.

Simon doesn't even blink when he says, "But you always leave."

The words pierce my heart like a blade. Admittedly, we

aren't close. He came into Trudy's life almost two years ago, and I've flitted in and then back out. It also hits hard that I'm trying to prove I'm stable when I haven't done anything to show he can trust me.

For some reason, I glance at Stone again.

"Well, maybe it's time for me to stay a while," I say, directing my gaze back to my nephew of sorts.

Simon doesn't respond, and I hate that I glance at Judd next for backup.

"Taxi wants to stay at the house with you and Trudy. Sounds fun, right, buddy? You'll have Grandma Trudy home and Aunt Taxi there."

Judd doesn't sound overly convincing about my presence.

Simon shrugs, and I hate the dismissal. Hate that I really haven't done anything to let this little guy see he can have faith in me.

"I know it's all still frightening," I say, dropping my hand to brush back his hair. "But Grandma Trudy will be just fine."

My voice lifts like I'm trying to convince myself as much as Simon. With a gentle tug at his long bangs, I try again. "You hear me? I'm here for you."

Simon nods, and I smile weakly, because he doesn't believe me. Not yet.

But I'll show him.

I'll show all of them.

I'M STILL SHAKEN by Simon's words hours later when Stone drives me back to Trudy's house. Simon is going to Judd's for another night.

Does he see me as a flight risk? Do I cause him the same apprehension I once felt?

Mama was unstable. Is that how Simon sees me? I don't drag him on adventures. I leave him behind.

The thought makes me feel a little nauseous.

"Why don't you shower?" Stone suggests, following me into Trudy's living room.

"You sayin' I stink, Superman?" I muster the energy to tease him.

Stone chuckles. "I'm saying, maybe wash off the day."

His suggestion isn't a bad idea. Today has been a lot.

The doctors in and out; nurses, too, then the social worker, and Simon's visit.

I'm still troubled by my relationship with Simon, guilt hitting me hard once again. I don't want Simon to feel uncertain or uneasy. Trudy is here for him, but I need to be more present as well.

When I return to the living room, I've wrapped my hair in one of Trudy's scarves. I've had the reminder of Trudy tucked in my pocket because I gave her my scarf yesterday. Despite sitting beside my aunt all day, I still wanted this extra little piece of her close to me.

While I thought Stone would question the vivid fabric on my head, he doesn't. He sits on the couch with his head tipped back against the cushions.

Earlier, I'd noticed how fine he looks in a tan button-up with a cowboy flare to it. Interesting color choice for a man who wears a similar palette in his uniform every day. He also has on faded jeans that mold to his backside and nicely accentuate the strength in his thighs.

He also looks tired. He's driven me here and there, worked a shift, after sleeping on that lumpy sofa last night.

"You don't need to stay," I say quietly, feeling a pinch in my chest at the thought of him leaving. "I can use Trudy's car and drive myself to the hospital tomorrow."

Something in my expression causes Stone to ask, "What's that look for?"

I shake my head. "What look?"

With the scarf on my head, and Trudy's too-large-for-me robe over a night shirt that hits my knees, I imagine I'm quite a sight. An August night, after a hot shower, and I'm bundled up like an Arctic blast is about to hit.

Stone points toward my face and circles his finger in the air. "That look?"

"I left my van in Alabama, but I need to get it here somehow." In my haste to get to Trudy, I left my van parked in the long-term parking lot at the Alabama airport. Seeing as I suddenly don't know how long I'll be staying in Sterling Falls, I want my Gloria.

He nods.

"And I have a mural I'll need to reschedule." Because, as I told Simon, I'll be staying in Sterling Falls. While the time limit is undetermined, I'll be here as long as it takes for Trudy to fully recover, like the doctors have promised.

My mind starts to race again, and Stone holds out a hand. "Come here."

I take his offered hand, causing him to tug me down to sit beside him on the couch. With the sudden effort, I sort of fall into his side, and then just stay there, leaning against him.

"How are you holding up?"

"Like a ton of bricks ready to topple," I openly admit. I feel shaken in all sorts of ways. Trudy's health. Simon's mental state. Stone.

"Understandable," Stone chuffs. "What do you need to stabilize that pile for a little bit? A movie? A glass of wine?"

I softly snort. "Trudy does not keep alcohol in this house."

Trudy is not a prude, but she preaches against the evils she's seen caused by alcohol consumption, and she never had liquor in her home while raising other people's children.

The thought hits me hard.

"Movie then?" Stone arches a brow, distracting me before my thoughts can take another detour into the past.

We both glance at the medium-sized television in the living room.

"*Superman*?" I question.

"What happened to alien invasions?"

A second passes before I remember the book I'd been reading when I first encountered Stone.

Daddy Dom Alien Invasion.

Since then, I'd gone on to read an entire collection of blue alien romances.

"Oh, I moved on to silver foxes."

Our eyes lock, and the corner of Stone's mouth twitches.

"As in shifters?" Stone asks, wiggling that arched brow.

"What do you know about shifter romance?" I tease.

"I've got a sister in a fake book club."

"Fake?" I snort. "What's a fake book club?"

"A group of women disguising themselves as a book club, meeting once a week over a yarn shop, where they drink wine, and the shop owner sells sex toys."

My mouth falls open. Stone laughs.

"You're totally kidding me."

Stone raises one hand, palm out with two fingers extended, and places his other hand over his chest. "Scout's honor."

I grip those two raised fingers and tug. "I bet you were the best Boy Scout as a kid."

Stone shakes his head. "Hate to disappoint you, but I didn't need that organization." He runs the knuckles of his other hand underneath his chin and scratches. "I learned what I needed to know by running wild on our property and in the woods behind it."

Still holding those two fingers for some reason, I scan down his body, drinking in his broad shoulders and firm chest.

"Outdoorsman?" I question.

He shrugs. "Not as much as I used to be. Go on hikes when I can." He glances across the room at the blank television.

I sense another story here, but Stone and I have had enough tough talks in the last forty-eight hours.

"How are you at technology?" I ask.

He turns his head toward me, and I nod at the television set. "You figure out how that works, and I'll go see if Trudy has microwave popcorn."

It's late. He should go home, but I don't want him to leave. Just like last night, there's something about his presence that brings me comfort.

We're both tired, but I'm also not ready to sleep. His rejection for something more last night was warranted, but I don't know that he'd willing sleep with me again, coiled around me like a human security blanket.

After a squeeze on the two fingers I'm still holding, I release them and head for the kitchen while Stone reaches for the remote.

When I return to the living room with a giant bowl of popcorn and two cans of soda, Stone reads a list.

"We have *Superman* with Christopher Reeves, a true classic, or *Man of Steel* with some Henry Cavill guy."

"Do not tell me you do not know who Henry Cavill is?" I add an *mm-mm-mm* to emphasize how fine that man is.

"Okay, we will not be watching *Man of Steel*," Stone states, narrowing his eyes and scrolling back through the list of options.

"And why not?" I laugh, taking a seat a little too close to Stone once again and tossing popcorn into my mouth.

"Because my fragile ego cannot handle you drooling over another man with me sitting right beside you." His eyes dance when he looks at me, but his smile is tight.

Jealous much? A little healthy envy is a turn on. "I don't

think you have anything to worry about, Mr. Sylver. That man is only a fantasy. And you are very real."

As real as a dance in an empty bar and a kiss in a vacant hallway.

If I had a man who curled my toes when he kissed me, I might cling a little.

Aunt Trudy was ridiculous. I didn't want to be a clinger like Mama, but then again, the situation with Stone is different. He's been attentive and kind, respectful and present.

With a spark in his eye while he's looking at me, I toss more popcorn in my mouth and chew, needing a distraction for my mouth, which might have already admitted too much.

"Delilah, you're dangerous," he teases.

I wink. "Just being little ole Taxi over here." I smile, still chomping on popcorn.

Stone rakes his gaze over my position next to him. I'm on my knees, angled toward him, while balancing a big bowl in my lap.

And that gaze of his is a brush stroke of flaming blue, the incandescent kind that pops to life, hissing and dancing, teasing with heat and promises.

"Somehow *Taxi* seems even more dangerous."

The corner of his mustache rises, his mouth slowly curling.

"Not sure I'm the only dangerous one in the room," I whisper, keeping my gaze on him.

His focus falls to my lips. Unable to stop myself, I smile, taking my time to curve my mouth, dragging out his attention there.

Irrationally, I want to dump this bowl of popcorn off my lap and climb into his instead. My blood rushes faster, pulse beating harder. I want this man with something deep within me I can't quite explain.

Stone swallows thickly, chuckles softly, and turns his gaze back toward the television. He clicks on *Man of Steel,* and we blindly watch a beautiful man act as a superhero, when a real one sits beside me.

Because Stone Sylver must be made of steel and iron and every other metal there is, holding him back from kissing me, when he knows I want him to kiss me again.

And I think he wants to kiss me, too.

24

———

[Stone]

few days pass, and Taxi and I fall into a routine. Nights on the lumpy couch. Drives to the hospital. Rinse. Repeat.

However, the monotony of the days is getting to Taxi. Trudy sleeps often and long hours at a time, and Taxi has kind of a nervous energy about her. Like she needs to get out of the four-walled enclosure of Trudy's room.

One afternoon, I can't stand the pressure I saw building up in her.

"Come on," I whisper, scooping my hand under her arm and gently tugging her up from the chair she'd been sitting in for days beside her aunt.

"What?" she questions, keeping her voice lowered. "Where are we going?"

"Out." I lead her out of Trudy's room and better explain myself when we near the nurses' station. "Nurse Betty here is gonna watch our girl for a little while."

I wink at the older woman who works in the intensive care unit. I've known Betty for years because of accidents and incidents in the community at large.

The white-haired woman giggles and waves a dismissive hand at me. "Get out of here, you two."

"What? I can't leave," Taxi argues. "And did you just use some Sylver charm to get your way with her?"

My brows lift. "I don't know about Sylver charm, but you absolutely *can* leave. Just for an hour. Give yourself a break."

"I really shouldn't." Taxi glances toward Trudy's room, crossing her arms, and chewing at her lower lip.

"Look, I understand your concern. And Betty here has me on speed dial if something happens. But right now, Trudy is resting as she should be. The doctors say she's doing well."

I pause, cupping her shoulders and lowering my head to meet her eyes. I'm not above pouting a lip, hoping that Sylver charm she mentioned might work on her.

"One hour?" she questions, glancing back at me.

"One hour." That doesn't give us much time, but I want to get Taxi outside for a bit.

It's a beautiful August afternoon. Still warm with the scent of change in the air. Soon enough, the leaves will shift colors, and the temperature will drop.

Eventually, Taxi gives in. Unable to help myself, I wrap my arm over her shoulder and tug her to my side, leading her out to my truck. Thankfully, she doesn't balk under the touch. Instead, she leans into me until we get to the parking lot.

We quickly hop in my truck and head out. "We're going to one of my favorite spots."

The place isn't the official trail I'd love to explore with Taxi one day, but a spot I'd discovered a few years back.

"I used to bring my brother Ford to Sterling Falls when he was young. We'd take a short hike until he blew off steam." I pause for a second. "My dad . . . he hurt Ford with his words, telling him he'd never be any good at baseball." Softly smiling to myself, I admit. "I think he did all right."

I'd say an all-star centerfielder for the Chicago Anchors for nearly a decade made him a success.

"Anyway, I found this little offshoot hike a while back." I steer down a bumpy trail that looks like it's nothing more than a two-tire lane. We veer off the lane and into a copse of trees.

"Stone Sylver, where the heck are you taking me?"

"Trust me." I smile again, popping open my door and reaching into the back. When I retrieve a picnic basket, Taxi raises her brows.

"Did I seem like a foregone conclusion?"

I chuckle softly. "That is the last way I would describe you." I'm still so uncertain about many things when it comes to Taxi, but we've cuddled every night, hunkered down on that lumpy couch, just being close to one another. That has to mean something, right?

I hold out my hand, and I'm pleased when she takes it, easily following me through the trees that quickly break apart, revealing a section of the river.

Taxi pauses beside me, staring at the water rushing past us.

"You mentioned how you grew up near a river," I remind her. "And I now realize you meant this one. Well, maybe not this direct branch, but we don't have time for the falls today. Maybe one day soon."

It's a sliver of hint that I'd like more from her. A future promise. A little more time.

Setting down the lunch basket, I drop Taxi's hand and pull out a blanket, shaking it out for us to sit on. I wave toward the square of plaid for her to take a seat.

"Stone Sylver, this is almost romantic."

"Almost?" I arch a brow. While I wasn't intending this spot to be romantic, I wasn't *not* intending it to be romantic either. I just want to give her some time outside of that hospital room and Trudy's home.

We take a seat, and I remove items from the basket. Two thickly layered sandwiches, mini bags of potato chips, and two whole pickles, plus bottled water.

"You make a mean sandwich," she teases, reminding me I made her one that first night. Every other night since then, we've eaten at the hospital or hit a drive-thru on our way back to Sterling Falls.

"Make a decent burger, too." I pause a second. "You should come to dinner at my place this Sunday. Judd's gonna bring Simon. The whole family will be getting together."

Taxi watches me as I hold up two small chip bags, letting her pick which flavor she wants.

"Sounds like a special occasion, I don't want to intrude," she states.

"No special occasion. Just a Sunday." I hand her the bag she selected, after I've opened it for her. "When my siblings were younger, I made Sundays a mandatory day to check in with everyone. Who had what, when, and who needed what."

I open my own bag of chips and pop one in my mouth.

"Ever the caregiver," she teases.

I shrug. "Something like that." I squint at the river. "Family is important to me. My mama wouldn't have wanted us to fall apart, and I'm the eldest."

I've tried to make her proud, even if she wasn't here to see me.

Taxi lowers her chip bag and stares into it. "I get that. Even though Trudy was present, I always worried about Sedona and Jolene. Especially Jolene. She's the wild one of us three."

I chuckle softly, knowing exactly what she means. "Sebastian was the wild one in our bunch. It's always the youngest." I shake my head, provoking a smile from Taxi.

Flipping my phone, I note the time. "Okay. No serious stuff. We only have forty-seven minutes. Tell me something fun."

Taxi laughs, the sound light and musical. "Like what?"

"You like to paint. Do you have a favorite color?"

"Blue," she whispers, and I glance up at her, meeting her eyes. "There's comfort in blue."

With her gaze locked on my eyes, I don't want to read more into her color explanation.

"But is that your favorite?" I lean toward her, teasing.

"I like violet. Well, more like periwinkle." Her mouth slowly curls like just saying the word brings her happiness.

"And what color is that?" I ask curiously before popping another chip in my mouth.

"It's blue and white, making almost a lavender, but not quite. It's kind of rare and not really found in nature," she explains.

"Sounds pretty."

Taxi chuckles. "No offense, but I'm not certain you under-stand pretty colors. Let me guess your favorite. Beige."

She eyes my uniform shirt.

"Don't have much of a choice." Sheriff's department stan-dard issue here.

"But even when you wear street clothes, you still wear beige." She grins, lips spreading wide.

"Well, I guess, I like beige. It's . . . comforting." I've never really thought about it, but I guess I just like the color. As she continues to stare at my uniform, an unease washes over me. I suppose my uniform isn't comforting for her, and suddenly, I'm second-guessing our current position, dressed as I am.

"Can I wear your badge?" she asks next, startling me.

"Um, no. But I can get you one of your own."

"Really?" Her brows lift.

"Yep. We have these plastic kid ones we give away. I'll get you one."

She tosses a chip at me, and I feign ducking when the chip doesn't even reach me. I laugh harder.

"You're mean."

"Okay, fine. You want to be a sheriff's deputy." I shift so I face her better.

"Sure." She shimmies her shoulders. "Chase the bad guys. Catch the thief."

I make her hold up her hand like she's taking an oath. Then I hold out my other hand, like I'm holding a Bible. "Set your hand on mine."

She sits up straighter, face becoming serious as she lays her small hand in my large palm. With my hand up in the air and hers matching my position, I begin.

"I, state your name . . ."

"I, state your name," she mimics.

I smirk. "No, really say your name on that part."

"Oh." She giggles. "I, Tallulah Alexander . . ."

"Do solemnly swear."

"Do solemnly swear," she repeats.

"That I will *not* . . ."

"That I will not . . ." She tilts her head, looking at me skeptically.

"Chase bad guys."

"Stone."

"Attempt to catch thieves."

"Very funny."

"Or throw chips at the sheriff."

She slides her hand against mine, retreating from her swearing in, but I catch her fingers before she fully withdraws from me.

"You're ridiculous," she says, still smiling.

"And you're beautiful." The compliment slips out before I can stop myself. I'm trying to be patient, giving Taxi the space she needs and the support as well. I don't want to pressure her in any way, but I cannot help how she takes my breath away.

"You're pretty, too." She quietly admits, dropping her gaze to where my fingers still pinch hers.

I use my other hand to cup her chin and tip up her face. "My favorite color is your eyes. Sterling grey."

Slowly, her mouth curls higher on one side. "Some say they are silver."

"They're the prettiest color I've ever seen," I admit. Unique and special.

"My mother was Egyptian. My father Black. People say I have my mother's eyes."

I shake my head, sensing she doesn't like the comparison. "I think you have Taxi eyes."

"What about you? Who do you look like?"

"All my siblings and I have varying shades of blue eyes. We get them from our mother. The dark hair was all Dad."

Taxi hums. "I think you look like a Stone."

I chuckle. "Hence, the color beige should not be ironic."

Taxi hums again, almost purring as her gaze lowers to my uniform. "The color is growing on me."

That's all I want. Her to accept me, be comfortable with me.

The longer she stares at me, those pretty eyes zeroed in, and her lips puckered upward just a smidge, the more I want to lean over this meager lunch and kiss her. Take those lips again and remind her of that moment we shared.

Then again, we're making new moments. Navigating who we are right now, not who we were fifteen months ago.

She reaches over and traces the badge on my chest. Running her finger along the edges, outlining the star. My heart hammers beneath the emblem, and I capture her hand once again, flattening her palm over the six-point metal.

With my other hand, I reach for her upper left chest and trace a star against the T-shirt she's wearing.

"I, Stone Sylver . . ."

She stares at me.

"Do solemnly swear . . ."

Taxi's eyes latch on mine.

"To wear another color, other than beige, sometime soon."

She bursts out laughing, and I release her hand, confident that my real oath was to make her smile for an hour, distract her from all the worries outside her control, and give her some fresh air.

"Eat your lunch, Tallulah Alexander." I wink.

"Yes, sir." She chews at her lower lip, keeping her gaze steady, but those pretty eyes . . . they are as playful as the first night I met her.

Absolutely arresting.

And I'm in danger of my heart getting caught by a thief.

25

[Taxi]

I wasn't exactly convinced I *should* attend a Sunday dinner at Stone's home. The day sounded important and full of family time, but Judd didn't allow me to excuse myself any more than Stone did. Judd picked me up when he came to Trudy's to gather more clothes for Simon.

The Sylver family collectively is loud and loving, and a bit overwhelming. Handsome men with beautiful women and gorgeous children. But their presence was more than eye candy. They were genuine and honest people. A quip of banter was met with an equal match of funny puns and teasing insults. They appeared to really like being in each other's company and reminded me a little bit of my younger days at Trudy's home. The original house overflowed with kids and imagination because we'd known worse days. Being together felt better.

My anxiety was bubbly when I first thought about the day.

Not like Stone and I hadn't been spending a ton of time together, but this was his time. His family time.

He'd been driving me to the hospital and sitting beside me. Feeding me dinners and giving me an escape, and I didn't want to encroach. I should give the man a break from me.

But the second I arrived, his instant smile put me slightly at ease.

This reunion at his home was nothing like the first time I arrived here. When I didn't know my Samson and Stone Sylver were one and the same, and my angry heart was still . . . angry.

Now, a strange giddiness overcomes me at seeing Stone in his element. Making certain everyone has a drink. Setting up the grill. Quietly smiling while his brothers tease each other, or him.

"He's good with his meat," his brother Knox teases.

"He loves his sausage," Clay playfully adds.

"Think he's more of a breast man now," Sebastian mutters, noting the boneless chicken on the menu.

Stone's responding smile is sheepish.

"Stoic Stone," someone says, and I see it, but I don't. He's been rather open with me, sharing pieces of his past, *showing* me who he is in the present.

Let me show you who I am.

I'm seeing it.

Family. Devoted. Protective.

Something inside me cracks a little bit. What would it be like to be part of that guarded bubble he's wrapped around the people he cares about most?

"Come sit with the girls." Genie loops her arm in mine, tugging me toward the other women seated in a circle with a lawn swing, Adirondack chairs, and blankets spread over the grass.

It's been a long time since I've been part of a group of

women. My job can be singular in some ways, while the teaching positions I've acquired in the past year have opened my eyes a bit. My need to share my art, share a piece of myself, with others.

Genie is amazing, and we chat about her latest calendar plans. We've talked intermittently when she and Judd visit Trudy, and her enthusiasm for art matches mine, even if our mediums are different.

"It's awesome having another artist in the family," Genie blurts.

"In the family," I parrot quietly, choking on the words. I'm not part of the—

"Hey, what do you think Halle and I are?" Cadence interjects, watching her toddler, Beck, who keeps handing her a ball and then taking it back from her.

"Oh, I'm definitely an amateur," Halle admits. Knox's redheaded wife smiles warmly at me. "I just like the creative outlet Art's offers."

"Art's?" I question, sensing she didn't misspeak.

"Art is a local veteran who owns Art's Studio. He likes to take trash to treasure there, but he also offers other opportunities in his place. Paint. Pottery. Sculpting. It's a cool place. You should check it out."

"I will," I say, excitement growing in me. I had no idea the studio existed.

Cadence clears her throat. "Music is art as well. Just saying." The brunette has a snooty air in her tone, but her smile says she's all tease. She is Cadence, after all, world renowned country music sweetheart, and I almost want to pinch myself being in her presence.

Then I remind myself she's just a woman. A girl married to a man who used to play professional baseball.

Wild.

"Just saying," Enya, Cadence's sister, jokes from her position in the yard swing, using her tiptoes to move the seat back and forth while she holds her daughter Annabelle in her lap.

The women continue to share stories. Anywhere from toddler tantrums to teasing about their men.

"Those are my brothers," Vale sighs about the minor complaints.

"Well, I could share how Ford does this thing and—" Cadence begins, but Vale holds up a hand.

"And that's where the sharing stops, because *those are my brothers*." Vale laughs, cutting off Cadence and what I imagine might be a little too much detail about what her husband does in the bedroom or otherwise.

I chuckle as well, finding I'm at ease with these ladies, even if I'm the quiet one among them. I don't have a toddler, and I don't have a man, but I don't feel excluded.

I feel present and accepted, and it's altogether strange while comforting.

I've been sitting on a blanket near Vale, and she leans forward on her Adirondack chair, whispering toward me.

"He must really like you."

"Who?" I ask innocently, glancing up and finding Stone watching me. He gives me that slow smile he has. One that looks sheepish, almost anxious, but is actually rather endearing on him.

"Why would you say that?" I ask, a bit more defensively than I should. I don't really doubt Stone's opinion of me. He holds me every night without taking anything to the next level. He spends time with me. But sometimes I'm curious what he sees in me. What do I bring to him?

"Sundays are kind of sacred around here." Vale's tone is still light and pulls my attention back to her. "For the longest time, Stone didn't allow anyone else to be present. Just family."

She nods at the woman seated in a circle, chattering away with one another. "Only the people who really mean something to someone could attend. You could bring a friend, but no girlfriends, or boyfriend shenanigans. A person had to have staying power to be here."

Vale's words hit with a soft punch. *Staying power?* Did I have it? Simon certainly doubted me.

"Anyway," Vale continues, not sensing my unease. "Stone has never had anyone here. Never."

She glances at her brother, shaking her head, but I don't know if that shake is disappointment or lack of understanding. Like she doesn't know why he's never invited anyone to Sylver Sundays, as I've learned Enya dubbed the day.

"What about Emerson?" I ask, before I can stop myself. I'm no longer jealous of her, just curious. Stone did pretend to date her, or at least, let everyone believe they were a thing.

Vale's head whips back in my direction. "Never." Her blue eyes are more playful than her eldest brother's set. And they impart all the answers I need.

I'm the only one who has ever been Stone's guest.

Suddenly, I feel overwhelmed with emotion, and I need a little break. Maybe it's the sense of community among this family that reminds me I've been alone a long time. On the outside, always looking in. A temporary addition on the periphery of something permanent for others.

Who's fault is that? Trudy's words come back to me.

"Bathroom?" I blurt, unfolding myself from the blanket and standing, keeping my gaze on Vale. I know where the bathrooms in this house are. I was caught in one over a year ago with the head of this household.

Eventually, I made my way to the one on the first floor back then and I found my way there again, after Vale reminded me where it is.

But just like last year, I'm sidetracked from the fib and find myself standing in what appears to be Stone's office. A large wooden desk and a worn leather desk chair behind it.

Another chair rests in front of the bigger piece. Bookshelves line one wall. An old corkboard hangs behind the desk, over-flowing with family photos tacked to it. Smiling faces of his nieces and nephews. Group photos of his siblings from various ages.

And among these photographs that seem important to Stone are the postcards I sent him.

"Lost again, little girl." His quiet, rugged tenor has me spinning to find him leaning against the entrance to his office.

"Snooping," I openly admit, caught, as it is, standing here staring at the picture on his wall. "You have my postcards up there."

My finger shakes as I point toward them, matching a strange tremor in my voice.

Stone presses off the door jamb and enters the room, closing the door behind him, but not shutting it completely.

"We haven't really talked about them." He nods toward the collection. His voice lowers. "I looked forward to receiving a new one every month. But I'm curious why you sent them?"

I twist to look from him to the images on the board and back at him. "Guess I just wanted to share a piece of me with you."

My throat feels thick, not so much from emotion but the admission. Sharing this information is also giving him another piece of me.

"When you left here over a year ago, you seemed pretty clear about how you felt," he reminds me.

"And I was an idiot," I whisper to the wall, my arms crossed around my middle. How silly I'd been to walk away so blindly before giving Stone a chance. Not that I would pull away from my work, but we could have had a more open relationship. We could have talked to one another while I was on the road.

"You never messaged me. Through Instagram," I counter, turning once more to face him.

"Didn't have a social media account until you shared that you had one. I saw your posts."

"But you didn't message me?"

Stone steps closer to me. Close enough that I have to tip my head back to look up at him. My arms drop from their protective hold on my midsection. I flex my fingers at my side.

"Didn't know if you'd want me to?" he admits.

He isn't wrong. I hadn't exactly given him an indication that I'd like to hear from him.

"I wanted to," I whisper, glancing from his eyes to his lips.

"I'm sorry I didn't reach out, then." Sincerity rings through his tone, like he truly regrets not messaging me.

Then again, he isn't a mind reader. He didn't know. I hadn't asked.

"You could always reach out now." My voice sounds steady, but inside I'm vibrating. Not with a sexual rush of need but more a simmering desire to have more from him. To feel his lips on mine again and remind me of how he kisses. Consuming. Confusing. A closeness I'd been afraid to admit I've longed for.

"What are you saying, Taxi?" His voice is equally as quiet as mine. His nostrils flare once. His mustache twitches.

"I don't know how to do this," I say, my words parroting what he said that night we first kissed.

When his hand comes to the side of my neck, and his thumb strokes over my cheek, my eyes involuntarily close.

"I need to be certain you want this."

My lids ping open, and something in my eyes must give him the answer he needs because his mouth is suddenly on mine, taking what he needs, giving me what I want.

I want this. This confusing, confuddling, comforting sensation he brings to me. The same feeling I had the night I met him, that something was different about him. He was special, unique in a way I couldn't define then.

His mouth is warm, lips in control, sipping along mine before stroking the seam, forcing me to open, allowing his tongue to meet mine. The kiss moves from a slow exploration to full investigation within seconds, and I lean forward, gripping his well-worn tee while he cups my jaw, holding the edge of my face like I'm precious. A sacred piece in his hands that his mouth continues to discover.

He pulls at my lower lip but doesn't release me, going in once again, deepening the connection. Tongues swirl, smiles spread, but our mouths never leave the others.

"Uncle Stone, I . . . oops."

We break apart like teens caught making out, and Stone spins, shielding me a bit from the interruption.

"What do you need, Zelle?" he addresses his young niece, clearing his throat while he speaks.

For my part, I fight a giggle and tuck my head against his shoulder blade, gripping the back of his T-shirt near his waistline.

"We wanted to have another dance off. We need you to judge."

Stone's hand comes around his back, brushing at the side of my thigh. "I'll be out in a minute."

"Okay." The young girl giggles and pulls the door closed behind her. The soft click of it latching shut sounds in the room, along with a shout from the hallway.

"I caught Uncle Stone kissing Miss Taxi."

Stone hangs his head, and the laughter in my throat finally escapes.

He spins to face me, capturing my face in both his hands. "Find that funny, do you?"

"Absolutely not, Stoic Stone." I laugh again, harder, until his mouth is on mine one more time, swallowing down the sound and stealing my breath once again.

When he pulls back, leaving me a little stunned and smiling like a fool, he presses his forehead against mine.

"How do you feel about being a dance-off judge?"

"Sounds amazing."

He has no idea how deep the answer is.

Sounds truly astounding to be part of this group, someone considered important enough to make the photographs on Stone's office wall and be his guest at Sylver Sundays.

26

[Taxi]

Watching Stone judge his nieces as they dance off like true professionals with awkward limbs and jutty motions is a sight to melt anyone's heart. He gives them all a rating that includes long numbers, like 9.875 or 10.321, to which they all giggle, except for Zelle. She takes the competition rather seriously and demands easier numbers to math.

Eventually, Cadence intervenes, declaring they are all winners and deserve dessert before dinner for their efforts.

"You all have the potential to be backup dancers one day," she announces.

"Really?" Dutton, Clay's son, squeals with hope.

Winnie, Ford's middle daughter and Dutton's best friend, rolls her eyes, clearly not interested in being a dancer. "I'm nobody's backup plan," she mutters.

"That's the spirit, girl," I offer, in spite of myself, and hold up a hand for a high five. She slaps my palm hard, and Stone chuckles when I shake the sting off.

June doesn't seem to care one way or another if she's a backup dancer. She's only six. And Stone scoops her up, blowing raspberries on her belly, before setting her back on the ground and patting her butt to follow the others for a treat.

"I need to get to the grill," he says, hitching his thumb over his shoulder toward the massive piece used to cook for such a large collection of people.

"Heard you make a mean hamburger," I remind him of our conversation from our lunch date by the river.

"Got a special one, just for you." He smiles and turns for the grill, giving me a good view of his backside in worn, ass-hugging jeans.

I hadn't noticed before, but it suddenly occurs to me he isn't wearing beige today.

He's wearing a blue T-shirt. One that says Chicago Anchors across it, but still . . . it's blue.

And I smile to myself before Genie nudges my arm.

"Still got the hots for him?" Her smile says she's caught me.

"He's alright," I counter, chewing at my lower lip.

Genie snorts. "Not a bad one in the bunch," she teases. "But Stone really is the best of them."

I'm beginning to really appreciate that fact.

FEELING guilty that I've had a good day away from the hospital, Stone gives me a ride to it later that evening, only to discover Trudy has been awake most of the day and is asleep for the night.

When Stone takes me to Trudy's, I don't need to invite him in. He follows me into the living room and then stares at the couch.

"Think Trudy would mind if we slept on her bed. Not in it, just on the top. More space. Better comfort."

"You complainin' about snuggling up with me?" I tease, but catch myself, curious if he is wanting a little space. It's been a great day, but a long one.

And his kiss still lingers on my lips.

"Never," he counters, not a second to consider his answer. "And I still plan to snuggle you. Just that this couch . . ."

"Is lumpy and old, well-loved but overused," I finish for him.

Holding out his hand, he tips his head in the direction of Trudy's room. For half a second, I feel like a girl sneaking into her parents' bedroom. Not that I ever did such a thing. Wasn't really into boys back then. I was focused on me. Moving forward with my dreams.

But I've been focused only on me for a long time.

And it's been kind of nice to feel like someone else is looking out for me.

Like Stone.

When we enter Trudy's room, I say, "Just give me a minute." Excusing myself to the bathroom, I change into my nightshirt and Trudy's robe, fixing up my hair in a bonnet.

When I reenter her room, Stone sits on the edge of the bed, one arm perched on his thigh. "My turn?"

I nod, and he takes the bathroom for a moment.

The entire process feels domestic, like something couples might do after years of living together. I'm getting ahead of myself with the thought.

It's only another night, snuggling up with this man.

But the air around us feels charged after that kiss we shared earlier.

No one mentioned the announcement Zelle made to someone down that hall, but sly grins and laughing eyes said the family knew the truth.

Uncle Stone was kissing Miss Taxi.

As I lay on my back, waiting for his return to Trudy's room, I tease him when he's still dressed.

"Gonna sleep fully dressed?"

"Gonna sleep in that robe?"

"I'm cold," I lie, using the heavy material as a shield. I shouldn't be shy. I propositioned the man a week ago, yet somehow, I feel self-conscious, anxious about exposing my body to him, despite us kissing again.

Because something tells me if a kiss can knock me off-kilter, sex with Stone Sylver might send me out of this world.

"I'll adjust the air conditioning," he says, his brows pinching with concern for my well-being.

I wave. "I don't want to fiddle with Trudy's settings." I'm not here to take over her home.

Stone nods before he slowly tugs his tee over his head, exposing the thick patch of hair on his chest and the trail that leads to his waistband. Most nights, he's kept his T-shirt on. Tonight, I get a show of what's underneath even his tee. Still no superhero S on his chest, but he still looks like one to me.

Love for his family. Sweet with his nieces. Concern for me.

Pure kryptonite.

Next, he shucks his jeans, exposing snug boxer briefs. I don't mean to stare, but I can't help myself. He's one *fine* looking man.

He gives me that lopsided grin of his before climbing up the bed and rolling me to my side. My back to his chest. Then we click into position.

His arm around my waist, the other underneath my head. His feet beneath mine.

I close my eyes, but I've already seen what he looks like bare-chested. The outline of what lies beneath his boxer briefs. The thickness of his thighs.

"You okay?" he whispers, and I realize I hummed. A signature *mm-mm-mm* escaped my throat.

"I'm good," I lie, covering my face with one hand as if that will hide me somehow. He's at my back and can't see the flame in my cheeks in the dimness of the room anyway.

Still, I'm warm all over.

His nose tickles my nape, just beneath the bonnet holding up my hair.

I loosen the sash at my waist, needing a little air in the heavy wrap. As I shift, I feel Stone's hardness against my backside and still.

"Sorry," I mutter.

I've ignored his morning wood every day, considering it biology and not anything else. But I cannot dismiss the firmness wedged against my ass.

Stone slips his hand into the opening of the robe, finding his typical position of palm against my belly, pinning me in place against him.

I fling a portion of the robe aside, needing more cool air on my skin, which suddenly feels like I'm burning up.

Is this a hot flash? Or desire?

When Stone flexes his hand over my belly, my core pulses, and I have my answer.

I cover the back of his hand with mine, holding over him a second, before slowly pressing his palm lower and lower.

I shuffle my legs, causing the robe to open more and my nightshirt to rise up my thighs.

Stone doesn't resist my lead. He lets me guide his hand until he's almost where I need him. His palm just covers the slight mound, blocked by the bunching up of my shirt and my boy-cut underwear, when he startles me.

In a move as fast as a superhero, he withdraws his hand and covers mine, flipping our positions, and forcing my fingers lower.

"Is this what you need, baby?" he whispers, his breath warm against my nape.

I hum, arching my back and forcing my backside against him, where the thickness of the robe's material does nothing to disguise the wedge in his boxer briefs.

"Stone," I whimper, wanting his hands on me but settling for my own, as he gently forces my hand between my thighs.

Burying my face in the pillow, I own our position. He's pressing on the back of my hand while my fingers graze the sensitive nub beneath the thin layer of my damp underwear.

"Do what you need, Taxi." He hums against the side of my neck, running his nose just below my ear. "Don't hold back."

With his hand like a cuff on my wrist, he pins my fingers between my thighs, and I swipe over my clit again. The brush causes me to flinch, and my backside bumps against his thickness.

"Stone," I whisper, needing him in a way I cannot describe and yet touching myself with him not even an inch behind me. While I want his fingers, this feels like so much more.

He releases my wrist and cups the inside of my thigh hard, tugging my legs apart and forcing my leg over the side of his thigh. Wide and exposed, my fingers have a mind of their own. I strum and pluck, and moan into the pillow, arching my back like a naughty kitty cat.

Stone's hand returns to the back of mine, fingers extended but not touching where I want him most. His entire body is a shadow of mine. He guides my fingers, adding pressure to the backs of them, but doesn't slip from his position of puppet master, pulling at my strings, winding me tighter.

I hum again, the sound an elongated moan, broken up by choked syllables. Flexing the noise, like I'm stretching out my body, rubbing against his.

"Is this what you want, baby?" His voice vibrates against my neck. "Want me between those sweet thighs?"

Holy shit. If he talks dirty to me, this will be over in seconds.

As my hips roll back, Stone rocks forward, grinding his hefty cock deeper against me. The pressure of his fingers against the back of mine is harder. The tips of my fingers stroke deeper. Our bodies dance in a way that makes me wish there were no layers between us.

When Stone runs that bristly mustache against my tender flesh, I tip my head as best I can, so he'll continue to tickle me. The rasp is a delicious sensation.

The push and pull between us continues.

"Want those thighs slicked?" he murmurs to my throat. "Want me deep, baby?"

He pauses as I groan at the thought.

"Let me?" he questions.

"Yes, please."

Then Stone is brushing aside my fingers, swiping my panties to the side, and sliding into me with one thick digit.

"Fuck," I cry out as I shatter, arching my back and moaning at the sensation.

Slickness covers my thighs as I melt around the thickness of his finger. He adds a second one, and I whimper again at the fullness, the pleasure, the relief.

The leg over his thigh clenches, holding onto him, keeping him close to me as I ride his fingers, swimming in the tide of release. I fear drowning, but know this man will rescue me.

I'm here for you. And he has been in so many ways.

"That's it, Taxi." He hisses before he nips at the juncture of my neck and shoulder, and I cry out again, clenching around his fingers, riding the rapids rushing up my center.

Stone thrusts hard against me from behind, and I counter the movement. While I want to remove the robe and any other barrier separating our bodies, I don't want to snap this dizzying frenzy between us.

Stone continues grinding against me, his fingers deep but

his palm still, cupping where I'm wet and sensitive. His lips linger against my throat, pinning him in place against me.

He grunts once, jolts hard, and stills.

"Fuck," he mutters, clutching tighter at me, like he's afraid I'll disappear. Like he doesn't want to ever let me go.

Eventually, he presses a kiss to the side of my throat, pinned there a long moment before pulling back.

Breathing heavily near my ear, he whispers, "That went a little further than I intended."

I chuckle, considering he just came in his briefs from grinding against me. The idea would be heady if I wasn't already a bit dazed by what's happened.

Stone touched me, and I came, reminded that not all orgasms are created equal.

The ones given by him were out of this world.

Biting back my grin, I twist my head, and Stone falls to his back behind me. I further shift to find his forearm draped over his forehead, blinking.

"You okay?" I whisper, glancing down at his boxer briefs, where the waistband is lowered and the angry head, now relieved, peeks over the edge.

Stone lowers the hand on his head to cover where he's spent. "I did not expect that to happen."

I glance back at his face; our eyes finally connecting.

"You are a little like kryptonite," he whispers. "Make me weak in the knees and lose my head."

I duck my head into his shoulder. "Same, Superman." He makes my knees tremble and my head foggy.

Thinking things like maybe I could belong here.

In the family, Genie said.

Might be a leap, like over tall buildings, but I won't mind a little skip.

A chance to test my own powers at staying.

Stone startles me with a sudden twist of his body, gently

cuffing my throat, so I lift my head. He kisses me, tender and sweet, and it's over too quickly, before jackknifing upward.

"I'll be right back," he promises, before exiting the bedroom to clean up.

I'll be right here, I whisper in my head.

Further taking that leap into staying.

27

[Taxi]

In the morning, when Stone gives me another ride to the hospital, with only the radio playing low, he holds my hand. It feels like such an innocent thing compared to what we did last night, but it's the touch I didn't know I needed. The reassurance that last night wasn't just a whim for either of us.

Thankfully, Trudy is more alert during the morning hours, but the nurses demand she continue to rest. As for me, I'm coming a little out of my skin sitting beside her. I need to do something. Stretch my limbs more than I stretched them last night.

With thoughts of Stone and what we did rolling through my head like a featured film, I squirm in my seat.

"You okay there, girl?" Trudy asks with her eyes closed. I swear she has Spidey-senses, which tracks because she's a superhero in my eyes.

"Just . . . antsy," I admit, as there's no sense lying to her.

"Need to paint?" she asks, eyes still closed, voice sleepy.

"Yeah." I do, and I had to reschedule my next project. With the decision to stay in Sterling Falls for a while, I need to cancel a few projects, something I've never done before. My reputation for being prompt and thorough is a thing of pride.

"You don't need to hover, Tallulah. I'm just lyin' here."

I snort. "I'm not hovering."

"But you're pinned in place, and I know how anxious that can make you."

This woman knows me so well. Like a mother. Better than my own mom.

"I'm not anxious." I shift in the chair again, causing it to creak. Trudy opens one eye and smiles weakly.

"Got other things on your mind?" That soft smile quirks higher on one side, like she knows something. "Seen Stone brought you in again today."

The chair beneath me makes another noise as I adjust my position one more time.

"Yeah. He's been giving me a ride."

Trudy chuckles. If she was a girlfriend, I might have joked about her having a dirty mind. But this is my aunt, and I don't have many friends. Not permanent ones. When you scatter like leaves in the wind in search of something new, you don't form long-term commitments, and friendship is a commitment.

My thoughts leap to Judd. And Genie. She doesn't seem like the type to let a friendship slide.

And Simon, who needs reassurance I'm not a flight risk.

And Stone . . .

"He's a good man," Aunt Trudy states.

I hum noncommittally.

When the chair beneath me squeaks once more, Trudy opens both her eyes. "Why don't you go grab a coffee or take a walk. A woman can't rest with all the noise that seat is making."

She isn't angry or even bothered, but she's detected my unease. My need to move or create or not think so hard.

Slowly, I unfold from the chair that isn't exactly made for comfort and lean over her. I swipe my hand over the silk scarf on her head.

"Do you need anything?"

"Peace." Her eyes are closed, but her smile says she's teasing me.

I pat her hand and exit the room. Wandering the hospital hallways, I don't get further than the cafeteria before I sit in an equally uncomfortable chair at a table and stare out the window.

An approaching man has me turning my head. He's wearing a security uniform, which makes him look like a cop when he's not. I don't know how much trouble a small-town hospital would have, but I appreciate the attention to keeping patients and visitors safe.

What I do not appreciate is how close this man comes to the edge of the table, pressing the tops of his thighs right up against the side. A quick pass over his features marks him as nothing special. Brown hair. Brown eyes. Pale skin.

Muddy comes to mind. Something clumpy and slick between my fingers.

"Jolene?" He hesitates, although excitement fills his voice.

When I turn and give him my full face, his crumbles a bit at the disappointment. I am not my younger sister.

I don't directly answer him, just give him a blank stare.

"You're one of Trudy Wallace's girls, right?" He gives me a sly smile that makes my skin crawl, and the fine hair on the back of my neck rises.

I keep my laidback position of feet spread wide and back tipped against the upper edge of the chair, however, I'm anything but at ease with his closeness and his assumption I'm my youngest sister.

"And you are?" Before I confirm I'm *one of Trudy Wallace's girls*, I want to know who he is and what his interest is in my sister.

Jolene could be a handful when she was a child. Finding trouble before it found her, and then rolling around in it like a puppy with an itch. This led to poor decisions and risky relationships.

He hooks his thumbs into the vest he's wearing, which seems like a bit of overkill in this hospital cafeteria. A room filled with soft murmurs and quiet conversations, plus the gentle *tink* of actual silverware on plastic trays. They up-cycle here. Rewash. Reuse.

"Andy Whitehall," he eventually answers. "You don't remember me?" He tightens that smile, forcing it in place, like he's a bit put out that I don't recall who he is. Something tells me my sister might not have fond memories of this man either.

"Sorry. I'm not Jolene."

He narrows his eyes a second, scanning over my face and dropping down to my breasts.

The creepy perusal causes me to sit upright and cross my arms on the table's surface. Andy scoots back, but not more than a slim inch.

"But you're one of them, right?"

"One of what?" I snap, a little harsher than I should, considering he's towering over me and trying to exert some false aura of authority. I don't want any trouble, so I should probably keep my tone steady. But I don't appreciate how he sounds almost accusatory, like it's a negative thing.

"One of Trudy's girls."

"One of them," I state, not offering my name.

"Your sister and I were . . . friends. Is she around?" He glances over his shoulder like he expects to see my younger sister. His voice lifts just a smidge, as if he's hopeful and eager to see Jolene.

Despite us not being particularly close, I think I'd remember hearing about a man who considers himself a friend of hers. Especially a man giving off strong stalker vibes.

"She's not here," I reply noncommittally, as I don't actually know where exactly my youngest sister is.

"Huh."

Huh.

He eyes me up and down again, taking in what he can see, considering I'm using the table like a weak shield of protection.

"She was one sweet taste of brown sugar."

"Excuse me?" I lean to my left while looking over my right shoulder, keeping my arms crossed on the table, when I want to flip it over. *What the fuck did he just say about my sister?*

I glare up at him, blinking like I didn't quite hear what he just said when I heard him loud and clear—and just get the fuck out of here!

"Andy." The short, stern, surprisingly loud sound of Stone's voice, along with a hard hand clap on Andy's shoulder, causes the man to jump.

Because of Andy's position, he was blocking my view of anyone else in the cafeteria, and I hadn't seen Stone's silent approach.

"Stone," Andy chokes out. His gaze flicks from me to the man standing a few inches taller and a lot too close to the lesser man. "Nice to see you."

Stone doesn't reply.

Andy glances at me again and offers a stiff nod. "Hope your Aunt Trudy is feeling better soon."

He saunters away, offering someone else a chin tip as he weaves around the scattering of tables. Stone and I both watch Andy's retreat before Stone turns toward me and pulls a chair from the opposite side of the table to the edge, so he can sit at ninety-degrees from me. He takes a seat and angles toward me, leaning forward to rest his forearms on his thighs.

"What happened to your arm?" I immediately question, reaching for his forearm, which is wrapped in a large gauze bandage.

"Did he say what I think he said?" Stone says at the same time, dismissing my concern for him.

"Stone. Your arm." What the hell?

"I'll tell you about my arm in a minute." He pauses, glancing quickly over his shoulder, then back at me and repeats his question. "Did he just say what I think he said?"

"What do you think he said?" I ask, falling back in my seat, crossing my arms over my chest again to steady the rumble inside me. My blood pressure is still on the rise, especially noting that bandage on Stone's arm.

When Stone doesn't repeat what he heard, I clarify. "He was talking about my sister."

His gaze doesn't leave my face. "Does that happen often? Comments like that."

I stare back at him, feeling the anger wavering around him like a foggy haze. His stoic, still nature looks ready to implode.

"You ever date a woman of color before?" I ask, keeping my arms crossed, my body tight. My tone is steadier than I feel.

Stone shifts in his chair, meeting my gaze head-on. "I haven't, actually," he admits slowly. "But I want to understand."

Lowering my arms, I clutch the edge of my chair and focus on the bandage on his arm. "Some people . . . they don't just make it hard, they make it impossible. You learn to keep your head down, swallow your anger, never make waves, because it never ends well for women like me. Being a woman is hard enough. Being a woman of color? It's like carrying a storm in your chest every damn day."

Stone's jaw tightens. "That's bullshit," he mutters, his eyes sharp, his focus on me unwavering. "You shouldn't have to put up with that. Ever. Not for a second."

I blink, caught off guard. His words feel deliberate, full of emotion, like he's thought about this more than I expected.

"Vale . . ." Stone's voice dips when he mentions his sister. "She's pretty open about the things men say or do. It's been a real education. So, I don't want anyone talking to you like that, or about your sister, or your aunt. No one. I don't care what color you are. You can be a fucking blue alien, and you still don't deserve a disrespectful tone, rude declaration, or questionable glance."

His normally even-toned voice grows louder, more agitated.

"As a *woman*, you learn to navigate all kinds of bullshit. Toss in this." I wave over myself. "And you add another layer to navigate."

Stone shakes his head. "I hate that, Taxi."

"I hate it, too, but I try to live my life as best I can. As only *I* can." I accept me, and that means I defend me when necessary.

Still, the protective alpha vibe Stone is giving off is a turn-on. I don't need him to stand up for me, but what if I had someone who did?

Stone continues to watch me. Maybe he has more to say on the subject, but he holds back, letting me have my moment.

Eventually, I snort. "Blue aliens?" The bitter chuckle that escapes with the question eases the tension in my body. I sit up again, leaning toward Stone.

"Taxi, I won't tolerate bullshit like that." He hitches his thumb over his shoulder, indicating dicks like Andy. "You're fucking stunning, so I imagine you need more than a stick to fight assholes like him off. I don't want you to ever think you have to take that kind of shit."

This might be the most worked up I've ever seen Stone Sylver, and it endears him to me even more.

"You gonna arrest everyone that talks to me like that?" I tease.

"I'll arrest anyone negatively breathing your air, if you want me to."

Something tells me he's serious, and I recall him mentioning how he'd arrest the man hitting on me in the bar the night we met. His face sobers, and he drops his gaze to my legs, covered in another pair of overalls.

I really need to get Gloria and my things to Sterling Falls.

"I try to be a fair person, an honest sheriff, but I'm not a perfect man." There's a hesitation in his tone that doesn't scare me as much as raise my curiosity.

What has Stone ever done that's bad?

I don't have the chance to ask because he continues.

"Now." His tone lightens, and he stretches his fingers, so they pluck the loose denim of my overalls over my knees. "I'd like to circle back to that dating comment."

"And I'd like to circle back to what the hell happened to your arm?"

"Tallulah." His tone is still serious, not giving in to my concern for his arm or letting go of something still troubling him about this situation that I'd like to put behind me.

I sigh heavily. "What dating comment?"

"The one where you asked me about dating."

"Someone brown sugar," I tease, lightening my tone so we can let this moment pass.

His eyes lock on mine. "Someone who takes my breath away when I look at her."

Dammit. Why does he have to look at me like that? Like he wants to pull me into his lap and wrap me in his arms. Like he believes those arms can keep me safe from jerks like the Andy Whitehalls of the world, which is an impossible task.

And why am I suddenly vibrating with the need to repeat what happened last night? Be close to him. Let him surround me again. Let him take care of me.

Because last night was more than learning Stone Sylver gives good orgasms. He did take care of me, making sure the moment was what I wanted, giving me all the power. And then his subtle touches, sweet kisses, and holding me again while we slept meant more than he'll ever know.

He wasn't out the door after what happened. He was clinging to me like he wanted to stay . . . wanted *me* to stay.

"*Are* we dating, Taxi?" He asks in such a hesitant, almost shy way, and his cheeks blush just a touch, reminding me of the man standing in a hotel hallway, doing a little left-right hustle. So cute. So sweet.

"Let me give you whatever you need . . . while you're here." He's been plucking at the denim over my legs, and I set my hand over his, pulling the one covered in a bandage onto my thigh.

While you're here, rolls over in my head. He isn't asking for a long-term commitment, isn't pinning me down, and I ignore that teeny-tiny pinch in my chest wishing he would.

Laying my hand flat over his, like he had ours positioned when we had a picnic by the lake, I say, "Do you solemnly swear to arrest anyone breathing my air that I don't like?"

Stone fights a smile. The corner of his mouth lifting, struggling, like he doesn't want to let the tension go, but he can't fight it. He's useless under my superpower—humor.

"Dammit, Taxi." He chuckles, unable to win the battle against laughter. "Pure kryptonite."

"Speaking of kryptonite, how do you feel about alien domination role-playing?"

Stone stares at me, his sky-blue eyes opened as wide as the heavens above, then he lets out a laugh. One loud and sharp and tickling my insides.

I grin. He lifts our hands and presses a kiss to my knuckles.

"I might be open to it, but I thought you were in a silver fox phase now."

Glancing from that mustache to his silver peppered scruff and then fixing on his bright eyes, I admit, "Definitely in my silver fox era."

I pause. "Now. Tell me about your arm."

28

[Stone]

"There was an accident on the highway," I begin, feeling like my own story is inconsequential compared to what just happened with Andy, but Taxi doesn't want to let my injury go.

"That's the reason I'm here so early." I glance down at the bandage. The EMT on call insisted I have the cut stitched.

"Two-car collision. Pretty bad crash," I explain, omitting the gorier details like how the passenger in one vehicle hadn't been wearing a seat belt and the driver of the other car had fallen asleep at the wheel. For now, the assumption is the person was going home after a long shift.

"Stuck my arm through the window to check the vitals of an injured victim." I twist my arm, glancing at the bandage again. My skin feels tight beneath the wrap, stitches pulling in my flesh, which is nothing more than a scrape compared to the physical damage done to the three victims. "Got cut on the glass."

"Stone." Taxi's voice grows louder as her hand hovers over my arm, which she's placed in her lap. "Does this kind of thing happen often?"

Her silvery eyes catch on mine, confusing me. She looks genuinely concerned for my well-being, but that's not the confusing part. It's that I can't remember the last time someone other than family looked at me like she is, worry etched between her brows, mouth tight.

"Accidents happen," I admit, swallowing thickly. Trying not to think about what could have happened to those three people, innocently making their way somewhere. Knowing I've thought about such accidents happening to Taxi, as she travels all over for her art.

But also, that thickness happens from an overwhelming sense that Taxi cares about me. The world has been unkind to her in so many ways, but she's worried about a little scratch on me.

"You need to be careful," she says, lowering her voice and her gaze. Her hand hovers over the bandage again. "Does it hurt?"

"Only a little." Going to sting and itch in a day or so, but nothing I haven't dealt with before.

"Would a kiss make it better?"

I chuckle. "Definitely."

She cups my jaw and pulls me closer to her, giving me a sweet kiss on the lips, instead of where my *ouchy*—as my niece June would call it—is. Her lips are soft and warm and gone too quickly from mine.

I'm still feeling a little rattled about seeing Andy in a security uniform at the hospital. Even more unhinged about what I heard him say to Taxi. His tone. The implication. The suggestion. She doesn't need that kind of comment in her life. No one does.

But I settle a little under her kiss.

Andy Whitehall previously worked for the sheriff's department, and I hadn't been contacted about his employment potential at the hospital. Legally, I couldn't say whether he'd been a good employee or a decent human being. I could only confirm he'd worked in the department, had they reached out to me for a reference. He was a little too squirrelly for my liking. Attempting to give big dick energy when he was a small man. He was the type of cop who had seen too many movies and was a little overzealous with his gun, as in, he liked to show it as a symbol of authority.

He'd been put on probation for an incident two years ago and was eventually let go from the department last summer. While working for the sheriff's office, he'd also taken a job working security at my brother Ford's baseball camp, but after a comment not too far off from the one he spoke to Taxi, made to our sister last summer, Ford fired him.

Andy did not have a good track record working with Sylvers.

"Let me take you to dinner tonight," I whisper, tipping my head close to hers as she continues to hold my arm on her lap.

"Let me check on Trudy first."

I nod to agree, and thankfully, an hour later Trudy gives Taxi her blessing to cut out of the hospital early.

"Get her out of here," Trudy turns tired, teasing eyes on me.

"Are you sure?" Taxi looks back at Trudy.

"Yes. Please." Trudy attempts to sound annoyed but offers a weak smile. "And don't come back 'til the morning."

"Aunt Trudy," Taxi admonishes.

Trudy responds with strained laughter that causes Taxi and me to meet eyes.

But the reality of Trudy's suggestion hits.

I don't want to let Taxi out of my sight until morning.

"YOUR HOUSE?" Taxi questions as we pull onto the gravel drive.

I shift my truck into Park and twist to look at her. "Figured you could use a home-cooked meal instead of more take-out or cafeteria food."

"You can cook?"

Her skepticism makes me laugh. "I have many talents." I tip a brow while shoving open my door. Rounding the hood, I get to Taxi's door just as she pops it open. Holding out my hand, I help her out of the vehicle and keep her hand in mine as I lead her into the house.

I haven't slept here in a week, and it's almost strange to return to my place. I've only taken quick showers here lately.

"Your sister lives here, right? With your nephew." Taxi looks around the living room after I've shut the front door and dropped her hand.

A year ago, when Taxi was here, Vale did live with me. "Actually, Vale got engaged in July. She and Hudson moved in with Cort a couple of weeks ago."

I nod toward the kitchen and place my hand on her lower back to lead her toward the back of the house.

"Did they live here long?" she asks.

I pause near the kitchen island and pull out a stool for Taxi, patting it for her to take a seat.

"Vale has lived here since Hudson was born. But essentially, she's lived here all her life, other than going away for college, just like me."

"Sounds like a story," Taxi teases.

I round the island and grab a bottle of wine, holding it up for Taxi's inspection.

"Yes, please." She smiles wide, curling those lush lips and

exposing beautiful teeth. I want to lean over the island and kiss her again. Skip the wine and dinner and conversation. But it's been a long time since I've entertained a woman, made her a meal, so I want to do this right with her.

I want to do it for me as well.

"I was born and raised here, just like all my siblings." I uncork the wine and pour each of us a glass, then hand Taxi hers. I tap my rim to hers and take a sip before continuing. "Went away to college on a football scholarship and had a chance at the pros."

"You were a professional athlete?" Taxi runs her gaze over my shoulders and down my chest.

I chuckle and spread my hands to lean against the kitchen island between us. "Not exactly. I could have been, but I wasn't."

Taxi takes a sip of her wine but keeps her eyes on me. "Sounds like more story," she says, encouraging me to continue.

"My mom died when I was twelve." I lower my gaze. "Pre-eclampsia." I glance up and around the kitchen as if it happened in this room. "Happened in my parents' bedroom. Clay found her. He was only eleven."

Taxi sets down her glass, eyes wide and focused on me. "I'm so sorry, Stone."

I shrug. I miss my mom, but it was a long time ago. "They were able to save Vale."

Swallowing thickly, I remember when Dad came home, stone-faced and worn. Exhaustion like I'd never seen before. He took Vale out of the car, left her in her car seat in the living room, and headed straight for the cabinet above the fridge where he kept the booze.

Everything changed.

"My dad shut down after my mom died. He didn't know how to raise a baby, although he had six sons from twelve to two."

Taxi whistles and gives a compassionate smile.

"Yeah." I chuckle. "My parents really liked each other." I laugh a little harder. "I have no doubt my dad loved my mom with everything he had. He gave her the children she wanted and the business she desired, and then . . . he just didn't know how to function without her."

I hang my head again, staring at the red wine in my glass. "I'll spare you the details of his behavior. Let's just say he changed toward each of us, going from bad to worse the younger down the line my siblings ran."

Taxi taps a dark nail on the island surface, signaling she wants my attention, and I lift my head, focusing on her face to finish my tale.

"I loved my dad, but I didn't know him by the time I left for college. He wasn't the same man he was when I was younger."

Taxi's head bobs as she says, "I totally understand that. I loved Mama something fierce, but with age came perspective. I couldn't make her have a relationship with me if she didn't want one."

Taxi and I have both had parents who walked away from parenting. Even if my dad was present, he wasn't involved with any of us. Taxi already told me how her mother shut her out. We both lost our mothers too young.

"Anyway, to explain why I was *not* a professional athlete, my dad died just before I graduated from college. I'd already been drafted, and intended for Tennessee along with my best friend, Cort." My mouth twists at the memory. Cort and me on the same team again. Always there for each other. Quarterback and receiver. We shared everything until . . ..

"But, when Dad died, Knox, Ford, Sebastian, and Vale were all still under eighteen."

"Stone," Taxi whispers, knowing where this story leads.

"And I couldn't let them be separated." I scoff lightly. "Trudy even offered to take them in."

Trudy had always been good to our family. As best she

could be, keeping her distance from Dad and his growing wrath toward the world. She'd offered to take in my younger siblings, but she was nearing the end of raising her nieces and nephews and foster kids, and I couldn't do that to her.

I couldn't part with my brothers and Vale.

I shrug. "I came home. Gave up my contract. Worked at Sylver Seed & Soil and did what I needed to do to become a sheriff."

The training was straightforward and easy enough, as Sterling Falls is the hub of Milton County.

"I took a job under a good man who endorsed my position after he retired, and I've been the sheriff for more than fifteen years."

Taxi stares at me for a long minute, and I almost worry I've told her too much. I know her distrust of the law, but I want her to believe in me.

"*You* are a good man, Stone Sylver."

My cheeks heat, and I deflect the compliment. "Haven't you heard? I'm Superman."

Typically, I wouldn't consider myself a superhero. I'm just a guy who loves his siblings and knew my mama would want us to stick together. I believe in my heart my father wanted his children all together as well, even though he disappeared in a bottle. We were a constant reminder of what he had with our mom. Their love was present every day in children who looked like her and loved like her, even if he turned into a hateful man.

Taxi scoots off her stool and rounds the island to stand in front of me. I spin, leaning my ass against the counter, and she steps between my spread legs. Her hand cups my chin.

"Hi," I whisper.

Her response is tipping up on her toes and kissing me. Kissing me slow and tender, pulling me under her spell.

Her hand comes gently to my forearm, and our kiss breaks. "How's the arm feel?"

"Feels like I can make you dinner."

She smiles but doesn't step back. Instead, she leans into me, returns her mouth to mine, and kisses me again with more intensity, more urgency, reminding me of the night we met. Her lips suck at mine. Her tongue seeks as well.

I cup her ass, and she circles my neck with her arms, lining herself up against me. Her breasts plaster against my chest, and I tug her tighter to me. The kiss continues with sympathy and compassion and understanding.

Life isn't always easy.

Moments like this make it better.

I spin with our mouths still connected and hitch her upward by her butt, setting her on the edge of the island. She breaks contact only long enough to move my wineglass and then wrap her legs around the back of mine, tugging me toward her. Tilting her head, our kiss turns hungry, almost desperate, and I bring her flush to me again, nudging where I'm long and hard against where she's warm and soft.

She's still wearing those denim overalls, and I can't wait to peel her out of them later. I want to strip her down to nothing and take her to my bed, but I also want to do this right.

Slowly, I pull back, setting my forehead against hers.

"You putting on the brakes?" she breathes heavily, and I watch her breasts lift and lower.

"Just making a little pit stop for dinner. Let me feed you, Taxi."

"Lots of innuendo in that statement, Superman." She pulls back and laughs. The sound is almost musical, lightening the tension in my chest I hadn't known was there.

"I like your laugh," I admit, stroking my finger around her ear to brush back her hair.

"I like your smile." She runs her finger along my bottom lip.

Her compliment only makes me smile wider, like a love-sick

fool. Deep down, I *could* love this woman if I thought she'd be open to it. If I thought she'd stay.

With my hands on her firm backside, I lift her off the counter and set her on her feet. I don't immediately let her go, but lean in for one more heated kiss to tide me over until after we eat.

"You're a dangerous man," Taxi says, smoothing her palms over my chest before stepping away from me.

"Made of kryptonite." I pat my chest as she rounds the island.

She laughs. "Ain't that the problem?"

29

[Stone]

Taxi is completely addictive. The way she kisses me. The stories she tells. During dinner, she told me more about her travels. The places she's seen and the murals she's painted.

I'm grateful the conversation shifted to something lighter. Neither of our lives has been easy and that could make us bitter. Instead, we try to be better people because of it.

After dinner, she hip checks me out of the way by the sink, insisting that she do the dishes. "You cooked. I clean."

The moment feels so domestic, so right, and I worry I'm getting ahead of myself.

While we've exchanged a lot about our pasts, the present Taxi is the woman I want to discover more about.

"Stay here tonight," I blurt, when the clean dishes are put away, and the wine bottle is empty. I tug her to me like I did earlier, pulling her between my spread thighs as I lean against the kitchen island. I like how easily she fits against me. How we click together. I run my hands over her hips and up her sides. "I just want you to stay a little while longer."

The invitation might have an even deeper connotation.

While I've heard her tell Simon she's staying, to take care of Trudy in the immediate future, there's no guarantee Taxi is staying for the long haul. I'd never want to hold her back. I've already been in that position once before.

Still, a deep-buried part of me wants her to stay. Wants her to know me better as well. The broken pieces I carry, because she's the first person I've let see them, and she isn't judging me for them.

Taxi leans into me again, tipping up on her toes to kiss me. Her lips are warm and soft, and she tastes like red wine and brightness. An array of colors I hadn't known I needed in my life.

"Plus," I mutter against her lips. "I have a bigger bed."

I don't have a problem sleeping at Trudy's, but I did feel out of sorts after what happened last night, and that it happened on Trudy's bed.

I want Taxi in mine, and I haven't ever had a woman here.

With Vale and Hudson in the house, bringing someone home felt like a monumental act, and I'd never had someone so large, so important, so consuming that I'd wanted to bring here.

Until now.

"We don't have to do anything you don't want to do," I add, knowing it's the truth. I'm happy to hold her and kiss her and nothing more. I'm not interested in pressuring her.

"What if I have things I want to do?" she hums, running her hands over my shoulders and down to my elbows then back up my biceps.

My body shivers, desire rippling through me in a way I can't recall ever happening. But it isn't the anticipation as much as her touch. I haven't been touched like this in so long, I almost feel deprived.

Her hands caress and her fingers tickle, causing another tingle to run up my spine.

When her fingers brush near the gauze on my arm again, she glances down at the bandage. Her brows pinch. "But I don't want to hurt you."

Her concern for me, over what I consider a minor scratch, also endears her to me. Taxi's concern for others is a common trait. The way she has explained immersing herself in communities and areas where she paints. She cares about others.

But that bone-deep concern, the one that comes from some place buried within her, is something I think she only shares with those she loves. Not saying she loves me, but the concerned expression on her face only comes from getting close to her. *Her* allowing someone to be close to her.

"I don't like that you were hurt on the job," she adds.

I press a kiss to her forehead and reassure her. "I'll be fine." Minor injuries like this one are part of the job. And my job is the last thing I want to think about tonight.

My hands glide over her backside again, and I pick her up, startling her by the move. The action pulls at the stitches, but I want this woman in my arms.

Instantly, she wraps her legs around me and circles her arms around my neck, trying to take the pressure off my arm.

"Let me see that bigger bed," she whispers, before kissing me again.

I carry her to my room, where we fall awkwardly onto the king-sized mattress.

Taxi's been picking on me for my love of the color beige, and I anticipate her having something to say about my room. A simple slatted headboard, the mattress on a low platform. Plaid green comforter. A matching set of nightstands and a single upright dresser.

But Taxi doesn't look around the room. Her eyes stay locked on mine as I perch up on my arm and run my hand down her body. Over the denim overalls that shouldn't look so enticing on a woman, and yet do. The coverup like a shield, constantly making me wonder what lies beneath the baggy clothing. Who is the woman inside the loose denim?

While I unhook one clasp, Taxi unsnaps the other. Then I cover her hand.

"I didn't get to see you last night. Didn't take my time with you," I admit, as what happened only last night was rather unexpected. But because I've been a patient man, having not been with anyone in years, I want to savor this moment. I can be patient a little longer.

"I want to take my time with you tonight," I admit.

Taxi's eyes lock with mine and her throat subtly rolls. "Okay." Her voice quivers.

When I pull the front flap of her bibs down to her waist, a form-fitting shirt hugs her curves underneath. From the sharpness of her nipples, I can tell she isn't wearing a bra, but it's the color of the shirt that holds my focus a second.

"I think you kind of like beige, too," I tease, running my hand right down the middle of her body, between the valley of her breasts and over her belly.

"This color is actually called nude."

"Hmm. A color I definitely want to see on you."

She chuckles, jostling her body and giving me a wide grin.

But I'm serious. "I almost don't know where to start. I want you everywhere." I feel like a horny teen on the verge of exploding, and yet, I want to take it slow with her. Discover every dip and curve. Every swell and valley.

With that thought, I cover her breast and squeeze, and Taxi's eyes flutter closed.

"Feels like a good place to start," she whispers.

I knead the firm swell, covered completely by my hand,

then pinch her nipple. Her mouth falls open and her back arches, forcing her deeper into my palm. Leaning forward, I blow on the other nipple, then open my mouth and nip her over the thin layer of her shirt.

"Stone," she moans.

"Let me take care of you." I circle my nose around her nipple, teasing the pert nub with the tip. I lower my hand to the hem of her shirt, pulling it up and over her head. Once she lies back again, my eyes drink her in. My personal mural of bronzed sunshine and deep browns. I'm not as colorful with language as Taxi. Not as appreciative of art, but I'm a converted man in this moment.

"Stunning," I whisper before diving in again, taking one pert breast into my mouth, swirling my tongue around her nipple before sucking at the full swell only to pull off her with a pop.

Her fingers dig into my hair, scratching over the back of my head and then trailing to the front again. Goosebumps ripple over my skin.

I move onto her other breast, cupping it in the palm of my hand, feeling the weight before diving in to give it a teasing flick with the tip of my tongue.

While I'm still in the midst of enjoying her breasts, Taxi gently presses my shoulder.

"Let's see what the color nude looks like on you," she purrs.

I roll to my back, and Taxi straddles me, letting her bib overalls fall to her waist, baring her upper half to me.

Slowly, she tugs the snaps of my shirt. I changed out of my uniform while dinner was in the oven and slipped into my favorite worn jeans and the same snap button shirt Taxi often teases me about.

With each snick of a snap being opened, my heart seems to skip a beat. I'm so hard. And with her in my lap, the worn denim on me does nothing to disguise what she's doing to me.

My hands come to her hips, plucking free the additional buttons along the waist of her bib overalls.

She rolls over the hard length in my pants and shoves the two sides of my shirt wide apart. Her delicate hands start at my belly and coast up my chest, fingertips sliding through the thatch of hair.

"Been wanting to run my hands here," she admits, speaking directly to my pecs. Her brows pinch like she's almost puzzled by the admission. As if she isn't certain why she likes it, but she does.

For me, I close my eyes, letting her explore. Letting her run her hands over my pecs and around my shoulders, then skip back to my chest and slide down my abs. My belly flinches as she draws around my belly button.

"Ticklish?" she teases.

I don't answer. I don't have one. It's been so long since someone's touched me, I don't know if I'm ticklish or not. But I'm sensitive to her touch. To her long fingers and warm palms running over my heated skin.

"Let's get this off of you," she says, and I jackknife upright, jostling her in my lap and catching her with my hand on her ass to keep her close. She presses at the fabric covering my shoulders, then slows, taking her time to carefully remove the right sleeve over my forearm.

Her brows pinch again at the sight of the bandage.

"Taxi," I whisper, drawing her attention back to my face. I cup the back of her head and pull her to me for a mouth-watering kiss. Teasing her tongue with mine. Invading the warmth of her mouth. Melting under the heat of us like this.

I lean back, bringing her with me, gasping into her mouth as her breasts brush over my chest. Her nipples are tight and hard, tickling against the hairs on my chest. She presses at my shoulders, breaking the kiss and sitting up over me again.

I drink in her body and lift my hand to the left side of her chest. I draw a star shape against her warm skin. I don't have words for an oath tonight.

Taxi flattens my palm against her chest instead, placing her hand over the back of mine.

We simply stare at one another, and while I want to beg to know what's in that pretty head of hers, she lets go of my hand and reaches for the button on my jeans, distracting me.

"Taxi," I whisper.

She doesn't answer other than scooting herself to my thighs and lowering my zipper.

"You took care of me last night. Let me have the pleasure tonight."

"That's not—" My thoughts cut off again as her hand covers the thick length of me, bulging out from the opening of my pants.

"Hush," she warns, working my jeans, along with my boxer briefs, over my hips and lowering them to my thighs. She gives me her signature hum, and I close my eyes, memorizing the sound.

When her warm fist wraps around where I'm hot and throbbing, my eyelids fling open again. Taxi is intent on where she strokes me up and back, squeezing me harder with each pass.

"Taxi. Baby." I groan. This hadn't been my intention. I didn't want to go first, but I'm totally under her spell, captivated by her and her touch. Her hands tugging with just the right amount of pressure, better than anything I've ever felt.

"Taxi," I warn, my eyes involuntarily closing again. My jaw clenches. "It's been so long and I . . ."

Suddenly, the tip of her tongue slides across the wet slit of my tip.

"Fuck," I grunt, reaching for the back of her head again. My other hand reaches up for the slats above my head, and I grip the iron, holding on, like my resolve is slim, losing my battle for restraint.

One of her hands comes to my hip, pinning me down a second as she draws me to the back of her throat, then glides to the top again. Back and forth, she slides up and down, teasing me with release and then swallowing me once again.

Eventually, my hips thrust upward, breaking her hold on me, and I feel her smile around my heavy cock.

I glance down the expanse of my body to see those silvery irises looking up at me. I'm mesmerized by the gleam in her eyes and her mouth surrounding me. She cups the heavy sacks at the base of my dick, gently rolling them through her other hand as she sucks harder, draws me deeper.

"Taxi," I choke, gripping the back of her head harder, while on the verge of snapping the headboard slat.

She hums around me, and I shatter.

Fucking break into a million pieces, like an asteroid striking a planet. I'm bright lights and shards of stone drifting through a dark sky.

The release is so intense my legs actually shake, and I hold tighter to the headboard, keeping Taxi's head in place as I ride out the aftershocks until I collapse back on the bed, like I've fallen to earth from the heavens.

With a slow, deliberate glide up where I'm spent, Taxi gives a soft kiss to my tip, then climbs up my body.

Our eyes meet again, and she swipes her thumb against the corner of her mouth.

"Pure kryptonite," I tease, digging my hand into the hair on the side of her head and lifting to kiss her.

30

[Taxi]

Watching Stone Sylver fall apart has to be ranked up there with the seven wonders of the world. A man so sturdy, so controlled, crumbling like he just did, and because of me . . . that is something powerful.

And now he's kissing me, tasting himself on my tongue, drinking me in again. Everything about this kiss is yearning.

As he said, it's been so long, and those words hold weight. If it's been a long time since he's been touched, it means it's been a long time since he's touched someone.

And he's touching me. His fingers in my hair. His mouth eager and hungry against mine. His chest brushing my naked breasts.

Stone shifts, flipping me to my back and breaking our kiss. He slips one leg between mine, scooting his body lower and lower as he peppers my breasts with kisses. One against the inside of the right one. One over the left where he drew a star.

What was his unspoken plea?

I know what mine was. *Take care of my heart*. The words were too much to speak aloud. Too soon for such sentiment.

For now, I melt under the onslaught of his lips on my skin, drawing something that makes no sense as he moves from one side of my body to the other, in a haphazard pattern, kissing me here and there and everywhere. Over a nipple. Against my belly button. On my hip.

He shoves at the fabric of my overalls, pulling them down my legs and off my feet, tossing them to the side. He cuffs my ankles with his large hands and skims up my shins, climbing back between my legs. Willingly, I spread my thighs, allowing space for his large body between them.

"Like I said earlier, Taxi. You take my breath away."

A woman could lose her head to compliments like that. And her heart.

He continues his slow travel up my body. Hands running over my knees and up my thighs, teasing where I want him most but only brushing his thumbs over the patch of coarse hair above it. His palms flatten on my belly, fingers spreading wide as he covers my hips and outlines the side of my midsection.

"You're a work of art," he says, his words worshipful. Something inside me cracks at the praise in his voice. The awe as he's looking at *me*.

He brushes over my breasts again, squeezing them in tandem before coasting down my stomach once more. Then he dips his hand between my legs, watching where his fingers split me open, and he easily glides one inside me.

I tip back my head and arch into his touch, feeling full but knowing I'll be fuller when he adds a second one.

"Been waiting for me, Taxi?"

My eyes ping open, gaze latching on his face to realize he's still staring at how his fingers slide in and out of me, pushing and pulling at my excitement, slicking those thick digits of his.

"You're so wet," he hums, again with surprise, with pleasant confusion. Like he can't believe how wet *he* makes me.

Last night was a rush. An unexpected high as I needed him. Needed to know if his touch would be as grand as I'd been imagining. Lying next to him every night, letting him weave around me like a vine, I needed to know how it would feel if something more happened.

Tonight is certainly more.

I hadn't anticipated the wonder in his tone or the praise of his touch. The sheer admiration through his hands running over my body and now slipping inside it.

He shifts lower, wedging his shoulders between my thighs and running one hand under the backside of my leg, hitching it over his arm. His hand cups the side of my backside, while his fingers continue to strum in and out of me.

His gaze lifts to my face, and I watch him as he lowers his head, eyes still on me. His tongue sneaks between his lips, and a hesitant lick tickles where I want him. My breath hitches, and he smiles before flattening his tongue, dipping his gaze, and stroking up that sensitive nub.

"Stone," I whimper.

His tongue circles the tight folds and laps harder, faster. His fingers inside me still as his tongue takes over, brushing against me, painting me in a world of color.

Pulsing red. Downy pink. Periwinkle.

He sucks at my clit and my legs twitch. He squeezes my backside with his other hand and hums against me. The vibration ripples up my body and settles in my lower belly, where an entire flight of something flaps inside me.

"Stone," I whisper, running my hands through his hair, spreading my legs wider as if he can get deeper. As if I can draw him into me, in ways he isn't already inside. His fingers. Then his tongue. His mouth on me so intimately.

My hips act of their own accord, rocking subtly, matching a rhythm only my heart hears.

And that mustache . . . it tickles when he dips his tongue lower and then pulls it back to the point that triggers all my pleasure. Where Stone treats me with delicacy, and yet with the full weight of his desire. His mouth becomes more insistent, and my hips roll a little faster, riding along peaks and valleys of a slow rising tide.

When Stone firmly cups my backside, practically lifting my lower half off the bed, his tongue is hunger and thirst. A man desperate to be full and quenched.

"Yes," I call out, affirming that I'm here to meet all his needs. "Yes. There." I say louder, almost as desperate as Stone.

No one as powerful as Stone, as masterful and attentive, has been this intimate with me in a long, long time.

Something in me cracks again. Like tectonic plates within the earth being ruptured, disrupted, and shifting. Something warm and molten fills the spaces, and my body trembles, anticipation building, heat rising.

"Stone?" I question the power of what's coming, of what's happening inside me.

I clutch harder at his hair, my fingers dig within the strands, holding onto him, like I need him to align my gravity. My hips rock faster, thighs spread as wide as I can.

Stone flicks harder, and I detonate. I feel like I've left this bed and hover above it, floating in suspension, the pleasure mesmerizing. If I thought my body could glitter and shimmer, I swear it does. My skin tingles. My toes curl. I cling to Stone's head and ride out the sensation that he continues to tease from me until I can't take anymore.

I fall back against the bed, legs limp, fingers loosening in his hair.

"Stone," I whisper, a warning, an appreciation. Enough.

He presses a final kiss against where I'm tender and spent, and then slowly lifts, climbing up my body.

One of his legs slips between mine. Half his body covers me. He falls into the cradle of my arm and my chest, resting his head against my shoulder. I run my fingernails up his back, and he presses a kiss right above my right breast.

"Thank you, Taxi."

The words surprise me, and I pull back my head, dip my fingers in his hair again, and gently tug his head back so he can look at me.

"For what?"

"For being here."

He settles back into the nest of my arm around him and his cheek against my chest, but I lie there stunned, eyes prickling.

Because no one has ever said such a thing to me.

31

[Taxi]

For the next few nights, I stay at Stone's place. Partially because his bed is bigger. Partially because I don't want to go to Trudy's home without her present.

Mostly because of Stone.

Being in a house that belongs to Trudy but is not the house I remember growing up in continues to feel strange.

Fortunately, we get the good news that Trudy can come home.

Trudy *and* Simon.

There's been so much to consider lately. Rearranging my schedule and figuring out how to get Gloria here, but the night before Trudy's return home, Judd brings Simon back to the house and I meet him there. It's the first night he and I will be alone together, and I think we're both a little nervous.

Judd offered to stay a while as a buffer. Stone offered as

well, but I need to do this on my own. I need to be here for Simon as well as Trudy.

We build our own mini pizzas. We blow up balloons and fill the entryway with them, and we make a Welcome Home banner.

Judd and Genie gave us a basket full of tomatoes, cucumbers, and beans from their home garden. Stone dropped off a large bouquet of flowers.

The house looks almost festive, and the night ends with Simon and me watching a movie. His choice: *Star Wars*.

He's such a good kid, but quiet, observant, hesitant, like Judd as a child. The similarities are almost eerie. But Simon isn't the same with me as I've seen him with Judd. He doesn't smile the way he does around Judd. Doesn't have private jokes with me or laugh at mine.

He's cautious around me, and I hate that for him and me.

The similarities between Simon and me are uncanny. Absentee parents. His father had custody of him and dropped Simon off at Trudy's home two years ago. It was the responsible thing to do, but I'm certain Simon feels the rejection. Mother never present. Father willingly giving him up.

My heart aches for him, but I've been equally not available to him. Guilt hits me in a new way. If I want to consider Simon family, I need to step up for family.

While my sisters and I have consciously gone our own ways, we've kept in touch as best we can. It's more difficult with Jolene as she's the wildcat in our trio. Still, she's my sister. I love her. I miss both of them.

After Simon is in bed, acting all responsible for himself by taking a shower and brushing his teeth, I lie on the lumpy couch again, staring at the living room ceiling. Missing Stone.

The way he's held me. The way he's been present for me from the second I returned to Sterling Falls. The way we came together each night.

We haven't had sex. We've had more. More kisses. More touches. More exploration.

He's so different. Awkwardly sweet and enthusiastically eager.

I can honestly say I adore him. Like truly adore him.

And Stone being here for me has shown me what he once asked of me:

Let me show you who I am.

He's an amazing man. He loves his family. He works hard. He's available for every single person who needs him. And I'm coming to realize how much I might need him.

Which is a dangerous thought that I drift off to sleep to.

However, hours later, a soft shout causes me to leap off the couch like that guy in 'Twas the Night Before Christmas. Only I wasn't expecting Santa Claus. The whimpering noise comes from down the hallway, and I race toward the bedrooms.

Simon's door is partially open, and he is sitting upright, breathing heavily. Slowly, I open the door, reminded of when Jolene was younger and had nightmares. Ones that would scare the bejesus out of me, but she didn't recall happening by morning.

"Hey, baby," I whisper, worried Simon might still be sleeping and not aware he's sitting up in bed. Cautiously, I approach the side of the bed. Simon looks up at me.

"You okay?" I ask.

He falls back on the mattress, blinking a few times before tears roll down his cheeks.

"Aw, sweetie." I take a seat on the edge of his bed and brush back his floppy bangs. "Was it a bad dream?"

He only nods, swiping hastily at his cheeks, but the tears keep rolling.

"Want to tell me about it?" I keep my voice low, continuing to stroke back his hair. His bright blue eyes remain glassy, and he blinks a few times. When he's near Judd, sometimes people mistake Simon for Judd's son. I never miss the slight smile that brings to Judd's lips.

"Grandma Trudy." He gasps. "She died." Another soft sob breaks from him, and I lean closer, curling my hand along the side of his face and cupping his chin.

"She's not going to die, baby." Not anytime soon with the stubborn attitude she's been displaying during her final days in the hospital. She's always been a feisty, respectfully outspoken woman, but she's a little more ornery than I remember. I'm giving grace because . . . heart attack.

"I didn't have anyone to take care of me." His tears flow faster. His lower lip trembles.

I remember that fear. Trudy had been a lifeline for me, but I remember that niggling feeling of *what's next*. What would happen to me and my sisters if Trudy were gone? What if she decided I wasn't worth the bother because of what my mother did to her brother, and she turned me out? I had worries for nothing because Trudy Wallace would never do such a thing. She'd never give away a foster child without just cause, which meant she kept everyone who came to her until they were ready to go on their own.

He's had a troubling life for someone so young, just like I'd had, so I understand his worries.

And I don't want him to be concerned.

"Oh, baby, no. You have Judd and Genie. And me." The ferocity of my plea hits me right in the sternum. I cannot prove to Simon I'm here for him if I'm not *here* for him. A child needs someone in their space. Someone reassuring him he's important and he's loved.

Simon cannot feel my love if I don't show him I have it for him. If he doesn't see I'm not a flight risk. I might work all over the country, but I don't forget him. I care about him.

But if I'm not steady in his life, he can't know that. Not yet. He's had too much upheaval as it is.

Just like I had when I was near the same age. It took me years of living with Trudy before I became comfortable, and I still never felt like I fully belonged. As if I didn't deserve to be with her.

"But you're going to leave, too." Simon hammers in my own fears, confirming my thoughts. He doesn't trust me to be here.

"I'm not going anywhere." *Not anytime soon.*

But how long can I really stay? I had commissions I had to put on hold. Work I couldn't give up, because I'm still young and I need the money. I live a simple lifestyle, but I still have expenses.

"Grandma Trudy says you're like the wind, always blowing around, never able to stay in one place for too long."

Trudy's assessment is accurate.

But what happens when the wind stops? Trudy might say it always starts up again. Never still. Never truly settled.

What if I want the wind to stop blowing, though? Do I need cement feet? Or do I just need to stop giving in to the gust? Do I need to build a wall, and paint it?

The irony isn't lost on me. How I decorate permanent places, making my mark on them.

But I always leave. Leave my art behind when I rush away to the next project. The next adventure. In the end, I'm so much like my mother that the realization sends panicked recognition along my nerves.

Maybe for once I need to stay. Need to make a longer-lasting impression.

For Simon. For me.

I need to decorate this fragile wall between us so he sees I can be steady.

I hold my gaze on his young face, remembering how I felt at his age. The abandonment that led to fear that no one would ever really want me. No one would ask me to stay.

I could stay for Simon. And Trudy. And even Stone, because I wasn't ready to let go of any of them.

"Grandma Trudy is rarely wrong. But sometimes, the wind can blow, and things stay in place. I'd like to be one of those things."

Simon has no idea how badly I'd like to stick in one place.

"Like a flagpole?"

I blink, uncertain what he means.

"The wind blows and a flag flaps around, holding onto the pole for dear life." He waves his hand like flimsy material battling the movement of the weather.

I chuckle softly. "I guess so. And I might need to hold on tight to someone to keep me in place." Or someone needs to hold onto me.

Suddenly, Simon is sitting upright again, and his thin arms wrap around me, holding onto me.

At first, I don't respond, so startled, so befuddled by the sudden embrace. Simon and I don't have that kind of relationship. I adore Simon, but we don't hug.

But this . . . him clinging to me, has me eventually responding with an equally tight hold on him. Breathing in his apple-scented shampoo, I smooth a hand down his thin back and embrace the moment.

"I can be your flagpole, Aunt Taxi."

Dang it. This kid. The back of my eyes burn, and my vision blurs.

"When you flap, I'll hold," he says.

A tear slips free, dripping from the corner of my eye and rolling over my cheek.

"You hold tight, kiddo." *And I'll hold you right back.*

Pressing a kiss to the side of Simon's head, I linger another second before pulling back.

"Do you think you can sleep now?" I ask, knowing he has school tomorrow.

Simon used to play sick to get out of going to school. Judd thought he might be bored because he's so smart. This year, Simon is in some accelerated classes, and the difference makes him more eager to attend. He's going for perfect attendance this year.

Simon nods and slowly lowers back to his pillow.

"I'll stay right here another minute." Or ten.

He rolls to his side, and I rub his back like Trudy used to do for me. And I once did for Jolene. He instantly closes his eyes.

Even after I'm certain Simon is sleeping, I sit on the edge of the bed, marveling at how people can come into your life at odd times, and loving them becomes as easy as if they've always been there.

And while my thoughts are full of Simon, I realize I also might mean Stone.

Flagpoles, allowing you to flap and flit with the wind, but holding tight during the roughest storms.

32

[Taxi]

Trudy and I wait for her final discharge, which includes instructions about a strict diet, exercise restrictions, and a demand for rest. Stone said he had something he had to do and couldn't get away, so I drove Trudy's car to pick her up. I don't want to turn Trudy's return home into a house party anyway. She'll want to fuss, treating people like guests instead of letting people treat her like the guest of honor. She'd never sit still, thus wear herself out, so her welcome home is only going to include Judd, Simon, and me.

However, when Trudy and I pull up to her house, I'm the one treated with a surprise.

Gloria, my 1970 VW Westphalia Camper, is sitting in Trudy's driveway with the back hatch open, exposing the engine, and a man bent over like he's inspecting the mechanics of the vehicle. The white topped, bright red bottom van contains all my worldly possessions, which includes my precious brushes and rollers, and a collection of denim overalls.

"What the . . ." Trudy whispers when I park next to Gloria in Trudy's sedan.

Stone straightens beside my girl, while I set Trudy's car in Park. Then he rounds the car to open Trudy's door and offer her his hand.

"Why, Stone Sylver, you're a sight for sore eyes, but my fragile heart isn't sure I can handle a gift so handsome as you."

My mouth falls open, and Stone's cheeks turn pink.

"Oh my." She turns and looks at the giant WELCOME sign hanging from the eaves. Her voice catches when she says, "My precious cottage."

If Trudy starts crying, I'm going to be a mess. Not that she isn't too strong for tears and always preaching a good cry clears the soul, but I'm feeling especially raw right now.

Aunt Trudy is finally home. Gloria is here. Stone is present. And Simon.

"Happy you're home, Trudy," Stone states, looping his arm around Trudy's shoulders as an embrace.

This man will be getting more than a hug from me once I can get away from playing nursemaid, which I can't and won't do for several weeks. Trudy needs me. Simon, too. And I won't let either of them down.

Stone helps Trudy toward the front door while I linger behind, turning to glance back at my van again.

She's a sight for sore eyes, but she'll also be staying put for a while.

Simon rushes out the front door to greet Trudy, and she folds herself around him like the protective guardian she's always been. Trudy is a superhero. Her hug is a giant cape of love.

With Simon's arm around Trudy's back, like his thin frame

is supporting her larger one, he leads her toward the front door where Judd awaits.

Stone steps back to me.

"What are you doing here?" I whisper, more relieved by his presence than I ought to be.

"This is why I couldn't go with you to pick up Trudy." He waves toward Gloria.

"How did you get her here?"

"Remember when I asked you for your license plate number and the make and model of her the other day?"

The other day, when he asked, I joked that he was going to call her in to be impounded. He laughed in that hearty way he sometimes does. A drumbeat sound strangely matching the rhythm of my heart.

"I was hoping she'd arrive yesterday, but there was some kind of hold-up. Not ideal for your surprise to arrive at the same time as your aunt's return home."

I remain quiet, speechless really.

"You okay?" Stone asks, watching me.

I swipe under my eye, uncertain where the sudden threat of tears is coming from. Maybe relief Trudy is home. Definitely joy that Simon will be back. Perhaps, a small pinch of concern that I'm grounded.

But the longer I stare at my van, I don't feel the itch to hop in her and drive off. Don't feel the need to disappear before I'm forgotten.

Glancing at Stone, I'm equally overwhelmed by his kindness. He's done so much for me.

"I'm good," I whisper, realizing the words are true. I'm scared about the recovery path ahead for Trudy and how I'll be able to best help her, but I'm also better than I've felt in a long time.

Like I just might belong . . . for a little while longer.

Stone pulls me into his strong arms and rests his head on mine a second. "Gloria. Good surprise or bad?"

"Amazing surprise, but how did you do it? And how much did it cost?" I'm living on a starving artist's budget. Towing a van across several state lines must have cost a fortune.

"Don't worry about it," he murmurs before kissing my forehead. With his arm looped around me, he turns me toward Trudy's front door, and I stiffen.

"What?" he asks, running his hand down my spine.

"I just . . ." I glance toward the front door and back at him. "I don't think I'm going to be able to get away anytime soon. I can't really leave Trudy yet. And Simon. Which means I can't spend the night with—"

Stone holds up a hand to stop me. "I'm not going anywhere. And neither are you."

It's not a statement as much as a question without the modifier.

For now.

I'm not going anywhere *for now.* And I'm realizing as much as I've been worried about people leaving me behind, I'm equally as guilty of leaving them.

"I also don't want to confuse things," I add.

Stone tilts his head, confused.

"I mean, we said we were dating, but I don't know how public I want to be about that right now. How public I can be about it."

Stone licks his lips and chews the lower one. His hands land on his hips, and he glances toward the street.

"Think a few people might already know something's going on. I've been at the hospital every night to pick you up and there every morning to drop you off."

"I know, but . . ." I dig my teeth into my lip.

"You saying goodbye to me already?" His face hardens, his

eyes narrowing. His tone isn't demanding but hesitant. Cautious.

"No!" My response is a tad loud, and I don't recognize the panic in it. Holding out my hands, I reach for his chest. "No. Just putting us on pause, I guess. I can't be at your house every night, and I don't know when I'll see you again."

"Like I said, I'm not going anywhere." He glances past me toward Trudy's front door. "Just don't shut me out. Please."

Don't leave without saying goodbye.

Something inside me breaks a little. Sensing this man has some of the same fears I do. He doesn't want to be left behind any more than me. He doesn't want to be abandoned.

The fear in his eyes and the honesty in his voice has me wrapping my arms around his middle and leaning my head against his chest. Beneath my cheek, his heart races.

"I won't." My mama didn't give me a proper goodbye. His mother surely couldn't say goodbye with her sudden passing. I'd never do that to him. I'd never close the door on him.

And I don't even want to think about goodbyes.

Stone presses a kiss to the top of my head and rubs his hand up my back one more time, but he doesn't hold onto me. Doesn't cling to me like he does while we sleep.

And I feel him slipping away a little bit when I'm not ready to let go.

33

[Stone]

As I don't want to overwhelm the heart patient, I don't linger long for Trudy's welcome home, and I'm a little uncertain where I stand with Taxi, which also sends me out the door early. I don't doubt that she is surprised to see her van and happy to see me in the driveway, but her decision to place us on pause is troubling.

Strange to think I'd had a public friendship that everyone thought was a more-than-platonic relationship, and now I have what I consider a budding relationship, and she wants us to appear like friends.

I don't fault Taxi. So much has happened all at once. Trudy's heart attack and Taxi's decision to stay a while. I just don't want to be shut out.

Taxi needs to see that I'm not going to abandon her. For a man previously opposed to commitments of the heart, my heart is certainly screaming at me to keep her.

She's strong, magnetic, loyal and someone who dropped everything for someone she loves. She doesn't trust easily, but I feel her opening up to me. She understands me in a way few people do. We share similar experiences with parents and family. The contrast of her strength and vulnerability attracts me to her. She sees the two sides of me.

I've been strong my entire life. Holding up my family, raising them, lifting them, but no one has done the lifting for me. Somehow Taxi does that. Her concern for my arm. Her fear for the risks in my profession. Her attention to me.

So this pause is a little confusing to navigate. Except almost immediately, Taxi acts opposite of what she requested.

I'm invited to stay for dinner when I visit, checking in on the patient and caregiver.

Taxi doesn't pass me without a simple touch, like she's confirming with a brush of her hand over my shoulder or a stroke of her pinky beneath the dinner table that I'm present.

We talk on the phone each night like classic teenagers. The ones who used to use the phone for the purpose of speaking to someone else, not just text messages. We even FaceTime, which is even better because at least I can see her.

And it's in one of these talks that I confess what happened to me.

"You ever been in *love*, Stone Sylver?" Her tone playful and teasing.

"Yeah," I admit, twisting my lips and glancing away from the screen. "Once."

When I look back at Taxi, her expression sobers. "Trudy might have mentioned something. A year ago, during that Fourth of July at your house. She said you'd been engaged." She pauses. "Want to tell me about it?"

No. Yes. I exhale and scrub a hand down my face.

"It was a long time ago. And I wasn't engaged. Not officially." I draw in a deep breath as I tip back in my office chair. "I met

Bailey my sophomore year of college. And I thought she was my everything." I openly admit, a weak smile meeting the old memory. A blonde beauty with an easy smile who seemed as attracted to me as I'd instantly been to her.

"We dated for years and I planned to propose. But then . . ." I pause, feeling my pulse pick up. "I told you about my dad dying, and my decision to take care of my siblings. Football or family, the choice was easy for me. Not that it wasn't hard to let go of the dream of professional football, but my family . . ." I drift off. I hadn't needed to think about it. "But I couldn't ask Bailey to make a choice."

"But did you ask her or did you make the decision for her?" Taxi defends, woman sticking up for another woman.

"I didn't need to ask."

"What do you mean?" Taxi perches her chin in her hand, staring back at me through the screen with confusion etched on her forehead.

"I didn't make my decision immediately or lightly. I was still in this state of grieving my dad and trying to figure out what happened to him. What would happen to all of them. Processing what I was going to do. Clay begged me to go. We needed the money."

The family business—Sylver Seed & Soil—was hanging on by a thread back then. Another one of our mother's dreams almost dead. Clay never went to college, throwing himself into keeping the business afloat as best he could. He was the only one able to tolerate Dad. Truthfully, he'd just found a way to work around the worn-out old man.

"I put us on pause," I admit. "Asked her to give me a little time."

Taxi's breath hitches.

"I figured if we could weather the storm of the moment, we'd make it through anything." My voice quiets, and I lower my gaze. "And I guess, a big part of me hoped she'd choose me anyway."

"If you didn't become a professional football player?" Taxi confirms, her agitation growing.

"If I took on the responsibility of raising my six siblings." I glance up. "But I knew it would never be fair to ask."

"So, she broke up with you? Because you put family first." Taxi shifts, sitting taller. Her irritation evident through the phone screen.

"Not exactly," I whisper, never wanting to fault Bailey for this sliver of our history.

"What exactly then?" Taxi is even edgier. Like she has sudden issue with a woman she's never met and she's bracing to throw down on my behalf.

My head spins a little bit, dizzy at the idea that Taxi is offended on my behalf.

Most people are upset for me, but they're more upset with someone else. Disappointed in him, like I'd been.

"She slept with my best friend. And they got pregnant."

"Cortland," Taxi whispers. Not as shocked as I'd expect, and I consider she must have heard the story like everyone else in this town has. People like to share it, feeling sorry for me, feeling shame with him.

"Un-fucking-believable!" Taxi blurts, throwing me off guard at her adamant disbelief.

She's not angry at me; she's angry *for* me. For the betrayal I endured. Her eyes are fierce, protective, like she's in my corner even if I didn't ask her to be.

"Their excuse was grief."

"What the hell had they been grieving? You lost your father, Stone. And your dreams."

"I know," I whisper.

And I remember it clear as day. Cortland standing in my yard, in front of the house I'm still living in. He'd gone to

Bailey's apartment because she called him over. At first, Cort said she seduced him, but quickly he reneged on the accusation, taking ownership for his part in the decision. There were two people involved. He'd been weak.

"Cort said he missed our friendship. A wedge had developed around the time Bailey entered my life."

"So he slept with her?" Taxi interjects, still appalled by the behavior.

I chuckle without humor. "Yeah, well, Cort and I had a relationship first, I guess. He was my best friend. Cradle to college."

"Stone," Taxi whispers, her voice softening.

"Anyway." I scrub a hand down my face and sit forward in my office chair, the damn thing creaking beneath me. "The hardest part was . . . well, there were several. For the first time in my life, I had something that was mine. Someone who was only for me."

I swallow an unexpected lump in my throat, which makes no sense being there because it has been more than two decades since I lost Bailey.

"I hardly remember much before I was twelve years old, and then I was thrown into raising Vale as a baby and caring for Sebastian and Ford as toddlers. Then my dad dies, and I'm back at it again. I'd been taking care of others my entire life, and I finally had someone who would take care of me. Or so I thought."

I choke back that thick lump. "I mean, I thought Bailey loved me. But Cort . . . Cort was the harder hit. He was my best friend. He stood by my side through all of it. He was my person as much as I thought she was, if that makes any sense."

"It makes perfect sense," Taxi confirms.

"Going off to college was the first break I'd gotten in life. A chance for me." I tap weakly on my chest, having never confessed these feelings to anyone before. "I had a future. I had a plan. And my fucking dad . . ."

The lump is back. Dammit. What is happening to me? Why am I opening up to this woman?

Because she's listening . . . to me.

"So selfish," I whisper, instantly chastising myself. He'd been heartbroken and then sick. Alcoholism. What a wicked disease.

"I'd wanted something for myself," I quietly admit. "And instead, I'd lost one of the most important people to me."

"Bailey?" Taxi asks.

"Cortland," I confess. The ache for my old friend was bigger than the loss of Bailey.

I'd never really asked Cort to stand by me either. He just did it. He'd chosen me. As his friend. As his brother from another mother. And then he chose her. One night. One mistake.

"I never had to ask Bailey what she'd do because her actions showed me who she was."

She'd only wanted the future. A professional footballer's wife.

"Cort married her instead. *He* played professional football."

"Stone," Taxi whispers again, sorrow in the single syllable of my name.

"They had a boy." I scrub down my face again, the thickness in my throat gone. "His name is—"

"Josh," she completes for me. "I'm so fucking sorry that happened to you, Stone."

She has heard my story.

"You deserve the world," she says.

"I have it. In my siblings. In my nieces and nephews."

Taxi watches me, her gaze intense. "But you deserve that one-on-one love, Stone. That red to your blue." She slowly smiles.

"How about periwinkle? Does that complement beige?"

Her mouth curls higher on one side. "I've never really thought about it," she admits.

"But you're thinking about it now, aren't you?" I just planted a seed. One I didn't intend to plant.

Like when dandelion seeds drift through the wind and then root somewhere unexpected.

Like in the cracks in a sidewalk or on the edge of a garden.

Taxi is quiet. Her grin growing larger, until another thought occurs.

"And now Cort is dating your sister?"

"Engaged to my sister," I correct, tipping back in my chair again, staring up at the ceiling despite holding the phone in a position Taxi can see my face.

"They're in *love*." I mimic her emphasis of the word earlier in this conversation.

"I don't know how you carry all that weight, Stone."

Then I whip my head forward. "What about you? Ever been in love?"

Taxi exhales and sits back in the kitchen chair. She glances to her left and shakes her head.

"No," she quietly admits, glancing back at me. Her sterling eyes focused. "And I'm sorry I suggested we put us on pause."

"That's not why I told you this story," I lean forward again, placing my arms on my desk top.

"I know. I asked a question and you answered. You always answer honestly, Stone. You give and you give, and you give. You need to take."

If I thought she meant I could take her, *have her*, I'd ask her right now to be mine. To give us a chance. Not just for the time she's here, but for longer. That commitment excuse I've used in the past feels like it's fluttering in the wind as well. Blowing out with the breeze.

We can work something out. Everything always works out.

Instead, I snort, dismissing the idea.

"Don't you be snorting at me, Stone Sylver," she teases again. "You take the next time you see me."

Her gaze remains focused, her suggestion still a little foggy, but her smile grows. "You hear me?"

"What about pausing?"

She licks her lips and glances to the left again before looking back at me. "Maybe I just want something for myself, too. Someone just for me, for a little while."

For a little while.

I don't let the words dissuade me from the rest of her statement.

I point at my chest, the jab forceful and direct, arching an eyebrow to suggest, *Me?*

"Yeah," she whispers. "I choose you."

She has no idea what those words do to me. How much I want them to mean something deeper than I'm certain she playfully means.

She picks me.

For now.

34

———

[Stone]

The next night, Taxi greets me in the driveway, rushing to kiss me. I don't need to take, she gives.

"Fuck, I want to touch you," I say, grinding up against her as I have her back pinned to the driver's side door of my truck, which blocks us from view of the house.

Trudy lives outside of town, so her closest neighbor isn't close enough to see what I want to do to *this woman* against the side of my vehicle.

"I need to taste you again," I murmur against her mouth as I bend at the knees to line us up and thrust at her covered center.

"Same," she whimpers against my mouth as we make out like randy teens, hiding from parents possibly spying through the front window.

The thought makes me chuckle.

"What?" she smiles, her lips swollen and wide as she pulls back. "What's so funny?"

"I was just thinking how I feel like a teenager about to get caught making out with my girl. Any minute I expect a front porch light to flip on and off, like a warning for you to come inside before breaking curfew."

"And you were thinking all that while kissing me?" she chides with giggles, especially when I angle for her neck and run my nose against her soft skin, the scent of citrus and honeysuckle invading my senses.

"I mean, besides the whole wanting to put my face between your thighs . . ."

Taxi hums with those three short *mms* and melts against me.

"How often did you do that?" she asks.

Abruptly, I pull back and focus on her eyes as best I can under the dark sky. "Put my face between thighs?"

She swats at my chest. "Kiss girls beside cars and watch for porch lights?"

"Oh." I chuckle and swipe my hand through my hair. "Maybe only a handful of times. Small town, remember? There were only so many girls, and when half of them dated half of your friends, it wasn't like I wanted to be second choice."

"First pick," she says, poking at my chest and tipping up on her toes, kissing me once again.

Eventually, I pull back. "We better get inside before I open this truck and lay us both down on the bench."

Her eyes flare like she likes that idea. "Promises, promises," she teases, before giving me one more quick kiss and then turning for the house.

"Wait." I tug at the crisscross backing of her overalls. "Come to Sylver Sunday again this weekend."

Taxi's eyes widen.

"Bring Trudy. Bring Simon. Get out of the house for a bit." All of them have been couped up since Trudy's return and as much as she needs rest, she could also use a little time outside of the house.

Taxi's brows pinch. "Let me see how she's feeling, but I'd . . . I'd like that. I'd like that a lot."

"Yeah?" I question for some reason.

"Yeah. I like your family." She plucks at the placket of my shirt, where the buttons connect the two halves.

"You should go out with the girls some night."

Taxi laughs. "You sound like Genie."

"Well . . ." I arch a brow at her.

"I'll think about that invitation, too."

THANKFULLY, Taxi didn't think too long about the Sylver Sunday invitation, and before I know it, we find ourselves in the upstairs bathroom. The same bathroom she cornered me in more than a year ago.

Taxi had excused herself for the bathroom, and within minutes of her disappearance from the backyard, I followed her.

I closed the door behind me, and at the same time she leapt for me, I stepped forward.

Our mouths crash together.

Her arms wrap around my neck and her legs around my waist, and I set her on the edge of the vanity. The kiss is hard, almost harsh, as we devour one another.

I didn't see her last night. Another incident of loose sheep in Mabel Wilson's yard that led to the discovery of a lost shoe, one believed to be linked to a child who disappeared three towns over.

The news was horrifying and had me hugging all my nieces and nephews extra hard today.

As for Taxi, the sense of anyone losing someone they love

has me kissing her harder.

"I fucking missed you last night." The admission might be more than she can handle, but I still want her to know I miss her when we aren't together.

Sometimes, I try to convince myself we are a fleeting flirtation, a fling based on circumstance and proximity. Then I remember when we met. How instantly I'd felt a spark with her, and how the Universe, or something other keeps putting this woman in my path.

Our conversation the other night certainly sounded like she's open to more.

I choose you.

Still, I'd never ask Taxi to make choices that go against who she is, what she wants. I only ask not to be shut out, like I said to her earlier this week.

As for right now, we're almost as close as we can get.

With her legs spread and my hips cradled between her thighs, she grips my ass and yanks me closer, matching where I'm hard with where she's soft.

"Superman," she whimpers, throaty and deep, and I pull back to see her lips swollen from my kiss and her eyes dazed from kissing me.

"What do you need, baby?"

"You," she whispers, her eyes meeting mine. Sharp and silver and seductive as hell.

I cup her throat and pull her back to me, crushing my mouth over hers. She makes my knees weak and my heart race. "Pure kryptonite," I murmur against her lips.

She smiles against me.

"Let me touch you," I quietly beg, wanting to feel her around my fingers, know that she's wet for only me.

"Yes." She tugs at the side of her skirt. The same one she was wearing the first night I met her. Layers of fabric in rich brown tones, each stripe a differing pattern. Her skirt is so symbolic of her. She's multi-layered—textured and complex, but soft, pliant—especially in this moment.

While she lifts her skirt, I slip my hands beneath the material, coasting my palms over her thighs and meeting in her center, where she is warm and as wet as I expected. I hook my finger around the slim fabric covering her and run my knuckle against her seam.

She leans back, hands falling against the counter to brace her.

We both glance at where my hand is hidden beneath the pile of her skirt over her lap. There's something extra about my hand covered, her thighs spread, the material hiding what I'm doing to her.

We can't see it, we feel it.

Her ankle hooks around the back of my knee, and she pulls me forward. "Superman."

"Been thinking about me?" Her body holds the answer. Her breath hitching as I easily slip a finger into her. *Taking* from her. Accepting the gifts she's giving me. Her. Her body. Her time.

"Yes," she whimpers, knees spread wide, ankle against my knee.

She rocks against my finger, and I add a second to the first, filling her as best I can.

Taxi cups my jaw and I meet her eyes. She sheepishly smiles and I match the curve of her lips as I work my fingers in and out of her. She crooks her finger into the collar of my T-shirt and tugs me forward. My lips meet hers, and my tongue seeks, mirroring my fingers in her channel with my tongue in her mouth.

I rock forward, mimicking the same motion with my hips. The desire to thrust into her. The need to fill her in other ways.

"Fuck, I want you," I murmur against her mouth. It's been a week since I've touched her like this. The intimacy. The rush. The need to be closer to her.

"Yes," she says again, like it's the only word she knows and she's giving it to me.

"Let me see," I say. "Let me see how I fill you up."

She hikes up even more of her skirt, holding it higher, so I can see how my fingers fit her, what they do to her. She's slick and hot.

"Please," she whimpers.

"Not gonna stop, baby." I almost want her to come undone more than I want it for myself. To know this strong yet vulnerable woman trusts me to touch her, to give her pleasure.

"No," she whispers, and I stop. It's the only word I need to hear.

She covers my wrist with her hand. "No. Us. Together." She gently pulls my hand from her and presses at my shoulder with her other hand.

"Taxi," I question.

She continues pushing me back until she can slide from the counter, and then she spins to face the mirror. I meet her eyes in it.

"Please," she begs, those silver eyes working their magic on me. She pulls up her skirt while at the same time reaches for me, squeezing at the bulge in my jeans. The thickness straining against my zipper, begging for release.

"Like this?" I question.

She chews her lower lip. "I need you, Stone."

Fuck!

The phone conversation and driveway make-out sessions, and all the little touches in between . . . I need her, too.

Hastily, I unbuckle my belt and unfasten my jeans.

"Next time, we go slow," I warn her. Her eyes meet mine in the mirror again.

"Next time," she slowly smiles, like the idea of doing this again makes her happy.

My chest expands. My heart hammers.

With my hand on her hip, I pull up more of her skirt, exposing her backside. She's only wearing a slip of underwear compared to the boy-cut shorts I've previously seen. I wrap my finger around the string and run my knuckle against her crease.

She shivers.

When I've reached where she's most sensitive, she arches back, forcing her backside toward me, willing my finger to brush where she's needy.

With my jeans and underwear shoved below my hips, I fist myself, the head weeping to be closer to her.

"I don't have anything in the bathroom," I admit. I've got a new box of condoms in my room, unopened. I haven't needed them in years, but I wanted to be prepared.

Still, every interaction with Taxi has been unexpected.

"I'm covered," she says, surprising me again. "And we both know it's been a long time for each of us."

"Taxi," I whisper, suddenly wanting to slow us down, despite my dick screaming in my hand and her center crying for my touch.

There might have been a time in my past when I wanted a child of my own, someone little who looked like me, and the memory tickles at my chest, but I'm well past raising more kids.

"Please. Don't deny me, Stone."

My head lifts, eyes connecting once more through the mirror. She looks vulnerable, aroused but still somehow scared ... that I would reject her.

"Never," I rush, then I'm at her entrance, and she leans forward. She's warm and so wet, and I easily glide into her, both of us humming at the connection.

"Holy ..." I cry out.

"Shhh," she purrs, taking me into her body.

With her hands on the edge of the counter, she presses back, pulling me into her, filling herself with me.

"So deep," I whisper as she drags me to the hilt, taking me completely inside her. "Fuck."

I wrap my arms around her middle, leaning over her back and rock my hips forward, gliding back and forth through her slickness. I shove her skirt out of my way to get my hand between her thighs, easily finding that sensitive nub. The point on her that causes her to rock back, almost tugging me deeper, forcing me faster, bringing us together harder.

"Taxi," I grunt, circling her clit and surging into her.

"Yes," she smacks the counter, then reaches behind her, clutching my hip. Her fingernails dig into my flesh. The sting spurs me faster.

"We're gonna make a mess," I warn, feeling my lower back tighten and my knees weaken.

"Make a mess," she hisses, pressing back harder.

"Fuck. Taxi," I groan, feeling the build, the spiral in my gut, and the twist of something deeper.

"Yes," she cries out, her voice echoing in the small space.

"Not without you." I flatten my other hand low on her belly, as if I can feel myself moving inside her.

"Stone." Her breath catches. Her hand covers mine, pressing harder. "Oh God. Oh *God*."

The pressure works magic, and Taxi stills a second before shoving her ass toward me, causing me to surge into her. She clenches and clutches, squeezing at me in a way I haven't ever felt. Like she wants to hold onto me, keep this connection as long as we can.

Everything inside me shatters and I let go, giving in to her warmth and her heart and the warm glow of this moment.

Me.

Her.

Us.

I can't form a coherent thought. Nothing has ever been like this.

I slip my arms around her middle and lower my head to the back of hers, coiling around her while still buried inside her.

"Taxi." I breathe out her name filled with a hundred questions and only one answer.

Stay.

Something I cannot ask.

Instead, I inhale the scent of citrus and honeysuckle and sex, and I squeeze her middle a little tighter, wishing I could keep us right here, locked in a bathroom.

A light rap comes to the door along with a throat clearing.

"Don't mean to interrupt, but your meat might be burning."

Both our heads lift and turn in the direction of the closure where Cortland speaks from the other side.

"Probably shouldn't let Sebastian take over, like he wants to."

I glance toward the mirror and catch on Taxi's eyes, which are wide and gleaming back at me. She covers her mouth to hold in laughter, and I press a kiss to her shoulder to suppress my own.

Easing myself out of her, I reach for a hand towel, using it to catch any spill. Then I snap the towel gently against her left cheek.

"Ow," she says, loudly, spinning to face me. Her skirt falls back into place. "What was that for?"

"So you remember me when you walk out that door." I nod toward the bathroom door.

"I don't think I could ever forget you. No matter where I go." Her eyes dip sheepishly, and I pull her to me, placing a softer kiss on her, letting the touch linger, distracting myself from what's been unsaid.

She's still leaving.

Not today, but someday.

35

[Taxi]

During the week, I finally take Genie up on her invitation to go out with the girls. After my second Sylver Sunday, the girls begged me to join them, and I didn't want to disappoint.

I also wanted to go out, not only for the break it afforded me from caretaking, but because I truly wanted to be with them. Their welcoming energy made me want to . . . belong.

Judd offers to stay with Simon at Trudy's, keeping Nolan with them, and giving Genie a little mommy reprieve as well.

"Jailbreak," Genie cries once we enter her SUV.

I don't mention how her comment hits hard, letting the joke go as Genie is just too bubbly with relief for a night out.

"Nolan is a breast man like his daddy," she overshares.

I wrinkle my nose. Despite my friendship with Judd waning for a while, I still consider him a friend. More like a brother, as he was around so often when we were younger. So, I do not want to hear this kind of talk, just like Vale doesn't like to hear the girls discussing the sexcapades they have with her brothers.

I'll also be attending my first Sterlet meeting, the weekly book club disguising a secret sex store. I've already learned that the Sterlets, a take on starlets for the women living in Sterling Falls, have an open-door policy, allowing attendees to come and go to accommodate their personal schedules. Vale is ever faithful in attendance.

"I consider myself an original member," she says, as we sit at a round table with a wooden keg barrel base. A ritual among the Sylver women who attend the book club is meeting up at Milton Roadhouse to pre-game.

Enya and, of course, Genie are also present. "Not a Sterling Falls resident anymore, though," Enya teases about Vale's move to Rogue River, the next town over. "How's it going over there?"

Vale dives into the trials of living with a man other than her brother after all this time.

I can't help myself, but I silently stew over the man who broke Stone's heart. No, shattered it, taking with him a life-long friendship. One that Stone misses. I heard it in his voice when he explained what happened when they were younger. When his entire world imploded again.

How many times has Stone's life been rocked only for him to remain sturdy?

"Stone and I co-existed. But having Cortland, my fiancé . . ." Vale's face brightens with the term. "It gets tricky with Hudson around." She wiggles her brows. "We find creative spaces and ways to come together."

"Speaking of creative spaces," Genie hums, lifting her glass of wine, and narrowing her dark eyes on me. Her smile makes them dance. "*You* were missing for a while this past Sunday."

"I don't know what you're talking about," I lie, as my cheeks flame.

"Funny," Enya adds, leaning on the table. "Stone was missing for a time as well."

"Was he?" I lift my drink, something off the special's menu, and take a sip of the sharp sweetness.

"Maybe we should ask him what you two were up to," Vale teases. "Oh, look, there he is."

"Where?" I ask, raising my head and giving myself away.

"Right there," Vale points to a high top across the bar.

Stone, in his uniform, is seated across from the beautiful blonde I remember seeing him with once upon a morning back in Tennessee. The same person he *hadn't* told me he was meeting for dinner. He'd only said he had a work-related meeting this evening.

"You should go say hi," Genie encourages, like we're schoolgirls and I should cross the cafeteria and talk to the hot guy on the other side.

"He looks busy," I say, pulling my gaze away and glaring at Genie. I like her. She's a woman I want in my corner, but I will not be afraid to tell her to knock it off. I don't need to go to Stone, he can—

"Looks like he's coming over instead." Vale's comment draws my attention back to the man in uniform who is now crossing the vacant space in the middle of the bar.

"Ladies." His low voice is smooth while equally rugged.

I do not know what it is about that sound that puts me at ease while turning me on.

"Hey."

"Hi, Stone."

"Big brother."

I snort at the last one from Vale.

"Mind if I borrow Taxi for a moment. I'd like to introduce her to Emerson."

My cheeks heat again. I could argue it isn't necessary to meet Emerson. We haven't needed to discuss her again. Stone told me that only Bailey was his one-time love, and Emerson is a friend. Plus, he did say dinner was work-related. I know he's the sheriff, she's the mayor, so logically, their meeting makes sense, but still . . .

When he holds out his hand, I take it, despite nerves rattling my bones like a Halloween skeleton. This shouldn't feel so monumental. She's just a woman. But she's also been important to Stone.

He helps me stand, but I instantly drop his hand despite the comfort of his palm. His hand goes to my lower back, instead, like he's announcing to the room I'm with him.

When we reach the high-top table, Stone introduces us.

"Emerson Milton, *this* is Taxi." Something strange rings in Stone's voice. The sound a little like pride, a lot like excitement. Like he's been eager to introduce me to her. "Tallulah Alexander, meet Emerson, mayor of Sterling Falls."

When she shakes my hand, her fingers are long and delicate, but her grip is strong and confident. "Such a pleasure to meet you. Stone has told me so much about you."

Glancing at him, I arch a brow.

"Because of Trudy," I clarify.

"No." Emerson laughs nervously. "Um . . . I believe it started when you met last year in Tennessee." Emerson looks at Stone for confirmation before her brows crease like she might have gotten something wrong.

"Nope. She's the one."

"The one what?" I ask, a little too defensively.

"The woman he wanted to—"

"Okay," Stone holds up a hand with all the authority he possesses as a sheriff. "Let's not give away all my secrets at the first meeting."

Emerson chuckles. "Well, knowing my secrets are bigger than yours, I guess I'll hold my tongue. If you'll excuse me a second, I'm going to use the ladies' room."

She slips from her stool, and I watch her walk away—poised, confident, not sizing me up even once. It throws me off. I was ready for claws, for competition, for her to claim she had him first.

But nothing. She seemed nice enough, confident in her place as his friend, respectful even of that position. Respectful of Stone. And as his friend, she seemed happy for him. Happy he has me.

The second she's gone, Stone takes a seat on his stool.

"I should probably get back to—"

"You didn't tell me you were going out." His hands come easily to my hips, like it's the most natural place for them to be. He spreads his knees to fit me between them.

"And you told me you had a work-related dinner," I counter, my voice coming out softer than I intended.

"Taxi." Stone's voice lowers, turns warmer. "Emerson is the mayor. I'm the sheriff. We're still friends, and sometimes we need to talk outside of the offices we work for."

I believe him, and a small part of me hates that I believe him, because believing him is dangerous. Believing him feels like stepping onto ground that might actually hold my weight, and that's never been my experience with men.

Stone is just a constant conundrum, steady as bedrock one second, and throwing me off balance the next by letting me get this close to his real life.

"Genie invited me to book club," I say, scanning down his uniform, my hand landing on that badge.

Genie. His sister. His sisters-in-law, more women, more of his family and friends, pulling me into their circle, arms open, hearts eager.

"Ah. Book club." Those hands on my hips draw me closer and glide up my side, like he can't help himself. He needs to outline my figure, confirm I'm standing here.

"And you're wearing that skirt again." He hums appreciatively. "You had that on the night we met."

"I had this on the other day," I remind him.

"I remember." He bites the corner of his lip. "I remember everything about you."

Soft pressure against my lower back forces me to step even closer to him.

"Stone," I whisper, like someone will hear him. Someone could mysteriously interpret what he means about the other night.

"So, book club?" He chuckles. "Let me know if you find a *selection* you like." He gives me a wink, knowing the truth about the club. He's so playful right now, almost silly.

"I just needed a night out." Stone already knows that I'm struggling with the day in and day out tasks of catering to Trudy's needs. Her house is only so big, and there is only so much cleaning, cooking, and laundry to be done. My creative itch needs scratching.

"I would have taken you out," Stone says, sounding a little hurt that I hadn't asked him.

I don't respond because he's already done so much. He comes to Trudy's every night, and he would have been there tonight if he hadn't seen me here first.

"This weekend is Founder's Day. We celebrate the birth of Milton County." He arches a brow toward Emerson's seat, implying this is the reason for their out-of-office meeting. "There's a barn dance held on the Milton property."

I nod like I understand when I haven't heard much about a Founder's Day celebration before.

"Tallulah Alexander, would you be my date to the dance?" Stone gives me that sheepish look he sometimes has. A bashful grin accompanies the gleam in his Montana-sky eyes.

"You askin' me out on an official date?" I tease. We might have gone to lunch by the river, but that was before everything reached a new level. A level that feels monumental and growing every day, building higher, getting taller, stronger.

I'm almost giddy, like that schoolgirl in a cafeteria. I've been invited to a dance by one of the most popular guys in town.

"Absolutely," Stone says, spreading those hands on my lower back and jostling me a little bit.

"Then absolutely yes is my answer." I pat that badge over his chest. "I'd love to go to the Founder's Day dance with you, Sheriff Sylver."

He grins. His mouth wide, teeth peeking out when he teases me.

"That's Superman to you, baby."

36

[Stone]

When Saturday night arrives, I'm nervous, like I've never been on a date before. Then again, it's been years since I've been on one, which doesn't sound any better.

The barn dance is casual, so I'm wearing my best jeans and a dark brown shirt, plus my cowboy boots and my light suede hat. Once upon a time, we had horses on our property. My mother loved them, and I thought I'd spend my whole life riding. Unfortunately, once she passed, my dad couldn't stand the gentle reminder of our mother, and he sold off her precious animals.

I never rode again, while Clay bought a horse as soon as he could afford one.

The night is perfect for a barn dance. The evening is cool, shrouded in mountain mist, hinting at fall coming just around the corner.

Autumn always feels like entering a new season of life, Taxi once wrote on a postcard.

I'm eager for the change brewing inside me. The excitement of having Taxi in my life right now. The ease of her being here, blending in with my family and friends.

Taxi often talks about community, and I want her to find it in Sterling Falls. I want her to find belonging . . . with me.

She was worried about leaving Trudy alone for the evening, but to her surprise, Trudy is attending the celebration as well. Emory Milton is sending someone to pick up her friend.

Simon will be at a friend's house for the night.

When Taxi opens the front door, she takes my breath away. Her bronzed skin has a dusting of powder on her cheeks, and her lips are deep red. She's wearing a floral print dress giving off country-girl energy that doesn't exactly match the urban artist vibe she typically has. Red ankle-cut booties match her lipstick. Her hair is pulled up on top of her head, tugging her curls into a wild ball of waves.

"Howdy," she says, kicking up one heel and giving me a wink while glancing at my hat.

"Stunning," I reply, still taking her in.

She laughs and tips up on her toes to give me a quick kiss.

"Where's Trudy?" I peek around her toward the living room.

"She already left." Taxi pauses, tilting her head and hitching her thumb toward the living room. "Wanna have a quickie before we head out?"

I laugh, loud and happy, uncertain if she's serious or teasing. "Don't you worry. I have plans for you later."

I tug at her waist and pull her closer, laying a better greeting on her. One that I hope conveys all my desire for her. When we break apart, Taxi sways a bit on her low heels. Never had that effect on a woman before, but her physical reaction is exactly how I feel.

Weak-kneed. Light-headed. Full heart.

"Now. I have a date to get to and a dance to attend."

Taxi flicks her thick lashes and plucks at the snaps on my shirt before laying her hand on my chest. "Anyone I know?"

With my hands still on her hips, like they were meant to fit there, I jiggle her. "Prettiest girl in Sterling Falls."

"Prettiest, huh? I might get jealous." She walks her fingers up my chest and taps my chin.

"I'm a devoted man, baby. You'd never have anything to be jealous of."

Taxi's face softens. "I've heard that about you. Devoted."

"Does devotion scare you?" I ask, still teasing but holding my breath a second.

"Not as much as I thought it would," she says, leaving me a little puzzled but mostly pleased. The last thing I want to do is frighten Taxi. Tonight, I just want us to have fun.

"Good." I tap her nose and lean in for one more kiss. "Now, your chariot awaits."

I sweep my hand toward the door, implying we should go, so we can attend the dance, have that date, and then get onto something that won't be quick. Because I want time with this woman. All the time she'll allow me.

"My chariot?" She jokes, swaying her hips before reaching for a leather jacket on a hook by the door.

Taking the jacket from her, I hold it open while she slips into it. With her hair pulled up, exposing her smooth skin, I can't help but take another sip of her, inhaling her citrus and honeysuckle scent.

She hums in her signature way before spinning to face me. "Is it true what they say?" She plucks my hat off my head and sets it on her own.

Wear the hat, ride the cowboy.

"Guess you'll have to wait and see." I wink, then tug my hat back off her head and set it on mine. With one hand on her lower back, I open the front door with the other and lead her to my truck.

Heading off for the only first date that has mattered in years. The kind that makes a man hope for more.

A change of season.

A change of heart.

THE MILTONS ARE old money in our community, and their home sits up on a ridge that has a clear view of downtown Sterling Falls, which consists of two cross streets, one stoplight, and a town green space. Their personal property is more like a compound, with a large main house mansion, and several smaller homes on the land, plus a giant barn that's been renovated and used as more of a gathering place than a shelter for animals. All Milton County residents are welcome to rent the space for weddings, parties, and more.

"I could never imagine being that settled, so settled that an entire mountain was named after my family," Taxi says, reminding me of how unsettled she can be.

I haven't missed how Taxi fidgets sometimes. We'll be at her aunt's, dinner finished, the day almost over, but her knee will be bouncing, or her fingers twisting together, like she needs to move, needs to do something. Needs to be more creative than just cooking and cleaning and playing chauffeur to her aunt and Simon.

"One reason Em and I were meeting the other night is the heightened security needed for the dance," I explain.

Taxi wasn't initially thrilled to find me having dinner with Emerson, and it was a good lesson in miscommunication. I haven't had to explain myself to anyone in years, but if I want Taxi to feel comfortable with who I am, what I do in this town, I need to be more open about my position.

"Everything okay?" she asks, concern etched in her voice.

"Just your typical small-town stuff."

When we arrive, the gravel lot near the barn is full, and a grassy area has been designated for parking overflow. I park my truck along the outer edge.

"I'm not on call tonight, but you never know when there might be an emergency."

Taxi's gaze falls to my forearm, where my sleeves are rolled up. The stitches have been removed, and I'll have a small scar if I don't keep up with the ointment the doctors prescribed.

"Always Superman," she teases, but underneath the cheerful tone is hesitation. A continued hint of wariness. Whether that's about my position or her fear of me getting hurt on the job, I can't be certain.

"Can't really turn it off." I shrug, making light of my job when I take it very seriously, which is why I agreed to meet with Emerson the other night. She's had an issue and the department is keeping an eye on the situation.

Once I hop out of the truck, I round to Taxi's side and help her out as well. She instantly loops her arm in mine, and we walk across the grass toward the barn that's lit up like Times Square, only the glow coming out of this space is one solid halo-yellow tone, giving it an ethereal appearance. Like something magical rests inside the old structure that's weathered on the outside and newly restored inside.

"How are we playing this out tonight?" I ask, knowing Taxi is hesitant about our relationship. We haven't exactly been discreet in front of Trudy and Simon, nor my family, and this space is public. This date matters to me.

"Playing what out?"

"Us."

Taxi stops short, forcing me to spin and face her.

"What do you mean?" Her brows pinch like she doesn't understand me.

I might be a little overtrained from my experience with Emerson, which isn't exactly fair to lay on Taxi. I want to shout to that barn rooftop this woman is with me, but I also want to respect any boundaries Taxi has this evening.

"Well, you said you wanted to put us on pause. But I . . ." I scratch under my chin, feeling like I'm already turning our fun date into something heavy. "You know what, never mind. I'll just follow your lead."

Taxi continues to stare at me, those silvery eyes reflective in the barn lights behind me.

"I hate that I said that. Hate that you think you have to play a role with me. I don't want any restrictions on us."

"I don't want restrictions either," I admit. I want to be free to express myself with her. To be open around others about how I feel about her.

"I don't want anyone doubting who I am to you or what we are," she says, her voice ripe with determination.

"Oh." My brows lift. "And who are you to me?"

"Shouldn't you be telling me?" She holds her head higher, eyes focused on me, like she's daring me to speak.

No restrictions. No holding back.

"You're everything I've been wishing for and everything I never thought I'd have."

Taxi stares at me, eyes still. I don't think she even blinks, then her gaze softens and her shoulders relax.

"Stone." Her hand comes to her belly. "You can't say something to me like that without it meaning something."

I step closer to her, brushing her hair around her ear and running my knuckles along the side of her neck.

"It does mean something to me, because you mean something to me." My shoulders fall a little, and I lean toward her. "I don't have much to offer you, Taxi. A small town. A big family. Devotion." I cover my heart with my hand.

I, Stone Sylver, do solemnly swear to serve and protect you . . . to honor and respect you . . .

"And I'll take whatever you're willing to give me."

Taxi's hand comes to my chest, where my heart is racing within it.

"We can be Samson and Delilah. Superman and Lois Lane. Blue aliens and their conquest."

She snorts, shaking her head. "I don't think you're ever going to forget that, are you?"

"Never gonna forget a beautiful woman jabbing me in the chest with a book and stealing my breath from the moment I saw her."

Taxi shakes her head again, dipping her eyes. "I'll never forget you either."

She rubs at her chin, and I chuckle, remembering how we bumped heads.

"Tonight, I'd just like us to be Stone and Taxi. On a date."

"I'd like that too," she says, stepping closer to me, running her hands up my chest and over my shoulders. "Just be us tonight."

I smile wide, unable to help myself. "Just be us."

She tips up on her toes and kisses me, soft and sweet, and shredding my resolve. I grip her hips and tug her closer, deepening the kiss before reminding myself I don't want to get carried away with her.

Not yet.

"Just to be clear," she says, pulling away and toying with the snaps on my shirt before meeting my eyes. "You're all I've been waiting for as well. And it scares me."

Panic takes me by the throat. "Enough to run?"

She slowly shakes her head, lowering her gaze again. Her voice softens. "Enough to stay."

One minute, my stomach is plummeting to my toes, and the next, my heart is leaping to my throat.

"Yeah?' I question, excitement having me in a chokehold. Hope wrestling within me.

"Yeah." She chews her lower lip, and I use my thumb to snag it free.

Then I'm kissing her again, pouring all my hope into the possibility.

Taxi might stay.

For good.

37

———

[Taxi]

Stone nearly lifts me off my feet. With his hands around my lower back and his mouth on me, I'm on my tiptoes once again, feeling light, feeling airy, almost giddy. He's so playful tonight, so carefree and honest.

Everything he's wished for.

Everything he never thought he'd have.

Every word was the same as my hopes, and all I hear now is the rushing of my blood and the hammering of my heart.

He wants me. He wants me to stay.

I hate that he questioned what we are, who we should be, and as much as I no longer feel threatened by Emerson Milton, I'm a little angry on Stone's behalf that he was used like that. As arm candy, as a plaything. Not sexually, just publicly.

Stone deserves happiness, and I want that happiness to be me.

"Now we're really making a statement," he teases, pulling

his lips from mine and placing me back on my feet, but I stumble on the uneven grass. Could also be because my knees tremble a little bit, my heart beating off kilter.

Stone Sylver has that effect on me.

"Giddy up," I tease, tugging his hat from his head one more time.

Save the horse, ride the sheriff.

I didn't think he was telling me the full truth about parking his truck on the edge of the lot, nor about the small-town stuff he'd been discussing with Emerson the other night, like heightened security, but I didn't pry. If Stone wanted to share sheriff business, I'd listen, but I also sense his hesitation to share that part of him with me, because of him. Because he knows how I feel about the law in general.

And now, I hope he knows how I feel about him.

He makes me want to stay. And it does scare me. Not enough to run, but enough to dig in my heels and plant in one place.

But tonight, I want my date, just like him, so I loop my arm back through his, and we approach the barn, with its sliding doors wide open on each side of the entrance. The place looks like Pandora's box, a warm yellow glow beaming out of the opening. A hint of magic and mystic inside.

The outside of the structure remains rustic and worn, while the inside is an explosion of light pine, like new construction happened within the aging confines.

Support beams and columns hold small light bulbs on wires, giving the place the country ambiance it deserves. Speakers are tucked into corners, and a live band plays on a raised platform. Completing the atmosphere are hay bales in corners as decoration and lined against the wall for seating. A bar runs the length of one wall, minus stools, allowing for standing room only.

"It looks like a Hallmark movie set," I whisper a little in awe. "Hallmark on steroids."

To my surprise, the female singer with the band starts singing about Texas, her voice throaty and rich, sounding exactly like Beyonce, while she cantors her tune.

I let out a little squeak of excitement and break into the trendy line dance associated with "Texas Hold 'Em".

Stone stands beside me a second, a smirk on his face as I bounce to the left and take one step to the right, but when the song mentions only wanting to slow dance with her partner, Stone shocks me.

His hand grabs mine, and I'm twirling underneath his arm. Spun away from him and then tugged back, lining us up hip to hip, my back to his chest. He dips his knee, and my body follows his lead, as we rock right then left. His arm is tightly secured around my chest.

We move like we've always been dance partners.

Like a couple who enjoyed a quiet connection in an empty bar once upon a time, and now we've landed here. In a crowded bar, but still acting like we only see each other.

Feeling as light as bubbles in champagne, I giggle as we finish the dance. Stone is a bit more rigid, less fluid than me. Stone and Taxi. We make excellent dance partners.

When the song ends, I'm still feeling a little high and lean heavily into Stone's chest. "That was fun."

He chuckles, a little breathless himself. "Sure was." He gives me that sheepish smile I've grown to love.

Love? Is it really possible? Falling for him might be one of the easiest things I could ever do, and that scares me, like I told him. But that fear isn't causing me to run, like he thought I might before we entered the barn, when panic danced in his blue eyes.

That buzzing sense of fear has me a little excited about possibilities. About the next season in my life. About him.

"Drink?" Stone asks, nodding toward the long length of the bar not yet crowded by the dance attendees.

"Absolutely," I say, looping my arm with his once again, making it known to anyone who questions it that I'm with him. He is mine. And I've never laid claim to anyone in my life before.

When we reach the bar, Stone quickly makes eye contact with the bartender and points at me to place my order.

"Whiskey sour," I say, wanting something sweet to match this dizzying sensation inside me. A warm hum. A crackling buzz. Just an all-over good feeling.

Stone orders a whiskey neat, then nudges my shoulder as we both lean against the bar. "Where'd you learn to dance like that?"

"Where did you?" I chuckle.

"You've seen the dance competitions between my nieces and nephew," Stone reminds me. "Zelle likes to rope me in, forcing me to learn the latest TikTok trend."

"Oh, she forces you?" I tease, leaning into his arm near mine and staring at him over my shoulder. "She's what . . . ten years old?"

"She's eleven. And persuasive." He smiles fondly. His nieces mean the world to him. Hell, his entire family means everything to me. He's told me such, but I see it too in every sheepish grin and warm hug. He'd lay down his life for his family. In some ways, he already has.

Devoted. What a heady thought that he could be that devoted to me?

"What other dances has Zelle wrangled you to learn?" I ask, curious about more.

"A man can't give away all his secrets," he teases, wiggling his thick brows.

But I want them. I want all of him.

Our drinks are delivered quickly and Stone salutes me. "To the prettiest woman in the room."

My cheeks heat, and I tap my glass against his, taking a sip of my drink as a snide, mountain-drawling voice comes from behind us.

"Well, that was some display."

Stone and I both twist to see Emory Milton standing with Aunt Trudy beside her.

Trudy looks surprisingly well, but I know she'll tire easily. She was rather excited to attend the dance, needing to get out of her house as much as I've needed to lately. She isn't used to being cooped up any more than me, even if her travels only take her around this small town. Trudy misses her work as a real estate agent.

"Emory," Trudy snarls under her breath at her short, blond-bobbed friend.

As witness to their friendship, one I still don't understand, I've seen these two women in action. One poised and polished, and insisting on respect, while the other grounds the first, reminding her she's as fallible and mortal as the rest of us.

"What?" Emory accentuates that drawl, like she's from the deeper South, but also like she's a teenager pretending she doesn't know what she's saying.

"You look beautiful, Tallulah," Trudy addresses me, ignoring her friend. "You do too, Stone."

Trudy has become a lot bolder with her compliments, flirting with Stone being a big surprise. Then again, teasing him is too easy, especially when the apples of his cheeks pinken, that warm color spreading to the tips of his ears.

"He sure does look fine. Just like his daddy always did," Emory states.

Emory's comment startles me and I glance at Stone, taking in the sudden stiffness in his shoulders. His chin rises a little higher. He doesn't like the intended compliment, and I understand why in many ways. Stone doesn't want to be associated with a man who lost his heart and then exorcised that ache on his children.

He's a forgiving man, but not a forgetting one. He's better than me on so many levels.

"Mrs. Milton," he addresses her, polite and contained, like I've seen him on occasion. He's courteous, dipping his hat in acknowledgement, but the edge in his jaw says he's offering his actions out of propriety, not earned respect. He's a gentleman, but he isn't blind to this older woman's behavior.

Stone leans toward Trudy next, easily offering her a kiss on the cheek, almost like tacking up a sign about the distinction between the two women. One he tolerates, the other he adores.

My heart expands in my chest when I consider how good he's been to Trudy over the years. Both Stone and Judd have taken care of her, when I should have been more present.

This woman has raised me. What have I done to deserve her? What have I done to show her how important she is to me?

"Now, you know you can call me Emory." Emory's voice simpers, cutting into my thoughts. "I'm practically a second mama to you."

Emory lays her hand on Stone's forearm, and I see red. A deep crimson color, blinding my vision for a second. Stone's hand comes to my back, running up my spine and squeezing at my exposed nape. Maybe he's touching me to steady himself, or hold me back before I pounce on this old lady.

"I was almost your mother-in—"

"Emory Aloysius Milton." Trudy hisses, shaking her head and *tsking*. I know that tone. I know that head shake. Trudy is not pleased.

Emory's hand leaves Stone's arm and comes to her throat, clutching at a set of pearls.

Pearls? At a barn dance.

"Did you just middle name me?" Emory asks Trudy, like a petulant teen.

Trudy glances at me and rolls her eyes before fixing me with a stare. A warning not to listen to Emory Milton.

I know the truth. Apparently, Emory hasn't gotten the memo.

To further prove *my* point, Emory continues. "Emerson is here tonight." She strains her neck, twisting her head side to side, as if looking for Emerson will make her appear out of thin air.

I return an eye roll to Trudy, while Stone gently tugs me by my nape into his chest.

Again, not certain if I'm shielding him, or he's toggling me in place before I strangle my aunt's friend.

"So is half the town," Trudy grumbles toward Emory.

Those two really do play off each other, like some poorly written comedy act.

"Yes, but Emerson and Stone are—"

"Just friends," Stone interjects over Emory, his tone suggesting he's done with this charade. Authority rings in that quiet tenor, enough that Emory straightens and Trudy fights a smile. I lift my drink, taking another sip to disguise my own grin.

He squeezes the back of my neck. "Now, ladies, if you'll excuse me. I'm going to dance with my date again."

The gentle pressure on my nape has me turning my head and looking up at him, meeting the sparkle in his blue eyes and the soft curl of his mouth.

His date. That's me. Prettiest girl in the room, he said. Everything he's waited for.

We leave our drinks on the bar as Stone takes my hand and leads me back to the dance floor. He's still a little stiff, tense maybe.

"You okay?" I ask him.

He glances down at me. With his arm around my back and his hand holding mine near his chest, we mirror the position we once had back in Tennessee.

How time has passed. How much of it I've lost by not being with him.

Still, I'm here now, and his gaze is fixated on me.

"You know better than to listen to the BS, right?"

"I know," I offer him a confident smile. Because I know him.

His mouth is slowly twitching upward when he stumbles toward me, forcing me backward a step.

Stone turns his head, holding tighter to me, while addressing the person behind him.

"What the—"

Sharp feminine laughter coming from Stone's sister cuts off his sudden irritation.

"She made me do it." Stone glances from his giggling sister to the man holding her in his arms.

"What are you, thirteen again?" Stone bristles a little bit, shuddering almost as a thought occurs to him.

I understand there's an age gap between Cortland and Vale. One Stone struggles to ignore, knowing Cort once changed Vale's diapers. I shiver a little at the thought as well.

Cort narrows his eyes at Stone's sharp tone, and Vale breaks out of her partner's dance hold.

"Easy there, cowboy big brother," she teases, her eyes lifting to the hat on Stone's head. "Are you trying to steal the title from Ford?"

Stone stares at his sister, blinking a second, before a low snort leaves him.

I can only surmise Vale means the playful nickname Cadence has for their brother. His wife is full of irony as she's the country singer and he was a professional baseball player. I haven't seen a hint that Ford is a cowboy at heart.

Other irony in the hat-wearing situation . . . Cortland is wearing a similar cowboy hat, but in black suede.

"You okay?" Cort asks Stone, sensing something in his old friend.

I glance from one man to another, knowing their history. The pain still lingering inside Stone. The sense of loss possibly deeper than the betrayal.

"Why wouldn't I be?" Stone snaps back, exhaling deeply afterward, mustering patience I sense he's struggling to find.

With my hand still in his, I squeeze, drawing his attention to me. Suddenly, I'm feeling very protective of him, wanting to wrap my arm around him and get him the hell out of here. Or step in front of Stone and shield him from whatever he's feeling in Cortland's presence.

Instead, Vale has her arm tucked into Stone's, and she's practically dragging him off the dance floor.

He glances back at me, not wanting to make any more of a scene than his sister is already making.

Cortland and I remain on the dance floor another second.

"If they break into a Ross and Rachel dance montage, I'm out of here," I mutter, hoping to lessen the tension, despite the irritation brewing in me.

Cort snorts, getting the joke about siblings on the popular show *Friends*.

I turn toward him. "And if you hurt him again, I'll be the wrath of that damn monkey."

Cort assesses me a moment before understanding, remembering that annoying pet Ross once had on the show. He dips his head, acknowledging my warning.

I don't let anyone mess with mine.

And Stone Sylver belongs with me.

38

———

[Stone]

As my sister drags me toward the bar, I glance over my shoulder at Taxi who gives me a wary look.

"Let's grab a drink," Vale mutters, pulling my attention back to her.

"I already had one," I tell her, because I drink responsibly and I planned to sweat out the alcohol by *dancing with my date*.

An angry vibe that rarely exists inside me is tickling over my skin. First Emory and her nonsense. Now this.

"What is going on with you?" Vale asks once we reach the bar, pulled away from our respective dates.

I sigh and glance back toward Taxi and Cortland, who remain on the dance floor another second, facing one another.

"Nothing," I lie, uncertain why I'm so worked up, but not taking my gaze off Taxi and Cort.

"Stone," she groans.

"Vale." I force my gaze away from my girl and stare at my

sister. I've missed Vale, but I have not missed these moments when she tries to mother me, even though I'm twelve years *older* than her.

"How's Hudson?" I ask, leaning one arm on the bar and glancing back toward that dance floor where Taxi's fists are clenched at her side. Her gaze narrowed on Cortland.

"Don't deflect," Vale demands. Out of the corner of my eye, I see her hands go to her hips.

"What was with the sharp tone toward Cort?"

"Vale," I groan, scrubbing a hand down my face. Cortland is the last person I want to discuss right now.

"You know he's concerned about you," she continues.

I tip back my head. I do not want to hear these things. Not now. Not tonight. I drop my head and glance back at Taxi. My heart hammers harder for some reason.

Does Cortland want her? It shouldn't be the first thing I think. He's engaged. To. My. Sister. But he stole a woman from me once and I'll be damned if he tries to steal Taxi.

While the thought further rattles me, I quickly shake it away, especially when Taxi turns in my direction, meets my eyes, and strolls toward me. Like she's tethered on a string, pulled in my direction. Roped and lassoed. It's how my heart feels when she looks at me like she is right now.

Like she's here for me. She's mine.

While I still have mixed feelings about Cortland Haven, I'm trying to give him the benefit of the doubt, which means believing he wouldn't cheat on my sister, wouldn't desire another man's girl. I can't be held accountable for my actions if he did it again.

And I'm confident in Taxi, and the way she's moving toward me.

I'm her choice.

"You know when you aren't your stoic self, giving off brooding alpha vibes, and interfering in all our lives—"

Whipping my attention back to Vale, I interject, "I don't interfere."

I let Judd fight until the others wanted to stage an intervention.

I let Knox run away when I wanted him to stay and seek counseling.

I watched Ford fulfill his dreams, and Sebastian fail before he picked himself up.

And I don't brood, or give off alpha, or even act stoic.

"This . . ." Vale points at my face. "Looks good on you."

Slowly, my forehead loosens and my shoulders lower. I lean more heavily into the bar beneath my arm, like it's holding me upright.

"What looks good on me?" I spare a quick glance back at Taxi, who is almost in front of me, Cortland trailing behind her

"Happiness," Vale states.

I don't pull my focus from Taxi. The concern in her eyes questioning. Her smile is tight but encouraging. She's worried about me. Because she cares about me.

"I'm always happy," I quip, keeping my gaze on Taxi until she's near enough I can stand upright and reach out my hand. Which she readily takes, stepping into my side, tucking herself against me, like it's where she belongs. Like it's where she's always wanted to be.

You're all I've been waiting for, too.

Cort snorts, and my gaze leaps to him again. I stare at him, trying to give myself another second before I react. He slips his arm around my sister and pulls her in front of him, wrapping his arm over her chest, like a shield. Whether he's using her to protect himself, or he's holding her in a way to keep her safe, I can never tell, but he knows I won't go through her to get to him.

"What do you know, dickhead?" I'm not much for insults, having heard them too often from my dad, but Cort started the dickhead thing a year ago, and we often sling it at one another under our breaths.

My question is in response to his snort, a knowing sniff, like he knows anything about me now and the person I am.

Taxi shifts under my arm, gaping up at me. Vale lowers her gaze and shakes her head.

"I know . . ." Cortland begins. "That loving a good woman, the *right* woman, can change a man."

Fuck, I hate when Cort says something smart, almost sweet about my sister. His comment is also a reminder of how bad Bailey turned out to be for both him and his son.

"Now, boys—"

"And Vale's right," Cort continues, cutting off my sister, keeping his gaze on me. "You look happy." He watches me, further assessing me. "You look good."

The compliment is strange to hear coming from him. I *am* happy, like I said, but I haven't always been. And I've never been as happy as I've been lately. Taxi is the reason for that feeling.

"I look good, huh? Want to date me?" The corner of my mouth twitches, and Taxi chuffs against me, tucking her head into my chest.

"I would, but I'm taken." Cort presses a kiss to the top of Vale's head while keeping his eyes on me.

"Yeah, well, I'm taken, too." And make no mistake, Taxi isn't going to belong with anyone else in this town.

"Good," Cort states, giving me a slow smile.

"Good," I counter, still sounding irritated.

Taxi glances between us.

Vale follows the same pattern before sighing. "How about you, Taxi? Are you good?"

"I'm good," she says, humor in her voice.

"Good. Now that we've established that we are all good, can we dance again?" Vale asks, impatience laces her tone, when she's the one who pulled me from dancing with my date in the first place.

"Sure, Little Bee," Cort says, using his nickname for her and standing taller, releasing her from his arm.

Vale surprises all of us by grabbing Taxi's hand and tugging her toward the dance floor.

"Come on, sister," Vale says, leaving Cort and me stunned for a moment.

Taxi glances over her shoulder at me, asking me with those eyes if I'm okay. She might be little but she's something fierce. A force I want by my side.

She's already tucked in my heart.

I nod, giving her a tense smile.

"I mean it, man," Cortland says beside me. "You deserve to be happy."

I pull my gaze from Taxi and stare at him. *He's damn right I do.* And the best way to make me happy is to get back to my date. Get back to this special night. Her and me. Us.

Leaving my focus on Cort for another second, I hesitate to clap him on the shoulder. An action once easily given and familiar between us. Hell, Cort has hugged me on several occasions a long, long time ago.

I've missed the friendship I once had. At times, I've convinced myself I only missed the idea of that relationship, but deep down, I know it's been him I've missed.

Cortland Haven. Best friend, cradle to college.

Giving in to the urge, I grip his shoulder. "Thanks." The word is simple.

Cort stares at me, gaze drifting only slightly to the hand on his shoulder before he relaxes a little bit. Just a smidge, suggesting he's been as tense around me as I've been around him.

And maybe, just maybe, he's missed me, too.

I know he's regretful. He's apologized. He's tried to atone in his own way. But maybe the thing I haven't seen is how much of a hole he's had in his life without me by his side.

He tips up his chin, acknowledging my gratitude.

"Now. How about we dance with our girls?"

We both glance toward the dance floor, where each of them is keeping a watchful eye on each of us.

Our girls.

Cort waves his hand toward them, and I lead us to the dance floor. Stepping up to Taxi, I set her back into the place where I want her to be.

In my arms.

39

[Taxi]

Hours later, Stone and I stumble out of the barn, drunk on dancing while exhausted from exertion.

As we're tripping over our feet and falling into one another, something out of the corner of my eyes catches my attention. A streak of blond hair just off the dark corner of the barn.

"Is that . . ." I narrow my eyes as the woman is pressed up against the exterior of the barn and then kissed by the person in front of her.

"Oh my God, that's—"

"Her secret," Stone interjects, running his arm over my shoulders and leading me toward his truck like there's nothing to see.

Like Emerson Milton, the town mayor, isn't getting kissed by the last person I'd expect to see with her.

As we continue to travel over the bumpy grass, I struggle

with what I just saw and reckon it with what I've known about Stone and Emerson's relationship.

I glance up at the man whose arm surrounds my shoulders, my heart softening even more for him.

He's been such a good friend to her. And I should have known from the first time he explained himself that he meant what he said. He was protecting her. Her secret.

When we finally reach Stone's truck, he helps me into the passenger seat, but before he closes the door, I reach for his shirt and tug him toward me, going in for a kiss I've been wanting to give him since we entered the dance.

He smiles against my mouth. "What's that for?"

"Just for you," I whisper, slowly pulling back. "Just for you being you."

He tilts his head, uncertain of my meaning, then he must decide it doesn't matter. Because he leans in to kiss me again.

"Been waiting all night to do that as well."

I sigh. He's so sweet.

Stone shuts my door and rounds the truck, hopping into his seat. He starts the engine with the press of a button, then turns toward me. "Got a curfew?"

He's so cute. "Little old for curfews."

Aunt Trudy hasn't put any parameters on my stay at her house. The self-imposed rule of being around her every second falls on me, but Trudy is nearly a month out from her heart attack. The doctors say she's a modern miracle, and she'll be starting therapy soon.

Only a few more weeks, Aunt Trudy told me. I won't *need* to stay any longer.

The words were only a tease from Trudy. Meaning nothing more than I wouldn't have to linger. She knows I have the itch to paint and the need to use my gift for communities. That part of me is ingrained into who I am.

Still, what if I wanted to stay? What if I wanted Trudy and Simon, and Stone, to be a new community for me? A family.

With all our broken pieces, we could be a whole.

I glance over at Stone as he drives us away from the dance.

He seemed genuinely excited earlier this evening when I mentioned staying.

Sister, Vale had called me earlier. And I consider Genie and Enya, and all the rest of the girls. How welcoming they've been. How easily they've pulled me in, considering me one of them.

Sisters. I have my own, and yet who would ever turn down more? Who could walk away from the friendships they are offering me?

With my eyes still on him, I question—how could I leave this man?

"Can you spend the night, then?" Stone asks, oblivious to my thoughts as we barrel over the mountain road.

"Maybe we should make it midnight?" I wrinkle my nose, still concerned for Trudy's well-being. She'd left the dance shortly after we saw her with Emory. She'll be asleep early, as everything still zaps her energy. Still, I don't like to leave her overnight.

He smiles as he reaches over for my hand and pulls it to his lap. "Midnight it is, Cinderella."

Midnight. Which means we still have a little while before the clock strikes the end of another day.

And I realize Stone isn't driving toward Trudy's home, but his own. Except, once he pulls onto the gravel driveway, he continues past the house, driving us deeper into the darkness behind it.

"Where are we going?" I question as Stone slows his speed, and the truck bounces over the rugged two-tire lane that looks rarely traveled.

"I'm the sheriff, so while I know all the places people make out, I can't get caught in them." He lifts my hand and kisses the back of it. "Plus, this is really the best place in town."

"To make out," I confirm.

He chuckles, resting my hand back on his thigh. "Am I getting ahead of myself?" His voice is playful, while hesitant. He won't press for anything I don't want from him.

"Hey, don't you remember? I'm the one who suggested a quickie earlier." Because I'm not stupid. Stone Sylver is one fine man, and I already know how he can wield his body against mine. I've missed him since last Sunday afternoon. The light touches and intense kisses have happened all week, but I still long for more. Joining us together, sleeping in his arms.

"Don't want to be quick with you, Taxi," he admits, slowing to a stop.

Jesus. This man.

He sets the truck in Park. He turns toward me, and I catch the wiggle of his brows in the dashboard lights. "Give me two seconds."

He pushes open his door and reaches behind the driver's seat. Tossing a blanket over his shoulder, he also picks up a small reusable bag.

"Don't peek," he warns, teasingly pointing a finger at me. "Just look through the windshield a second. Count the stars." He points toward the glass.

"What stars?" I ask, but as soon as I gaze forward, he reaches forward and shuts off the ignition, immersing us in darkness.

And I'm mesmerized by the bright display of pinpricks that look like perfectly placed dots, decorating the sky. While science can explain how stars exist, they look hung from a black curtain and the beautiful backdrop to a romantic night.

When Stone opens my door, I'm startled only because I'd been concentrating so hard.

"Cinderella." He holds out his hand, and I set mine in his to slide off my seat. My legs are still a bit shaky from all the dancing we did, so I say, "I don't think I can dance any—"

My breath hitches as I catch a glimpse of the truck bed.

"Stone," I whisper.

The rim of the truck bed, along with the inside edges, are lined with lit candles. A thick blanket is spread down the center with pillows tucked against the storage box near the cab.

Silently, Stone leads me to the tailgate because I'm still too stunned by the setting to speak. He helps me up and follows after me. I slowly spin, taking in the low votives and tall hurricanes, each flame dancing in the slight breeze of the cool evening.

Stone stands behind me. "Take a seat." His quiet, rugged voice sends additional goosebumps over my skin. Pleasant prickles of excitement.

"It's so beautiful," I whisper, afraid to disturb the low flames.

"So are you," he says.

"Stone." My breath catches.

He slides his hand down my arm, lowering himself to sit. Gently tugging at my wrist, I follow his lead, folding down beside him, still in awe of my surroundings. The low flickers. The dark sky. The man next to me.

"Where did you have all this?" I question.

Stone has fallen to his back, one hand behind his head, the other on the notch of my waist. He's taken off his hat and set it on the slim storage box behind his head. He knocks on the box, giving the answer to my question. The box shortens the space, so Stone's feet stretch onto the tailgate, where he crosses his ankles.

"Come here, baby," he quietly commands.

Snuggling in next to him, I shiver despite the heat of him.

"Cold?"

"No." Overwhelmed.

All of this is so unexpected. The night. The dance. Him.

He's sturdy and kind; confident and sweet. Romantic. Not to mention, a human heater and I cuddle closer, hitching my leg over his.

We remain quiet, both looking up at the stars.

Make a wish, my mama used to say. With thousands of stars, and hundreds of dreams, which star was I supposed to wish on? What dream should I ask for? Wasn't it a shooting star you wished upon? The ones moving across the sky.

For thousands of years those stars have existed, ever moving but never really falling out of place. Gravity keeps them aligned somehow.

Could Stone be my gravity? Allowing me to still move at my own speed but still have a sun to center myself around?

"Do you know how to read them?" I quietly ask, like I'll break the silent spell around us, although the night is hardly devoid of noise. The rustle of the tall autumn grass in the breeze. The soft hum of crickets despite the cooling temperature. Even the flickering flames seem to whisper.

"Not as versed as I once was, but I recognize a few." Stone points toward the sky. "See that one that makes an M or a W."

I do not see it, but I keep looking.

Always searching.

"That's Cassiopeia. The seated queen of the heavens."

I hum in response. The sound of his voice is soothing, even if I don't see what he sees.

Always chasing.

"And that one there, that looks kind of like a strung bow with an arrow, is the Swan." He points toward another pattern, pausing a second. "Zeus in disguise."

I settle into letting him quietly point out a few more constellations that I still don't see.

Always waiting.

His heart is a slow drumbeat beneath my ear, and my hand rests on his belly. He aimlessly rubs his fingers along my arm.

What if I stopped spinning like the stars? Would I fall from the sky? Would I burn out my glow? Or would I become something softer, quieter, more settled?

Still.

Between the calm sound of Stone's voice and the heat of his body against mine, I sort of melt into the night. Not sleepy or drowsy, just relaxed, just comfortable, just . . . still.

A girl could get used to this.

When I realize Stone is no longer speaking, I break the silence with a little lie. "You're an excellent teacher."

"And you're not a great liar." He chuckles against me and presses a kiss to my temple. He knows me so well.

"What are you drawing?" he asks.

"What?" I lift my head and he taps the back of my restless hand. I rest my cheek on his chest again. "Oh." I hadn't realized my fingers had been moving over his chest. Outlining something, filling it in with imaginary color.

"I don't know," I admit.

"Always moving," he whispers, tugging me tighter to him.

"Meaning?" I say too defensively and clear my throat.

"I've seen your knees bouncing and your fingers twisting. You're like one of those stars, Taxi, but out of her orbit. You're holding yourself in place, but your body senses the need to move. Or is it your heart?" His voice is low. "Do you feel like it's time to go?"

To leave a place.

"I need to paint," I admit, my voice a little too loud.

He pulls back, glancing at me, eyeing me. "You need to create." He stares at me a long moment, as if he might get it. Or at least he's trying to understand.

I nod, almost sheepishly, almost embarrassingly, when I'm

not ashamed of who I am in the least. I'm an artist, and I need a canvas to let out all the emotions swirling inside me.

The red of passion, and the blue of peace. The yellow of happiness, and the green of my addiction to this man. Basic colors. Basic needs. A kaleidoscope of want.

Eventually, Stone hugs me tighter, setting his lips to my head and lingering there.

When the silence goes on too long, and his lips don't move, I take action. Turning my head, meeting his eyes, I lean in and kiss him. Needing the red and blue, yellow and green of him, filling in the outline of me.

The kiss stays slow at first, deliberate as we connect in soft sips and teasing tugs. But as we move into something deeper, desperation flares inside me. Broad strokes of passionate purple and vivid orange merge together, driving my tongue to seek his.

Within minutes, we're making out as he suggested. Kissing with fervor. Our lips remain locked, hands only subtly moving. His fingers in my hair. Mine around his neck. But our bodies roll into one another, seeking, chasing.

Legs skim along legs. Belly meets belly. My breasts crush to his chest. And still, I'm not close enough.

"Stone," I whimper.

"I'm here," he says, kissing along my jaw and down my neck, and I tip back my head, giving him full access to me.

He sips along the column of my throat and ticklishly licks along my collarbone. I palm the side of his face, feel the bristly scratch of his stubble. His mustache scrubs playfully at my skin, along his trail of kisses.

"We need to go slow," he says into my flesh as he moves lower on my body. "The candles."

I glance at the wall of them along the edge of the truck bed. It would take a force to jostle this sturdy truck, and yet I have no doubt reckless motion back here could topple a few of them.

"Fire hazard," he mutters, moving toward my breasts.

He's a fire hazard.

I sigh as he reaches the deep V of my dress, where a few buttons have come unbuttoned. The calico print isn't something I'd typically wear, but it fit the theme. Barn dance. Small town. Stay still.

A blaze of desire rips up my center as Stone nuzzles my breasts, and I press at him, pushing him to his back and climbing over his lap.

My dress rides up my thighs and Stone's warm hands cover my bare knees, skimming up my legs, forcing my dress slightly higher. He strokes back in the opposite direction, cupping my knees again.

"Queen of the stars," he whispers, looking at me, like I've placed them all in the heavens.

With my hands on his chest, I paint over him again, the image unclear. Just a rough outline of dancing fingers before I tug at the two halves of his shirt, forcefully opening it so I can run my fingers through that coarse hair, feel the heat of his skin, take comfort in the strength of his chest.

"Be gentle with me, Taxi." His voice is tight, quiet, serious while sweet. The underlying tone says so much more.

"I will be," I promise.

I, Tallulah Alexander, do solemnly swear to embrace your spirit, to be tender and kind. To take my time.

I unclasp his belt, undo the buttons, and lower the zipper, giving the hard bulge in his pants some relief.

My mouth waters with the possibilities of what this man could do for me. And it isn't only the physical pleasure I know he'll give me. It's the heart-stopping, breath-stealing reality that I could love him.

His gentlemanly ways and his patience. His low voice, sweet smile, and quiet awkwardness.

I lean forward, caging in his head with my braced arms. My

hair flops forward on my head, the ponytail suddenly feeling too tight, too confining.

"I don't know where to start." I sound like he did when we first stripped each other. When clothes were removed and I felt bare to him in so many ways.

Stone taps his lips. "Start here."

I stare at his mouth for a second, realizing his entire body is a map. Uncharted territory for me. Again, not just the physical, but this sensation of being close to him, *wanting* him.

So, I start with his lips, then move to his throat, dragging my body down his.

"Taxi," he groans, as I pepper his chest with kisses and suck harder at the space just above his hip, before running my nose along that trail that leads lower and lower, beneath his waistband.

With his pants already loosened, and his shirt opened, I tug the remainder of the material free from his jeans, running my palm over his flesh, mapping out the terrain.

The curve of his hip, the flat of his belly, the scratch of his hair.

In this half-undressed state, he's almost as sexy as if he were fully unclothed. Somehow, he looks more seductive. More tempting.

Pure kryptonite.

I reach for the edge of his jeans, hooking my fingers into his boxer briefs as well, and he lifts his hips for me to tug everything lower, until his dick is free. Free to be admired and explored.

When I wrap my hand around the thickness, fisting it with a tight grip, Stone groans.

His eyes roll back a second and his head tips as well.

"Taxi." My name is a plea, a prayer, a need. *For me.*

Queen of the stars? I don't need it. I'm queen of this moment. This man is giving me all the power.

I lower for him, teasing the tip with the edge of my tongue before opening wide without more preamble. His stomach flinches, and he hitches upward slightly, hips thrusting.

"Fuck," he mutters, cupping the side of my head with one hand. "Easy, baby."

I don't know how to go easy with him. He's so hard, and I want him too much.

I draw up his length, then slip back as far as I can take him, until he stops me.

He cups my chin. "Inside of you again."

Our eyes lock, mine scanning up the span of his body. Slowly, I drag my lips up him and pop off the end.

Our minds are on the same scene. Him behind me, buried inside me, filling me up.

Everything happened so fast, and yet I wouldn't change a thing. We need to get that moment out of the way in order to prolong this one.

I shrug off my leather jacket.

"Panties off," he demands, watching me with lust-drunk eyes, brightened by the flickering light around us.

I toss away the jacket and reach to push my panty to the side.

"Take them off," he demands, watching me with lusty eyes, lit by the numerous candles surrounding us.

Scrambling to my feet, I stand, straddling his body with spread legs. I lift my dress, as if I can discreetly remove them, slipping my hand beneath the material and shoving my underwear to my knees before I need to step aside to fully remove them.

I reach for my dress next.

"Keep it on. Unbutton the rest." Delicate buttons dip lower than my breast line, and I fold to my knees, straddling him, settling where I'm warm and wet directly over his solid length.

Stone hisses.

I continue to tease him, taking my time to undo each button, opening the bodice of the dress farther, exposing the strapless bra underneath.

With my dress open to my ribs, my soft heat against his hard length, Stone sits upright, digs his hand into the back of my ponytail, and cups my head, pulling me to him, kissing me firm and deep.

Hunger fills the kiss. Desperation to let go of that control he's mastered. A fight within him to remain slow and patient when the tension between us is so thick, so tight. So hot.

Stone tugs my ponytail holder, snapping it, and releasing my hair to tumble over my shoulders. He slips his hands inside the dress, wrapping around my body to fumble with the clasp of my bra. Removing it in a few snaps, he tugs it forward, releasing me from the confines.

With my dress open, braless and breasts free, he rolls down to the truck bed again, staring up at me as I straddle him.

"Breathless," he whispers, before placing his hand on my belly and sliding it up between the swells that ache for his touch. He cups one, and I gasp. Squeezing at the weight, I arch into his touch. His fingers firm, his thumb flicking over the hard, sensitive nub.

"Stone," I whimper, wanting more of him. More of this.

I rock over him, his length still nestled beneath me, where I'm slick and easily glide against him.

Stone watches me. His hand on my breast. Mine on his chest. Slipping along the thickness of him.

He tucks his other hand behind his head again, like he has all night to watch the show. Me gliding over him. Him squeezing me.

"Stone," I whimper again.

He smiles slowly, teasingly, removing his hand from my breast and walking it down my body. His other hand releases his head and works the skirt of my dress up my thighs. Both hands eventually land on my hips, lifting me the slightest bit over him.

My brows cinch, my eyes questioning him, until his hand slips beneath my dress, fingers disappearing but knowing their way to where I want him.

Two fingers enter me at once, and I suck in a breath.

"Too much?" he questions, stilling them.

"Too good," I answer.

His lips curl out of that pucker of concern into a full-blown grin.

With one hand bracing my hip, the other works his magic, sliding up and down inside of me, filling me. His thumb joins the mix, flickering over where I'm sensitive and slick, like the flames dancing around us.

I'm twisted up, spiraling like a climbing blaze.

"Stone." My breath hitches as I ride his fingers. I pitch forward, resting my hands on his belly, balancing on my shins, as I drag myself along his fingers.

My hair around me. My dress covers my thighs. My breasts spilling from the top of my bodice.

And I move like I'm a skilled horsewoman. Like I'd know the first thing about country living when I don't know a thing about cowboys.

I only know what this man does for me.

"Now," I grunt, needing this, needing something, as my belly flutters and my legs start to ache.

I need more. I need him. Inside me.

"Not yet. Come for me first."

Typically, I would hate commands like that one, but in that quiet tenor that's deep and rough and a little demanding, I acquiesce. Giving in to that spiral inside me, letting it snap and release, rushing rapidly through me.

I squeeze at the sides of his abs, digging my nails into his flesh as I arch my back, thrust down on his fingers, and scream into the night. "Fuck!"

I'm a banshee, reckless and wild, hair streaming in all directions. I'm a goddess in the stars, glowing and dancing among the heavens. I'm me, centered over this man. This incredible man, who has me undone in more ways than one.

Sticky release coats my inner thighs. I know what just happened to me, what he did to me, and I tug at my dress, whipping it over my head. I'm naked, other than my boots, and I reach for his hat on the box, setting it on my head. Living out a fantasy.

I shove at his shirt, forcing him to be as exposed as I feel, at least on the upper half of him.

Fisting his firmness, I balance on the tip only for a second. One painful beat where both our breaths catch, and time almost stands still, before I bring him into me, surrounding him, embracing him. Full to the hilt, the suddenness of the motion jostles the truck ever so slightly.

The candle flames flare, matching the rhythm in my chest.

A blip on a heart monitor. A beat I want to repeat again and again.

Stone grunts from the suddenness. He clutches my hips, squeezing at spots that feel permanently marked by him. Only his hands fit there. Then he's moving me, guiding me, up and down again, slower this time.

Patience.

The unspoken word whispers between us.

I follow his lead as we dance to a new song. One set by two heartbeats and ancient lyrics. The oldest dance in existence.

I try to make eye contact, but the intensity eventually feels like too much. Too intimate. Too real. I gaze where he enters my body instead, marveling at how well we fit.

And not just like this, but in so many other ways. Ways my brain cannot process in the moment. Instead, I give in to this one. This point in time when nothing else seems to matter.

Only him and me. Us.

"Fuck, I don't know if I can continue this slow," he eventually admits, his head lolls to the side. His eyes close with each tender surge.

He bucks a little sharper, deeper.

"Yeah," I whisper. Drawing out this connection is almost making the result happen faster.

He's so hard, and I'm so wet, and together we're making a mess.

I want to be messier.

I want the joy of sticking with this man and the fear of leaving him as a reason to stay.

I want what I've been waiting for my entire life. The one I might joke about in bars but search for in every new corner of the world, only to learn he's right here in the place I once called home.

Waiting.

Suddenly, I'm moving faster.

Chasing.

Gliding up and down his slick shaft, teasing us both with release, only to hug him back into my body again. Through the push and pull, we tease one another until I'm nearly galloping over him and he's following my pace.

Searching.

The candles are humming, vibrating against the metal of the truck. The flames dance in wicked flashes, and yet we can't stop.

"Stone," I call out, desperate to finish. To stop waiting, chasing, searching.

"Taxi," he grunts, my name a warning. He's close. He's almost there.

His hand comes to my lower belly, and his thumb stretches

to reach that sensitive point. He slams me down on his cock, letting loose inside me, nearly shouting as he pulses and jolts, marking me in a new way.

His release sparks mine, and I leap off the cliff with him. Not feeling so alone anymore, because he's holding my hand. He's holding me.

I catch a glimpse of my hand over his chest. Fingers splayed out like their own unique five-point star. A badge over his heart. And his hand is right over the back of mine, holding it in place on him.

I do solemnly swear . . .

The release in me rips apart any promise I could formulate. I have only one promise to make.

Stay.

I lean forward, cupping his jaw and planting my mouth over his, kissing him with all I have as I ride out the bliss. A jump without a parachute.

Only him.

Stone.

Eventually, I realize, we aren't kissing so much as just holding our mouths against one another, breathing in each other.

"Taxi, I—"

I kiss him again, swallowing whatever was unsaid, not wanting words in this moment.

Let me show you who I am.

He has.

40

[Stone]

Holy shit.

I blink, trying to make sense of what just happened.

We made love, I have no doubt about it. Yet I also realized I've never done what we just did. I can hardly explain it to myself. The way she moved. The way I responded. Following her lead and almost telling her—

A blaring bleat vibrates my phone against the storage box behind my head, and Taxi and I both flinch. She's collapsed on my chest, her hair wild and draped everywhere. My hand is flat on her back. I'm not certain I can move a limb.

I don't want to move.

But the annoying sound continues to rhythmically blast.

"What is that?" Taxi laughs, burying her face in my chest.

"I set an alarm, so I get the princess home before the carriage becomes a pumpkin."

She lifts her head, eyes bright with color but sated. "You're really up on your fairy tales."

I shrug. "I've got more nieces than nephews." Plus, I'd been reading fairy tales to Vale forever.

Slowly, Taxi peels herself off me.

Not yet, I want to shout. Just a few more minutes. But then I'll want a few more, and a few more. And she needs to go.

I tug up my pants as she reaches for her dress. With my pants in place, but not fastened, I take the dress from her, wanting to do the honors.

"Up," I nod for her arms to lift, and I spread the material to cover her. Sitting above me, breasts spilling from this dress, the skirt hitched to her hips, she was a fucking vision. A downright goddess.

She's still just as lovely as I take my time to tuck each one of the buttons through the holes. I love how innocent the dress looks, knowing the woman underneath is a queen.

I snapped her ponytail holder, so her hair remains a wild, dark halo around her head.

"Where's my bra?" She giggles, knowing I tossed it aside. I find it and stuff it in my back pocket.

She eyes me suspiciously but doesn't comment.

While she steps into her underwear, I hold out my hand to help steady her, then I put my shirt back on.

The air has cooled considerably. A few minutes ago, I wouldn't have noticed. I didn't feel a thing other than the snug fit of her around me. Her knees around my hips. Her hands on my chest. All Taxi. Only Taxi.

Together, we blow out the candles. The containers are too hot to stuff back in the larger storage box, so I set them in the original plastic container I had inside the truck chest and set the container at the edge of the tailgate once we are ready to drive Taxi home.

I'd really like to bring her to take her to my home, lay her down in my bed, and wrap around her, like I did that first week after she arrived. When she was put in my path again.

With her hand in mine, settled on my thigh, I drive her home, understanding her need to stick close to her aunt. At least for a little while longer.

When we get to Trudy's house, I step out of the truck and walk Taxi to the front door.

"I had a good time tonight." I sound lame. I had a phenomenal time. I didn't want it to end, but I'm not a man of words.

Her mouth slowly curls at the corner. "I had a good time, too." Her silver eyes flicker in the pale glow from the porch light.

Yeah, *good* doesn't describe the night for me either.

"So, how'd I do?" I ask next, like I'm a rating scale. "For a first date?" First one I've had in years. Might even be my last first date ever.

"First everything," Taxi whispers, and I reach for her jaw, cupping the edge of her face.

"First everything," I repeat. "Want to do it again?" Another date. Another night like this one.

"Again and again and again." With each repetition, her voice falls quieter.

"Good," I whisper, that damn word once more.

I decide to stop talking and just kiss her, soft and sweet, like a front porch kiss should be. But also achingly sad, because we're going to part for the night.

Suddenly, the porch light flickers on and off. On and off.

Taxi pulls back, glares at the light, and tucks her head into my chest. I watch the lights flip again.

"What the . . ."

"I might have told Trudy about your porch light scenario. She caught me swooning over you one night after you left."

"Swooning," I chuckle, still watching the lights blink.

"I'd fallen against the door, a little dazed after you kissed me one night."

I lean closer, curious. "Which night?"

"All of them," she whispers, but as the light flickers once more—on, off, on, off—Taxi grumbles. "Guess I better go. I wonder what Trudy is even doing up so late."

We made it here by midnight. Not a pumpkin in sight.

Suddenly, the front door opens, and a woman shouts, "Got you."

Taxi lets out a scream.

The woman behind the screen door screams.

Then Taxi is out of my arms and through the door, hugging the other woman, rocking her side to side.

"Jolene Amaryllis Wallace, what are you doing here?" Taxi addresses the woman I now realize is her youngest sister.

"It's a long story," Jolene says, blowing out a breath. She's just as beautiful as her sister but in a different way. More curves. Less curls.

Taxi glances back at me. "Jolene, this is Stone Sylver. Do you remember him?"

The younger woman holds out her hand. "Oh, I remember him. Had the biggest crush on you as a kid."

"What?" Taxi says, snapping her head in her sister's direction, practically growling.

"Thank you?" I hesitate, feeling my face heat.

"Stone and I were—"

"Just kissing on the front stoop," Jolene teases, leaning against the open front door and giving me a wink similar to her sister's.

"I was going to say coming home from the Founder's Day dance. How's Aunt Trudy?" Taxi glances around her sister like she expects her aunt to be nearby.

"She was asleep when I got here. Scared the bejesus out of me."

"You mean, you scared the bejesus out of her. You'll give her another heart attack," Taxi chides.

Jolene waves her hand like that isn't possible, and I smile at the scrunched nose and pursed lips she gives me. "Not Trudy. Her heart is too strong."

That's what we'd all like to think. That love makes our hearts strong enough to withstand anything, but we're only human. Other factors come into play where our bodies are concerned.

"Anyway, I'll let you get back to it," Jolene says, waving toward the front step but not making a move to close the front door or give Taxi and me more privacy.

Taxi looks at me, her expression apologetic.

"I'll call you tomorrow," I say, giving her a reassuring kiss on the cheek.

"Thank you," she says, before glancing at her sister, and then back at me. She mouths, *I'm sorry*.

She has nothing to apologize for and nothing to thank me for either.

I'm the grateful one tonight.

This evening has been . . . everything.

FOR THE NEXT WEEK, Taxi and I don't see much of each other. I'm focused on that case with the shoe that was found near the falls, a child who was still missing from the area. And Taxi takes extra time to spend with her sister.

But after our fourth phone call about Taxi and Jolene bickering over the littlest things, I suggested Taxi take a break and meet me for lunch. I've been working on something for her anyway, and I'm ready to share it with her.

We plan to meet at the diner for lunch. They serve the perfect grilled cheese with tomato soup.

As I'm early, I already have a seat in a booth toward the back when Taxi tosses herself on the bench seat across from me.

A sharp huff exits her, and I chuckle. "You alright?"

"Define alright. I'm always confused. Is it one word or two?"

I chuff. "What's wrong?" Jolene has been at the heart of Taxi's frustrations this week.

"If I thought taking care of Trudy was exhausting, now I have Jolene to contend with. And while living room campouts were fun as kids, they are *not* fun as adults."

Taxi goes into a long tirade about her sister and their fight over the use of the couch.

"Like I want to be couch surfing at my age. Playing eenie-meenie-miney-moe to see who gets that lumpy old thing."

She sighs heavily and waves a heavy hand. "I get it. We probably have unresolved issues from our childhood. Some psychology book somewhere has a case study about us."

"Really?" I ask, a bit surprised.

Taxi shakes her head. "I'm being dramatic. I'm learning from Jolene." She squints, looking out the window at her side.

"It's just . . . she's my sister. And I love her. I do." She glances back at me. "But she can just get under my skin."

I snort, knowing exactly what she means. Sebastian was never easy. Ford was so determined. Judd closed in on himself. Even Knox could be evasive. Only Clay and Vale were the open ones.

"And I try to be understanding." Her voice lowers. "Our mother is in jail. Killed their father." She whispers. "I only ever had Mama, but she took their daddy, too."

From what I remember, her sisters were pretty young when their dad died. I don't know how strong their memories of either parent might be. Vale certainly has none of our mother; Sebastian and Ford both admit their memories of her are weak.

Trudy and Carlton Wallace are the only parental figures

they've known, but that doesn't mean they aren't without their own personal trauma. Hurt and frustration that only they understand.

"We aren't close," Taxi admits. "But we do stay in touch. When we can. When we have cell service. *I* try to stay in touch with them."

She rolls her eyes. Apparently, this must be an excuse for a lack of communication. However, there are places that still don't have the best service.

And I understand again. Taxi wanted to keep her sisters close, maybe. Keep tabs on them. Make them feel like they have her. Whether that's to ease the unnecessary guilt she harbors or because she truly wants a relationship doesn't matter. It's most likely both.

"Ugh." Taxi leans forward and presses the heels of her hands against her eyes. "And I'm trying to be so good for Aunt Trudy." Her voice is thick; watery but resolute.

"Taxi," I say slowly. "Take a deep breath."

She keeps her eyes closed, elbows on the table, and blows harshly from her lips.

"Try again. A little slower." I slide my hand across the table, wanting her to take it. Wanting to comfort her some-how, ease her burden. Wanting her to know she doesn't have to feel alone, be alone. I'm here to shoulder what she'll give me.

When she still doesn't look at me or my hand, I breathe in, hold a second, and slowly release, willing her to follow my lead.

She tries again, but her breath is still choppy, eyes still shut. She swipes underneath one of them, and something in me cracks. I do not want to watch this strong, proud woman fall apart.

She's given up so much. Her art. Her work. And she's dedicated all her time to Trudy and Simon. I'm irritated that her sister blew into town only to upset Taxi.

Then again, sometimes it's the people closest to us that hurt the most.

I would know.

"It's so like Jolene to be missing for everything important and then waltz in at the nth hour and demand to be treated like she's a fucking savior."

"Taxi," I whisper, tapping the back of my hand on the top of the table. She lowers her hands from her face, one of them falling flat against my palm. I squeeze.

"Jolene's been to Africa to work with underprivileged young women. Jolene's been to Honduras to assist in some Doctors Without Borders program. Jolene, Jolene, *Jolene*," her voice sings.

I clear my throat, holding back from telling her how well she carries a tune.

"I'm sorry," she eventually mumbles, acknowledging my hand holding hers with a gentle squeeze. "You didn't ask me to lunch so I could lose my shit."

"I asked you to lunch so you could definitely lose your shit, if you needed to."

Taxi lifts her head and chuffs again. "What is wrong with you? Why do you have to be so amazing all the time? Can't you have a fault?"

I chuckle. "I'm certain I have many."

"Tell me one. Just one, so I can stop thinking you're perfect."

"Hey now . . ." I hold up my free hand, teasing her. "You can keep thinking I'm perfect all you'd like."

Slowly, she leans forward again, her smile not quite full yet. "Families are so complicated."

"Yes, they are," I easily agree. Mine certainly has been. So has hers.

Out of the corner of my eye, I catch a glimpse of Curmudgeon Bakery. From this angle, it's across the street, catty-corner to our position, and it reminds me of how very complicated families can get.

"Uh-oh. You've got that look."

"What look?" I sling my attention back to her.

"A pensive one."

"I'm not pensive," I say, sounding a little too defensive.

The waitress suddenly appears and takes Taxi's drink order, then asks if she knows what she'd like to eat.

"I haven't even looked at the menu," Taxi admits, rushing to reach for the plastic-covered card tucked behind the condiments.

"I recommend the grilled cheese and tomato soup special," I state.

Taxi glances at me and then looks at the young waitress. "I'll have what he's having."

For some reason, I chuckle. The waitress notes the order and walks away.

"Come here," I say, stretching both hands across the table. Taxi slips her hands against my palms, holding on a little tighter than before.

"You cannot take on everyone," I start.

Taxi snorts, tugging her hands back, but I catch her fingers with my thumbs, pinning her in place.

"For a long time, you've only had yourself to take care of," I remind her. "And you're doing amazing with Trudy and Simon."

Taxi looks toward the window again, blinking a few times.

"And all you can do, as the eldest sister, is love the rest of them."

She nods, closing her eyes.

"You can't change who they are. How they are built or what they carry inside. You can only love them as they are." I squeeze.

Taxi nods again, her head bobbing. She hears me. She understands me, but it's still hard.

I'm forty-seven, and I still worry about each and every one of my siblings like I'm still responsible for them. I was never responsible for who they are. I acted responsibly *for* them. I kept us together and gave them a home, and provided what we could afford until the Seed & Soil took off again.

It was hard. The frustration in Taxi's face is exactly how I felt for *years*.

But Taxi's sisters are adults now. They're accountable only to themselves.

"The best you can ever do is just be there for them," I state. Be present. Like she's been doing for Trudy and Simon.

"When the cell service works," I add, hoping to ease the tension in her hands, which are suddenly gripping mine hard.

Like she's holding onto me to ground herself.

"You're a strong, beautiful, capable woman, Tallulah Alexander. Don't you ever forget it."

A tear leaks down her cheek, and she releases my hand to swipe at it.

The waitress returns with the sweet tea Taxi ordered, and we sit back like we've been caught almost kissing.

"Better?" I ask, once the waitress walks away, knowing a few words might not make the situation any better, but I'm here for her, and I remind her of that as well. "I'm always here for you, Taxi."

I'll always be right here in Sterling Falls, where sometimes our cell service *is* spotty. But I never leave. Wherever she goes, I'll still be right here.

She nods again, brushing at her other cheek. She blinks a few times, then reaches for a paper napkin in the metal container. She dabs at her eyes.

"Two grilled cheese specials." The waitress slides the sturdy plates onto the table.

Taxi and I break apart again.

"Thank you," she soggily says to the waitress, continuing to break my heart.

"Eat your sandwich, Taxi." I watch her, her eyes still avoiding me. "And then I have a surprise for you after lunch."

"Stone," she groans, like she can't take any more surprises.

"I promise. This is a good one."

When she glances up at me, I have my hand over my badge, making a silent vow to her.

She's going to love the surprise. I hope.

She picks up a French fry and bites, slowly chewing, while I reach for the ketchup. With a sharp whack, I send a giant dollop to my plate. Then I dip the corner of my grilled cheese in the red sauce.

Taxi stares at me. "What are you doing?"

I shrug, like it's no big deal. "Dipping my grilled cheese in the ketchup."

She wrinkles her nose. "Don't people typically dip it in soup?"

"Do they?" I say, knowing the answer.

She continues to watch me as I take another swipe through the ketchup and bite into the sandwich.

It's . . . awful.

"See," I say, chewing quickly and swallowing fast. "A fault. I told you I have many."

Her eyes widen before she chews at the corner of her mouth. "You're ridiculous."

But she's smiling again. Not a full smile. Not a sterling, gleaming, Taxi smile, but a smile nonetheless.

"Eat your lunch." I nod toward her plate.

And thankfully, Taxi picks up her sandwich . . . without ketchup on the corner.

41

———————

[Taxi]

While I'd come into the diner ready to burn this whole town down, Stone extinguished my irritation with a breathing exercise, a listening ear, and a grilled cheese sandwich.

But once we ended our meal, I'm apprehensive again. Like walls are rebuilding around me, or bars cage me in.

I wasn't ready to return to Trudy's and face my sister.

I heard what Stone said and appreciated his comforting words. My sisters and I were complicated.

We'd scattered to all corners of the world, and sometimes I felt guilty about that as well. Like it was somehow my fault.

They'd lived with Trudy and Carlton most of their young lives. They hadn't really known Mama or their dad. Trudy and Carlton were their parents for the most part. So why had they left? Why had they gone wherever they went?

A big part of me thought it was because of Mama. An inherent part of our DNA to wander.

Another part reminds me of Simon and his words weeks ago.

You always leave.

Maybe, just maybe, my sisters fled because they felt abandoned by me. My need to disappear. My fear of staying in one place.

I didn't travel from a desire to see the world. I traveled because my art caused me to move around. I was searching for communities that needed help feeling cohesive. Towns that wanted to show how proud they were of who they are.

A reflection of me, scattered here, there, and everywhere, when I should have been looking in one particular direction.

Sterling Falls. And my sisters.

Did my sisters know I was proud of them? Did they know how much I missed them?

Who's fault is that, Trudy said about not having a backyard.

So many faults were mine. Because I didn't stay put. I didn't build community where it mattered most—with my family.

As we stand on the corner of Corner and Main Street, Stone takes my hand, startling me out of my musing. We cross the street, facing Frederick's, originally an alchemist shop, then a pharmacy and eventually an ice cream store.

The signature red, blue, and white striped barber's pole, originally attributed to pharmacies, is still on the corner of the building.

I'm full from my sandwich and don't think I can handle ice cream right now, but Stone doesn't stop in front of the shop.

Instead, he walks along the side of it, stopping midway down the walk, and then spins us so we face the wall.

In front of us is a dull red brick building, dirty and weathered, yet in decent condition.

Stone releases my hand and steps behind me, setting his

hands on my hips like they belong there. And I marvel at how perfectly they fit.

"What do you think?"

I glance at him over my shoulder, then back at the wall. "It's a brick wall."

He chuckles at my stating the obvious.

"Let's activate that artistic brain of yours." He lowers his voice, setting his mouth near my ear, and lulling me to tip my head against his shoulder. I stare at the two-story expanse in front of us.

"Try again," he says, like he's a mystic of sorts.

Focusing on the wall, I try to imagine what I might paint. Something that represents this town. What it has always meant to me. What it means to the man standing at my back.

"What do you think should be up there?" I ask.

"Oh, I'm not the artist here." I can hear the smile in his voice.

"Humor me," I say, finding a smile myself, before I chew at my lower lip. "What comes to mind when *you* think of Sterling Falls?"

"The Falls."

"Come on, dig deeper." I clutch my fist and tap it over my heart. But now that he's mentioned the local falls, I visualize them. Clear streams of water, billowing to white caps crashing on the river below. Dark, dirty rock formations. Green vegetation. Blue sky overhead.

The water has a silvery tint to it when the sun hits it just right. The sterling color is a mystery as silver isn't something mined in the area.

Rumor has it star-crossed lovers died there. Opposing sides of a new county. Very Romeo-and-Juliet-esque in nature. On rare occasions, some say you can see the couple behind the waterfall where there is no ledge big enough to hold humans.

Others say if you drink the water with someone present, you'll know if that person is your true love.

All of it is folklore.

And endears me even more to this small town.

The color green glides over everything, like a filter, representing the blue-green mountains of West Virginia. Green is often a symbol of rebirth, new growth, thriving.

I grip Stone's wrist over my shoulder and tug his arm around my chest. He leans into me, or maybe I just press further into him.

"What else to you see when you think of Sterling Falls?" I ask my voice hushed, like the wall can hear us assessing it.

"My family, of course," he says, the people who bind him to this mountain town. A ribbon around his heart, holding him in place. The gift of himself he's given so easily to all of them.

Clay. Judd. Knox. Ford. Sebastian. Vale.

Seven siblings. One great man at the top of the list.

Stone.

"What else do you see?" Asking one more time, needing just a little bit more.

"Community," he says quietly. "The town. The people. People, like Trudy and Carlton, make this area great."

Trudy and Carlton Wallace. People who never had children of their own, and yet loved so many children. Three sisters. One cousin of sorts. Countless teens coming and going. And one left-behind boy. Simon.

Tears prickle my eyes again. I'm so sensitive today.

And yet, I see their faces on that wall.

Sedona, Jolene, and I. Rowan Lyons, a hero from the community. Simon, loved by all.

The blend of differences making this mountain what it has always been.

Home.

"Is this for real?" I whisper, staring at the brick, no longer seeing just red rectangles on the side of a building, but a mural of color, bright and dark, rich green, soft blue, and a multitude of every other color to represent everyone who lives here.

"What?" Stone asks, answering my question with his own.

This moment. Us. A future.

"Are you giving me this wall to paint?"

He presses a kiss to my temples. "Technically, Frederick's is allowing you to paint the side of their building, and Emerson approved a mural as a town improvement, giving you a limited budget for paint and your services."

I spin to face him. "You don't even know what I charge?"

"I'll pay any difference necessary." He waves up and down my body. "As long as it gets you out of your head, and into your art."

He pauses a second, looking me directly in the eyes. Cobalt swirls in those blue orbs. "You need to paint, Taxi. And selfishly, I want to give you a reason to stick around a little longer."

A reason?

He's my reason.

Stone Sylver is as sturdy as they come. He's attentive without being overbearing. Sweet in all the right ways, and undeniably sexy.

But I also know a decision to stay is bigger than us. It's about me.

I like the road, but I'm tired of traveling. I want some place to call home. I want a backyard. I want to build my own community, one where I'm active and permanent.

"I want to see your work," Stone adds. "A new item on my bucket list is to travel to all your murals, but for now, I want to see one created right here. One I'll get to keep in my town."

One he'll keep.

And one I plan to make extra special, just for him.

I turn toward him and throw my arms around his neck. "Thank you."

I've never had someone gift me a wall. The canvas is blank, and my fingers are already itching to sketch a design for the town's approval.

But first, I kiss Stone Sylver, town sheriff, ultimate man, right here on Corner Street.

Let this small-town be put on notice, he's mine.

I intend to keep him.

Stone kisses me back before smiling against my mouth. "I have one final suggestion about the couch trading dilemma."

"What?" I say, still hanging on to him, grinning like a fool.

He gave me a wall. A freakin' wall.

"Come stay with me. Let Jolene take the couch. You can have my bed," he says, still holding on to me. His hands slip to my hips, keeping me in place against him.

"I was planning on sleeping in Gloria," I admit.

I don't know why I've been arguing with Jolene. I have an escape hatch. I've slept in my van plenty of times. And yet, something inside me doesn't want to bundle up in the van in my aunt's driveway, alone again.

"I don't like that plan," Stone states.

Our eyes meet. It's not up to him to like the decision or not, but I appreciate his concern all the same. I also might agree with him. I don't like the plan either.

"If I take your bed, where will you sleep?" I tease, smoothing my hand down his pressed uniform, gaze catching on that shining star over his chest.

"Right next to you." He tugs my hips and pulls me closer, giving me another meaningful kiss.

If a man kissed me enough to curl my toes, I'd cling a little bit.

No need to chase. I didn't need to go anywhere. He was right here in my hands.

I hold on tighter.

"Think about it?" Stone says, eventually pulling back before we're arrested for indecent exposure or behavior or whatever someone wants to call the town sheriff doing to me on a public sidewalk in the early afternoon.

"For now, maybe, I can bring some stuff to your place? Use your dining room table to spread out my pens and paints and do some sketching?" Trudy's home doesn't offer the wide space I need to start the creative process. I've used plenty of public spaces before, but Stone's dining room table feels most fitting.

I'll also need wall measurements and then my iPad with the scaling software and—

"Take whatever room you want." Stone interrupts. my mind already spiraling. "Come over later?"

"I'll be there."

I can't wait.

42

[Stone]

Later, Taxi lies across my chest while I wind her curls around my finger and watch them spring back into place. For her part, she runs her fingers through the thick patch of hair on my chest.

She was rather excited when she entered my house, her art supplies in two overstuffed bags. And nothing made me happier than watching her spread everything out on my dining room table. Paints and brushes. Colored pencils. A large roll of paper.

Then we ended up in my bedroom.

But despite what we just did, how we joined together, Taxi feels like she's drifting away from me.

"What's on your mind?" While I want all Taxi's truths, my biggest fear is that she still wants to leave. Even giving her Frederick's wall as a commission would only prolong her visit. There isn't a guarantee she'll permanently stay.

"I'm thinking about Jolene again." Taxi shifts, craning her head back against my bicep, so she can look up at me. "Sorry. Not very romantic to think about my sister after what we just did."

I quietly chuckle and continue winding and unwinding her hair around my finger. "You can think whatever thoughts you want, darlin'."

While I wish she was thinking about me, her sister's presence weighs heavily on her mind. And I'm not certain the words I offered earlier as wisdom were necessarily wise.

I have my own failures with siblings, and don't feel like I'm fully qualified to give her advice on how to handle hers.

"I'm still so angry about her showing up out of the blue, acting like she's been overly concerned about Trudy when she couldn't be bothered to get here sooner. And all this time she's been God knows where. Plus, she's acting like she has a medical degree by association because she works for a world-renowned organization that helps others." Taxi snorts, and unknowingly pulls one of my chest hairs.

"I don't want to begrudge her concern for others, if it was genuine, I just . . . I don't know what I *just*."

I smile and press a kiss to her pinched brows. "Like you said earlier, families are complicated. I know about being the worst sibling."

I chuckle, but honestly, Taxi talking about Jolene earlier, sensing she thinks she's somehow failed her younger siblings, has me thinking about Sebastian.

Taxi blinks. "You? Never. You're like the poster child for the perfect eldest brother."

I snort. "But I'm not." I clear my throat. "I've had my moments."

"Name one."

With a heavy inhale, I blow out a breath and tuck my other arm behind my head.

"I arrested Sebastian."

The instant I confess my greatest regret, Taxi tenses beneath my arm. Her back straightens, her hand stills on my chest. I swear she even inches a little away from my side, and I immediately realize that telling her this story might be disastrous.

Given her history with law enforcement, she isn't going to like my tale.

She presses up, balancing on her outstretched arm. Her body distinctly no longer touching mine. She pulls the sheet with her, covering herself breasts, holding her hand against her chest.

"As in, your brother?" She blinks several times, her voice incredulous.

"My brother." I reach for her lower back, my arm having fallen off her when she shifted upright. When my fingers tickle the base of her spine, she flinches, and I drop my touch. Instead, I fist the sheet behind her and stare up at the ceiling.

"Why?" The question cracks in her throat, disbelief still ringing high.

"When I was still young and only a deputy, there was a small-time drug circuit happening in the woods behind the original Wallace Farmhouse."

Taxi continues to stare at me, but I don't look at her. Her distance, while only inches, suddenly feels like a great divide.

"Where Sebastian lives now?"

"Same place." The ransacked farmhouse outside of town was purchased a few years back and renovated into a gorgeous modern home.

"He'd been dealing drugs, getting deeper involved in the use of them, and I'd turned a blind eye." My throat is thick again, shame and regret clogging it.

The signs I'd seen but ignored. The disbelief. He was too young, right? He couldn't really be involved in drugs. Where was he getting them? What was he doing with them? All things I should have asked.

But I was going to be up for sheriff soon. Beau Wilson was backing my election.

"We'd needed the money," I confess again, shamefully. I hadn't known for certain that Sebastian's money came from drugs. I only had an inkling. Still, I dismissed the niggling in my gut that said my brother was in trouble.

When he paid for Vale's dance lessons.

When he bought Ford new sports equipment.

When he gave me an expensive pair of Aviator glasses when I graduated from training.

"So you'll look like a bad ass sheriff."

The glasses cost more money than he could possibly have made as a young kid working at the Seed & Soil, getting paid on the family discount of pennies. The gift was my first hint he was doing something he shouldn't be doing, but I didn't question him.

"When he beat a man to death, I had to arrest him."

Taxi gasps, her hand moving to cover her mouth.

I'm tainting her image of my brother. The now local business owner, devoted husband, loving father of two. But I've already started this story.

I'll never forget the call, arriving on the scene. The man was black and blue, and red from Sebastian's blood. The victim looked like he'd been strung out. There was no saving him.

The last thing I wanted to believe was my youngest brother could kill a man. Then again, our father displayed the ultimate crimes against his children, and that bitterness, that hatred, could have built up in Sebastian, waiting for a moment to strike.

I just didn't know.

"He was charged with manslaughter and sentenced to seven years." The sentence was relatively light, and a relief considering the circumstances. He needed help. Help I hadn't given him.

Guilt sucker punches me in the gut again.

"I thought going to jail might have been the best thing for him."

"Don't say that," Taxi whispers.

But I continue, feeling at the time, like there hadn't been another choice. "He was forced to get clean. When he finally got out, he was changed." Still hard. Still a fighter, but more focused.

"He opened his bakery on an honest dime and became a successful businessman."

Taxi remains silent and I rush to finish my sorry tale. "He met the right woman at the right time." *Enya.*

"Wow," Taxi whispers, her tone tight, almost sarcastic.

My hand still fists the fitted sheet behind her. She still holds the top sheet to her chest.

"Did you visit him in jail?" she asks, her voice still quiet, eyes lowered. Taxi's mom had refused to see her own children.

"All the time." I didn't want my brother to think I was abandoning him, like our father had abandoned us. I took his displeasure in the situation, fighting against my guilt, eager for his forgiveness, but first he had to forgive himself, which took time. More than just his seven-year sentence.

I exhale heavily and look at Taxi. Her shoulders hunched forward, her hair curtaining half her face.

I've fallen from grace in her eyes, and I feel sick. But in order for Taxi to ever love me, she'd need to know all of me. And acting on behalf of the law is still who I am. My faults are more than ketchup on the corners of a grilled cheese sandwich.

"My point in telling you this is because no one is a perfect sibling. And even the worst decisions can be made with love."

I love Sebastian. Love him something fierce, and he slipped

through the cracks in our household. The one I tried desperately to keep together, but failed on several occasions.

Taxi remains quiet. "All I ever wanted to do was protect them."

"Like I said earlier, maybe Jolene has her own reasons for staying away from Sterling Falls. Ones that don't involve you."

Taxi huffs, glancing up and across my room, like the opposite wall is the most interesting space. It also holds the door, and I'm bracing for her to bolt any second.

"You hadn't been exactly eager to get back here either." I cautiously remind her. "Or stay for that fact."

"But I *am* here." She whips her head in my direction. "For Trudy. And Simon."

I'm not arguing that point, she's given up weeks to be present for them. And my next question is wrong before I even say it, but I ask anyway.

"Those the only people you're here for?"

"Stone," she whispers, her eyes still avoiding mine. She can't even look at me, tell me to my face that I've disappointed her. I've somehow proven I'm exactly how she's typecast everyone in law enforcement, and I don't even blame her.

I'm sick myself when I consider how I treated my own brother. Once he was incarcerated, there was no getting him out. He risked a higher sentence. The judge wanted to make an example of him, and thankfully, we caught the rest of the ring with Sebastian's cooperation.

"Yeah," I counter her quiet voice, lifting my arm that had painfully been clutching at the sheets behind her. "You don't need to answer that."

I fling my arm from around her, and lunge upward, swinging my legs over the side of the bed. "I'm gonna clean up."

I need a minute.

We all want to be picked by someone. Be their first choice.

Looks like I'm suddenly not it for her.

43

[Taxi]

I didn't like leaving Stone's house feeling like things were unsettled between us. We'd had a great start to the evening, but I had to go.

The story he told. Arresting his brother. The situation just hit too close to my heart.

The entire day had been filled with upheaval. Another fight with Jolene. The grand gesture of the wall. Another round of mind-blowing sex with Stone. The truth hitting me in the chest.

He's still a law officer.

I knew I needed to separate the man from the badge, but I'd already been on the struggle bus, and I needed to get off the ride.

I was emotionally exhausted and just wanted to crawl into bed. Preferably with Stone, but tonight, I just needed to be alone with my thoughts. Or maybe, not think so much for a little while.

Those the only people you're here for?

How did he not see he was also part of the choice? The choice I'd only decided earlier in the day.

I want to stay.

But I also need a minute. Or a good night's sleep.

Instead, I walk into Trudy's, preparing to check on her before retiring to Gloria, and run into Jolene again.

"Where the hell have you been?" The sharpness of my youngest sister's tone as I enter the house startles me. She's sitting in the small blue and white kitchen on one of Trudy's hard-backed chairs with a cup of tea in front of her and a glare that might melt a weaker person, but not me.

"*Excuse me?* I didn't realize I had a curfew or that you were my mother." Bringing up a term like Mama isn't fair, and I'm about to apologize when Jolene continues.

Jolene purses her lips, her tone still cutting. "Trudy needed dinner and Simon had a school project."

I blink a few times. "So you cook, and then you tackle homework."

Jolene snorts. "I'm not his mother."

The jab hits. I'd like to think Jolene is only tossing out the line because of what I said, still, it isn't fair to Simon.

I glance over my shoulder, toward the hallway. "Would you keep your voice down? Where is Simon?"

Jolene brushes her hand through the air. "In his room."

When Stone is present, Simon stays in the kitchen or living room, because Stone is engaging. He knows how to talk to a child and encourage conversation. He easily shows interest in whatever Simon shares, and on occasion, the two of them have gone into the yard to play catch.

When Stone leaves, often Simon goes to his room.

The thought gives me pause, the images of Stone with Simon conflicting with the story he'd told me earlier.

Letting his brother slip through his fingers. Guilt and shame riddled his voice as he shared the story.

But I couldn't think of Stone and his brother right now. I had my sister to contend with.

I cross my arms, keeping my voice low. "No one said you have to be his mother to show compassion, Jolene."

How many times did we sit at Trudy's dining room table amid the other kids and do our homework? Trudy wasn't *our* mother and yet she did the best she could to understand complicated math and tackle last-minute science projects.

"We need to discuss the kid." The words are blunt and not to my liking. Not one bit

Maybe Stone was right about my sister, maybe she's damaged in a way I can't possibly understand. Because no one ever spoke about her the way she's speaking about Simon.

"Simon," I correct, glancing over my shoulder again, hoping he is in his room, preferably with headphones on and not able to hear this very un-adult-like interaction.

"He can't stay here." Her gaze drops to the teacup in front her. She pinches the handle and twists the cup on the saucer.

My mouth drops open, letting her words settle faster than sugar in her tea.

"Why the fuck not?" I flail my arms outward, anticipating some *un*scientific reason. Not to mention, who made her a judge. Trudy has every right to have Simon with her. A court of law gave her custody of him.

A floor board creaks and I turn my head again, stepping toward the entryway.

"She's an old woman with a heart condition. She shouldn't be raising another child."

I turn back toward my sister, disheartened by the lack of

empathy from the save-the-children philanthropist she claims to be.

"Who says I'm old?" Trudy snaps, causing both of us to look in her direction, where she stands in the entryway wearing the bathrobe I wore when I first stayed here. She fills it out much better than I did. She also looks tired.

"And would you two keep your voices down. A woman can't get some rest in her own home."

"You're nearly seventy," Jolene reminds Trudy.

"I'm sixty-eight, I'll have you know. And my ticker is ticking just fine again. The cutie at physical therapy says so." She smiles at her own joke, but her eyes are wide and blazing at Jolene. "And what's this about Simon?"

"I don't think he should live with you," Jolene argues, holding her head higher, poised like she's the smartest person in this room and her word is law.

"And just where do you think he should live? With you? Jet-setting all over the world?" Trudy counters, slipping her hands into the deep pockets of her robe.

"I'm not jet-setting, I'm doing good deeds."

Trudy snorts. "You're following a certain doctor on trips he won't take his wife on."

Wait. *What?* I swivel my head toward Jolene.

"Aunt Trudy," she quietly groans, shifting her eyes to me and back to that ultra-interesting teacup.

"Are you *chasing*?" My voice is hardly above a whisper, aghast that my sister sounds just like our mother. A woman she hardly knew. The person who abandoned her at two years old.

The three of us remain silent while I process that my sister's idea of good deeds is doing a doctor *who has a wife.*

"He's going to leave her," Jolene mutters, still twisting the teacup. I want to pick it up and pour the contents over her head.

"You are not seriously falling for that shit," I argue, arms flailing again. "You don't actually believe that statement?"

I cannot believe this is the first I've heard of this situation.

Jolene keeps her gaze averted.

"Does he have kids?" The question flies from my mouth.

Jolene runs her finger around the rim of her cup. Her silence says everything.

He's a cheater *and* he has children.

"Now." Trudy's tone is firm. "I'll hear none of this nonsense about Simon."

For thirty seconds, I forget Simon, still focused on the other elephant in the room.

My sister. Her braggard ways. Her good deeds. Helping children.

I shake the thought. The lies. And draw myself back to the issue at hand. Was Jolene wrong? Taking care of Simon is a lot. Maybe it is too much for Trudy. Maybe . . . maybe . . . maybe he should come with me.

But where was I going?

I don't have a backyard.

Who's fault is that, Tallulah?

Still the words tumble free. "She might be right." I pause a beat. "These are supposed to be your golden years," I remind Trudy. "Visiting grandchildren and raising them are two different things."

"Simon isn't hers," Jolene states.

I turn toward my sister again. The reminder is a cold dose of truth. I am not blood to Trudy either.

"That boy is every bit of mine, as much as your backside is, sitting at that table, young lady," Trudy snaps. She's not one to raise her voice as much as strike with a hard tone that makes you rethink your thoughts.

Jolene doesn't argue.

Trudy turns on me next. "And what do *you* think I should

do with him?" The question is rhetorical. "I have no more mind to turn him out than I did any of you."

Completely chastised, a heavy pause follows in the kitchen. Her admission is another smack of truth, one that hits as hard as Jolene's claim that Simon is not Trudy's grandson.

"You..." Trudy points between my sister and me. "Belong to me." She jabs at her chest to accentuate her meaning.

"We . . ." she circles her finger to indicate the three of us in the room and then points toward the hallway leading to Simon's room. "Are a family."

The moment is a reminder that families can be *made*. Families are communities and families can be found, built from whoever is present. Broken pieces glued together, forming a whole.

I glance at Jolene, remembering what Stone said earlier.

You can't be responsible for the people your family have become, you can only love them for who they are.

I still love Jolene, but I'm disappointed in her, and right now, I'm disappointed in me.

Watching Trudy's chest rise and fall with the tone of her voice, I worry she's working herself up, causing her ticker to tick too much.

"Take it easy, Aunt Trudy," I warn, easing compassion into my tone despite the gravity of the words.

She holds up one hand, warning me to shut my mouth, while holding the other hand over her heart, which I can almost see racing beneath her robe.

"I will not send that boy anywhere." Determination fills her voice. "He needs me. And I need him."

"He can't take care of you," Jolene quietly admits. "He shouldn't be taking care of you."

She's right on that point. A child shouldn't be responsible for an adult.

"That's why I'm staying," I announce, like I promised Simon in the hospital. Like I told Stone I wanted to do.

Trudy looks up at me, slowly shaking her head. "I'm not asking you to do that."

"You don't have to ask. I want to stay."

Those the only people you're staying for?

No. No. Stone was a big factor as well. Maybe even the biggest factor. I wanted to be with him. I wanted someone for me.

"Baby girl, you're like those autumn leaves, falling off the trees, preparing to be scattered in the wind."

"But what if I don't want to scatter?" I argue. "What if I want to stay put?"

Jolene gasps. "Here? In Sterling Falls?"

"What's wrong with Sterling Falls?" Trudy narrows her eyes at Jolene, a silent warning to check herself.

But I won't let Jolene dissuade me from arguing my point with Aunt Trudy.

Autumn always feels like a change of life season.

"What if I've changed?" I step closer to Trudy. "What if I want to stay with you?"

Please don't turn me out. The ten-year-old inside me who never would have asked is coming back to life. The little girl huddled in the back of a police car, holding both her sisters while watching our mama go in another direction, knowing we might never see her again. We didn't see her again.

And I hadn't known then how much I needed Trudy Wallace to accept me. The last thing I want is for her to tell me to leave now.

I clear my throat. "Well, I don't mean here. In your house. I just mean in Sterling Falls."

Aunt Trudy's hands come to her hips. "And now what's wrong with my precious cottage?"

I glance at Jolene, then back at Aunt Trudy. "Well nothing,

other than it's a little small for the three of us." I'm thinking Trudy, Simon, and me, because Jolene won't be staying, and that's an issue for another day. "And your couch is lumpy."

"Understatement," Jolene attempts to say under her breath.

Aunt Trudy turns her glare on my sister. "Says the girl supposedly sleeping in tents in the jungle."

It appears Aunt Trudy is questioning Jolene's stories as much as me. Who knew?

Jolene is quiet, but I feel the anger brewing beneath her skin. Her own battles, like Stone said.

Three siblings can be raised in one household and each of them will turn out differently.

"Why would you want to stay here?" The underlying disgust in her voice makes me wonder what *she's* doing here.

Instead, I ignore my questions about her life and point at Trudy. "Because she's family and I love her."

I turn back toward Trudy, knowing I've never really said the words with the same emotion I feel in this instant. *Love you* had been a throwaway phrase in response to her salutation on each phone call, where she proclaimed she loved me.

"I love you, Aunt Trudy, and I'd like to stick around a little longer. Probably a lot longer."

Slowly, her lips curl. Her mouth widens. Her eyes soften. "I'd like that, baby girl. Simon would like that, too."

Simon. Oh God, I don't want him to think he isn't wanted. I want to get to know him better. Our journey has only just begun. We're making progress, slow but steady progress. I can't turn my back on him. I promised him I'd stay, and I want to prove myself.

Let me show you who I am.

Oh, God. Stone.

"Now, if we're done trying to dictate my life, I'm going to bed," Trudy states, lifting her chin. Then points between Jolene and me. "I suggest you two do as well."

Once Trudy leaves us, I glare at Jolene, not certain where to start with her, and then decide I don't want to start at all.

She's a grown ass adult. I cannot change her. I don't want to change her. I accept her. Okay, well, not her sleeping with a cheating man, but it isn't my right to judge her decisions. It isn't my place to dictate her life. I can only love her, even if I don't like her choices.

Family. It's complicated.

"I'm headed to Gloria," I state, excusing myself.

Once I climb into my camper van, I stare up at the ceiling, questioning all my life choices.

Staying away from Sterling Falls for all these years. Keeping myself distant from Trudy.

Chasing, chasing, chasing.

Not a man.

A dream, perhaps.

Then again, I'm living a dream. Maybe what I've been searching for all this time is me. I've been living a life but not loving it as I should. Chasing something I wasn't going to find anywhere other than the only place I've ever considered home.

Stone.

His name so easily comes to mind when I thought Trudy would take the top spot.

Waiting. I'd been waiting for what?

Stone slips into place again.

He made decisions in the past that shouldn't be held against him in the present. He's mournful, ashamed, guilt-ridden. I heard it all in his voice.

He's there, and I'm here, because I left him behind. I always leave first and look where I am.

The loneliness hits deep as I curl to my side and stare at the front seat of my van. In my forties, I'm still living like a vagabond. Here. There. Nowhere. When there are people in Sterling Falls who want me to stay.

Trudy. Simon.

When I think of the boy, everything in me seizes up. I never want him to feel unwanted, abandoned, left behind.

Let me show you who I am.

Fuck. I haven't done a good job. Not by any of them, including Stone. And that stops now, here.

Okay, tomorrow.

Because maybe Trudy is right. Here she is, and here Simon is, and they need each other.

Simon, who doesn't need just a house, but a home and love, and I want the same things.

And Stone is here, and I am here, and I need him, too. He can provide that home, that love, I desire.

And yet I walked away tonight.

Home isn't a location, Trudy once told us. *It's a safe space. There's a difference.*

Trudy has been that safe space for so many of us.

Stone feels like a safe space, too.

With that on my mind, I toss and turn until my brain seems to think it can't think any more. I close my eyes for a little while, which feels like no more than a few minutes, before Jolene is rapping on the back window of Gloria.

"What the fuck?" I mutter, sitting up, feeling my back pinch as I brush my hair out of my face.

Jolene is yelling at me through the glass, and I can't exactly make out what she's saying, so I scramble to the sliding door and flip the latch.

Jolene rounds to the side of the van.

"What did you—"

"Is Simon out here?" she questions, sticking her head into the van and forcing me back so she can scan up, down, and around like a ten-year-old boy won't be blatantly visible in the small vehicle.

"Simon?" I parrot. "Shouldn't he be getting ready for school?" A quick glance at my phone says it's seven-o-eight.

I'll need to drive him to school in about fifteen minutes and then I'm headed back to Stone. We need to talk more. He needs to know I'm not leaving.

"That's just it," Jolene says, her eyes wide, her cheeks sallow. "Simon isn't in the house."

"What do you mean?" I push past her, finding my legs shaky from lack of sleep, but also creaking because of my curled-up position.

I'm wearing a shirt I stole from Stone and a pair of his socks, which are oversized on me.

"Simon," I call out, rushing into the house, repeating his name like my sister simply missed seeing him.

He's in the bathroom. Or the kitchen. Or even Trudy's room.

But Trudy stands just outside his bedroom with her phone to her ear.

When I reach Simon's bedroom, the bed is unmade, and I scan the space for clues. Anything that says he's just hiding.

Only, the backpack he keeps near his bed is gone, and his favorite gym shoes which are normally tossed near the sack are also missing.

"I'll head out," I warn Trudy, running my hand down her robe-covered arm as some form of reassurance. He couldn't have gotten far. I hope. "I'll see if he's along the road somewhere."

My thoughts race to every bad scenario.

Trudy's voice trembles as she speaks into phone, nearly deaf to my muttering around her.

"Judd, Simon is missing."

44

[Stone]

"Stone, Simon is missing." The moment I hear Taxi's voice, relief hits me, until her words register.

My instincts immediately kick in. "Tell me what happened?"

As I pace my kitchen, drinking my final cup of coffee, prepared to start another long day, thinking I'll be alone again at the end of it, I listen as Taxi explains how Jolene woke her up, discovering that Simon was gone.

His room empty. All the typical places checked. Bathroom, Kitchen. Yard.

Being that his backpack, favorite shoes, and a light jacket were also gone, my gut didn't like what it told me.

"He's run away," I state. Foul play couldn't be ruled out, but it couldn't be ruled in yet either.

"When did you last see him?" I ask, doubling back on details.

"Trudy had seen him around nine when he went to bed."

"What about Jolene?"

"Same."

"And you?"

Taxi is quiet a moment. "After school. I picked him up and dropped him off at Trudy's before I came to your house."

My house. Where we spent the early evening in my bed, and then she left.

I clear my throat. "Okay. Did anything unusual happen last night? An argument with him? Something to upset him?"

A long pause fills the phone. "Taxi?"

"Another argument. Jolene and I were fighting."

I don't want to think about the two of them sparring again. More disagreements. More to upset Taxi about her stay in Sterling Falls.

"What were you—"

"Simon," she whispers, cutting me off. "Oh God, Simon. He must have heard us."

I pause, confused. "Simon heard you fighting? Or the fight was about Simon?"

"Both," Taxi says, her voice struggling. "Jolene. She . . . And I . . . And then Trudy."

"Taxi, slow down, baby. Take a breath." I wait a beat. "Where are you?"

Panic surges inside, as if I know the answer before she gives it.

"I'm driving, searching for him."

"How? Do you know where he went?"

"No." She breathes out, exasperation seeming to hit her as hard as it hits me. "He could be anywhere," she whispers again.

"Okay, look, first, where is Trudy?" We need to hope that Trudy stays put, so Simon can call her. She still has a landline despite the popular use of cell phones. Simon has his, although apparently, he hasn't been answering it.

"She's at home. Jolene is with her. Trudy called Judd. Jolene is calling the school." Taxi exhales. "Perfect attendance. He doesn't want to miss a day."

Her voice lifts, hopeful that me might head to the school and I hear her blinker through the speaker of her phone.

"I'll head there now."

"Okay, good. But I don't like you being on the road." She sounds distraught, and I don't want her getting into an accident because she's searching the roadside and side streets instead of paying attention to traffic.

"I have to do something," she snaps at me.

I wait another heartbeat, knowing her anger isn't with me. Not directly. She's upset because Simon is missing.

I need to call Judd, maybe Simon headed toward him. It'd be a long walk, but not impossible Simon went in that direction.

"Can you tell me more about the fight?"

I've already tucked my wallet in my back pocket, adjusted my belt and holster, and I head for the front door, listening.

"We fought about Simon. Jolene doesn't think he should stay with Trudy."

"Why the fuck would she say that?" My voice rises as I reach my truck and climb inside, switching my cell from hand-held to speaker in the truck.

"You still there," I ask, always worried I've disconnected someone. I reverse out of my driveway and head toward the sheriff's office.

"Yeah. Jolene . . . she said Trudy was too old to raise another child."

"She's not even seventy," I argue.

"That's what Trudy said." A faint smile fills Taxi's voice, and I can almost hear Trudy defending her age.

"So, just to reiterate, you and Jolene had a fight, Trudy overheard. What about Simon?"

Taxi remains quiet another second. "I need to back up. I agreed with Jolene." Then she rushes on. "Only for a second. I agreed that Trudy should be in her golden years, traveling or visiting others."

"Who does she have to visit?" I question, thinking I know everything there is to know about Trudy Wallace. Other than distant cousins, her siblings have all passed. Her older brother dead. Her younger sister gone. Most of her foster children are scattered, and most don't have children of their own. Simon's the only grandchild of sorts I'd ever heard about.

"No one," Taxi breathily admits. "Everyone important to her is in Sterling Falls."

I sigh, knowing the sensation. "So tell me again. Did Simon hear the argument?"

"I don't know," Taxi sighs, frustration in her voice. "But he could have. Jolene wasn't exactly quiet, even though I told her to hush."

I smile, imagining Taxi scolding her younger sister, although they are both around forty.

"So, he was last seen around nine o'clock last night. Items missing," I confirm. "And an argument about him. What time was the argument?"

Taxi calculates. "Around the time I got home, so maybe nine-thirty?"

Had it been that late? Had Taxi and I lingered in bed that long? When I consider what we'd done, how I kissed her by the dining room table, and then laid her out on it, among her paints and brushes, thinking I'd only get her off first. But then we ended up in the bedroom, and I confessed my greatest sin . .
.

The sky had been dark. It had been late.

"Okay." I clear my throat. "Has anyone called the department?"

"I-I don't know." Taxi's distrust rang through her hesitation. "I called you first."

Something swells in my chest. Relief that her first thought was me. That she remembered I'm always here for her, no matter what.

"Maybe Jolene could call a few of his friends, see if any of the other kids have heard from Simon. You said Judd knows?"

"Trudy called him."

"Good. I'm gonna call this in, and then I'll start searching as well."

"Where?" Taxi asks.

"Everywhere." I turn a corner. "You keep to the school and then double back. Be careful, Taxi. Watch the road. Traffic."

"Yes, Sheriff Stone." A tiny tease registers. The slight edge of relief because humor might be the only thing she can grasp right now. Her nephew is missing.

"We'll find him, Taxi," I state, confident, determined. I will not let anything happen to that child.

"Thank you." She exhales. "Stone, I . . ."

"Later," I state. "We can talk later. Simon is the priority."

"Yes." In my head, I see her nod, agreeing with me.

"I'll call you back in a bit," I say as I reach my office, setting my truck in Park. The first parking space is reserved for me. "Be safe, Tallulah."

We hang up without saying goodbye. It's almost a relief. I'm not ready to say goodbye to her.

Simon is the first priority.

Stomping into the department, I'm a man on a mission. "Crupkey. Crowley." I bark as I enter the bullpen and head straight for my office. The two young deputies lurch out of their chairs and follow me. When we enter my office, I tell them to close the door. I pace behind my desk.

"We have a missing person. Amber alert. A child. Simon

Gilbert. Age ten. Dark hair. Blue eyes. Last seen last night around nine." Fuck. It isn't much to go on.

The two are scrambling to type notes on their devices.

"Family members are contacting the school, friends, and important family members." I pause looking at Crupkey, his name not lost on me. He takes the heat for having a famous last name related to a fictional cop in a classic musical.

"My family members," I reiterate. "Simon is close to my brother Judd." I rattle off Judd's address. "I'm going to assume he might have gone there."

Crowley lowers his tablet. "Boss, is the kid missing?" he hesitates. "Or did he run away?"

"What's the difference?" I snap, knowing that voluntarily leaving his home isn't the same as being taken involuntarily. Either way, a ten-year-old is out there somewhere, having possibly left in the dark. The mountain nights are growing colder as autumn approaches. Even if Simon knows his way to Judd's, any number of things could have happened to him. He's on foot.

Brown bears. Mountain lions. Another person.

Crowley and I meet eyes. My hands rest on my hips. "There was a possible kidnapping in Wrightwood." Several cities away, a child went missing weeks ago. His shoe turned up in a field near Sterling Falls.

My stomach drops to the floor.

"We need to find Simon." My fists clench at my sides. "Now," I bark when I hardly ever raise my voice. My team is a good group. They work hard. They show compassion, empathy for others, and self-reflection.

I won't ever allow another Andy Whitehall to work for me. My department is clean.

And a little boy is missing.

"Why are you both still standing here?" The second they scramble out of my office, I realize I can't just sit here either.

I fire off information to Fern the dispatcher as I near her, telling her I want all hands on deck. Those on traffic duty need to be on the lookout. Those not actively working on something else need to be part of the search. We have no time to lose. We've already lost hours.

Thankfully, there isn't easy access to planes or trains in Sterling Falls. A bus headed out of the area picks up just outside of town, where the big box stores are starting to gather. Simon would need to take the highway to get that far.

And my only hope is he didn't head for the busier thoroughfare.

Please be somewhere local.

Please let us find you. Or better yet, come home, little buddy.

Taxi is worried about you.

Trudy must be scared out of her mind.

I make another set of calls as I settle into my truck, heading toward Trudy's. The simplest place to start is at the beginning.

The calls I've made include Knox at the fire department and Sebastian at the bakery, hoping he can spread the word to the local businesses.

Maybe Simon went downtown.

I contact Clay, although he's on the opposite side of town from me, and Ford, who is more north. We seem to have the four directions covered. Judd is already scouting the winding roads near him, but he's further up the mountain and deeper in the woods, and as much as I want Judd to be Simon's safe haven, I do not want to think about him walking to Judd's place. Too easy to get lost. Or hit by a reckless driver on the switchbacks. Or . . .

I refuse to think of the alternatives.

My profession says I must. My heart says don't go there. Not yet.

I have Trudy at the house, Jolene with her. Taxi covering the route to school. I run off the checklist in my head.

I even call Vale, hoping she and Cort can keep a lookout in Rogue River, in case Simon made it over there somehow. Twenty minutes away by car is pretty far for an evening stroll, but we don't know how long Simon has been gone.

When I reach Trudy's house, I park in the drive, hopping out to look for clues. Something. Anything. Footprints in the soft shoulder that might hint about which direction he took.

Right or left, buddy. Which way did you go?

Taxi's camper van is still gone, and I should head inside to check on Trudy, but every second is a second lost.

Jolene is in there, I remind myself, getting back in the truck.

Looking left, then right again, and picking a direction.

Hoping my instinct is correct.

45

[Taxi]

I'm beside myself. The worry. The panic. The fear. My heart races.

"Where could you be?" I say aloud, scanning the side of the road as best I can while paying attention to the road itself. I'm hardly going the speed limit, and a few annoyed drivers have given me the one-finger salute or a long horn honk.

I ignore all of them, my focus solely on finding Simon.

"Come on, buddy," I whimper, like he can hear me. Like he knows he has everyone concerned.

Trudy . . . oh, God, I can't even think about Trudy right now. The mess she'll be if something has happened to Simon.

"Stop it, Taxi," I scold myself, taking the warning to not let my imagination get the best of me.

Instead, I beat myself up for suggesting that Simon should not be with her. Who else could love him like she does? Of course, I can love him. And Judd and Genie love him, but Trudy's love is just different. It cannot be replicated. Her love is unique.

Just like Stone's.

Next, I berate myself for leaving him last night. It wasn't like I slipped out the door, but we didn't actually have a warm fuzzy goodbye. Not like the hour earlier, when he gave me another mind-blowing orgasm on the dining room table and then took me to his room, worshipping me the way only Stone ever has.

I curse. "Get yourself together, Tallulah Alexander."

Everything I've ever wanted is right here, and it can be shattered in an instant. The situation with Simon is reminding me that a person can be gone in minutes. Lost to you forever. Like Mama. Like Sedona and Jolene's daddy. Like Stone's parents.

I don't want to be broken anymore.

Messy pieces can still be put back together again. For some reason, I think of that Japanese art where pottery is created from bits and pieces. Golden joinery. *Kintsugi.*

Mural paintings are similar. The staggard bricks are the canvas. The connecting of angles and edges linking together, creating a final, beautiful artwork.

I want that image to be family. *My* family. The family I make with Trudy, Simon, and Stone, bleeding outward and blending with his large family, and hopefully, one day, maybe bringing back my sisters.

"And I want a backyard," I blurt as if my Gloria will answer. She's been a good listener over the years, having traveled miles and miles with me. But I'm ready for something real, something concrete, something solid as a stone to hear my story.

The ups and downs. The silvers and golds. The black and white. And all the colors in between.

Beige comes to mind. A color I typically consider bland and boring has become one of my favorite shades on the color wheel.

The hue of Stone.

And once we find Simon, because we *will* find Simon, dammit, I'm going to tell Stone how I feel. No more holding back. No restrictions or pauses.

Plot twist.

I love him.

And I want to start building on that love as soon as I tell him.

My phone rings as if Stone knows I've been thinking of him. I answer breathlessly.

"Yes," I say, hopeful, expectant.

Stone's voice rings through the phone. "I found him."

Oh, thank God.

46

[Stone]

I took a big chance, and it paid off.

Because Simon wasn't answering his phone, Judd started to believe either the phone was forgotten or the charge dead. Judd also had a people search app on Simon's phone, being over cautious about Simon's whereabouts, but the feature didn't seem to be working. It can happen, he explained. Depending on manually powering off a phone versus it simply being dead or the service being spotty.

The thought was hopeful in a roundabout sense. At least something hadn't happened directly to Simon. He could simply be lost without a way to make contact. Or be contacted.

The sliver of hope still did nothing to put me at ease.

So I took a risk and headed to a place I'd run to if I were running away.

A greater fear was that Simon intended to hurt himself.

Something I didn't want to consider, but also didn't have a choice to ignore.

Given how my father died, suicide was something I had experience with.

I didn't want to think about it for Simon.

He was a smart kid with so much potential. He had Trudy's love and Judd's devotion, and he had Taxi trying to be another person in his corner.

The effort was there. Time was what Simon needed with Taxi.

And I didn't want to think about it being too late. He was only ten.

As I pull into the gravel lot, so many memories come back to me. Bringing Ford here to walk off frustrations after ballgames. Coming here with Clay and Vale on occasion. Hiking with Knox. Judd and Sebastian were never interested, which is ironic, as they each have a motorcycle now and make this spot a destination when they ride together.

Sterling Falls, the trail marker reads. There were several ways to see the famous falls.

Long hikes along the river. Shorter climbs up the boulders. There was even a hidden grotto of sorts off to the side of the falls. The trail to that spot was more locally known and harder to travel, and I hoped Simon wasn't there.

Still, I call out his name, hopeful, desperate, eager to find him among the rocks and trees, boulders and water.

But not in any of them. Not in a sad ending kind of way.

"Simon," I call out, optimistic, something in my gut saying it wasn't too late. We could find him.

After several minutes, walking down the first trail that leads directly to the river's edge, I double back, still hollering his name.

I should have gotten an entire crew out here, but the

distance to the falls, especially on foot would have taken Simon hours.

Maybe he isn't here, I second-guess myself.

"Simon, please," I call out. "If you can hear me . . ." Give me something, kid.

Whatever he overheard, whatever he thinks Jolene and Taxi intended, Trudy Wallace isn't letting him leave his home. She isn't letting him leave her.

Traveling the path in reverse, I stop by a smaller one that veers off to the left. People often venture off the designated hikes despite the warnings. Still, less worn, less traveled paths exist, and something tells me to start down this one.

"Simon," I call out again, my heart beginning to race. The climb is steeper here, the path narrow, almost a divot in the earth. A stream might have run here at one point, water trickling down from the snow caps, making its own way down to the larger river.

"Simon," I holler one more time before I hear rustling. The crack of a twig. The shuffling of leaves.

And then a small boy of ten, with dark hair and crooked glasses on his nose, steps into sight.

"Stone." His voice is small as he hugs his backpack to his chest. His face is dirty.

I rush forward, picking him up and tugging him to my chest before remembering I should check for injuries. My hands shake as I set him on his feet and examine his face.

"Are you hurt? Tell me where it hurts."

He shakes his head, and I comb my fingers through his hair. He looks so much like Judd did at this age, it's almost uncanny.

"What are you doing out here, buddy?" I ask.

He shrugs, keeping his gaze lowered and his backpack against his chest.

"A lot of people worried about you. Grandma Trudy and

Judd." I softly say, keeping my hand gently on the back of his head. "Aunt Taxi."

His head lifts. "They don't want me." His voice cracks.

"That's not true," I say, feeling like I've taken a spike to the chest.

"She said it."

I nod, not willing to argue with him. I don't want to tell him he heard wrong. He heard what he heard. He might have misinterpreted what he heard or only heard half the conversation.

"I don't think she meant it the way it might have sounded," I state, knowing that Taxi's already told me what happened. A misunderstanding. A fight that wasn't for little ears. Especially for little ears that have an anxiety complex.

He's in therapy for it. And maybe a little family therapy wouldn't hurt.

I didn't have the luxury as a kid. Couldn't afford it for my siblings either. But we take therapy seriously now. There are so many benefits.

And I want Simon to have every benefit.

Simon doesn't argue back with me. Instead, he pushes at his glasses like Judd sometimes does, imitating his role model. "I broke my glasses."

I chuckle softly, squeezing gently at the back of his head. "We'll get you some new ones."

Simon nods. Might be Judd who does it. Might be Trudy. Might even be Taxi. But Simon has a number of people watching out for him.

"A lot of people love you, Simon."

A tear leaks from one of his eyes.

"Ready to go home?"

He shrugs.

"We could hang out here a while longer if you want." I don't need to rush him. He's safe and whole. A bit dirty and with broken glasses, but he looks relatively unscathed.

He tilts his head like he's thinking about it. We could linger in the woods. Take a walk. But I imagine his legs are tired.

"How'd you get out here anyway?" I glance around us, emphasizing I'm not in a hurry.

"I walked." So direct. So innocent.

"Yeah, but how did you get up here?"

"Judd brought me here once. Said he comes here to think sometimes."

News to me, as Judd has a whole pond in his backyard and woods surrounding it. His house is relatively hidden in nature.

"He said coming here brings him closer to his mom."

Fuck. My eyes prickle. Judd was exceptionally close to our mother and at the tender age of eight or ten or something like that when she passed away. No older than Simon is right now.

"Do you miss your mom?" I ask, before remembering that Simon doesn't recollect her. "What about your dad?"

He shakes his head and I'm confused.

"Judd says Violet is always listening when he's troubled. I thought maybe she'd listen to me, too."

Violet. My mother. I pull Simon to me again, placing our foreheads together.

"Buddy, you ever want to talk to Violet, you don't need to go into the woods to find her."

Mama is always listening, watching over us, and taking on anyone else we bring into this family.

And I'd like Simon to be part of mine. He already is in some ways because of Judd.

Maybe he could be even closer because of Taxi.

"I got lost," he admits, and I pull back, chuckling a little bit.

"What do you think Violet was going to tell you?"

He pauses a second, tilting his head again. Terms like 'precarious' and 'precocious' are often used to describe Simon. He's giving me a look that fits the words.

"I think she'd tell me to go home."

I purse my lips. "Sounds like a plan." Slowly, I rise from crouching in front of him.

"Ready?" I hold out my hand for him.

"What do you think Violet would say to you?" he asks, going for a sucker punch.

I hope she'd say she was proud of me. That she knows I did the best I could. That I didn't screw up too much.

I chuckle softly, swallow thickly.

But what would Mama have said if I ran away? She'd probably have laughed, telling me to be home before supper, and invite Cort to stay, too. For a second, I think I hear a laugh. A familiar tinkling sound. Something carefree and easy.

Then I decide it was only the breeze playing tricks on me. And I tell Simon what I hope my mother would think.

"She's proud of me. You're doing the best you can. And people love you, no matter what."

He stares at me. Maybe I got a little too deep there. I clear my throat, preparing to go with my other thought.

"I don't want to disappoint anyone," he admits. "And I am trying real hard to be good for Trudy and do well in school."

I lower back to his level. "You're doing amazing, buddy." He's a great student from what I've heard, and he is a good kid.

"I don't want Trudy to send me away."

"No one is sending you anywhere," I tell him, gripping his shoulders and jostling him a little bit.

"The only place you're going is home, okay? Back to Trudy. Back to everyone who loves you. We've missed you these past few hours."

He glances up at me, through the broken lens. "I was only right here."

I chuckle. "Only right here," I repeat, bringing him back to me and hugging him once more, before holding him at arm's length.

"How about we get out of here now?"

"Sounds like a plan." He takes my hand, and relief washes over me.

Maybe Violet . . . Mama . . . had been in these woods after all, watching over this boy who is so special to so many.

Thank you, I mouth to the treetops before leading Simon to my truck.

And the first call I make as I get back in the truck is to Taxi.

47

[Taxi]

The second Stone pulls into Trudy's driveway, I'm rushing to his truck. I've been pacing outside since he called me. A phone tree of calls went out after I spoke to him.

The department was notified. The school informed. Stone's family told the joyful news.

They're so relieved that many of them are here, showing up unexpectedly.

Full of relief, they arrived with a breakfast casserole, baked goods, and booze, although it's only ten in the morning.

Stone rounds his truck, popping open the door for Simon. I don't look at the hero of the moment.

I need to lay eyes on Simon first.

The second he slips free, I rush him, falling to my knees and pulling him into my chest.

"I'm sorry, Simon. I'm so sorry." For all I know, he heard the entire fight, but missed the part where Trudy adamantly said Simon wasn't going anywhere. Maybe he only heard half the argument. Maybe he misunderstood the entire thing.

All that mattered was that he was home and we were going to fix everything.

Meaning nothing was changing.

Simon is staying with Trudy, right where he belongs.

Clinging to him, I cup the back of his head and hold him crushed to my chest. Then I push him back by the shoulders.

"Don't you ever do that again?" I warn. "You scared me, and Jolene, and Grandma Trudy."

My voice is tougher than it should be, fear and relief colliding inside me.

"Taxi," a stern but gentle voice speaks from beside Simon.

And I pull the boy back to me. "I love you, Simon. I *love* you." Tears fill my eyes. "Please, don't leave me."

His fear mirrors my own. The fear that others would leave me behind, wouldn't want me around, but he needs to know that fear so we don't have more misunderstandings.

He's afraid I'll go.

And I'm afraid he won't stay.

Simon wiggles, signaling me to release him, and he stares at me.

"Your glasses." The frames are off kilter, one lens cracked. "Are you hurt?" My hands hover over him, scanning his shoulders and arms, glancing at his legs and feet, before returning to his face.

He shakes his head.

"But I hurt your heart, didn't I?"

Tears begin to leak from his eyes.

"I'm sorry, Simon. I didn't mean it. I don't want you to go anywhere. I want you to stay right here so I know where you are. Where Trudy loves you." I swallow thickly. "I'm gonna stay right here, too. So Trudy can love me as well."

My vision is completely blurred, like I'm the one wearing cracked glasses.

I pull Simon back to me, afraid to let him go.

"Are you gonna keep sleeping on the couch?" he asks, like nothing else matters right now.

I chuckle, watery and thick, and pull back. "Well, I'll probably live someplace else, but here in Sterling Falls. Where I can be close to you, and we can keep drawing."

"Can I paint a building with you?"

"Absolutely." I tug at the thin jacket he's wearing and jostle him again. "You can be my apprentice."

"What's an apprentice?"

"A student. An understudy."

"Sounds magical," he says, tilting his head.

"It can be."

As my smile starts to spread, the tears still fall, and I hear Aunt Trudy call out Simon's name.

He looks up, rushing around me, no longer interested in my apology or my offer or magic. And none of it matters, as I twist, falling on my ass to sit in the grass and watch Simon reunite with Trudy.

That's magic right there.

That woman. Her hugs.

More people filter out the door, the first in line being Judd, who embraces Simon hard and picks him up. Words are whispered by Judd to Simon, who nods into Judd's neck. Genie stands nearby, eventually running her hand up Simon's back. Only when he's on his feet does he get a hug from her.

I sit in awe, in wonder, admiring how much this family loves. Not just each other but others around them.

Trudy and Simon.

The Havens, even Cortland.

Seven siblings. Six with partners. And a multitude of kids.

Stone is the rock for all of them.

And me.

His presence is felt behind me. He crouches in a way that one knee rests against my back, the other near my front, as if he's caging me. Not a prisoner, but protection.

"Taxi."

There is so much to be said, and yet I can't get the words out. I only nod my head, leaning into him, sobbing against his shoulder.

"Shh, baby. He's alright now. He's home."

I keep nodding, reaching for Stone's neck, until the next thing I know, I'm up in the air, cradled against him. He spins for his truck, the passenger door still open, and he sets me on the seat.

"No," I reach for him, shifting to keep hugging him, unable to let him go.

"I'm not going anywhere, sweetheart." He rubs a hand up my back. The other holds my head to his chest.

"I'm so sorry," I finally mutter. "For leaving last night, and reacting to what you told me about Sebastian, and—"

"Shh," he whispers again. "None of that matters right now. Simon is home. He's safe, unharmed. We don't need to talk—"

"But I have so much to say," I lift my head, meeting his gaze. His cloudy eyes look tired, concerned, with a twinge of sadness … because of me.

"I … I didn't mean to overreact to what happened between you and Sebastian."

Stone covers my lips with two fingers, but I need to get this out.

"I just needed a minute to process it," I speak against his fingertips, and he pulls them back, lowering his head to listen to me.

"Since the moment I've met you, you've been such a . . . conundrum."

He glances up at me, his thick brows pinching.

"Okay, maybe not the best word. It's just that there are so many sides to you. Playful and protective. Family and friends." I wave in the direction of the house. "You're a great brother, uncle, father-figure."

I watch as he swallows thickly.

"And you have an important job."

His gaze meets my eyes.

"You are a superhero, Stone. You save people." I point toward Simon, then toward myself. "You saved me."

"Taxi," he whispers. "You're strong and independent, you don't need saving."

"But I did. From myself. I've been running my entire life." Not chasing, just running. "Thinking if I left first, I couldn't ever be hurt again. But I'm so tired of running, Stone. So tired of never having a place to call my own. I want a backyard," I blurt.

Stone straightens a little bit, narrowly missing the roof of the truck. He stands tall, staring back at me, before setting his forearm on the lip of the doorframe.

That forearm. Where he'd been hurt on the job, helping someone. Saving someone else. Marking him with another scar.

"I heard what you said to Simon. About not leaving Sterling Falls. Maybe finding a place around here." His voice is cautious, hesitant.

I hurt his heart, too.

And I cup his jaw, running my hand over his bristly stubble before holding his chin in my palm.

"I'd like to stay in Sterling Falls, Stone. For a long, long while." I glance around him again, noting his family spilling into the yard. Then I glance back at him. "There's a great community here."

"Heard we need a mural," he teases.

"But what do you need, Stone?" He blinks a few times, tipping his forehead to that arm on the roof.

"I just need you, Taxi. If you'll have me."

"I'll have you. Yes, please." I clap my hands together, like a child begging for a treat.

He slowly smiles, reminding me of that man in a hotel hallway in Knoxville. A little embarrassed by our collision. Definitely cute but awkward. And so, so lovely to look at . . . both on the outside and the in.

"I know Trudy's a real estate agent, but maybe you know somewhere I could live?" I arch a brow.

"A place with a big backyard?"

"Well, it doesn't have to be big. Maybe just a yard swing, and a few Adirondack chairs, and picnic tables."

"Might need more of them soon. Our family keeps growing."

Our family.

"I love you, Stone, and I don't want you to ever doubt that. And, oh—"

I'm cut off by a kiss so powerful it almost knocks me backward on the seat. His hand cuffs the back of my neck, and his mouth locks on mine.

The kiss is a mixture of sweet and claiming. A kaleidoscope of colors.

Beige being the center of all things.

When Stone eventually pulls away, I hear a few catcalls coming from his siblings behind him.

He doesn't turn around, keeping his gaze locked on me.

"I love you, too, baby." He leans his forehead against mine. "So much."

He pulls back and focuses on my eyes. "I want you to stay, Taxi. With everything in me, I want you here. With me. But I don't ever want to think I'm holding you back. Keeping you from your art, or your need to travel."

I pluck at the edge of his uniform shirt.

"Maybe you could come with me sometime. I can't give it up forever, but I'd like to slow down. Maybe find that teaching position I mentioned in one of my postcards."

His smile grows slowly, like a lazy river. "Yeah?"

"Yeah," I whisper.

"I told you seeing all your murals was my new bucket list."

"*You're* my bucket list," I admit before placing my hand over his badge.

He glances down at my thin fingers over the star.

"I . . ." I pause, meeting his eyes. "Tallulah Alexander, do solemnly swear . . ." I smile slowly. "To protect your heart. Honor your love. And chase away the demons."

His brows lift, knowing we both have them. Our personal bad guys that need to go. No more locking them up inside us, but releasing the past.

Stone sets his hand on the roof of his truck and the other comes to my chest, drawing a star over my left breast.

"I, Stone Sylver, do solemnly swear . . ." He pauses, arching a brow like he's thinking. "To always be a safe place for you. To be your home. And to love you with all my heart." He flattens his palm over my chest.

"Jesus, just get married already," one of his brothers says behind him.

Stone does respond, giving that one-finger salute I'd gotten earlier when I was driving. Someone chuckles, and Stone softly chuffs as well.

"Someday," he says, keeping his eyes on me.

I lean back, awkwardly patting the space for the driver's seat. "I've been saving this seat for someone."

"Oh yeah?" Stone arches a brow.

"Been waiting a long time for someone to fill it."

"Ready to have it filled?" Stone teases.

"Someday." I smile. "Hopefully, soon."

He tips his head back and laughs, the sound easy and loud, and filling a space in my heart.

The one I've been holding, waiting for him.

48

———

[Stone]

My family turned Simon's return into a party of sorts, but by noon, I was shooing everyone out. Simon and Trudy looked exhausted. Taxi and Jolene as well.

Earlier, I'd caught the tail end of a conversation between them.

"I'm leaving," Jolene said.

"Already?" Taxi says, surprised but also not surprised.

"Soon," Jolene says. "Tanzania."

"Really?" Taxi arched a brow. "Is that the story you're going with?"

Jolene shrugged. "It's better than being alone."

Taxi opened her mouth, then shut it. She reached for her sister's shoulders. "You do you," she said softly. "I'll be here if you need me."

"You're really staying?" Jolene questioned.

"I'm really staying," Taxi confirmed.

Jolene looked like she didn't know how to respond. She just nodded at her sister and stepped away from Taxi.

When Taxi looked at me, she mouthed, Later.

I'll hear all about it. Later. Because we have more time together. In fact, we're just getting started.

I'm taking out the trash when I find Taxi standing near the side of the house, staring at Trudy's backyard, where Judd built a giant playset after Simon arrived.

"Whatcha doing out here?" I ask, following her gaze.

"Looking for blue aliens," she teases.

"Did you find any?"

Her arms are crossed, and she twists toward me. "Nope. Only a silver fox."

My face heats, and Taxi reaches for my cheek, following what I assume is a blush over the tops of my cheeks and around my ear.

"Lucky man," I chuckle.

"Lucky woman." She points to her chest.

"Darlin'." My throat is thick for about the hundredth time today. The past twenty hours have been a whirlwind.

Taxi leans closer to me. "How would you feel about getting out of this place?" She tips her head toward the house. "Simon and Trudy need to rest, and I think everyone could use a little space."

I rub my hands up her arms.

"What did you have in mind?"

"I could invite you into my room." She glances toward the driveway, where we see a sliver of Gloria, before looking back at me.

"Or we could go to mine." I settle my hands on her hips, loving how easily they fit there, pulling her closer to me.

Taxi giggles. "You did say you had a bigger bed." She walks her fingers up my chest.

"You still trying to get into my pants?" I joke.

"Always." Her voice is breathy as she looks up at me, then pats over my badge. "But I'd rather be in your heart."

"Always," I confirm, leaning in for a kiss. One that seals my vow and sets forth all the promises. To love her, honor her, protect her.

Be here for her, because she'll be here for me, too.

She chose me, and I picked her right back.

"I love you," I say to her.

"I love you, too, Stone Sylver."

EPILOGUE

One year later

"**N**ervous?" Clay asks as he stands beside me, his voice a teasing buzz amid the hum of crickets in the field. The August sun is high and the day gloriously vibrant with wheat-colored yellows, effervescent blues, and the curl of green in the nearby trees.

Taxi has taught me to look deeper at the colors all around me. The kaleidoscope of our lives.

But one color will stand out above the rest today.

Periwinkle.

I've learned what the color looks like and appreciate the subtle mix of blue and white, which makes the soft purplish hue that highlights the features of my future wife.

My wife.

The thought alone might make me nervous, but it doesn't. It's something I've been wanting my entire life without ever voicing it, without believing it could happen for me.

But Tallulah Alexander is about to become my wife.

Surrounded by our two families and a small gathering of friends, my backyard has been transformed into an intimate space where Taxi and I will vow to love one another forever.

"Nah," I finally answer Clay. My best man. My best friend. And the best brother. We've come a long way from the hungry, angry kids we were, running around this property, causing innocent havoc, and eventually raising our family.

The Sylver Seed & Soil is thriving. Each of my siblings has a partner and children of their own in some form or other.

I've witnessed all those happy moments, but today is my turn to celebrate. To promise, before my family and underneath the heavens, to love and honor someone who makes me a better person.

This is the biggest commitment of my life. I've avoided this kind of bond in the past but now I look forward to embracing it. I'm ready to race toward a beautiful future.

Taxi already lives with me. The house is *our* home. One filled with our entire family every Sunday and intermittently filled with overnight visits with Simon and Hudson. Occasionally, my other nieces and nephews stay over, giving another couple in the family a deserved break and allowing Taxi and I to play house for a while.

But at the end of the day, we are each other's home, and we don't mind the quiet when we are on our own.

A slow smile blooms on my mouth as images pop into my head of all the ways we make our own noises in the absence of others.

The places we've fucked and the ways we've made love throughout the house I've always lived in.

While the minister stands near me, an arch of flowers behind him, I survey the guests assembled to witness our wedding.

Trudy, of course, and Simon, along with our families. The

Haven clan. Emerson Milton, whose secret temporarily derailed my romance with Taxi, but who has now become a good friend to her. Art Simms, whose maker's studio provides a regular outlet for Taxi's creativity and became an additional reason for Taxi to remain in Sterling Falls. Art introduced Taxi to the Dean of Fine Arts at a local college, who, in turn, offered Taxi a position as visiting professor, fulfilling her desire to teach.

The people present today represent community, something Taxi always wanted for herself. Their presence in our lives strengthens the roots she was ready to lie down. The promise of our future amid these special guests gathered here fills my heart.

However, my attention fixes on the back door of the house, breath held but not anxious. I'm just . . . excited.

Any minute, Taxi is going to walk out that door. Walk toward me. Where *we* will chase the future together.

First, though, comes Vale. My sister is radiant in her own right. Smile wide and eyes seeking Cortland, who sits in the front row of white folding chairs.

With such a large family on my side, having everyone stand with me was just too much. My brothers are here, supporting me in every way, whether they stand at my side, like Clay and Judd today, or sit among the gathered guests.

Vale winks as she approaches me, her mouth forming words she's easily given over the years.

I love you, big brother.

The backs of my eyes burn.

Vale has always been more than my sister. She's been the child I nurtured from birth and my roommate when she had a child of her own. We're close in ways some might not understand, and yet, I'd never change a single thing about our relationship.

Next down the aisle comes Genie, Taxi's new best friend. Her sister from another mister. The one forever friend Taxi never knew she needed. Their combined love of art and Judd has brought them closer, along with Simon's help. He's been the glue to put so many people back together again. Genie smiles at Judd, standing on the other side of Clay, as Taxi's once brother-like best friend.

Taxi toyed with asking Simon to walk her down the aisle. Then, she thought about asking Trudy. But in the end, Taxi wanted to walk herself toward me. Her bridal march making it clear she was giving herself to me and not being passed along by someone else.

"Might even skip down that aisle," she teased me the other day.

As long as she was coming in my direction, she could cartwheel for all I cared.

Chasing, she'd told me about the adventures her mother had led them on during their nomadic lifestyle.

The only thing I wanted Taxi to chase was me. She wasn't going to have to run very far. I was willing to be caught.

Taxi's sisters sit among the guests. Trudy is in the front row opposite where Cortland sits. Her smile so wide, her round face is radiant. Happy tears leak from her dark eyes.

I only needed Taxi's permission to marry her, but I still went to Trudy for her blessing, knowing how important she's been to both Taxi and me. To my entire family.

"Your mama . . ." Trudy said, choking up over the remainder of her thought about her long-gone best friend. She didn't need to tell me my mother would be proud. Be happy for me.

I knew it. I felt it.

Violet was watching over me right here, right now. In the place I've always been.

"If you'd all please rise, if you are able," the minister addresses everyone, and people stand, shifting to face the back of the house, where the door opens.

A door I've walked in and out of a million times in my life, yet I'd never focused harder on the opening that would deliver the one woman I've been waiting for my entire life.

Taxi.

Her hair is up in an intricate sweep. Only a single curl dangles near the side of her face. She's as bright as the sun, blinding and stealing my breath like she always does.

Her dress is periwinkle, because why not?

As for me, I'm wearing a beige suit. She told me the color is actually stone brown.

Doesn't matter to me. She's the rainbow in my life.

Her eyes are focused on me, and that prickle in the back of my own liquifies. I blink several times, not wanting to miss a single moment of her walking toward me, filling that space that's been vacant most of my life. The spot right beside me.

"Hi," she whispers as she nears me. Her mouth curved so big those silvery eyes of hers sparkle.

"You look beautiful," I greet her, leaning in to kiss her cheek.

She slips her arm through mine as we face the minister. We've already discussed how there might be a few things not so traditional about this wedding. We aren't going to stand with space between us.

And eventually, we share our vows in our own way.

A private joke, of sorts.

With my fingertip, I draw a star over her heart and begin.

"I, Stone Sylver, do solemnly swear . . ."

Taxi chuckles, her eyes suddenly welling with tears.

"To love you. To honor you. To chase the wind with you, but also to hold you steady when the gusts are too strong."

A single tear drips from her eye, and I catch it with my thumb. She soggily smiles.

When Taxi goes next, she slips her hand into my jacket,

spreading her fingers like a special kind of five-point star over my heart.

"I, Tallulah Alexander, do solemnly swear . . ." She chuckles a little despite the seriousness of what she's about to say next.

"To love you. To honor you. To plant roots with you, but also to dance with you when the breeze blows."

I lean in to kiss her again, this time taking her lips, sealing our deal, our vows, our promises.

The minister clears his throat. "We'll be getting to that part in a minute."

The crowd snickers.

And the rest of the ceremony passes in a blur before he pronounces us wife and husband, because ladies always go first.

Eventually, we travel back down the aisle to cheers and whistles. Our celebration will continue in the yard like a typical Sylver Sunday when there is nothing typical about this day.

This is our wedding day.

And because of it, I steal Taxi away for a few minutes, leading us into my office where I can shut the door and kiss her like I really want to kiss her. Full lips. Seeking tongue. Hands on her hips where they belong.

After a few minutes, she pulls back, resting her forehead against mine.

"I love you," she exhales. The hum that follows emphasizes how happy she is.

"I love you," I whisper, cupping her face and forcing her to look up at me, matching the happiness in her eyes with my own.

"Can we leave on our honeymoon yet?" she teases, slipping her fingers into the waistband of my suit pants and tugging me closer to her.

"Already trying to get in my pants, Mrs. Sylver?"

Her smile widens. "Always, Mr. Sylver."

I hum like she does, taking her mouth again.

We aren't actually leaving on a honeymoon any time soon. Much to my surprise, Taxi wanted to stay right here.

Deeper on the property is a house. The original homestead, from what we've imagined over the years. A once crumbling shelter, missing a roof, with only one solid stone wall. When my brother Knox returned from the Navy, he needed something to do, and together, we rebuilt the original structure with bricks and stones.

Ironic considering his nickname and my actual name.

And that small rectangular space with a single door and one window will be our honeymoon retreat.

Taxi said she didn't want it any other way.

She wanted to spend time with me ... at home.

A homey-moon, she teased.

"Soon," I whisper when I release her lips, stroking my thumb over the softness of her skin.

"Don't make me wait too long," she playfully warns.

"Never."

Neither of us will ever have to wait again.

Because she is here. And I'm next to her.

We are home.

Want a little more of Stone and Taxi?
How about the entire Sylver clan?
Check them out ten years in the future here.
Ten Years Later.

Not ready to leave Sterling Falls?

Come on over to Rogue River, the small mountain town next
door,
and read the romances of the Havens.

PROMISE
When Trinity Haven's ex-husband returns after seven years on
a racecar circuit, she learns she's still married to him, but she
has a surprise all her own for him.
Read about their later-in-life, second chance, marriage in
repair.

Want to read the Sylvers in order?
Start with Sterling Heat.
Sebastian Sylver has always been a bad boy. but when he's
finally on the up-and-up owning the local bakery, the last thing
he expected was to deliver a baby of a striking single mom, and
then pretend to be the dad to help her out.

AUTHOR NOTE

In the middle of writing this story, it hit me how much I loved a 1994 television show called *Party of Five*. If you're old enough to remember the series, in which the oldest brother puts aside his personal goals to care for his siblings, you might see how Sterling Falls relates.

I originally thought this series was more *Seven Brides for Seven Brothers*, which is an entirely different story.

The idea of an older sibling raising his brothers and sisters is a tough concept. First, because the parents are gone. Then comes the struggle of raising children when a person is just out of childhood. And finally, the trials of giving up personal dreams to ensure the dreams of others.

One thing so phenomenal about the television show was the complexity of the five siblings. Each tackled modern-day issues in the 90s. Some might say the issues were timeless.

Struggling with failed dreams. Creating new goals. Seeking purpose. Finding love.

Somehow, it made sense to me that a family would not only struggle with these concerns once, but maybe twice in their lifetime, and those struggles would stem from old baggage.

Loss of parents. Loving (or difficult) relationships with a parent cut short. And relationships with siblings.

I once read a study that your siblings raise you more than your parents. Commonalities result from the closeness in age; the experiences of being raised by two older people; and the timeliness (different generations), and I've been fascinated by the truth in that study.

All this to say, I've loved every minute of the three-plus years I've been planning and writing the Sylvers, and as I'm not ready to let Sterling Falls disappear, I'll be headed to Rogue River next to tell the romantic tales of the Havens.

Because I love a big family with lots of siblings, who all need a second chance to find love.

MORE BY L.B. DUNBAR

<u>Sterling Falls</u>
Seven small-town siblings muddle their way through love
over 40.
Sterling Heat
Sterling Brick
Sterling Streak
Sterling Clay
Sterling Fight
Sterling Touch
Sterling Stone

<u>Chicago Anchors</u>
When your eyes are on the silver fox coach more than the ball.
Elevator Pitch
Catch the Kiss

Parentmoon
When the mother of the groom goes head-to-head with the
single father of the bride.

Holiday Hotties (Christmas novellas)
Holiday novellas certain to heat the season.
Scrooge-ish
Naughty-ish
Grouch-ish

Road Trips & Romance
Three sisters. Three destinations. All second chances at love over 40.
Hauling Ashe
Merging Wright
Rhode Trip

Lakeside Cottage
Four friends. Four summers. Shenanigans and love happen at the lake.
Living at 40
Loving at 40
Learning at 40
Letting Go at 40

The Silver Foxes of Blue Ridge
Small mountain town, silver fox brothers seeking love over 40.
Silver Brewer
Silver Player
Silver Mayor
Silver Biker

Sexy Silver Foxes
When sexy silver foxes meet the feisty vixens of their dreams.
After Care
Midlife Crisis
Restored Dreams
Second Chance

Wine&Dine

Collision novellas

A spin-off from *After Care* – the younger set/rock stars
Collide
Caught

The Sex Education of M.E.
The original sexy silver fox.
When a widowed professor decides she'd like to date again,
and a local fireman volunteers to give her lessons.

The Heart Collection

Small town, big hearts - stories of family and love.
Speak from the Heart
Read with your Heart
Look with your Heart
Fight from the Heart
View with your Heart

A Heart Collection Spin-off
The Heart Remembers

BOOKS IN OTHER AUTHOR WORLDS

Smartypants Romance (an imprint of Penny Reid)

Tales of the Winters sisters set in Green Valley.
Love in Due Time
Love in Deed
Love in a Pickle

The World of True North (an imprint of Sarina Bowen)

Welcome to Vermont! And the Busy Bean Café.
Cowboy

Studfinder

THE EARLY YEARS

<u>Legendary Rock Stars Series</u>
A classic tale with a modern twist of rockstar romance and suspense.

<u>Paradise Stories</u>
MMA romance. Two brothers. One fight.

<u>The Island Duet</u>
Intrigue and suspense. The island knows what you've done.

<u>Modern Descendants – writing as elda lore</u>
Magical realism. Modern myths of Greek gods.

ABOUT THE AUTHOR

www.lbdunbar.com

L.B. Dunbar loves sexy silver foxes, second chances, and small towns. If you enjoy older characters in your romance reads, including a hero with a little silver in his scruff and a heroine rediscovering her worth, then welcome to romance for those over 40. L.B. Dunbar's signature works include women and men in their prime taking another turn at love and happily ever after. She's a *USA TODAY* Bestseller as well as #1 Bestseller on Amazon in Later in Life Romance with her Sterling Falls, Lakeside Cottage, and Road Trips & Romance series. L.B. lives in Chicago with her own sexy silver fox.

To get all the scoop about the self-proclaimed queen of silver fox romance, join her on Facebook at Loving L.B. (Dunbar) or receive her monthly newsletter, Love Notes.

+ + +

CONNECT WITH L.B. DUNBAR

www.ingramcontent.com/pod-product-compliance
Lightning Source LLC
Chambersburg PA
CBHW070237200726
48293CB00005B/1655